MOON CHILD

EWA ZWONARZ

ACAMAR PRESS

PRAISE FOR *Moonchild*

Zwonarz's coming-of-age tale functions on multiple levels: vision quest, family saga, spiritual memoir, paranormal mystery. Rich and sensuous descriptions of nature and the inner life, give the storyline a velvety lushness, which is deftly blended with page-turning suspense. If Nancy Drew and Rumi would have had a love-child, and raised her in the land of Oz, she might have looked and felt a lot like Moonchild.

- J. Biscello, Author of *Freeze Tag and Broken Land*

Layered with both the mysterious and the mystic, the twists and turns in Zwonarz's Moonchild *will keep you guessing, and keep the pages turning. An impressive, original debut novel.*

- B. L. Bruce, Author of *The Weight of Snow*

Ewa Zwonarz superlatively weaves a story tapestry in her breakout debut novel Moonchild. *The chilling dreams her main character experiences become more shockingly real for the reader as they turn each new page.*

- R.J. Jeffreys, Associate Editor of the *Tiferet Journal* and Executive Producer of Tiferet Talk Interviews Radio

To Mom and Dad, Grandma and Grandpa,
and all who came before them. . . .

*In Your own Bosom
You bear Your Heaven And Earth,
and all that You behold,
though it appears Without, it is Within,
In Your Imagination
of which this World of Mortality
is but a Shadow.*

- William Blake

MOON CHILD

PROLOGUE

Time, time . . .

The seed needs time and a fertile ground before its essence can blossom.

Far away in a place long forgotten, deep beneath the ground's crust, for eons their silent pleas have gone unanswered. Punished for acting on their desires, their attainment became their downfall. Human women—the objects of their lust—perished in childbirth, writhing in pain. The fruits of their consummation gave rise to a generation of giants leading to the degradation of the living kind. The era ended with a catastrophic flood sent to eradicate sin.

The story of the Fallen Angels became a legend, its fragments preserved in but few lines of text on yellowing pages of ancient tomes. And as is often the case with very old stories, the pieces that survived were incomplete.

When one night, the moon began speaking to me, I discovered that the angels' souls never left our earthly plane. They kept drifting through space in search of their human consorts. What if love could bring them back? I wondered looking at the moon's face. The more I attuned myself to its whisperings, the more I remembered. And when one day he finally found me, what once was a legend became my destiny.

PART I
FAMILIAR STRANGER

I.

November 7, 1995
Niemodlin, Poland

Gasping, I opened my eyes at the break of dawn. It wasn't the first time. The dreams started three months ago in September, lasting for a few days around the time of the full moon, their intensity waxing and waning with the orb's luminosity.

In my dream, I traversed barren plains of gray rock—a silver desert sprawling beneath a starry sky. I was lost and the landscape offered no landmarks to follow. Howling voices grew louder, as I approached a precipice—a place where the ground ruptured, forming a gateway to the underworld. Here, the kingdom of shadows ruled and phantoms roamed free and unchecked. I sensed their presence all around me. Impeded by nothing, they knew how to lure me deeper into their secret domain, their rough, ancient voices baying incantations, against which I had no power of resistance.

In my waking life, the repetitive nature of existence left me feeling dull and unfulfilled. He must have known how to reach me with his bitter sweetness, how to lure me into his realm with such uncommon invitation, offering an escape from the ordinary. He found me in my dreams. I was fifteen years old.

The moon illuminated the obscure path of my soul's nightly wanderings, fulfilling the dual role of a connecting cord and a catalyst. With each subsequent cycle, my ordinary reality kept filling with images and feelings that opened doors to new dimensions giving my life a whole new meaning. As my humanity transformed, my womanhood blossomed, and with it emerged a desire impossible to resist. This is how, unknowingly, I re-opened the doors that were meant to remain closed.

The chilling dreams held a promise of something new that wanted to unfold in my life and engulf me in its mystery. So I walked on, aiming for the edge of the chasm, drawn by some inexplicable force. Once I'd reach the edge of the precipice, close enough to look down into the void, the cadence of voices would grow to overwhelming proportions. Usually the dream would end as soon as I saw steam rising from the mouth of the gorge. At that point, the tension would become unbearable with two opposing forces—fear pushing me away, and fascination luring me in—tearing me apart. Emotions would engulf me, with terror and anticipation grabbing at my throat and disrupting my focus, too hard to sustain within the delicate matrix of a dream.

But this morning was different. Armed with unbreakable curiosity and even an inkling of confidence from having been here before, I promised myself that I wouldn't back down until I'd seen what was in the gorge. I fought hard to prolong the vision. Pushing my mounting fear and the haunting wails to the background, I leaned in to look down toward the abyss, my toes curling over the edge, heart pounding, and blood rushing into my head. *I know this is a dream, but please allow me to stay a little longer*, I stated my plea. On my bed, I felt my body grow tense, pulling my consciousness away from this land of dread and fantasy. *Reveal yourself*, I whispered softly and waited with bated breath.

The currents of swirling steam came up to my face, warming me with their heat and blinding me with milky vapor. But once they receded, beneath the drifting fragments, I noticed the contours of a face.

It was a strange face; a man's face frozen in time, bearing snake-like features with high cheekbones, a long jaw and narrow eyes that remained shut. I squinted mine, a distant memory hurtling at me from afar. But that inner flash of rumination shattered into pieces the moment his eyes opened and ignited with sulfuric flames, making me almost lose my focus.

So many epochs have gone. A voice escaped his dry lips painted with the rusty hue of blood.

His voice crashed into my chest melting the rigidity of my ribs. Another flash of memory, this time a feeling, opened within me like an encrusted rock spilling lava to my farthermost extremities. That moment felt like I was coming home. And to my own shock, I was willing to never wake up in order to continue feeling this way. He smiled, as if welcoming me but I also saw a warning in his flaming eyes. Still, I readied myself to jump into the gorge. Fire was now coming out of his lips. My feet caught the spreading flames. I took a step forward and saw myself catch fire. And then another, louder voice broke through.

Ninsal . . .Awaken!

The next moment I was panting, eyes scanning the gray rectangle of the grainy ceiling in my room, mind slowly landing in my body. I turned my head to look at my clock, catching it just as the arm that trailed seconds passed twelve, snapping the minute arm in place with a subtle click. It was six in the morning. I pressed my palms into my lids and let out a groan.

Who's Ninsal?

Each day since first dreaming of the abyss, the void consumed another piece of me, enticing my imagination with alluring content. I became obsessed with trying to disentangle this vision that was haunting me with chilling regularity.

Since my grandfather was diagnosed with lung cancer in the spring, I thought that the dreams were a reflection of my primal fear of an eternal, thoughtless emptiness—a total nihilistic end to everything, his illness bringing me face to face with the possibility of death for the first time in my life. But I also sensed that the mystery originated in some deeper and more personal place, and I wanted to explore it. There was something waiting for me inside this darkness. And after today, this longing turned from nebulous to precise. It was him—that face, that voice that called for me—I longed for.

The heavy feeling from the dream lingered in my body. I glanced around my room, bathed in the smoky silver of dawn. The air seemed to shimmer. Everything was the same yet different, as if the contents of my spellbound mind had spilled onto the tapestry of my life like a tipped bottle of ink, soaking every fabric of my existence with some portent prophecy. The house was quiet, my parents and sister, Rena, who had just turned seventeen, still resting in the arms of slumber.

I rolled out of my warm bed in an effort to move the

dream's weight off of me and looked out the window. The weather outside was dreary, dirty puddles scattered over the ground by distressed rain and winds indicating seasonal transition. Winter was around the corner. I could smell it in the faint breeze that snuck into my room through the cracks in the window frame. Shivering, I threw open the door to my small closet to put on a few layers of black before all heat evaporated through my skin. Something was pushing me to leave the house early, perhaps to catch Ben before the morning school bell announced the first class of the day. He often lingered on the concrete plaza in the back of the old movie theater, which stood across the street from school, where a bunch of renegades usually gathered.

At seventeen, Ben was two years older than me, and the only person who seemed to be able to grasp and explain the strange things going on in my head. Our relationship was far from conventional. It wasn't exactly romantic, but it wasn't strictly platonic either. There was a palpable tension between us—which frightened me, as I had no idea what to do with it.

Conversing with him, talking about things most people didn't talk about, such as extra sensory perception and mysticism, felt safe. I was too timid to go beyond that and afraid that any change would destroy the purity of our friendship, which to me was priceless. My parents liked and trusted Ben enough to allow me to stay out late as long as he was with me. As a result, all sorts of rumors circulated. At first they were annoying, but later I learned to shrug them off and continued to see Ben on a daily basis, between classes during the day, and either in my room or in his inky candlelit attic after dark. In Ben, I found a confidant and a loyal partner in our joined quest to decode life's greatest secrets.

Last night, when Ben was over, we sat on the floor in my room, drinking copious amounts of tea and gobbling up waffle cake while an audiotape played softly in the background. Tuning in to the music, I painted pictures for Ben, explaining in detail the successive images the melodies evoked in my mind. But no matter how well I dressed the song with visual interpretation, its meaning remained elusive, dwelling in some ungraspable realm. I was left yearning for something essential, some revelation that would allow me to go deeper into an exquisite territory where complete unity of minds was not only likely but fully attainable. I shared my thoughts with Ben.

"What do you think could help you get there?" Ben asked.

I thought for a moment before answering. "I think that could only be possible if our thoughts matched the creator's at the exact moment of creation."

"You mean telepathy?"

"More like being there, sharing that same instance and set of circumstances."

"I think it can be even simpler than that."

"How so?"

"Interpretation causes miscommunication. Meaning slips through the cracks. You must focus on the feeling," Ben said.

"Do you think there is such thing as objective reality? Or is it a construct made up by people?"

Ben shrugged. "I don't really know. Maybe it's a combination of both, objectivity glazed with subjectivity."

I smiled, my gaze drifting out of focus. "What is reality anyway?"

"I think it's whatever we accept," he said, his palms briskly slapping his jeans. "It's what we give meaning."

"Is it the same with our dreams?" I asked, getting up to flip the tape. "If I believed them, if I gave them meaning, would they become real?"

Ben thought for a moment, his finger tracing a circular pattern on my carpet. "I think it could be possible. But I think believing is not enough. You need action. By acting on your thoughts, you transport the immaterial particles of the mind from the dark realm inside into the outside world of forms."

"What books have you been reading?" I asked, staring at him.

He shrugged. "I'm just guessing. Pulling ideas out of thin air."

"Sounds like you've tapped into a vortex of high knowledge. Are you hiding something from me?"

"No," he cleared his throat. "Are you? What's all the talk about dreams?"

I shook my head and looked away. I only hoped that he couldn't see that I was hiding. The dream had already created a distance between us. It was too private to talk about.

I hadn't told anyone about my dreams, although once in September I came close to telling my mother when the same dream occurred three nights in a row. But Dad interrupted me, storming into the house and yelling at Mom with so much volatility that she ordered me to go to my room. The accusations Dad hurled at Mom jabbed my heart like little pointy knives. Crying, I sat in a corner nook between my closet and the wall, pressing a small weathered picture of an angel to my heart. It was a picture I found at the bottom of Mom's credenza, tucked in between the pages of Hans Christian Andersen's book of tales. But to me, the angel looked too fierce to be a guardian. A scantily clothed, muscular long-haired male wielding a sword, he was born to command the elements, not guard the fearful. His image and the visions it conjured in my imagination ignited a fire within me that lingered for days, until one day the feelings retreated and I lost the picture.

Dad's jealous outbursts seemed to be gaining in frequency. He would charge his wife with infidelity, an accusation he himself was guilty of the night of their wedding. My mother was a beautiful woman, but her attractiveness seemed more of a curse than a blessing. Still, Mom would say that his suspicions had no solid base in reality. They were only his fears, *projections*, she would explain.

Their argument that afternoon made me forsake my intention to tell her about the dream, becoming a sliver of a secret I kept locked up in the treasure chest of my soul, where it incubated.

When a few days after the first dream Ben had asked me why I looked so sick and pale, I blamed the full moon for not letting me sleep. "I don't really believe in astrology," he had said to me, "but being a water sign, I've heard that it can make you more sensitive to the phases of the moon." He even found a book on alternative medicine for me. "Maybe there is an herb that could help you," he had said. I thanked him, sliding the book in between two others on my shelf. No herb could help me, I deemed.

This was more complicated than being born in March. Besides, I wasn't sure I wanted help.

I walked over to the bathroom and caught a glimpse of my reflection in the mirror. I looked worn and nearly sick. My skin was pale, lips chapped, eyes sunken, dark circles like shaded half-moons obscuring their blue radiance. I turned away from my image to wash my face, brush my teeth, and peel the dry skin from my lips. Looking around the bathroom for an herbal salve with which to protect my skin from the frosty air, I found my mother's cosmetic bag. Having no experience with make-up, I carefully applied a dab of powder and blush. The color breathed some life into my tired face. I reached for the mascara next, applying a thin, black layer to my eyelashes. I quickly replaced the items, but before I zipped the bag, a small object fell to the floor and rolled beneath the sink. I picked it up, my heart beating faster since I had hoped to keep my frivolous act a secret. It was crimson lipstick in a black sheath that had cracked. I'd never seen it on my mother so she might not notice, I thought. I put the bag away, slipping the lipstick inside my pocket. I threw on the sheepskin coat I had inherited from Dad, grabbed my school backpack, and slithered out. It was Tuesday morning.

Rapid fall winds tangled the naked crowns of trees as I walked to school. Flat clouds shifted over the landscape, which by now was almost entirely devoid of life forms. I kept on, stepping around frozen puddles of melted snow with crumbled leaves, decaying remnants of summer memories, submerged in my inner obscurity, wishing I could see that face again.

Fifteen minutes later, I reached the plaza behind the old theater. Even though the space was littered with cigarette butts and broken glass from beer and cheap wine bottles, I preferred this place to the school halls that smelled of sterility and wet chalk. The building's back wall was a backdrop for colorful graffiti arranged into a multi-layered jumble. Young people gathered here to forge bonds with one another and express themselves freely. Dressed in dark clothes, most of us liked similarly dark music, which made us stand out from the neat pullovers and colorful leggings of the techno crowd.

I stopped beside a small tree, dropping my heavy backpack on the ground to watch for Ben's approaching figure. But he was nowhere in sight. I shivered and sighed.

"Morning!" a male voice startled me from behind. I turned to see a stranger sitting a fair distance away on the concrete steps that led to the building's bolted back entrance. A tall mohawk crowned his head, stiff spikes nudging the air with hardened blue paint. He was hard to miss, but I did not see him walking by.

"Hi!" I replied with a burst of confidence to cover up my anxiety. I wished I wasn't alone. Unfortunately Ben and I weren't on the same wavelength this morning. The stranger jumped off the ledge and started to walk toward me. He was dressed in a partially decomposed leather jacket with a plastic white and blue chain drooping from his left shoulder clasp, and a pair of torn-up jeans inscribed with a medley of pen drawings and credos.

"Going to school?" he asked, approaching with a bouncy, casual stride, hands in his pockets, mohawk cutting a crease in the sky.

"Yep," I replied, my breath turning into steam. "You?"

"Nope, school's not my thing," he said with a crooked smile and narrowed his smudged-with-black-liner eyes. "Life's my school."

I can tell, I thought, but kept my lips sealed while my hands nervously tried to scrape something off my faded suede gloves.

"Is it that obvious?" he asked, scanning his own outfit and not holding back the chuckle that escaped his lips. I attempted a smile. He looked up, his eyes meeting mine for a long moment. He lowered his voice. "Everything okay?"

"Yes . . . w-why?"

"You seem scared. Am I scaring you?"

I shook my head. "It must be my nerves. I have a math

exam today," I said and went back to scraping my gloves.

"I can only sympathize," he pretended to scowl. "Didn't prepare?"

I shrugged. "Something like that."

"How many classes today?"

"Several. Why?"

"Any plans after school?"

"Not yet. You?"

"Not yet," he said without budging. He just stood there, staring at me, and I at him. It seemed like he was examining me. Seconds elongated and I felt something warm stir in my abdomen. A blush climbed up my neck and wanted to run before it spilled over my face but my feet seemed glued to the ground.

"Where are you from?" I asked, trying to interrupt the effects the stranger was having on my body.

"No place in particular," he said, making it sound as if it was an actual place that really existed. "To be honest, I'm not even sure how I ended up here," he laughed, rubbing his hands together. His fingers were purple from the cold. "I mean I took the train, it's just that—" He broke off mid-sentence and went back to staring at me.

Moments passed and the warm feeling invaded me again. I felt my breath grow in cadence, the steam generated by my exhales becoming more opulent and turning sight into mysterious visions of past and future, with his large blue eyes at the center of it all. While my body was melting and opening like a springtime blossom, a placid lake was expanding inside my over-stimulated brain, sending calming signals to my nerves.

My body jolted the moment the bell rang. I had five minutes to make it to my classroom.

He blinked his eyes as he took a step back. "You must go."

"Yeah, I should." I turned to pick up my backpack.

"I want to see you again."

"Yes, me, too," I said, startling myself. "I mean . . . sorry, I don't know you and it feels kind of strange to be saying this. I don't really understand why I want to talk to you more.

Actually, I don't even need to talk to you. It's just that your presence here, you are making me feel . . ." My words trailed off. "Sorry. This must sound like a bunch of gibberish. Why do you want to see me?" I blurted out, swinging my backpack over my shoulder.

"Because now I am certain that you are the reason I came to this town."

Throughout my entire history lesson, the stranger in the plaza kept interrupting my focus. When the bell finally announced morning break I was out in the blink of an eye, pushing away the table and tearing my coat away from the chair. The last thing I heard was the sound of my pencil hitting the worn-out wooden floor of the classroom.

The plaza was quickly filling up with goths, metals, and punks, lighting up cigarettes and carrying on loud conversations. Someone was sounding off a guitar riff, someone else calling for a light.

"There she is!" Ben's voice found me across the growing cacophony of voices. I picked up my pace, aiming for the area where he stood with Art and Rock.

"Morning. Want one?" Ben held out a box of cigarettes. "You should stop, though, you know? These can't be good for you," he withdrew the pack with a wink. "Do it for your grandpa," he said, referring to my grandfather's lung cancer, which everyone attributed to his heavy smoking habit.

"Cut it, please. A smoke is exactly what I need," I mumbled, my teeth already chattering from the cold, my hands curling in the pockets of my coat.

"You look better today. Slept okay?"

"Hardly. It's make-up."

"Make-up?"

"Desperate times," I said, scanning the space, looking for a trace of blue. A wall of bodies obscured my view.

"Still, looks good," he said, pulling a cigarette out of his pack. He lit it with the embers of his own and handed it to me, enveloping my face in a bluish cloud of smoke. I took the cigarette and sent him a lopsided grin. "What?"

"Nothing, I just hoped I'd see you this morning," I said, sliding the cigarette between my lips.

"Sorry, Eve. I was in bed. My telepathic skills abate when I'm in dreamland."

Art and Rock laughed while I cringed.

"Did you ditch school again?" I asked.

He shrugged. "I have more important things to do. Speaking of, are you free tonight?"

"Why? What's going on?" I asked, and exhaled, watching a waft of smoke get caught in a vortex of air.

"We are leaving the jurisdiction of our small province to excavate newly discovered ruins left to us by our medieval forefathers," Ben said, stepping back to get a better view of my reaction. "You'll love it. You are loving it already, I can see it. Game?"

I didn't hide the smile that broke out across my face. "What exactly are we going to see?"

"A castle. Early thirteenth century. You'd be amazed at what gems lurk in our dreary villages. Should be spectacular." Ben added that tonight would mark an evening when we ditched books and dove straight into time travel and the realms of myth, sidling among gothic ruins, searching for hidden truths in every crack and crevice. "Plus it's a full moon so the lighting will be perfect."

"Right, I know," I said, shaking off the ashes. "About the moon, I mean."

Rock and Art confirmed their attendance. Just like Ben, they were seventeen, taller than most peers their age, and wore long coats with scarves neatly tucked around their necks. All three were very different from each other, and striking, though this morning I thought I could see even more symmetry in their faces, more shine in their hair, and a brighter glow emanating from their skin.

Art saw me looking at him and smiled, blinking his green eyes twice. "I was there last night. It looks frozen in time."

"Did you see any ghosts?" Rock asked, reaching to the back of his neck to pull his curly jet-black ponytail from beneath his scarf, his face turning pink. Rock blushed often when he spoke, which some girls found charming.

"I've heard they are only visible when the moon is full," Art replied, once more batting his lashes at me. Art's hair was short and the color of shiny graphite that contrasted with his olive skin, always giving the impression that he was tan. Irrespective of the subject matter, his face expressed a kind of subdued indifference, a mixture of serenity and cynicism. Regardless of the topic of discussion, his voice remained steady, carrying the message with a certain melody, green irises catching light beneath arched brows. It was often hard for people to follow Art's train of thought and his stoic demeanor didn't help. In other words, Art could be intimidating.

Rock, on the other hand, was an awkward introvert. He lacked the self-confidence that both Ben and Art exuded in abundance, instead expressing the side effects that arise from being overly self-conscious. Often tripping on his shoes, his flawless skin would redden whenever he said something that was supposed to have evoked laughter but instead was followed by deafening silence. Rock dreamed of becoming a rock star, hence his nickname, something that we teased him he could accomplish solely with his looks in the event that his skills failed him. A novice myself, in some strange turn of events, I had become his music teacher.

"So you're coming with us, right?" Ben asked again.

"I was supposed to go with my parents and Rena to visit grandfather in the hospital tomorrow. Even though I don't need to come to school in the morning I still need to be up at dawn. Dad wants to get on the road early."

"Is he getting better? Your grandfather?"

"I'm afraid not. He's having an emergency surgery as we speak. They found more tumors."

"Sorry to hear."

"Thanks. Still, I'd rather not go. I don't like hospitals. We'd be spending the night and driving back Thursday."

"Can you get out of it?" Ben asked.

"Maybe. If I could convince Mom."

"Would you be okay with staying home alone for a night?"

"It would be better than having Rena breathe down my neck," I said, and dropped the cigarette to extinguish it with my boot. "It would be only for one night. I should be fine."

"I could always come over and keep you company."

"No. I mean, we'll see. Maybe." Ben's proposal felt both like an intrusion and salvation.

As the trio began arranging tonight's ride to the castle, I moved to where the crowd was thinner, at last catching a glimmer of blue. I was relieved to see that he was real after all, not a figment of my imagination. Surrounded by a handful of chattering kids, he looked up once he sensed me looking at him. His eyes drew me in and soon I was floating inside his world, both of us weightless, rising above the school scene. The sounds muffled and surroundings faded until only his watery eyes remained, moving across the opacity of space and closer to me—soothing, communicating.

I inhaled slowly, feeling the cool air fill my lungs. I blinked and the vision dissolved.

"Enthralled?" I heard Art's voice behind me.

"No," I snapped, turning my body toward his imposing frame.

"I would disagree. You looked quite entranced," he added, squinting his eyes at me and making me blush.

The bell rang but Ben and Rock kept talking, unfazed by the sound that meant nothing to them. As most youth began to depart, I turned back once more, my eyes scanning the dispersing crowd, but the place where the stranger stood just seconds ago was now empty. I turned to Ben who offered to walk me to the school gate. He and Rock made arrangements to meet up later.

"I really want to see you tonight. I have a lot to talk to you about," Ben said, pacing next to me.

"Like what?"

"I'd rather wait until tonight."

"Can you at least give me a hint?"

He wavered. "Fine. It has to do with our conversation last night."

"The telepathy part or making dreams a reality part?" I muttered, stopping by the gate.

"There is something I haven't told you, Eve. I've been hiding something, and you detected it."

"I did?" I asked, hardly remembering that part of our conversation. "What have you been hiding, Ben?"

There was a rift growing between us that had deepened since last night. I wondered how much of it he felt, but judging by his expression I determined he felt enough.

"It's this dream I've been having," he said with downcast eyes. "It's about you and it's been haunting me, pushing me to do something for days. I've just not had the courage to do it."

My face paled. "Pushing you to do what?"

Ben chuckled and kicked the tip of his boot into the ground. "Forget it. Like I said, this is not the place to talk about it, really."

Ben pulled his hands out of his pockets. I noticed they were shaking. Hesitating at first, he placed them firmly on my shoulders. He was a whole head taller than me. Nearing his face toward mine, he bent his knees, the glimmers in his hazel eyes absorbing my full attention. He looked as if he was about to break down, his eyes seemed to water, his lids quivered. He tried to say something, but instead shook me lightly and kissed my forehead, his lips leaving a warm mark in its center. I shivered.

"I just want you to know that I'm here for you, okay?" he said, withdrew his hands and walked away with a slight hunch.

II.

I spent the short break before my dreaded math exam gazing out a hallway window at the desolate landscape, unable to construct one cohesive thought. Standing with arms folded over my chest and the nail of my thumb rubbing across my lips, I listened to the chaos unfolding around me. Groups of all sizes were forming, some in circles, some shuffling past each other to make it to the next class, their random murmuring interspersing with recaps of formulas in an effort to hammer them deeper into their brains. Those who did not have an exam to worry about stood in small clusters, watching others and sharing their observations in hushed whispers.

The bell rang, breaking up the human constellations and one by one the students settled behind their desks. As soon as the teacher wrote our test problems on the blackboard with white chalk that kept breaking, I put my pencil to the paper in front of me with the intention of finishing the test in record time. I turned in my exam without even double-checking my answers, all in the hope that I might catch the stranger before anyone else showed up.

Walking briskly, I exited the school, and crossed the gate, and street before rounding the corner that led me behind the theater. But the plaza was devoid of life. There was only the cold wind howling between naked branches of the trees, amusing itself by rolling empty bottles across the cement. The time I had hoped would have allowed us to have an impromptu private conversation now seemed long, empty, and stripped of opportunity.

My stomach growled. I walked up to the same tree I had stood beside this morning and dropped my backpack onto the frost-covered ground.

Squatting, I reached my hands inside it in search of my sandwich.

"Who are you?" I felt his gaze on my back and smiled to myself.

"Do you always materialize out of thin air?"

"Most of the time, actually. Who are you?"

"My name is Evelina, but most people call me Eve,"
I said, standing up and turning toward him. He stood a few
paces away, hands burrowed in his pockets, steam coming out
of his nostrils. "What else do you wish to know?"

"Everything."

"There's only one problem."

"What is it?" he asked, eyes fixed on my face.

"I can tell you where I was born, where I live, and
how old I am, but something tells me you don't care about that
stuff." He smiled and his body budged a little, confirming my
conjecture. "I no longer know who I am," I said to him. I had
a strong feeling that he was somehow aware of the internal
battles I'd been fighting with myself. The outside world not
only failed to provide clues, it kept muddling the waters,
blurring my vision. But the gaze with which he penetrated
me, seemed to reach all the way to the core of my soul, the
place where the pulse of my existence and the truth of who I
was laid bare and obvious for him to see. For a moment, in his
eyes, I caught my own reflection.

"That does present a problem," he said, and walked
up to me until he was an arm's reach away.

My lids grew heavier and my feet sank deeper into the
soles of my boots.

"Not knowing who you are or at least what you want
makes you vulnerable to outside influences," he said, and his
eyes brightened as if someone flipped on a light switch inside
of his body. The outside world grew dimmer.

"But I actually do know what I want," I said and bit
my lip.

"I'm all ears."

I realized there was little point in evading this
stranger. He could see right through me. "I want to understand
the meaning of my dream."

"Tell me more," he leaned closer.

"It's this thing, this chasm that keeps luring me in.
I'm sure this sounds weird to you, especially because I suck at
describing it, but—"

"You are being called," he said, and I looked
around to make sure he was talking to me. "Something is

summoning you."

"How do you know?"

"I can feel it through you."

"Who are you?"

He put on a lopsided smile. "I'm what I want to be. And that changes daily."

"What a great way to live," I said, with a tinge of sarcasm. I felt completely exposed while he was doing a superb job at camouflaging himself with elusive answers.

"You'd think it's all about being free and unbound, huh? But it's more of a pain than you think."

"How so?"

"Like you, I'm always searching for lost traces of myself."

"Always?"

"For as long as I can remember. It's not easy being me," he said. "How much time do we have before the bell?"

I checked my watch. "Seventeen minutes."

"Come," he beckoned. I grabbed my backpack and followed him to the concrete stairs spilling out from back doors of the theater.

A black raven flew closer and landed by the stairs. "Sit here and just relax. Put your back against the door. Close your eyes. And now tell me everything that comes to mind," he said, leaning his forearms over the railing at the top of the steps on which I now sat. The cement was cold, but I quickly forgot about that detail.

"What are we doing?"

"Taking the fast lane to getting to know each other. You need help interpreting your dream, don't you? I can be of better help the more I know about the inner workings of your mind." As if sensing my hesitation, he added, "Don't fear. I mean you no harm."

The conviction flavoring his words made me relent and follow his lead. I closed my eyes until my inner blackness expanded, muting the sound of the wind outside. The world under my lids spun a little and the visions arrived.

Pangs of fear mixed with anger. My fear, my father's anger. I only asked a question.

Why did you hit her? I repeated, as another thundering sob shook my aching chest. The hot tears burned my cheeks. I was eight years old.

It's between her and me! You stay out of it. He yelled back, the deafening sound of his reply bouncing off the walls of his garage, loaded with hardware and rolled-up cables of various colors and thickness. The place smelled of paint, engine oil, and benzene.

My family was a quadrant of clashing personalities, my mother and I occupying the more submissive corner and my father and sister, oppressing us from the opposite end. The way Rena treated me often didn't make sense to me. The more I worshiped her, the nastier she got. In the early years, my sister was my idol and I used to follow her everywhere. I did not resent the authority she commanded. In fact, I used to be her devoted sidekick. That was until the day she belittled me in front of her peers. The event was distressing enough to kill my trust in others and question humanity's innate good nature, something that school further reinforced.

From that point onward, a feeling of alienation began to sprout within me. I learned that showing any sign of weakness was like begging for a jab. And the kids were merciless in their menacing attacks, never missing a slip-up. Each day required a new level of skill in proactive self-defense. With time, I learned to pay less attention to the visible and spent more time inside of the malleable sphere of my thoughts. Gradually, that became my favorite thing to do, especially during the warm months when I had my meadows.

The swaying plains of tall grasses stretched far and wide beyond the edges of the little development where our house stood. To reach them, I had to cross our strawberry garden, traverse an open field with a lone oak at its center, and descend down a steep, narrow, and shaded dirt path that dropped between old swooning oak trees. The path lead to a creek. Its waters were murky and brown, the result of the officials' relaxed approach toward regulating municipal waste. Its bed was shallow and sometimes I could see the bottom. But the creek had unpredictable currents, which at times swirled and shifted the mud beneath. When approached carelessly, the waters had the power to suck a body into its slimy underbelly, as it did one day when it took the life of a small boy, traumatizing our neighborhood. I had to cross that creek on an aging narrow bridge, two long overlapping pieces of wood held together in the middle by a series of protruding nails. Each time my feet stepped on it, it squeaked and quivered, sniveling in protest.

A handrail made of a thin wooden pole nailed to two trees, one on each side of the creek, ran along one side of the bridge. I usually tried to steer clear of touching its rugged surface, so as to not have to pull splinters out of my hand later. I had to be watchful of every step, but all the effort would be worth it because the moment I jumped off the bridge's ledge and reached the other side, I was in a different world—one that much better suited my unconventional proclivities.

"Someone's coming," the soft murmur of his voice broke through the mist of remembrance. My body felt heavy, as if I was waking from a dream. I opened my eyes just as his hands rose to his temples, fingers lightly tapping his pulse. "Thanks to you I am also starting to remember more," he said, before turning toward the interloper.

"Do you guys have a smoke?"

"Sorry, mate!" We shook our heads and displayed our empty hands in unison. The youth left to mind his business elsewhere, kicking an empty can in front of him.

"I'm going to have to go soon," I said.

"I want to tell you something before you go." He reached for my hands. "It's about a vision I had of a girl walking across the surface of the moon. She was searching for something," he said, his aqua-blue eyes once more freezing upon mine, making me shiver. "She looked like you," he added without blinking. The world around us became silent and still. New memories began to form in my head: the surface of the moon, the searching. And then the memory snapped, like a branch breaking, and disappeared. He jumped off the ledge and coughed a couple of times, scaring the raven.

"Are you cold?" I asked, alarmed by the state of his physical body, and chastising myself for not paying better attention.

"Not really," he blurted, wiping his runny nose with a white sleeve peeking from underneath his battered leather jacket. "Well maybe a little, but I'm used to it."

"Here," I said, reaching into my backpack and handing him my untouched ham and cheese sandwich, wrapped in grease-marked parchment paper. "It might warm you. It's yours if you want it."

"You must be hungry, too. It's your lunch."

"When was the last time you ate?"

He thought for a moment, "I don't know. Yesterday, I think."

"Please, take it! I have more."

"Thanks." He grabbed the package and began to unwrap it with quick movements. "What's in this town anyway? Besides you, of course," he asked, after a couple of bites.

"Dreary buildings, lots of mud and bored-out-of-their-mind youths looking for trouble. Or escape. But maybe if you were to look deeper—"

"Are you looking to escape?"

"Maybe."

"Your town sounds like everywhere else I've been," he said, his mouth full. "But things seem different now, at least for me. Some parts are starting to make sense."

I hung my head, "I still feel muddled."

"Tonight will be a full moon. Maybe that will help . . . illuminate things?"

"Or maybe next time I dream, I should just jump?" I said, thinking of the chasm.

The sound of the school bell scattered my focus.

"Soon we will no longer be alone," he said, looking around, and brought the uneaten half of the sandwich toward his lips. "Good sandwich by the way."

"I don't feel like going to class. Maybe I should just stay?" I said, desperately wanting him to agree and suggest we go somewhere to continue our explorations.

"It's not your style. You might regret it later."

I knew he was right. Skipping class would only add to my growing anxiety and piles of homework. I would be already missing school during two consecutive days if I went with my parents. It's just that I didn't want to end our exchange so soon.

Groups of youth were arriving at the plaza. I could hear the growing stampede of their footsteps behind me.

"Keep following the breadcrumbs," he said. "I will find you when the time is right." He raised his hand in a goodbye gesture and turned to walk away.

III.

I climbed the stairs to the second floor of the school building and dropped my bag at the end of a sagging line of backpacks that stretched in a long row against the wall. The hallway, as did my mind, was reverberating with incessant chatter. Leaning against the wall, I slid down to the floor, joining the backpacks and pulling my knees up to my chin. Suddenly, a feeling of heaviness and exhaustion descended over me, like an armor made of steel. The teacher was late so I contorted my body into a small ball with my forehead nesting between my knees, and thought of Ben.

The day I met him I was sitting atop the front steps in the front of the theater, waiting for my music teacher who wouldn't show. The theater also served as our town's concert and rehearsal hall for young musicians. With my guitar tucked inside a black case lined with red velvet, I sat on the concrete stairs, looking into the distance and feeling the evening autumn breeze caress my face.

From a distance, my eyes glimpsed three tall figures in long billowing coats. I watched them approach and ascend the stairs next to me, our eyes meeting in passing, one by one. Rock avoided looking at me, already blushing. Art's gaze felt like a cutting blade before he peeled it away, releasing my breath. The two of them passed by and joined others gathered in a circle. But Ben didn't follow. Instead, he sat right next to me and began asking about my instrument, sidestepping introductions. We quickly lost track of time. After a whole evening spent in conversation, he walked me home, carrying my guitar and only pausing to point out constellations floating above our heads.

"Isn't it strange how the light that is reaching us now left the stars years ago?"

I looked at his face, part of which was illuminated by moonlight, and nodded with a smile.

"Most people don't care about these things."

The next day I couldn't wait to see Ben again. And it had been like that until today. I feared seeing him this evening

22

and hearing his words, what they implied, and the changes they would bring.

The clattering of the teacher's keys returned my attention to the hallway. My classmates began stretching their arms and lifting bags to line up along the wall. I got up, the armor still weighing me down, and took my place in line.

Inside, the arms on the wall clock hanging over the blackboard moved as if they were forcing their way through a thick gelatinous substance. One minute felt more like ten. The classroom was soon overheating and the droning voice of the teacher repeating phrases in Russian, syllable after syllable, put me in a trance. Hardly anyone paid attention, but the teacher's bad sight prevented her from noticing. *I could be using this time so much better right now,* I thought with regret, and gazed outside the window.

Leaning my forehead into my hands, I closed my eyes, waiting for a storm of random thoughts to come and sweep me away. But instead, as soon as my lids drew down, the void began spreading inside me like an ink blotch sucking me in. While the darkness seemed dismal and threatening, it also contained a grain of mystery that glistened like a pearl inside of a murky shell. *You're being called*, the stranger had told me. I drew a deep breath and sunk back in. I recalled his features until only his blue eyes remained, drawing me in with their serenity. *Who are you?* I asked, and the stranger's face contorted into a grimace as if he was trying to say something but couldn't. His blue eyes became yellow and his features began to transform. I heard a distant cry followed by a deafening silence. The face from my dream stood before me. No longer veiled by steam, it was clear of obstructions. A memory surfaced. I knew him. His face was gaunt and darkened from coal and fire. But his eyes still expressed the same passion. *It happened before the flood,* a voice broke through, and I understood.

The teacher's keys landed on my desk. Forcing air into my lungs, I snapped and opened my eyes.

"Evelina Sopel! Are you in the clouds?" the teacher scolded. Someone laughed. She picked up her keys and pointed her finger at me. "Daydreaming never fed anyone. Wake up, child, or I will have to call your mother!" More laughs. "Silence!" she yelled, before returning to the blackboard to write our assignment. Avoiding eye contact with anyone, I reached for my pen and began doodling squares and spirals in my notebook, hoping for my vision to return. Shapes soon became words.

Silver moon spins above my face
A mirror reflecting an ominous dance
When a crown of dejection slips off with a nod
The surface stills, freezing the pond

My spine ignited, spreading fire across branches of nerves. I straightened my back and touched the cold end of my pen to my quivering lips. I lifted my head. The arm on the wall clock that indicated seconds became still. While the students were busy jotting down the assignment, I returned to my poem.

Trailing the surface, I scout for your face
Lost, I listen for the peal of your wings
Dropping to the ground, I wait in silence
For a sight of the feather to bring me peace

The bell rang. I tore out the page with the poem and folded the paper slipping it inside my pocket.

Outside, the chill had lost some of its earlier biting sharpness. Thick clouds hung low, piling on top of each other like layers of whipped cream, signaling a snowstorm. I walked past the theater, noting a small cluster of people but no one I wanted to talk to, and toward a path that led me home through an avenue of oaks that looked glorious in the summer but tragic during winter. Instead of turning left at the fork, which would have taken me home, I went in the opposite direction.

The old library, a two-story building covered with a black veneer of soot, stood on the fringes of our town, halfway between a gothic church that towered over a short market street and a cemetery sprawling on a plateau above. I followed the silhouette of a man who had just exited the church. He was dressed in a long black coat, and feeling my gaze pinned to him turned to look at me, his eyes lashing me with an icy chill. I slowed my pace and waited until he disappeared beyond a bend. I pulled the paper out of my pocket and reread my poem before I decided I had given the man enough time to make significant headway.

I walked up the stone steps of the library, bits of dirt and sand grinding under my boots. I pulled on the massive wooden doors and went inside. A musky wall of heat glazed my cold face. I crossed the short empty hallway of the first floor, which housed administrative offices, and followed the stairs to the second floor.

The library was empty, save the librarian. I greeted the young woman absorbed in the newest tome of imported literature, and moved on to scan the long shelves for hidden treasures, my index finger moving across the tall round spines, my boots leaving muddy stains on the green carpet. While plenty of classics and romance novels graced the rows, this library lacked the esoteric section. Still, I hoped to discover that somewhere, perhaps tucked in a corner, the rows held that special book left just for me, a find as good as a dusty trunk found in relatives' attic.

I heard a rustle and turned, catching a glimpse of a dark coat rounding a corner behind a shelf. My heart jumped. The librarian and I weren't the only people here. Just then, my eyes landed on something that looked off—a small book with its yellowing pages rather than its spine facing out, its corner protruding at an angle. I reached for it, pushing away the compressing tomes. The book looked old; its pages were uneven and craggy, its leather cover stamped with an embossed circle, nothing else. No author, no title. I fanned the pages and the spine creaked. The entire book was handwritten, parts of it in a different cursive than the rest. The writing was elegant, like it belonged to a trained hand, but the black ink was starting to fade in a few places. The book even had drawings.

I turned to the first page:

I open the gates, gazing inside the lion's den, unsure whether this fear is my foe or my friend. He speaks: the

*answer, my dear, is within your heart; so don't let illusions
tear you apart. And as you gaze up into the light and look for
traces of familiar faces, before you turn away, remember that
most profound truths hide in the darkest places. . . .*

The passage was signed with the initials J.G. and
below it glared two words: *Forgive me.*

I shut the covers knowing I had to take this book home
with me. But it lacked a library stamp and card listing
its previous users. I hesitated, looking around and wondering
what to do. If I bring the book to the librarian and point out
its lack of registration, it might take awhile for her to add it
to the catalogue. I might never see the book again. Besides,
it didn't look like a normal book. With cheeks burning with
shame and nascent guilt, I slipped the manuscript under my
coat and exited the building.

IV.

Liberty Street was a small development of thirty-two homes, the oldest of which was erected less than twenty years ago. The street had a shape similar to the angular number "two" displayed on digital clocks. My house stood close to its far end. I walked the street, smelling the coal smoke that for over a month now had been spewing out of stained, concrete chimneys, stinging nostrils like chlorinated water. Black particles of soot danced with crystals of ice, graying the white of snow wherever they settled, especially near the sidewalks. It was twilight.

Walking up the cement steps, I smelled the cozy familiarity of home that always hovered outside its front door, a mixture of ground coffee beans and fabric softener. I entered the small foyer crowded with shoes and squatted to untie my boots, which must have weighed a kilo each. Besides my own breathing and the quiet music in the kitchen coming from Mom's radio, my ears detected two voices, both coming from my room. Never too fond of surprises that could compromise my privacy, I barged in. Two girls—one sitting on my spinning desk chair and the other cross-legged on the floor by her feet—went silent. Instinctively, I scanned the space for open drawers and objects that were out of place. Everything seemed to be as I left it, so my shoulders dropped a centimeter.

"Hi, Eve!" said the girl in the chair. Her name was Paula, and she was one year younger than me.

"Sorry . . . I completely forgot that you guys were coming," I said, somewhat bummed that I wouldn't be able to read more of the mysterious book that waited in my backpack.

"No worries," Paula waved her hand. "We just got here. Your Mom let us in."

"Hope you're ready," I said to Paula, dropping my backpack and my coat onto the floor and closing the door behind me.

"You bet she is ready!" said the second girl, one of my classmates. "She can't turn away now, even though she's about to undergo a bloody torture. Isn't that right?" Her name was Marta and she never held back her opinions. In fact, she was known for her ability to be so direct, it hurt, which allowed her to avoid most confrontations due to intimidation, but at the same time made her the subject of much behind-the-back gossip by the girls who eschewed her intimidating presence.

"Is it going to hurt more than, you know, doing it the normal way?" Paula asked, her face turning pale.

"It may," I shrugged, bending over my desk to open a drawer. "But that depends on you."

Someone knocked on the door. I recognized Mom's slim silhouette through the glass. The moment she entered, the faces of my guests transformed. Her serene smile always put people at ease.

"I made sandwiches. Are you girls hungry?" she asked. I looked at the plate filled with tiny sandwiches made with ham, cheese, and egg salad sprinkled with red paprika and chives, and thought of the stranger to whom I had given my lunch. *Where was he now?*

"That would be sa-weeeet!" Marta said, clapping her hands. She loved to eat and it showed in her distinctly plump figure.

After our impromptu supper, Mom delivered three cups of hot lemon tea and leftover pieces of cake from Rena's birthday party, which had been two days ago, further delaying our procedure.

"Okay, ladies. Let's get down to business. It's getting late," I declared, putting my plate on the edge of the desk and shaking the breadcrumbs from my lap. I went to the bathroom to wash my hands and tie my hair back, and when I returned I pulled out a bag of white cotton balls from my desk drawer, along with a bottle of rubbing alcohol and a bundle of the thickest syringe needles I could lay my hands on.

"These must be fun to get," Marta remarked.

"I get raised eyebrows from the pharmacist every time," I muttered.

"She must think you are feeding a nasty habit. Careful, your parents might go through your room!"

I gave Marta a lopsided smile, "No one ever goes through my room." I turned on my desk lamp and lit a small candle. "Why not make it a little ceremony?"

"Woo . . . mysterious," Marta whispered, kneeling next to the desk, then looking at Paula "Hey, don't panic, it's not a big deal. I've got five in every ear!"

"My business survives, thanks to this girl," I sent Marta an exaggerated smile.

"How many do you have, Eve?" Paula asked.

"Eight total," I replied, brushing my finger across the tiny silver hoops in my right ear. "Five in this one and three in the other."

Paula wanted her piercing to be at the tip of her left ear, just below the fold. That meant going through cartilage, which could be tough. I rubbed her skin with a cotton ball soaked with an ample dose of alcohol. I took the needle out of the plastic wrap and snapped it out of its little plastic shaft. Just then, his yellow eyes flashed before mine, throwing me off balance. I steadied myself by grabbing my desk.

"Are you okay?" both girls asked at once.

"Yeah, I'm fine. Just a little dizzy, sorry." The stirring sensation returned and suddenly I got the urge to be alone. I felt him so close to me, his hot breath on the back of my neck.

"Are you sure you're up for it?"

"Positive," I said, brushing my thoughts aside and taking control of my mind with one deep inhale. "Let's get this over with. I'm going to count to three and do it at three. Ready?"

"Yes. No! Wait," she drew a breath. "Okay. Go." Paula shut her eyes and lips, making small creases in the skin of her face.

"One. Two . . . " I pushed in, never getting to three.

Two long tears streamed down Paula's cheeks. I felt something inside of me implode, a new kind of awareness entering my body, like the cold blade of a sword. The needle was moving slowly, encountering much resistance as if the tissue was made out of wood. I stood there, bent over Paula's ear, squeezing my legs and lips tight, trying to hold on. *I'm waiting for you to open, to allow me to come through...* I heard him and groaned before making it to the other side with one solid push.

Both of us were perspiring, our hearts pounding. Paula's temple vein pulsated under her flushed skin, which was sparkling with a thin film of sweat. It was a breathless rush every time, but never quite like this. With the needle stuck in her throbbing ear, Paula sat up straight, her spine at once turning into a staff while I dropped lifelessly onto my mattress bed.

"Intense stuff!" Marta said. "I better open the window or else I'll pass out from all this excitement."

"Please do," I murmured, pressing the heels of my palms to my eyes.

"How much longer?" Paula asked.

"We're almost done," I replied, knowing well that the real labor had just begun. The frosty air coming through the window helped clear my head. I searched for any lingering sensations inside my body, but only found his afterglow, an echo shimmering in the distance like rain.

I got up and tugged on the needle stuck in Paula's ear. A drop of blood oozed out of the opening. "Let's give you and your ear a little rest." I reached for the tiny silver hoop earring that Paula had brought with her and swabbed it with alcohol-soaked cotton ball. My hands were trembling.

"So, what are you up to tonight?" Marta asked, scanning through my music library of close to two hundred audiotapes, most of which I had inherited from my cousin, who at the age of twenty-four deemed himself too old to still listen to Iron Maiden. "Usual assembly behind the theater?"

I nodded, and Marta suggested we walk there together, since she and Paula lived nearby. While I enjoyed my solitary walks, I didn't mind having company at this late hour when the oak-lined avenue resembled a dark tunnel.

"Have you guys seen the new visitor in town?" I asked, and bit my tongue. It was too late now. The cat was out.

"Which one?" Marta asked, pulling out a Slayer tape before shoveling it right back in.

"The punky-looking guy with the blue mohawk," I

said, walking up to my desk to collect cotton balls stained with crimson droplets.

"No, I haven't. But he sounds interesting. I like punky guys with mohawks."

Paula broke out laughing and I picked up her earring to resume my labor.

"I need you to hold still so that I don't make a second hole with the earring."

"Sorry, I just imagined Ben getting jealous."

"Yeah, wouldn't that be something? I mean the guy always has the same expression on his face," Marta laughed. "Look at me, I'm so calm, cool and collected," she intoned in a low voice.

"Oh, shut up, you two! Ben and I are just friends. No one is getting jealous of anyone," I said, gearing up to pull the needle out of Paula's ear to insert the hoop.

"I think Ben might have a different opinion about that, but, oh well. How's he doing by the way?" Marta asked, before moving over to scavenge through my bookshelf.

I didn't answer, instead remembering why I usually eschewed the company of girls. They were nosy and talked too much.

"What's this?" She forced out a book that was tucked between two larger tomes, its spine facing away from her. "Are you studying black magic?" she asked, the tone of her voice exposing enthusiasm and condemnation. My mind made a connection with the book that was still in my backpack. They seemed related, although the book Marta found contained forbidden knowledge shrouded in darkness. The one I had just found seemed to emanate light rather than absorb it.

"Sort of was reading it, but I stopped," I mumbled, trying to control my mounting frustration. I wanted her to leave my room at this point. The wet ring slipped through my fingers and fell onto the carpet. I cursed under my breath.

"Does it have spells?" Paula perked up, forgetting about the hole in her ear.

"It's full of them!" Marta answered for me. "Wow, this is great! Can you cast a spell on someone to make them fall for you?"

"I wouldn't go there if I were you," I said, disinfecting the earring again and forcing it into the hole in Paula's ear. I wanted to finish this job before Marta got her hands on other things she and the rest of my town shouldn't know about. "You should check out the alternative medicine book instead."

"I'd rather cast a spell than make herbal teas."

"Eve is right, though. Doing that wouldn't bring you true love," Paula winced and hissed. "It's like cheating."

"Okay, fine. You want to know about alternative medicine? Take this: my aunt said that an acupuncturist told her to never pierce ears. The needle does something to the energies, messes them up or something."

"Don't listen to her," I told Paula. "Just breathe. I need to focus now."

This was by far the most difficult part of the procedure. Clenching my jaw, I pressed the sharp end of the earring into the hole, curved it slightly, withdrew the needle, and felt a small snap. The ring passed through. I breathed out a whole lungful of stale air.

"And I heard that you can wake people up from a coma if you insert the needle in the right spot in their ear," Paula replied.

"Feeling more awake?" Marta said, and all three of us laughed.

"Better than after two hours of trying to sleep with my eyes open," Paula said.

"I'm telling you, this girl is crazy," Marta said, rolling her eyes at Paula. "Sleeping with her eyes open."

"It's technically called mediations. But back to the black magic book," Paula said, "I once heard that just having such a thing nearby could attract bad spirits."

"Hear that Marta? You should listen to Paula," I said, cleaning her ear of bloodstains. "There, all set," I proclaimed, putting a mirror in front of her face. "Marta, please put the book away."

"Looks great," Marta said, holding the book open on her lap and watching Paula caress the ring with her trembling fingertip. "Okay, back to your little black book, where did you get it?" she asked, her attention back on the page in front of her. "Ben?"

"He gave it to me to get rid of it." I said, which wasn't entirely true. Ben warned me about this book when he showed it to me one night in his attic. He had borrowed it from some guy at his school, who supposedly had received it from a practitioner of magic who had *moved on to more advanced stuff*. Aside from letting me browse through it, Ben wouldn't let me take the book home, so I took it without his permission. I promised myself I would return it within a couple of days, but then school ramped up and I forgot about it until Marta reminded me it was still here.

"Why would he want to get rid of it?"

"Because it is like playing with fire!" I snatched the book out of Marta's hands and shelved it back. "It's getting late. Let's get out of here."

Paula was already reaching for her coat. "Do you think my ear will be all right in the cold?"

"Yes, yes. The cold will do it good," I replied.

"Thanks," Paula said, tucking tightly rolled-up cash into my palm.

"Coming?" Marta asked, her hand already on the doorknob.

"Yeah," I said, and untied my hair, letting it fall loosely onto my shoulders. The three of us stepped into the cold night as the full face of the moon climbed over rooftops, quietly echoing my name.

V.

The storm clouds returned to empty their contents over our town. Barely the size of coconut flakes, most of the snow melted before reaching the ground, and could only be seen floating within the halos of two streetlamps outside my house, one of which was erratically flashing, its bulb on the verge of going out. We left the warmth of my house and descended down the steps onto the deserted street, the marks of our footsteps letting through the raven-blackness of the asphalt that matched the color of the sky.

Passing by a neighbor's house, I turned to the girls. "I left a burning candle a couple of nights ago on this street corner," I pointed. "I wonder if it's still there. Mind if I check?"

The girls nodded and followed me to the area where two ends of a fence joined at a right angle, pausing a few steps behind me as I squatted down to investigate.

"Why would you leave a burning candle here?" Marta asked.

"Long story," was all I was willing to say in an effort to sidestep her instinctual nosiness. I moved a thin film of snow and clumps of grass to the side, and took off my gloves to feel for remains—a frozen puddle of red wax. Even though strong winds had raged through our town the night before last, the candle managed to burn itself to the ground. Peeling its edges with my bare hands, I retrieved the hard shape in one solid piece.

"Let's see the shape it casts on a wall," Paula suggested. We were nearing Andrzejki, the eve of St. Andrew's Day, a holiday Polish people celebrated at the end of November. That evening, females of all ages would gather together to melt candle wax, then pour the liquid through a keyhole and into a large bowl of cold water where it would instantly solidify. The shadows created by the shapes of wax would be carefully examined on a wall illuminated by a lamp, and were believed to foretell the future of the young women related to their matrimonies.

We spotted a suitable place where a halogen lamp illuminated a stack of large, empty water pipes waiting to be used in one of the neighborhood's construction projects that usually commenced in springtime. I held up the wax and angled it, my hand freezing in midair, the blood draining from my face.

The shape revealed the profile of a man. He had a long slanted forehead, a pointed nose, high cheekbones and long jaws; the back of his head was swathed in long disheveled hair. Without a doubt, it was a profile of the serpent man from my dream. This version of his image was twisted and grotesque, menacing even, and yet I was able to still recognize him.

"Does anyone else see what I see? Or is it only my sick imagination?" Paula broke the silence.

"I think it is pretty clear to all of us," Marta divulged. "This face is unmistakable."

"Eve?" Paula began.

"Yeah?"

"Your candle made the face of a devil."

What was terrifying to them was mesmerizing to me. Seeing it so close ignited a flame, melting the frost of fear that had been collecting over the glass of my perception, turning it into crying droplets of dew. My breath sped up and a subtle trembling overtook my body. Memories were returning and assembling into patterns. Some may have been fragments of dreams, others of things real, maybe partly imagined.

I couldn't tell. It didn't matter. The fire grew, making me feel naked and exposed. I wanted the girls to go and leave me there with his image. Sure, his face looked demonic, but their reaction was overblown. They didn't know what I knew.

"It's this satanic music you listen to!" Marta was quick with her verdict.

I swallowed and slowly lowered my arm.

"Do you think the black book may have something to do with it?" Paula asked.

"Definitely!" Marta said. "I'd give it back to Ben right away if I were you, and destroy the wax."

I shivered, considering the weight of her words that reawakened my fear.

"I don't think it's as serious as you make it," I said, running my bare fingers across the effigy's rugged surface.

"Break it up, Eve!" Marta said. "Look, your hands are shaking."

Holding the object with both hands, feeling cracks furrow across my heart, I broke it into two pieces. Just then an intense stabbing pain in my abdomen nearly made me fold over. But the girls insisted so I kept on breaking the wax into smaller pieces watching the little red fragments fall onto the carpet of snow like drops of blood. With each piece that fell, I grew colder and more rigid inside, until only a mere shadow of sensation lingered on the surface of my empty hands.

"Do you want me to go back and get the book?" Marta asked.

"Sure, why not," I shrugged, feeling the pain slowly recede.

While Paula and I waited for Marta to return, I tried to put some order to my thoughts. If the girl's suspicion was correct and the book helped manifest the effigy, I could use it to bring him back.

"Maybe you should pray tonight," Paula suggested and I nodded. Arguing made no sense.

When Marta returned, she held the book in one hand and a cookie in the other. "Please get this thing away from me." She nearly threw the book at me. "It's making me dizzy."

"Can we go now?" Paula asked, after I stuffed the rolled-up book into my pocket. None of us said anything; the sounds of our footsteps and Marta's rhythmic chewing were the only noises that filled the night's vacuum.

As we turned the corner, the contours of the gray theater building came into view, people sticking to its stone steps like black clumps of tar. I quickly spotted three towering figures. Seeing me approach, Ben broke away and began his descent. Marta pinched my arm. I jabbed her with my elbow. A moment later he was within an arm's reach.

"What happened to you?" he asked, ignoring the girls. I knew he could barely tolerate Marta. In his view, she was the epitome of sensationalism and gossip.

"It's a long story. . . ."

"I have lots of time," he replied.

"She made a devil out of candle wax," Marta couldn't help herself. The girls giggled and I wished I now had a spell that would make them vanish.

Ben looked at me. "Why don't you and I go on a walk? Alone," he said, pulling me away. I heard them depart in whispers.

Ben and I walked until we reached a nearby children's playground. Before we sat on rusty swings, I turned once more toward Paula and Marta, feeling our glances brush against each other.

"New friends?" Ben brought me back.

"Nah. Just needle work."

"I see. But seriously, you look like you saw a ghost."

"It's not that far from the truth," I said, and recounted what had occurred. "You heard them, they said it looked like the face of the devil."

"Did it?"

"Kind of."

"Are you scared?"

"I was a little earlier. But not anymore."

Ben drew in a breath. "Maybe it's because of the candle?"

"It was not the best idea, was it?"

"Told you so." He did ask me to think twice. Even Art had muttered something under his breath about the lunacy of my decision. But in those moments when I wanted to do whatever I set my mind on, I didn't listen.

"Right. What idiot takes candles off people's graves?" I tried to make light of the situation, but neither of us laughed.

The red candle had rested atop a German soldier's crypt. It came to my possession the night of All Saint's Day, when the four of us went roaming the cemetery.

It was almost midnight when we had reached the necropolis, meandering in silence through a labyrinth of graves and catacombs, the smallest of which made me shiver. The burial grounds were set ablaze with thousands of flames carrying prayers across dimensions. Passing by a war tomb, I spotted four candles lining its edges, and had decided to take one with me to *light my way home*. I glanced into its flame all the way there, reciting made-up words as I traversed the last portion of the path alone. "Good luck!" the guys called out after we split at the fork. Even Ben hadn't proposed walking me home that night.

By the time I reached the bridge, warm winds were picking up strength and rushing clouds obliterating the face of the waxing moon. Less than a finger in length, the candle had continued to burn, the wind occasionally tugging on its flame. Rounding a corner to my house, I set it down, wary of taking it inside, convinced that the gale would put it out.

"Maybe it's the candle, but maybe there is more to it," I said to Ben.

"Any ideas?"

"Here is one," I said, handing him the rolled-up book.

Ben took it, rolled it back into a compact tube and stuffed it in the pocket of his coat. "I told you not to take it, Eve."

I froze, marinating in shame. "I meant to give it back sooner. I'm sorry."

He jumped off the swing and started to walk.

I followed.

"Are you mad?"

"No, just disappointed. You've been making bad choices lately. First the candle, and now this. What else have you done that you are not telling me?"

His comment stopped me in my tracks. "Nothing. I'm just confused," I said, well-aware of the secrets I'd been keeping from Ben. "Everything has just been strange lately."

"How strange? Come, let's keep walking."

"I've just been feeling . . . odd."

"Why do you think that is?"

"It's like some foreign force has entered my life. I just can't put my finger on it," I said, and quickly added, "Do you think that this book has something to do with it?"

Ben shrugged. "Remember our talk last night about what's real? The more power we give to something, whether it's a thing, a thought, or a belief, the more power it will have over you. It works both ways."

"Great, thanks. That makes me feel like I am the ruler of my life," I said, "forever at the mercy of thoughts and objects."

"That's not what I said. Thoughts maybe, but not objects. But objects can tell us something. They are like mirrors, reflecting back parts of ourselves that otherwise would remain unconscious."

"Mirrors?"

"As above, so below. The outer reflects the inner," he said.

"How do you know all these things?" I said, trying to match his pace.

He shrugged again. "I don't know. It just came to me. Although I admit, I too have been feeling strange lately. Everything seems easier."

"It's been the opposite for me."

"Sounds like it."

"How has it been easier for you?"

"I've been acing all my tests, for example. You know I don't study. I don't even go to the damn class or open a textbook, but my tests get perfect scores. My teachers are baffled and so am I. I only hope it continues."

"So, if you know so much and have gotten so clairvoyant, what do you think is causing all these things to happen to me?" I asked as we made an arc around the theater, sidestepping the chattering clusters of youth.

"I don't think they are so much happening to you, but rather that you are creating them. You didn't have to take the book or the candle. But you did. Free will. The question is, what's been motivating you? And you should be the one answering it."

I shrugged, searching for words that wouldn't betray what I knew about *him*. "I don't know the answer to that."

"I could help you," he cleared his throat, and turned to look at me. "If you let me."

We passed the swelling crowd and entered a side street. It had stopped snowing and whatever had fallen on the road before had already melted. Moonlight cast a silver pillar in its center. The night was calm and the sky had cleared in a few places. The moon's partly unveiled face hovered higher, giving the black sky a hint of blue. The air smelled of moist earth.

"What do you mean if I let you?" I asked.

"I could tell you. But it will be better if I just show you," he said, slowing us down.

The theater was out of sight; only sleeping houses with dark windows surrounded us. Ben turned to face me. The air sighed, tickling my face. He reached out his hands to move the hair off my cheeks. His warm touch lingered on my skin. I looked up at him and once more noticed the radiance emanating from his face, a light blue tone on the backdrop of the night sky. How come I'd never noticed it before? Cradling my head with his palms, he leaned his face closer. An avalanche of thoughts poured through my head before everything came to a standstill.

"I've been wanting to kiss you for a very long time, Eve," he whispered, and touched his lips to mine, soft and tender.

I gave in to the caress, hoping it would melt the wince off my face and thaw my icy lips. His breath warmed my face as the wind continued to blow through my hair, oblivious to my inner battle. Ben's open palm pressed into the small of my back, sealing all spaces between us, the metal button of my jeans pressing into my stomach. I gripped his shoulders. Crowded with curtains and smoky mirrors, I ran across the labyrinth of my mind until I thought of the blue-haired stranger, and an electric current jolted my spine. I gasped and peeled away.

"Are you all right?" Ben asked, still holding me tight.

"Yes," I said in between breaths. But I wasn't. My surrender to Ben was a lie.

"Good," he said, and pressed me toward his warm chest. "I'm glad you now know how I feel about you."

His words sizzled my brain before guilt twisted my gut. I lied to him, I betrayed him. But he couldn't hear my soul's desperate calls. From this point forward, I knew that things could never be the same between us. With great sadness, I realized I had just lost a friend.

"Everything will be all right. Just trust me," he said, cradling me in his arms. "You have had way too much on your mind lately. You are simply stressed and trying to hold it all together. Plus your grandfather . . . I mean it is easy to make things into more than they really are when you are under this much pressure. But this is also why I like you so much. Because you are so sensitive and vulnerable. It makes you impossibly beautiful."

"Stress? You really think it's that simple?" I asked, on the verge of crying.

He nodded and released me. "Yes, I do. I really do."

I touched my hand to my mouth. The space between us seemed impossible to cross.

Ben smiled. "We should go. It is already half past ten," he said, and seized my hand before I had a chance to hide it inside my pocket. I felt Ben's grip tightening around my lifeless palm as we approached the theater and could swear I saw heads turn and the wave of conversational noise died down, only to pick up again ringing with a new intonation. Nobody said anything directly; they just kept whispering and flashing glances at us.

Two cars with headlights and engines turned on were parked by the stairs. Ben pulled me in the direction of a black Audi, inside of which Art and Rock sat fiddling with the stereo. Then I saw Mila, my music teacher's younger sister and a talented pianist, and asked Ben to let me go so I could talk to her, in an effort to liberate myself from his grasp.

I approached her with relief, as if finding a family member in a crowd of strangers. But upon seeing me, the girl threw her locks to the side with dramatic aloofness and walked away, sending me a cold glare. Surprised, I strolled past her until I was alone in the dark shadow of the theater's windowless sidewall, walking blindly toward the back.

"Eve, c'mon! We're waiting!" I heard Ben's voice trailing behind me.

"I need a moment alone. Please." I curled my hands into tight fists and continued to walk toward the void. In the distance, I heard muffled voices. Something portent was brewing, almost ghoulish.

"I don't think it is a good idea for you to go there!" Ben called.

"Why not?"

"Those kids, they can act stupid sometimes," he warned me. But I kept on. "Eve, please. Turn around and come with us!"

Making my way around the building's corner, I could make out about a dozen moving shadows next to the stairs where the blue stranger had me sit this morning. Some had their cigarettes lit, the light from their embers hovering midair like orange fireflies. Someone threw a glass bottle to the ground, shattering it into pieces. Then someone else started to howl and dissonant shrieks followed. The cacophony anchored me in place. Ben caught up to me and lightly tugged on my sleeve, but by then our presence was known.

"Is this a girl? Am I smelling a female?" one of them said, his voice growing louder with each approaching step.

Ben was right. It was a mistake for me to have come here. My breathing became choked with fear. "Because if you are a girl, you couldn't have picked a better place to visit."

"Hey, guys! It's Ben and I'm with her."

The voice turned toward Ben. "But girls can appreciate beauty much better. They were made for it. Wouldn't you agree?"

"Don't do anything stupid," Ben said.

"Stu-pid?" the voice answered slowly, accenting each syllable. I recognized whom it belonged to and my body trembled. "Who said stu-pid? Nobody would ever think of such a thing! No, not stu-pid, my friend. What we have here is something so spectacular, it begs to be seen. Something meaningful, which says a lot in a world that suffers from its lack, am I right?" he asked, casting the question over his shoulder toward his companions. They cheered on Crass' ghastly spectacle. "Have you ever witnessed a ritual? Not candles and holy water and shit, but a real ritual with real sacrifice?"

"Okay, enough. Let's go, Eve. Now," Ben said to me. I knew I should've left right then, but I couldn't move. Crass came closer until I could feel the force of his exhale. It smelled of alcohol. If I reached my hand, I could touch the greasy blond hair falling down his shoulders.

"She wants to see it. Let her see it," he repeated with a growl, stepping behind me and placing one of his hands over my eyes and slipping the other under my arm.

I was annoyed at Ben for not intervening more strongly. But didn't I just want him to back off and let me be moments ago? What was wrong with me? I realized I was filled with conflicting thoughts and desires, which made me reconsider Ben's proposition. Maybe he was right. Maybe I was overstressed and should just trust him.

Crass nudged me forward. His hand on my face smelled of cigarettes and something akin to a mixture of dirt and iron. I opened my mouth to avoid the repugnant scent. We took about two dozen steps, with Ben shadowing us. I felt the space around me with my free arm, wary of where I was being taken, but all I could feel was empty space. Crass took away his hand.

"Open your eyes," he said in a husky voice.

Moonlight poured into my eyes.

Crass spoke in a hushed tone. "No matter how hard you try, you cannot turn back time. You can scream and shout in protest, but ultimately there is only one thing you can do to feel peace again. You must accept it. You must accept death. Passive acceptance. So feminine, so dark, so beautiful," he said, pulling me closer.

The orb of the cold November moon became the backdrop for the cat's hanging silhouette. It dangled on a rope attached to a tree by its neck. The sight triggered a chill similar to the one I had felt upon having the coated man's gaze fall upon me. I felt a rage rising in my heart, difficult to restrain.

"Please, tell me it was dead before you did this," I said. "Or that a car ran over it, that it was deceased! Tell me that!"

"But that wouldn't be a proper sacrifice, would it? That would be wrong. That would make the spirits angry. The animal before you was healthy and strong and it fought well for its life. Its fur glistened in light. Its body lean and supple," Crass said, his words inciting a wave of nausea.

I turned to Ben, "And you knew about this? Why didn't you do something?"

"Eve, let's go."

Tears burned my cheeks like hot lava. "You are sick!" I screamed and turned to run.

"Sick?" Crass laughed. "Obviously you know nothing about rituals," his words stomped on my heels. "You know nothing of invoking the fallen."

Rock and Art were in the car waiting, the engine still running. More cars were coming, loading people and departing. I crawled onto the back seat and saw Ben chase away some kid who wanted to hitch a ride. We drove off with a sharp squeal of tires. Ben put his right arm around me. I was sobbing and trying to hide it. Rock turned on the stereo and soon the familiar sounds reverberated out of the speakers:

Well it's a righteous dream, out of my mind.
A righteous dream, out of my mind . . .

Art lit a cigarette and opened the window. I shivered from the cold wind that whipped across my face, drying my tears. Ben squeezed me tighter and with his free hand brushed away a wisp of hair lashing my face. He tucked it behind my right ear and brought his head closer to mine.

"I want you," he said. But my heart was cold.

VI.

The lights outside the car window seemed to elongate like small comets through the glass as we drove. Besides the occasional glimpses of man-made brightness, the rising moon continued to bathe the onyx world in a cold glow, turning the frosted crop fields into sheets of glistening sandpaper.

I looked over my shoulder. Ben was looking away, his thwarted exhales occluding the car's side window. As much as I wanted to alleviate the pressure that had mounted between us, I was at my wit's end, unable to make a move. I felt that the person I used to call my best friend had moved so far away from me that he almost belonged to another world. Or maybe it was I who had crossed dimensions? After all, shadows were obscuring what I used to take as common reality, with demonic acts, strangers and faces popping up around me, even finding me in my dreams. Or maybe they had always been there and I was just now beginning to see them?

The road led us away from already scarce sources of night-lights, and toward a village submerged in deep sleep, over which shone a single, faint streetlamp. Rock slowed down and turned onto a dirt road, carved between two houses with barns. Gravel churned beneath our tires. We crossed a short narrow bridge fashioned out of uneven wood planks, which ricocheted our bodies and made the seats squeak, and entered an open lot, our headlights blinding the people who had gotten there before us. Another car was approaching closely behind. I glanced at Ben, who was still immersed in deep thought, his chin leaning into his curled fingers, and wondered if I had lost him forever.

My hand was on the door handle before the car came to a full stop. I pulled the lever, got out, shut the door, and walked away. Cool autumn air swirled over my cheeks. Dizzy from exiting the stuffy car so fast, I stopped and pressed the heels of my palms into my shut eyelids. Darkness exploded into a spangled eruption, fireworks on a backdrop of darkness. I withdrew my hands. As the murk receded, the castle's imposing silhouette emerged, the inky velvet sky peeling off its contours. I kept walking away from the car, feeling Ben's eyes following me. He stayed back. I felt his silent defeat in my bones.

I passed circles of people, but they were too absorbed in conversation and lighting their cigarettes to notice me. Approaching the castle, I looked up toward the first of its two front towers, one of which had nearly collapsed under the weight of time. A gaping hole in the middle of the tower's cylindrical wall exposed a spiral staircase inside which starlight splashed across the uneven surfaces of stone. I passed by decrepit oak trees with branches like claws, and thorny bushes that scratched my jeans, and walked into what many centuries ago may have been a lush garden. My eyes skipped upward toward the apex of a tower surrounded by a ring of predatory bird effigies that lunged beneath the tip of its turret, bringing back the mood from my abysmal dream.

A gust of wind hit my wide-open eyes; I blinked and two tears rolled down my cheeks. Stumbling, I neared the castle wall, and almost fell, my bare hands grabbing onto the fortress' rugged surface in time. A feather stuck in a dry branch grazed my cheek. Startled, I jerked back and a waft of dense air ran through my hair like the fingers of a ghost. I plucked the feather off the branch and hid behind a wall of shrubs, stomping among stones and decaying leaves. Leaning my back into the wall, I closed my eyes, letting out a long exhale that merged with the wind. I listened to its howling as it snaked through the forest and licked the insides of the castle walls, its arms stretching in multiple directions at once. It soon dissipated and I inhaled the silence that descended, letting it bloom inside the still center of my being. It was the most peaceful I'd felt all day.

There, beneath my closed eyelids, floating on the wisps of feather-like clouds, my imagination brought me to a small, blue pond nestled among high mountains. I flew above its frozen surface, which, like a mirror, reflected the glowing face of a full moon shining above. *I am the knowing that crushes all doubt. Ancient, numinous, rising . . .* I heard its whisper. I opened my eyes and gazed up. *What you seek is within you. Follow the trail.* The whisper continued. *Release your doubt. Trust your feelings.*

A sharp cramp took my breath away. I folded over, one hand on my stomach, the other gripping the stone wall, its sharpness cutting into my skin. I straightened up, just enough to draw a breath. With oxygen's aid, the tightness in my stomach unraveled a bit, and a glob of thick mass detached from my diaphragm and ascended upward. It crossed the gorge between my lungs and crawled across my arteries, squeezing itself through the clenched chambers of my heart before reaching my throat, where it held me in a strangling grip.

Convulsions shook my body and images swirled. I slid down the wall to the ground, and I grabbed a hold of my head. My scalp was tingling, a sandstorm raging beneath, scraping the inside of my skull. In an effort not to faint, I kept breathing and holding on with everything I had. When I could not fight it any longer, the top of my head burst open and like a geyser, the sensations left my body.

Release your doubt, the voice bellowed in the empty chambers of my head.

Still holding onto my stomach, I flung my lids open and looked at the moon. It looked back at me with its uncompromising, watchful eye. I was no longer nauseous and the cadence of my breath returned to normal. I could taste the freshness of air, devoid of the coal tinge, which was typical in town.

I heard footsteps, followed by a glimpse of a bursting flame. I shivered and froze. The last thing I wanted was to be discovered by Ben and smothered by his attention. But it wasn't Ben. The stranger moved the branches aside, and without uttering a single word joined me on the cold ground. Moonlight bespangled his face with a spray of a thousand cobalt flickers.

"You found me," I said.

"I told you I would," he smiled. "You feel different."

"It's the moon. I think it cast a spell over me."

"Could be," he said. "It has the power to enhance our ability to see things that are normally hidden."

"Like what?"

"Like the deepest cravings of your soul," he smiled at me. I felt a rush of scarlet warmth on my face. "Tell me more about the meadows."

"The meadows…" I echoed his request. "The place where I found scattered pieces of myself." I closed my eyes and let my mind carry me to the land of daydreams and wildflowers. "They spread just beyond my house. They became my private kingdom. There, I felt—"

"Free." He said the word slowly.

"Right, free. I remember running across them laughing for no reason, joy bursting out of my heart. Or I'd lie on their soft bed, tracing the sky's changing cloud formations. But then, one day something happened."

"Yes, that. What was it?" he asked in a shaky voice.

"I found a new place. A hidden place."

"Take me there," he said, and I did just that.

It was a small forest of densely growing young trees, easy to miss, surrounded by soft, moist turf. That day something had lured me in its direction. I put the crown flower wreath I had just finished making on my head and got up, shaking bits of plants off my dress and stepped across the damp ground. Water welled up around my sandals, wetting my bare toes. Slowly, I made it to the forest's edge. Bees electrified the herbal air. Up close, the small forest had the shape of a dome, its tangled tree branches leaning toward each other. In a place where a tree had fallen, piercing the thicket, I found a passage. I stepped onto the horizontal trunk and forged ahead, arms outstretched for balance. Without a scratch, I passed through the thorny fence and looked ahead. Before me was a shaded glade sprinkled with primrose flowers, moist grass sparkled in sunlight, fresh and untainted. With trees ending their bloom, white petals were falling to the ground in swirls like snow.

"You found something there, didn't you? On the grass," his voice entered my world.

"A feather. The most glorious one I'd ever seen."

"What did you do with it?" he asked and I blushed.

"I caressed my skin with it. I liked to run the long firm quill between my fingers. I let it paint my cheeks and tickle my neck. I liked its gentle touch."

"But you lost it. How?"

My mind took me back to that day in late fall when my grandparents came for a visit to our house, which was something that did not happen often. The leaves were falling off the trees and it was raining. Dad picked me up from school. Mom made supper and the six of us ate together at a table, another rare occurrence. I kept the feather in a tall flower vase on top of a cloud of white cotton on my windowsill. When after the supper I came into my room, the vase was empty. There was no feather in sight. "I never found it again."

"Open your palm," he said. Nesting in my hand was a mangled quill, the rusty blood from my scratched hand rubbed into its fibers. "Do you know what the girl in my dream is searching for?" he asked.

"A feather?"

He shook his head. "She is looking for the entrance to Tartarus, the place of his imprisonment." He paused before continuing. "The one from your dreams is a fallen angel. The feather you found in the meadow belonged to him."

"How do you know this?"

"Long story. Maybe one day I will tell you."

"Who are you really?" I squinted my eyes at him.

"Friends call me Punk."

"But that can't be your name."

"Why not? Don't you think it's fitting?"

"What's your real name?"

"I gave it up long time ago."

"Why?"

"It no longer fit," he said. "Names have vibrations that can influence a sense of self."

"Maybe I should change mine, then? Maybe that would help?"

"He is looking for you," Punk said changing the tone of his voice.

"Who?"

"The guy in the long coat. He wants to protect you. I think he feels responsible for you."

"Protect me from what?"

"Yourself," Punk said and got up.

"But I'm not doing anything to myself. He should stop worrying."

"It's that curiosity you have. You won't stop until you find what you're looking for..." he reached his hand to help me up.

"And what's wrong with that?"

"It can take you into strange territories," he said, let go of my hand and shook the leaves and bits of grass off his pants. "You should go now and find Ben. He will take you home."

"What about you?"

"It's time for me to go, too," Punk said stepping around the bushes. "Be safe, Evelina. Oh, and one more thing," he turned toward me. "If you are really serious about finding the truth, you should go with your parents tomorrow."

I looked at his back until the shadow of the forest swallowed his silhouette, leaving behind a yawning gap. Punk's last words hung suspended before nature's breath dispersed them into nothing. He was a strange person, this Punk, his presence always evoking so much, leaving me feeling cold and alone each time he departed.

Wondering how it was possible to feel so close with someone who less than a day ago was but a stranger, I began walking toward the front of the castle. Slowly, avoiding spider webs and sharp branches, I made my way back to the parking lot. Ben, Rock, and Art were waiting for me by the car. I went inside without saying a word and they followed. As the engine ignited and tires begun to turn over the gravel, my eyes fell shut and I realized how tired I was. But I was no longer angry or confused. I had found my answer. The man from my dream was a fallen angel eager to communicate with me.

"Eve," Ben said, gently patting my knee with his fingers. "I don't quite know how to tell you this, but I don't want you to grow anymore distant from me than you already have."

"Just say what you have to say," I said, leaning my head onto the headrest.

"Something strange is happening to me. I don't feel like I'm myself."

"Right, you told me that. Acing the tests and

what not."

"No, but I also feel like I'm losing control. It kind of freaks me out," he said, low enough so the others couldn't hear. I placed my hand over his palm. "Thank you," he whispered in reply to my gesture. "Thank you for that."

"The world does feel like it's gone to hell, doesn't it?"

"It does and the worst part is losing you. I'm sorry about today. I don't know what came over me. I just wanted to let you know I cared. But now I see I went too far."

I wasn't sure what to think of his confession. "Can we talk about this later? I'm really tired now."

"I will come over in the evening, if that's all right? Your parents and Rena will be gone. I'll bring supper."

"I won't be home. I decided to go with them."

"I see," Ben said, retracting his hand from under mine. A few moments later he spoke again. "Maybe we can talk tonight then? I can stay a little longer. I don't mind walking home—"

"I have to go to bed," I said. "I will need to be up in a few hours. You better get some sleep, too. Clear your head. I'll call you when I get back."

"Eve," he lifted his hand to caress my cheek with its back. I looked down and then up at his face. "I feel like I am losing you and I don't even know how to express how bad it feels."

"I really need to be alone right now, Ben. It's better this way."

"If that is what will bring you back to me, then sure, I'll leave you alone," he said. "Until you return."

The car stopped in front of my house. I thanked Rock for driving, and exited the car waving at Rock and Art from the outside. Art's eyes were piercing and I could feel them trailing me all the way to my door. I slid the key into the lock and as quietly as I could, turned it, and slipped inside my warm house.

I took off my heavy boots, walked into my dark room, and dropped my coat, sweater and jeans onto the floor. I washed my face and brushed my teeth without turning any lights. The exhaustion that had weighed me down earlier wore off once I was home. I lit a candle in my room, retrieved the book from my backpack, and perched myself on the edge of my mattress. I flipped through the pages and ran my fingers across the handwritten text tracing the depressions left in paper. A cold shiver rolled up my back, but I didn't feel like getting up to put on a robe. Instead, I let myself soak up the text in front of me.

> *Death—unsightly warrior of time*
> *Measuring my strength to your might, I cannot.*
> *Your dark empty caverns*
> *Shall not suit the affections of my mind,*
> *Only inspire the song of my dying heart.*
>
> *You level us across the gamut of truths and desires,*
> *Your teachings are stern in their rule,*
> *Your laws uncompromised.*
>
> *You shall not deny my undying trust,*
> *Though your void awaits,*
> *As I near my journey's end.*
> *Soon, you and I shall be one.*

I closed the book and hugged it to my chest. What kind of ode was this? Was the one who wrote this on the verge of death? I decided it would be best to start at the beginning. My legs were tingling from the squatting position. Ready to hide under the covers, I stood up to stretch and pulled the jeans off my bed. My hands stumbled upon something hard that nested in a pocket—Mom's red lipstick. I opened the shaft that was loose from the cracking and turned the bottom, watching the crimson cane emerge. Gazing into the candle flame, I applied a layer of the creamy substance, rubbing my lips together to evenly spread the color, a forbidden taste lingering on my tongue's tip.

A gust of cold wind broke into my room, banging the window open and blowing out the flame. I shivered and got up to close it. But when my hands touched the sill, I was no longer cold. I squinted at the moon's full glowing body and the orb began to grow. Its radiance spread through my bones raising my temperature. The wind kept blowing through my hair, but its frigid touch had no effect on me. I took off the rest of my clothes. Wearing nothing but the lipstick, I leaned into the sill and continued staring at the moon.

The sphere cast off a second halo that reached all the way to my room. I squinted more, blurring my vision, and watched the shadows on its surface liquefy and shift positions. Like drops of quicksilver, the shades melted together to mold a figure. It stirred before rising and showing off its full majesty. I could see his face, those distinct features that were etched in my memory. His bright yellow eyes were bewitching, body descending toward me down a celestial stairway. Cold wind tangled my hair while a descending drop of sweat tickled my back.

"Who are you, shining one?" I asked, swaying.

From the back of his body, two black wings unfurled.

Innocence is torment, I heard his deep voice reverberate within me. He reached his arms toward me. I saw dried blood on their surface. Soon his cold breath was on my neck, his hand touching my chest, fingertips drawing a straight line from my collarbone to my bellybutton. My legs folded under me. But he caught me before I fell, surrounding my body in a warm cocoon of feathers. All movement ceased and I felt I was home at last.

I am Sariel. Free me, he said, and for a brief moment the walls separating our worlds fell, and I found a piece of myself I had lost so long ago.

PART II
DANIEL

VII.

Where am I? Tongues of fire lick my body, searing my wings. I try to hang in midair, but the loss of lift and force of gravity are dragging me down. A gaping black hole of the abyss looms beneath me. I feel my feathers detaching, heat transforming their tips into ember dust. Unable to ascend, I'm starting to fall. The fire liquefies my lower body. Wax drips down my legs. I am made of wax. I am an effigy, alive and dead, caught between resistance and release. Losing substance, drop by drop, I become lighter. Drop by drop—the dripping reverberates like tears falling into a well. My descent slows just as the fire reaches my heart. With the flames consuming the last vestiges of my form, my body vanishes and I fly free toward the moon. The cold, cold moon.

I awakened to the window in my room clamoring open, the lacy curtain flying to my ceiling. The temperature inside must have been close to sub-zero. The world was still dark, but I could hear Mom and Rena shuffling around and Dad loading things into our car and slamming the doors.

I stretched and shivered. I couldn't remember when sleep took me away. The last thing I managed to recall was how bright the moon was, and me standing naked by the window— not the smartest idea. I could've gotten sick. My scowl brightened into a smile. It was all worth it because I got to see him, feel him even when his black wings closed around me. He told me his name. What was it? I thought hard, trying to remember, making a crease between my brows. *Sariel.* Sariel was his name! And he asked me to free him, something that brought up another memory before everything faded. But what was it that I could possibly free him from? And why did it make sense to me when he said it, like pieces of a puzzle snapping together for a fleeting instance? I felt the weight of the angel's request press against my logic and a pinch of fear spread inside me like ice freezing the surface of a lake, halting all movement. Clearly, I was not in control. The thought crossed my mind that some form of a chain reaction had been

57

initiated and there was not much I could do to stop it.

But maybe all this was only a delusion? I've always had a rich imagination, and it was possible that I'd outdone myself with this recent fantasy. But even if it was only my imagination, last night's dream was a very visceral dream, a prurient dream.

I stirred to break my mind's immobilizing spell. My sheets were tangled and binding my legs. My hands stained with blue ink, and my bed sheets soaked with sweat. I noticed crimson marks all over them. Blood? I scanned my hands looking for traces of cuts but couldn't find any. It must have been the lipstick. My body felt tender, as if I had just caught the flu. But there was something else happening as well, a strange feeling in the lower part of my belly, a burning that felt like all my nerves had coiled into a tight ball down there, hypersensitive and fevered.

Wrapped in sheets, I leaped out of bed, shut the window and left the freezing room, aiming for the bathroom. The smell of fried eggs and coffee wafted through the air in the hallway making me hungry and think of Punk. I worried if he'd get to eat today. I knew so little about this strange youth and yet was beginning to feel closer to him than Ben. Last night he said I should I go with my parents if was serious about understanding everything better. Mom should be happy to hear I changed my mind.

I locked the bathroom door, turned on the shower faucet, and waiting for the water to heat up, looked in the mirror. I saw a solemn face looking back, her features sharper, more serious, before the steam obliterated the reflection. Stepping under the searing hot flow, I stood with my eyes closed, breathing slowly and letting the heat seep into my bones.

I left the bathroom wrapped in a fluffy towel and walked into my room, now also much warmer, my eyes fixed on the black book lying next to my bed, and shoved it into my backpack. I dressed in my usual black attire and walked into the kitchen. Dawn was beginning to break.

A cape of worry slipped off Mom's shoulders once I told her that I would be coming with them to visit the most pensive of our family members. She liked having all of us close. Grandpa never spoke much, but when he did, he'd choose his words deliberately. He had told me many times that words had the power to move mountains. Since I was little, he had stressed how important it was to err on the side of the good, especially in most trying circumstances. He'd tell me war stories and sing Russian songs to me as we picked wild mushrooms in a forest laced with pre-dawn mist. Then after we returned home, with his blue pen he'd make drawings for me on scraps of baking parchment paper.

I knew that Grandpa Jan had almost died at the hands of the Soviets who had invaded Poland from the east in 1939. The country needed young and able men to fight the Red Army. His small battalion had been captured near the border and held in confinement for weeks. Many had died. Grandma would always call Grandpa's escape miraculous. Battered and starved, he vowed never to fight again, his soul traumatized by the horrors he'd witnessed. He had hid in the woods until the war was over, had become a farmer and soon after met his future wife. They had three children. Watching them interact, I would notice that while he was firm with his two sons, he'd look at Mom with deep sadness, his eyes growing opaque. One Sunday, after a bad fight between my parents, I overheard Grandpa telling his wife how he wished he'd listened to his daughter when she was pregnant with Rena asking for permission to raise her child on her own, without having to marry Dad. But my grandmother wanted to hear none of it. According to her, the times were hard and my father was a resourceful man, and marrying him guaranteed Mom a level of security her own parents couldn't provide. Besides, her daughter's reputation would've been ruined, though I suspected that she also worried about her own.

The ride to the hospital that should have taken four hours, took almost twice as long due to roadwork delays and subsequent detours, many a time testing Dad's self-control, and our ability to handle his outbursts. The day was wet and bleak, as was our collective mood, which Mom tried to alleviate with her sunshine smile and playful winks. Pools of ice had melted overnight, lining streets with uneven puddles and scattering muck on cars and passersby. Mom arranged a night at a motel for us to allow for a double visit and to break up the driving.

As we entered the city, Dad had to turn on windshield wipers because the soot that floated in the air hindered our visibility. It landed on the glass like black specks of dry ink, which the wipers only smeared. The soot came from welding factories that lined the streets, and a ring of coal mines surrounding the city. This region boasted the country's highest child mortality rates due to leukemia. The public channel on late night television aired stories about those innocent victims making Mom feel sad and helpless.

Leaning into the car window and away from my sister, I tried to focus on reading the black book. Every few minutes my eyes would go out of focus and my memory of Sariel would return. I smiled in those moments, my little secret pulsing with life. Whenever I picked up on Rena staring at me, I would bring my eyes back to the book. It was harder for her to try to interrupt me when I was engaged.

The first pages described in verse the early life of a boy and his search for identity. From what I could glean, as the language was full of metaphors, he spent that time in constant motion. The landscapes were changing page to page, from mountains to sea, to dreary places swathed by clouds of coal smoke, much like the city we were in. It was becoming clear that he was an orphan, often mistreated and lonely. But he had a clairvoyant gift—he knew how to interpret dreams. I wanted to keep reading but the driving made me nauseous so I had to take frequent breaks, my eyes returning to the gloomy landscapes until my body reminded me once more of my recent encounter with the angel.

It was early afternoon by the time we parked our car in the hospital lot. Outside the front of the building, rusty ambulances were lined up like train wagons. We entered the fluorescent hospital lobby filled with the sterile smell of dry medicine. The front desk was empty. Mom tried to smile, though I could see repulsion torque her facial features beneath a layer of forced pleasantness. She and I exchanged distressed glances while Rena and Dad took seats in the waiting room, my sister diving right into a youth periodical she grabbed off of a newspaper pile.

"What a sad place," I said to her.

"Do you remember the little boy we met in the hospital when you were four? The one who got ill because he ate too many green apples?"

Of course I remembered. It was the only time I was ever hospitalized, which was due to a severe drug allergy. The little boy came to visit me each day, holding my hand as Mom read to us. He stayed there after I was discharged. The nurses told Mom that there was nothing wrong with him and that he'd been there for over two weeks because his parents never came to pick him up. "I often wonder what happened to that boy," Mom said, looking at Dad who appeared as if lightning had struck him, and immediately got up from his chair and stormed outside. Mom's eyes followed after him. "He can't stand when I bring it up."

"Why?" I asked

"He wouldn't let me take the boy home with us."

"But, Mom, that would have been more complicated than just taking him home."

"At least we could've tried," her eyes glazed with tears.

"How can I help you?" the nurse's hoarse voice rattled my eardrums. She asked questions with the speed of a charging locomotive only Mom knew how to answer, and then pointed her pen up the stairs while looking down at her desk. "Room twenty-nine."

Seeing the commotion through the glass doors in the entranceway, Dad put out his cigarette in haste and came inside. The four of us ascended the stairs that ended in a long train-like hallway, with rows of windows on our left and patient rooms on our right. Judging by ascending numbers, Grandpa's room was on the far end.

The hallway smelled of illness and pain. Some of the rooms we passed had their doors open and while I tried not to peer, my head involuntarily turned, catching a heartbreaking scene. Pale afternoon light seeped through the window stained with long, white smudges, as if someone had thrown a carton of milk onto the pane and left it to dry. Three bald children sat on their rusty beds. One child was rocking back and forth, another was crooning a lullaby while dressing a doll, and the third child sat still, looking out the window. Something made me stop for a moment, and the third child turned her head and looked at me. The girl smiled at me through her tears. I swallowed a hard ball down my throat and continued walking.

The next two doors we passed were closed. The corridor was eerily quiet save our footsteps on the stone floor. Just as we were passing the middle door, I had a strong feeling that the density of air had shifted. It became thinner and cooler. Tripping on my loose shoelace, I quickly bent down to tie it. My family passed me, drifting forward in slow motion. I looked up and a ray of light struck my eye. It was coming from a crack in those middle doors, a crack that was getting wider. Soon I could see the whole window inside the room. The clouds parted to let the sun through, bathing its bare walls in sepia light.

A slim figure stood by the door. He had a glow to him, enhanced by the sun illuminating him from behind. It had a textured radiance I could touch, shining from within. I could feel his gaze fixed upon me. I stood up and held still. Seconds dripped like honey, transfixing me in layered folds of time. With his slim hand, he beckoned me to come closer. I gazed down, watching my rugged boots step over the invisible line that divided his tiny room from the hospital corridor, until we were an arm's reach apart. From up close, his body resembled a pale winter of frozen blue rivers snaking underneath his translucent skin. My gaze traveled upward: bare feet, yellowing pajamas draped over his thin frame, mossy patches of hair growing back, green eyes piercing right through me. My mind told me that he could've been on the verge of death, but to me he was glowing brighter than the sun.

"At last," he said. "You came."

"You sound like you know me."

"You are a seeker. But I must warn you. The truth will make you the loneliest person in the world." He reached his hand toward my face and touched the space surrounding it. I closed my eyes and felt the tickle of his touch transfer through air particles. He dropped his hand and coolness returned to my face. I opened my eyes. "You came here to see someone so I shouldn't delay you."

"Yes, my Grandpa."

"You must come back and see me again later."

"Come back?" I chuckled trying to imagine sneaking out of a motel room unseen in order to break into a hospital to spend the evening with someone I hardly knew. But he seemed serious.

"Best time is before the lights go out at nine, but after the evening walk-through. The front doors lock just after eight so you will need to get inside before then. Do you have a watch?" he asked innocently.

"No, but—"

"Get one. And bring a candle. It will be much better with light. It can get dark and cold in here once the lights go out." I was amazed how convincing he was, already paving a way for me to return. "Don't worry. You will find a way."

"I will try," I said, and stepped back, the heel of my boot bumping into the doorframe.

I walked into the hallway just before Rena peeked out of Grandpa's room.

"Gosh! Can you be any slower?" she said, her voice carrying across the hall.

"Shhh!" I shushed her with my pointer finger on my lips. "Be quiet. People are trying to rest here," she raised her brows before furrowing them again, surprised by my audacious reply.

When I entered the room, my eyes zeroed in on the shrunken man lying on a narrow bed surrounded by IVs and cables. I barely recognized Grandpa. He was thin, his eyes sunken and able to communicate only with faint smiles and occasional nods, motions that must have cost him great effort, due to the tube in his throat. He looked tranquil under the heavy load of medication, but seemed hardly at peace in his quiescence. His eyebrows were tense and the space between them marked by a deep wrinkle, a chasm of pain.

Mom relayed what the nurse had told them. The surgery had been successful and the surgeon was quite certain that he was able to excise the entire tumor. What Grandpa needed now was lots of rest.

Grandpa reached toward me so I rushed to his side and sat down on the edge of his bed. He took my hand into his. Inwardly I thanked Punk for convincing me to come here today, and immediately after, the thought of Sariel crossed my mind, shooting an electric current through my body. As if receiving the signal, Grandpa squeezed my hand, his eyes widening. I looked at Mom. Two long tears glided down her cheeks, leaving wet marks on her face.

"He just woke up," she whispered, wiping her tears.

"We want you back home with us," I said to Grandpa, prompting another hand squeeze.

"Yes, we do," Mom stepped in and began to recite all that had transpired since his most recent departure, bringing him up to date on family affairs. There was not much to talk about, but she did her best trying to elevate the somber mood. "Your sister-in-law is visiting. She came for All Saints Day. She and your wife have been cooking up a storm, could feed an army," her bubbly voice dispersed the tense silence. While she spoke, Dad sat bent over in a chair, grinding his jaws and studying his nails, while Rena looked out the window. " And we just celebrated Rena's birthday. It was a feast. We are still trying to eat all the food. . . . Eve will be graduating soon and she is beginning to narrow down her high school choices. It looks like she may have to move away," Mom continued her report.

Grandpa blinked and let go of my hand. Unfurling his forefinger, his hand bruised from IVs and bandaged around a needle that delivered nourishment to his tired veins, he pointed first at the ceiling, and then behind him toward the other patient rooms. My body dimpled with goose bumps.

"The boy. . . . You know him?" I whispered.

Grandpa inhaled deeply, his face contorting before a violent sob shook his chest.

VIII.

"Eve? Eve! Evelina! Where are you?" Mom waved her hand in front of my face. "You barely touched your supper. Are you feeling all right?" She, Rena and I were at dinner in the motel's cafeteria, while Dad went outside to smoke.

"Yes, Mom. I'm all right. It's the hospital. And it's hard to see Grandpa this way," I said, sculpting mashed potatoes with a fork in one hand, cradling my head in the other. I'd created quite the mountain trying to devise a plan of action that would get me back inside the very place that I had just blamed for stealing my appetite. I couldn't stop thinking about the boy.

"I know, honey. It is hard for all of us."

"What do you think made him cry?" Rena asked with a raised brow. Grandpa got very upset before we were asked to leave. A nurse came in and gave him a strong sedative so that he could calm down.

Mom shrugged, "I really don't know."

"I think it's because of whatever she said to him," Rena pointed her fork at me.

"I'm surprised you even noticed. I thought you were admiring the cityscape," I said to her.

"Shut up, Eve. You are the one barely paying attention, not me!" she said as Mom put away her utensils. "Always somewhere else but here. You'd better stop living in dreamland or else your delusions will land you in a room next door."

"Rena!" Mom shouted.

"Which is where? I don't get it. Next door where?" I inquired.

"The psych ward."

"Rena, stop!" Mom hissed.

"I'm just sick of her constant mood swings! And you're always buying into it! Oh, poor little Eve," she said, making a face.

"Have some compassion for once!" Mom snapped. "Your sister isn't well."

"She's probably pretending so that you feel sorry for her!"

"I don't need anyone's pity, especially yours," I said, reaching for the shaker and creating a salt storm over my potato mountain.

"Smartass!" she scoffed from across the table.

"Enough," Mom said, as Dad returned to the table. "This has been a hard day for all of us. The last thing I need is to witness this," she buried her forehead in her hands.

The motel stood less than a block away from the hospital, a favorable detail in tonight's quest, I thought, standing outside. Mom got us two rooms rather than one, which was also good, except for the tedious fact that I was to share mine with Rena. Still, sneaking away from one person was easier than trying to evade the watchful eyes of my parents. I wondered how Rena would behave this evening, considering our latest squabble. And then it struck me. Rena liked to stay up, listen to her Walkman, and read magazines. She would raise an alarm loud enough to wake the whole city if she saw me gone. The more I thought of it, the more absurd the whole escapade seemed.

The temperature outside was very low, freezing in fact. As the rain clouds departed, the dry frosty air returned, stilling all life, its coarse fingers pinching my exposed cheeks. I huddled inside and quietly snuck into the room I was to share with my sister. The room had vaulted ceilings and, save the red rug, was entirely covered in orange lacquered wood. Laying with her headphones on and facing the opposite wall, Rena didn't even budge when I entered. I took it as a good sign and I looked at the clock ticking on the wall. It was five minutes until seven. Hopefully, she'd get tired soon.

I reached for my backpack and retrieved the small book. Stretching on the squeaky bed, I opened it slowly, running my fingertips over its pages. I read until my eyes fell shut and I drifted away. Seven rings of a church bell nearby reached my ears, and the book fell of out my hands. I had one hour to make it inside the hospital.

I became restless, so I put on my coat and stepped out

to take another look. On the backdrop of the inky sky above rooftops towered a cathedral, its apex aglow with a cross. I heard his words echo in my mind. *You will find a way.*

"What are you doing outside, honey? Aren't you freezing?" Mom appeared from around the corner, grayish-blue smoke leaving her mouth.

"Just getting some air."

"Let's go inside," she said, grabbing my hand and nudging me toward the door.

"Actually, Mom . . . would you mind if I went to that church over there?"

She twisted her head to look where I was pointing. "You? In a church?"

"I feel the need. To pray."

She looked at me in disbelief.

"Besides, I cannot go back to the room with Rena right now. She is still fuming at me. I need time alone. Please?"

"It is way too dark for a young girl to walk around alone in a city at this hour."

I was losing hope, my intention fading like a dying bloom.

"But if you really want to go that bad, I can go with you."

"No, Mom, it's okay. Don't worry about it. I don't have to—"

"But actually, I'd like to. I could use a walk to clear my head. And it won't hurt to say a prayer for Grandpa either. God knows we can use all the help we can get."

I watched my plan dissolve like a cloud of steam and sighed in surrender.

Mom had me put on my wool hat as she and I traced the edges of deserted streets, the bright moon hovering over the city skyline behind clouds. We crossed the street and stepped onto a cracked cement sidewalk, its uneven planks jutting in front of my feet, making me stumble. Rows of heavy gray apartments like stone monoliths lined the street with the blue blinking glow of television screens radiating from behind yellowing lace curtains. At our next turn, the winds picked up, blowing my hair into disarray and Mom's scarf off her head.

"What strange weather we've been having," she called out, as strong gusts of air rolled over our lobes, deafening our ears. We fought our way against the wind, our hair whipping our faces. I pulled my hat tighter over my ears. We continued our silent walk until the winds subsided and a single ring of the cathedral bell reached us, announcing seven-thirty. Feeing disappointed I slowed down my pace.

"Everything all right?" Mom asked, turning toward me lagging a little behind.

"Yes, fine. Just tired."

"We can walk slower. We are not rushing anywhere."

"No, in fact, I'd rather get there faster," I said, looking at her face, which I'd been avoiding since she had said she'd join me on my jaunt. Her blue eyes smiled at me with love, while her gloved hand took hold of mine, pulling me closer.

The air brushed my face with nascent droplets of moisture. Up above, yellowish clouds, reflected the sulfuric light of the city, obliterating the moon's face.

The two blocks turned out to be four, and by the time we reached the cathedral, tiny snowflakes were swirling around us like little ballerinas. Kindling lights inside tempted us with their warmth. We climbed the stone steps that spilled like terraced layers of lead onto the sidewalk. The slight indentation in their middle made me think of the masses of people that had climbed them over the years. Faith indeed can melt stone, I thought, reaching for the brass handle anchored in the massive doors, and pulled hard.

The view dazzled my eyes. Emptiness had a shape here, a definite form. It cascaded upward, like a reverse waterfall, converging at the apex, blanketing the walls with frescos and gold. The air was dense from candles and myrrh, whispered prayers and worship songs still lingering, charging it with intent. A half-dozen old women continued to kneel, bending their kerchief-covered heads over folded hands with tangled rosaries, lips reciting prayers, their murmurs rising on freshly extinguished candelabras smoking at the altars. Mom led us sideways to where a slanting shelf blazed with a hundred flames, a collective plea for miracles. The fiery semblance warmed hearts, cold hands, and cheeks.

"We should light a candle for Grandpa," I murmured, and she nodded, pointing toward a box of unlit white candles, handing me donation money. I picked up a candle and extended its wick toward another, before anchoring it in place.

"Come," Mom whispered, extending her hand.

She led us toward the front altar where we kneeled on a step that led to the tabernacle. I closed my eyes, letting the murmur of an adjacent prayer wash over me. Under my lids, the afterglow of candle flame became the outline of the moon, a glowing tapestry of Sariel's descent. I fantasized about him coming to surround me with his wings.

"Ready?" Mom shook my shoulder.

"Can you wait for me at the door? I want to see something," I said, and walked back to the field of flaming candles. My window of opportunity to see the boy was quickly narrowing, but I still had hope.

A lone figure stood facing the flames. The man turned toward me slowly. He seemed old and frail, his lips twisted in a mocking grin, gray spiky hair like needles protruding from his cheeks and chin. He wore a weathered hat and a long black coat, not unlike Ben's, but his showed clear signs of overuse. He narrowed his eyes at me. They were dark but milky, their rims red, lids droopy. I felt a cold breeze skim my face. He held out a candle for me and shook it when I wavered, so I took it from his hands and hurried toward the exit. Mom was waiting for me by the door, her eyes closed, lips moving in supplication. I turned to look at the man again, to evaluate his strangeness from a distance, but he was no longer there. Mom made the motion of the cross with her hands and we exited the cathedral.

"Did you see the old man by the candles?" I asked her.

She shook her head. "No, I only saw you."

The outside air smelled of pungent coal. Large snowflakes blanketed the urban landscape with a cape of purity that was quickly turning gray. I walked down the steps letting the flakes fall on my face, my warmed fingers rubbing the smooth surface of the candle in my pocket. In the other pocket, I held the poem I wrote in class yesterday. A thick ball of snow hit my chest. I heard Mom giggle so I bent down to scoop a handful of snow and worked it into a hard ball and ran after her.

Breathless and wet, with our hair and coats covered in blotches of snow, we made it back to the motel in good spirits. We stood outside as Mom finished her cigarette, me casting nervous glances at the hospital across the street.

"You know what my father once told me?" she said just as the cathedral bell started to ring, announcing eight o'clock. "He said that prolonged moments of silence mean that an angel is passing by."

Mom and I hugged goodnight and I went to my sparsely lit room, closing the door with a click. The wall clock showed three minutes past eight. Rena was lying on her side, still facing away from me. Her bedside lamp was out, but in a kind gesture, my sister had left the bathroom light on for me. I took off my coat and reclined on the lumpy bed. Rusty springs creaked under my weight, my eyes drifting aimlessly among the cracked wooden boards of the slanted ceiling. I had no idea what to do next.

I tried to read the book but couldn't concentrate so I closed my eyes and imagined that all the walls and obstacles that separated the boy at the hospital and me had become transparent. With my mind I made hard matter turn into liquid so that I could swim through the plasma toward the room where he was resting. Outside, falling snowflakes turned into droplets of rain, but soon evaporated, dried by the winds before touching the ground. The darkness of night receded and the stars descended closer, lighting my path, while the gales propelled me forward.

I floated across space until I arrived at his bedside, where he laid peacefully, with a serene smile. I landed on my feet and walked up to him. I could see his glowing heart beating softly underneath the thin fabric of his pajamas.

"You can light it now," he said, and my eyes traveled to the white candle he was holding in his hand.

"But I forgot to bring matches."

"It's quite fine," he smiled, and asked me to sit across from him while he positioned his body with his back resting against the wall. "Cup your hands around the wick."

"Like this?" I asked, and he nodded.

"Breathe slowly and focus on the tip. Soon you will feel the heat rise in your body. Then you will need to project it out."

I did as he said, breathing in and out, but without a clue as to how to perform the projecting. Minutes passed and all I could feel was my heart growing restless.

"I don't think I can—" I said, but he put his finger on my lips.

"Don't think. See it light up."

I tried again, ignoring my agitated mind and deepening my breath.

"That's it. Stay with it." He cupped his hands around mine and looked at me with his almond-shaped eyes. "Now all you have to do is imagine the flame." I felt a tingling rush on my skin, tiny droplets of sweat oozing out of my pores. "See it, Eve. See it now."

His warm palms closed around mine, and the tip of the wick sparked. A small flame brightened our faces and my lips broke out into a victorious smile.

"See? You can," he said, withdrawing his hands.

"But how?"

"Mind over matter," he shrugged. "This is how it works. You can create whatever you want. What do you want, Eve?"

What do you want? His words echoed.

"To know who I am."

"So you shall," he said.

We gazed at each other while the candle flame grew to the size of a torch flame. The fire kept rising until it swallowed the space between us. Flames soon consumed his sheets, moving toward the paltry curtains. They licked the wooden floor and walls, heating the metal frame of his bed. Both of us were burning now. I looked at my hands and watched them liquefy. Only his eyes remained still and firm in their message.

Come. There is still time.

I opened my eyes and looked at the ceiling. Everything in the room was still, and there were no signs of flames or smoke. Rena was lightly snoring in her bed. Getting up before dawn caught up with her at last. It was a quarter to nine. I'd fallen asleep for almost an hour. I went to the bathroom to splash cold water on my flushed face. I returned to the bed and turned over the open black book that was laying face down over a pillow. My eyes landed on a passage:

> *Just as a candle cannot burn without fire,*
> *Men cannot live without Spirit. . . .*

"The candle," I groaned, then quickly covered my mouth and glanced in Rena's direction. She turned and the book fell out of my trembling hands, right in between the bed and a wall. Rena slapped her lips and folded her fingers under her cheek. I held still, frozen, until I could hear her breath settle. I reached for my coat and searched the pockets until I found it. On my tiptoes, I walked to the night table by Rena's bed and gently picked up her watch to fasten it around my wrist. I decided to borrow it since he asked me to bring one, though I wondered if I would even need it since I was running so late. I stood there studying the contours of my sister's body, rising and falling like the ocean's tide. She looked much less threatening while asleep, the sleeves of her wool sweater pulled over her palms.

I looked toward the door and then at the bed behind which the black book had fallen. The bed seemed too heavy to move to allow me to retrieve the book. Besides, the noise could wake up my sister. I decided to wait until the morning. I put on my coat and zipped it up to my chin.

Was I courageous enough to follow my hunches? Or was I following some mirage, a trick of my mind? I didn't like the sour taste of doubt, and I remembered Punk's advice telling me to go with my parents if I wanted to know more. I didn't feel that what had happened today came even close to satisfying my hunger. If anything, it had only made it bigger. My hand ventured to the doorknob. Perhaps what I was about to do would once and for all prove to Rena that her sister was indeed out of her mind. But I decided to act now and rationalize later.

IX.

The snow crumbled beneath my feet. Grasping the candle in my pocket, I crossed the street in haste leaving behind my footsteps embossed in white powder before anything would make me change my mind. Led by instinct—and a whiff of intuition—I took an abrupt turn to the right, sidestepping the main entrance that, by now, would be locked anyway.

The rear side of the building looked desolate, a veneer of cement covering the ground cracking in many places. The space was littered with scattered pieces of black rocks surrounding piles of coal—moonlight making it sparkle like some subterranean treasure. I squeezed the waxy cane that was beginning to soften in my hands and aimed toward the piles, discovering a downward sloping set of stairs leading to the building's basement. I approached the stairs and hearing a door squeak, squatted behind a short ledge that ran alongside the stairs. My heartbeat tripled in cadence and my nose caught the dry, sulfuric scent of smoke that invaded the night air.

After moments of silence and lack of movement, I peeked over the ledge. The door that led underground had been left ajar. Next to it stood a wheelbarrow, loaded with coal. I waited with bated breath, listening for the person feeding the incinerators, but no steps came so I plunged ahead slithering through the door into a narrow tunnel. My throat constricted from the smoke. I could not go straight, only left or right. Which direction to go? I took a few steps to my left and immediately felt the air thicken and the temperature rise. The furnaces must be close. I braved my fears and not registering any suspicious noises, made a sharp turn in the hallway, stopping suddenly, pinned flat against the wall. Battling my fear, heart racing, the orange glow dancing on the walls,

I was starting to melt in my sheepskin coat, but I had an idea and decided to follow through with it.

I shuffled my feet sideways, hands grinding over the rough surface of the basement wall, feeling the heat climb to hellish proportions. Once I could go no further, I turned my head and peeked around the corner. The furnaces were massive, flames converting matter with the roaring sound of a hurricane. Stacked atop a small shelf was a pile of matchboxes. Shielding my face from the heat, I reached around and grabbed one box before a moving shadow appeared on a wall. I broke out into a blind run in the other direction. With each step, the air got cooler and the space grew darker. I reached out my hands until they touched a wall. Feeling my way through, I turned left again and continued my dash, stumbling over a set of stairs. Panting, I raised my head and looked up.

Up above, dim light outlined the edges of a doorway. Thinking that it must be the hospital floor, I picked myself up and ascended the dozen steps. My fingertips ran along the door's coarse surface, drops of hardened paint frozen in time. Suddenly, I heard a noise, and I was sure it wasn't coming from the other side. I froze in place, hearing footsteps below. Holding my breath, I put pressure on the handle, but it stalled. I ran my fingers alongside the frame, looking for bolts and locks, as the footsteps behind me neared. Desperately searching, I couldn't find anything that would indicate why the door wouldn't open. My shaky hands returned to the doorknob, my fingers examining its shape in detail. In the meantime, whoever was behind me was now at least halfway up the stairs. A draft of cold air reached the exposed skin of my hands. I could smell my own trepidation, like the fear of a hunted animal. My sweaty hands were slipping over the metal when I located a tiny lock and twisted it. Squeezing my lips together, a knot in my stomach, sweat on my temples, I pressed down the handle once more and pushed open the door just as someone's fingers brushed against my hair. The door yielded with a faint pop.

I stepped into the bright hallway and turned, my eyes skimming the face of the one pursuing me. Looking at me with an inkling of a smile, was the same man who had held out the candle for me in the cathedral.

Fluorescent lights buzzed above my head, reflecting off the gray linoleum floor as I scuttled on my tiptoes down the silent corridor. Still shivering from angst, and simmering in my coat, I turned to look behind me, but no one was there. I slowed my pace. *Who was this strange person? And what was he doing following me?*

Approaching the nearest staircase I looked around, lost. I had no idea where I was in relation to the patient rooms. I must have reached the main floor with the administrative rooms, which at this hour were free of important people in starched white uniforms. Like a ghost, I drifted through the dimly lit corridor, an apparition traversing a sterile duct of an abandoned spacecraft. Part of me could not believe that I had made it this far, ignoring the perils of danger, instead thrusting my head into the tiger's mouth, hoping it would overcome its hard-wired urges to bite. I was scared, but also thrilled.

As soon as I began to climb the stairs, two at a time, I heard female voices approaching. Stopping in my tracks, I pressed my back to the wall. Completely exposed and with no place to hide, anxiety rolled over me, further rousing my boiling blood and searing branches of nerves. If I was caught, the consequences could range from disciplinary escort to something more severe. Just this summer the police had gotten involved in a case with a classmate who had broken into our school at night. The episode was humiliating, not only to him, but also to his entire family who resided in our town.

This was the closest scenario I could think of, and since my case involved a hospital, not a school, the consequences could be worse.

The conversation above me took on a casual tone and was not growing any louder. I was safe, but probably not for long. I sped up the stairs, rounded the corner, and plunged into the closest bathroom. Grabbing onto the sink and breathing hard, I looked down at the floor, spotted with inky splatter marks, which in this dim light could have been blood. I shivered. I turned to look past the open doorframe and listened in. The voices belonged to two nurses in a room dangerously close to me. This floor was much darker than the one below me, sparse light diffusing from the nurse room and the bathroom that glowed reddish in hue. I decided to take a risk and climb up one more floor, hoping to find the boy's room there. I exited the bathroom, and sped up the stairs trying to do so as quietly as possible.

Stalling at the top, I eavesdropped again, working hard to calm my breathing. My ears registered the distant sound of a beeping apparatus, located behind one of the closed doors. The corridor on the top floor was even darker, and I glided through it with soft knees, carefully placing each foot in front of the other. I reached the right floor. Passing by my grandfather's room, I imagined him submerged in a drug-induced sleep. As I looked for the boy's room, trying to discern between three middle doors, my vision grew cloudy. I squinted and noticed slight movement around one set of doors, as if its frame was trembling. Then, the doors began to open. I held my breath, not sure whether I was just imagining it, but then he stepped out into the hallway.

"You didn't lose faith," he said, and reached out his hand.

"I came close to doubting everything," I replied walking towards him and feeling my hand soften under his touch.

He led us into his room, closed the doors, and took my jacket to hang it on an old wooden hanger standing by the door. I felt like I had just shed a layer of skin. The lights in his room were off, but his white pajamas seemed to glow in the dark.

"Give me your hand," he asked, coming closer. The warmth of his body poured to me like a ray of sunshine. "And the other." The smell of his skin reminded me of the scent of a newborn. "Now, close your eyes."

Immediately, everything started to spin, as if I was riding on a carousel, my mind erupting with a volcano of thoughts. It kept picking up momentum, becoming a raging tempest. The images blurred and sounds roared like helicopter engines. I saw my mother crying, my father screaming, Rena laughing at me. There was Ben trying to kiss me, followed by the distinct sensation of the needle going through Paula's ear. Fear, anger and desire . . . I felt them all at once. I saw the silhouette of the hung cat and the moon beyond, which got brighter and bigger until it filled my entire vision with silver light. The light faded into darkness, out of which emerged the face of the angel looking at me with his burning eyes. Those eyes then became blue, and I saw Punk biting into the sandwich before he lost all his hair and became the one now holding my hands.

"So much on your mind," he said. "No need to be afraid. These are only thoughts, noise you can learn to let go."

"Who are you?" I asked.

"My name is Daniel. I can help you understand your dreams."

X.

Outside, violent winds rattled the windowpane. Daniel let go of my hands to peek outside, and I was quickly getting cold. But I decided to brave it, as he was wearing an even thinner wardrobe.

"What just happened? And how do you know about my dreams?" I asked.

"I don't know how I know. It was something I was born with, both a blessing and a curse," he said, and turned to look at me. "As to what just happened, you can call it a slate clearing. Your mind was filled with so much stuff, no wonder you've been confused. Amplifying the speed of your thoughts helped diffuse some of the static."

"Sounds so simple."

"It really is," he smiled.

"Why are you here? I mean, this hospital . . . there is sickness and death all around. You don't seem to belong here."

"Maybe my body is paying the price for my abilities?"

"What are the doctors saying?"

His hands ventured to his bald head. "Brain tumor," he said, and added that his doctor had discontinued his treatment and Daniel had stopped eating. I asked him how he could just give up like that, and he said that trying to hold on would only prolong the inevitable, dragging out the pain. "It hurts living on this side," he said, and showed me his thin bare arm covered with bruises and needle marks.

"But you seem fine!" I said in protest. "You're just very thin and malnourished. Your hair . . . it looks like it's growing back. And your hands, they are so warm."

He smiled and said that it's easy to be deceived. His hands tend to get hot like irons when he uses his abilities. But that can be draining, leaving him exhausted for hours afterward. "The heat evaporates and I turn into a block of ice." Daniel touched his hands to mine, and I noticed that they were already much cooler. "The doctor told me that it's a miracle I survived this long."

Every nerve in my body contracted. I squeezed

my fists, trying to get a hold of myself, as if preparing for an emotional tsunami, for once forgetting about my own trivial problems.

Daniel smiled at me as if trying to cheer me up. "But then I had a dream. And I understood why I held on."

"What kind of a dream?" I asked.

"A prophetic one. Of you coming to this place."

"You saw me coming here?" I asked, blushing, but he couldn't see that in the dark. He was the second person I had met in a two-day span that dreamt of me without even knowing me before.

Daniel nodded. "Did you manage to find a candle?" he asked, and I walked to my coat to retrieve it. "What are we waiting for? Let's light it!" he beamed.

Daniel invited me to sit on his bed while he pulled up an elevated aluminum tray on wheels used to hold his meals. He lit a match and melted the candle's base, anchoring it to the tray. I watched him move with grace and poise, relishing every gesture. He handed me one of his two pillows and positioned himself on his bed across from me with his back against the wall, our knees almost touching.

"Will you do me the honors?" he asked, handing me the matchbox.

I took out a match and stroked it on the coarse strip on the side of the box, watching a golden flame explode on its sulfured tip. Daniel surrounded the small fire with his palms, grinning like a child, exposing his white teeth and a dimple in his cheek. I transferred the flame to the virgin wick until it caught and blew out the match.

"So tell me," I looked into his glistening eyes, "why do I keep having my dream?"

"That I don't know yet," he said, his fingertips massaging the flame's halo. The light made his face look like a living painting. His eyes seemed too big on his bony face, the backdrop for the shadow's play of chiaroscuro. Daniel also seemed healthier than he did when I first saw him, his face taking on a more vital tone. The thought was like soothing oil on my soul.

"Do you want me to tell you about it?" I asked.

"I'd like you to just think about it so that I can tune into the undercurrents."

I nodded and closed my eyes to take a deep breath. I noticed that it started to rain outside, drops tapping the pane like someone's fingertips. As my body grew heavier, my mind became unbound. In an instant, I was back there, standing over the pit, looking at Sariel's face.

The angel's eyes opened, his yellow gaze pulling me into his realm. I became engrossed in his presence, a desire to touch him once more igniting my nerves. I tried to resist, as I didn't want to feel this way in Daniel's presence. But it was only stalling the flow. Reluctantly I let go, relaxed my legs and let the usual melting take its course. Feet, ankles, shins, knees, thighs . . . The angel's lips parted and he looked at me with pleading eyes before the image dissolved and pure sensation took over. I traced waves of heat rising up, uncoiling at my tailbone, until my entire spine was on fire.

Show me the parts that remain hidden, Daniel's voice entered my mind and the vision of the angel returned. He stood before me in full frame. His body emaciated, amber skin stained with dirt and coal, marked by cuts and bruises, wings folded behind his back.

Why do you keep coming to me? I asked the angel.

Sariel's lips parted. *Free me.*

I reached out to touch him, but encountered resistance, a wall made of glass.

But how? How can I free you? I called, watching his silhouette become obliterated with water running down the glass. *Sariel!* I called his name but his image was starting to fade until I couldn't see him at all.

I looked around, finding myself alone in a stone cave with feathers scattered on the ground. Sorrow descended upon my shoulders like a cold wet cape. Waves of sadness kept washing over me, annihilating any remaining vestiges of sensuality, withdrawing everything toward a single point in my center, a black hole of my soul.

I called out Sariel's name again, but heard no reply. Heat swirled in my chest and my hands and eyes ventured there. I had become transparent with a red flicker of light pulsing inside my heart. I scooped my hands toward it until I held the light in my palms encapsulated by a figurine made of thin glass, as delicate as a bird. I lifted it toward my eyes it shattered into a thousand little pieces, bathing the cave in crimson light.

Come back now, Eve. Come back, I heard Daniel's voice and my mouth opened to take in more air.

XI.

The storm had entered Daniel's room, slamming the window against the wall. Raindrops pelted the floor. Instead of a flame, the wick of the candle now only emitted a tendril of smoke. Daniel's head was resting on my lap, his arms were around me, shoulders shuddering. My hands still pulsated with heat, an aftermath of the vision. Without thinking, I placed them on Daniel's head. I curled my fingers, their tips tracing the landscape of his cranium, where a long scar like a crescent lined its base.

The wind blew pieces of debris into the room, diffusing the precious heat that had accumulated, but I couldn't make myself lift my hands off Daniel to get up and shut the window. He seemed to have emerged more shaken from the experience than me.

"Why are you crying?" I asked.

"All this sadness and suffering. It broke my heart."

"It breaks mine to see you like this."

"This is not a mere dream you are having. The angel is real. You must turn back," Daniel said as the wind tipped over the clothing hanger that fell with a thud.

"But I don't want to turn back. I want to help him."

"You don't know how."

"But I want to know."

"If you do what he's asking you to do, his pain will become yours."

"Why, Daniel?"

"Because even if you give yourself to him, he can never be yours. You cannot meet him in this life. He is not human. You must turn back."

"But love can overcome everything! You are seeing only the dark side, and forgetting about the light!"

"The forces he is a part of, they are dangerous to those who don't know how to command them."

"Daniel, I cannot turn back. I need to go on. I need to disentangle this, understand why it is happening."

Daniel lifted his head and blew his nose. I was

83

beginning to understand what he meant when he told me that his abilities were as much a blessing as they were a curse. He felt so much.

I got up to close the window, the wind pushing against me, but soon silence and calm returned to the room. Daniel sat up and pulled the blanket over his shoulders. I found the matches and relit the candle. Kindling light returned to our space, surrounding us in a golden halo.

"Sorry, I just don't want you to suffer in vain."

"Why do you care?"

Daniel dropped his gaze. "I don't know. I just do."

"In that case, maybe it will be better I told you how everything started. Maybe then you will understand?"

Daniel agreed and pressed his lips together. I told him about Ben, the black magic book I had taken from him without permission, the details of my dreams—the gray terrain, the wails, and the steam rising from the gorge. I told him when the dreams started and how they matched lunar phases. I told him about the red candle I took off the soldier's crypt, and finding in its remains the image of the angel frozen in wax. I told him how noticed Ben's behavior change, about meeting Punk and what he had said to me about coming to the hospital when we sat with our backs against the wall of the castle. And finally, I told Daniel about the meadows, the feathers, and even the red lipstick. Daniel listened, nodding here and there, absorbing every word with a scholarly focus. When I finished, his face was expressionless, eyes on the flame.

"Your friend Ben can feel it, too," Daniel said. "He is trying to hold you back, warn you."

"How does Ben know about the angel?"

"He doesn't. But the heightened activity around you summons opposing forces. It is invading his subconscious, much like the angel has invaded yours."

"But the angel didn't invade anything. I let him in," I said in protest. "Willingly."

"Your friend Ben, is trying to pull you away from falling for the angel by making you fall in love with him instead."

"This is just too much!" I got up and walked to the

window, wringing my arms over my chest. The storm had subsided, but the rain was still falling, its big drops producing small creeks in the asphalt's dips and cracks.

"Ben is only a vessel, a vehicle for something much larger, something he could never comprehend."

"Is this why Ben told me he feels like he's losing control of himself? That night, when he kissed me… it wasn't even him, he said. I shouldn't be mad at him." If Ben only knew of the forces that stirred in the depths of his mind…I leaned in closer toward the pane, espying a movement down on the pavement below us. A lone figure crossed the street. The man wore a hat, but had no umbrella. I wondered why anyone would be out in this weather at this late hour.

Daniel cast his blanket aside and stood up. "But all that could fade and things return to normal if you turn away. You still can."

But I wasn't eager about the prospect of turning away. I kept the thought to myself, only telling Daniel how disappointed Ben would be at losing his ability to ace his tests without ever opening a textbook.

"Love is a double-edged sword. It first brings delight, but its loss causes worse pain than the worst physical wound," Daniel said, and reached for a towel slung over a chair next to a small table with a pitcher of water and a glass. He bent down to his knees and began wiping the wet floor. I waved in protest and tried to take over, but he wouldn't let me. He finished cleaning, placed the folded towel in the corner and poured himself a glass of water, asking me if I wanted any. I took a sip and shuddered. The water tasted very bitter, so I passed. He took two gulps and set the glass aside.

"Why are you so against love?" I asked him.

"I'm not against love."

"Were you ever hurt?"

"It doesn't matter. It is not about me."

"But I want to know more about you."

"What do you what to know?" Daniel asked.

"Where were you born?"

Daniel smiled, but his expression was jaded. He went back to sit on the bed, placed a pillow between his back and the wall and drew the blanket around his shoulders. I sat on the edge of his bed and waited. The candle had lost about a third of its volume.

"I'm not really sure where I was born. Nuns raised me until I was four. Then I lived with a family of orchard growers in the north until I was six. Then a nurse, who couldn't have children, and her husband, adopted me. She died before I turned twelve. I lived with her husband for four more years until he drank himself to death."

My throat constricted. Here I was concerned about my dreams while Daniel's life must have been a living nightmare.

"Have you ever been close with anyone?" I asked.

"I once had a friend," Daniel said. "I met him the day my adoptive father died. He helped me a lot. I had no family left and no place to go and I was scared about what to do. He was about my age, but unlike me, he thrived alone. I admired that. He taught me how to be self-sufficient and believe in myself. We spent most of that summer together. We'd forage for food, swim in lakes, and sleep under the stars.

"What happened to your friend?"

"One morning I woke up and he was gone."

"Just like that?"

"Just like that. But before he departed, he left me with something that changed the course of my life."

"What was that?"

"The motivation I needed to go back to my roots." Daniel told me about the night before his friend had left. "We sat by the fire and I told him that I wanted to be free like him. He said no one could truly be free until they made peace with their past. He also said that we were of the same kind."

"What did he mean?"

"I don't know. But the next morning I was on my way."

"On your way to where?"

"The orphanage."

"Did it help you find your parents?"

"I found clues that led me to my mother. I still don't know who my father is."

"Who is your mother?"

"I haven't met her yet. But I now know that she didn't want to give me up. That alone makes things easier."

"Did someone make her do it?" I kept on.

"Her father did," Daniel said, looking uncomfortable. "The nun told me they brought me in on a cold January day. Mountains of snow were piled up everywhere. She said that my mother's face was swollen from tears, but she was resigned to doing what her father told her to do," he said, and his voice broke.

"Did you try looking for her?"

Daniel nodded and his eyes watered. He rubbed them and I helped him lie on his back. He was starting to look pale and ill again.

"Sorry, I shouldn't have pushed you. You should rest now," I said, and he nodded again. I reached for his hand feeling faint pulsations of his palm, listening to his breath settle into a rhythm. After a few minutes, he seemed to be asleep. I let go of his hand and walked to the window. It was still raining but not as hard. I wondered if anyone at the motel had noticed my absence. To my surprise, the figure I spotted earlier was still there, sitting on a ledge, motionless. I could've mistaken it for a statue. As I kept looking down, he raised his head and looked straight at me. As he did, a cold gust of wind skimmed my face. He was the man from the basement. I heard a noise, turned around, and saw Daniel stirring in bed. He stretched his arms and blinked.

"How long was I asleep?"

"Not long at all."

"Strange," he said. "I just had a dream about the nurse who took me in years ago. I never dream about her. It is always her husband who keeps asking me for forgiveness, hunched over a bottle. But this time, she came. She sat next to me on this bed where you just sat and said, 'You're going home, Daniel.'"

I walked up to him, and sitting in that same spot again, let myself get carried away telling him how he would surely get better, and how I would then help him find his parents. His dream was a premonition. It must have been. But Daniel said that he thought she had meant him going home to be with

God. Not wanting to give in to his grave mood, I asked him to tell me about the dream he had of me.

"A girl came here, to this hospital, to visit her grandfather, and to see me too. The dream was very short but it felt very good to have someone visit me. The next day I saw your grandfather and he said—"

"Wait, Daniel, you know him?"

Daniel confirmed, looking lost, as if he had been caught saying something he wasn't supposed to. But I was happy they had met, and that another piece of the puzzle had snapped into place. This is how Grandpa knew of Daniel. This is why he cried when I mentioned him. Grandpa must have been aware of Daniel's critical condition and felt sorry for him.

"What did my Grandpa say to you?" I asked.

"He said that you had the sensitivity of your mother and the stubbornness of your father and wouldn't stop looking for something until you found it," he said with quivering lips.

"He's right. Once I latch onto something, I tend to become obsessed until I figure it out. But how does he know about my dreams?"

"He didn't mean your dreams."

"What did he mean?"

"I don't know," Daniel said quickly and looked away.

"You are hiding something. I can sense it. What did he mean Daniel? What did he say I'd never give up searching for?"

"I can't say. He had me promise."

"Promise what?"

"That I wouldn't say anything. I already said too much. I'm sorry," Daniel shifted on the bed, looking uneasy.

I let go of his hand and got up to pace around the room with my arms folded at my chest. "Grandpa wept when I mentioned you to him. Why Daniel?" I turned to him.

"It's his guilt for hurting you. It's been eating him alive," he said, kneading the edge of the blanket in his hands.

The sight filled my heart with unbearable pity.

"But he didn't hurt us! The worse thing he's ever done was getting ill, but we can't blame him for that, can we?

Mom depends on him so much."

"Your grandfather told me he felt so bad because he could've done more for her."

I sighed. "Grandpa shouldn't be stressing now. He needs to get well. That's the best thing he could do for all of us. That's what Mom would say. And now, I would add you to this wish. You too will heal, Daniel. I walked up to his bed and placed my palm on his forehead. Daniel's skin felt cold and I noticed that he was starting to shiver.

"I feel better just having you here. Thank you," he said.

"Why did you give up so soon? For goodness sake, Daniel, you need to start eating again."

I reached for the glass, and brought it to his lips. He took a few gulps and I took one small sip and set the glass down. That water tasted nasty. I wished I had had the foresight to bring a sandwich from the motel. And a cup of hot tea. Yes, I could go for some hot tea now, I thought, feeling homesick. I walked to the hanger by the door, retrieved my wool hat and scarf, put the hat on Daniel's head, and wrapped the scarf around his neck. I positioned myself closer, so that I could blow warm air on his cold hands that seemed to only get colder. Once they were sufficiently warmed, I slipped my gloves over them.

"You are turning me into a snowman."

"I wish Mom was here. You know what she used to do to us when we were little?" Daniel's eyes increased in size. "When we'd come home from playing in the snow, she'd take off our wet socks, roll up our pants and put our feet in hot water that she had poured into a bowl. It was the most blissful sensation, especially with something warm to eat in one hand, and a remote control in the other."

Daniel looked spellbound. "Your mom sounds like a very caring person."

I nodded, and told him that to me she'll always be the best mom in the world. I wished she had a happier life, but her sensitivity was also a part of her beauty. "She suffers, too. Sometimes I'd find her curled up on the sofa crying. For a long time, I thought she was haunted by something, but as time went by I realized that this is probably how she just is."

"I miss her," he said. "The mother I never knew. I wish I could meet her. Just once. Feel what it feels like to have someone love you just because you exist."

Daniel took off one glove and reached out his hand to touch me. I cupped my hands around it, wondering where I had the strength to be here with a person that may just die in my arms.

"Daniel, will you please tell me what my Grandpa meant about me never giving up searching. Please. I need to know."

"He was right when he said that you were stubborn."

"Daniel, please."

"You don't know what you're asking."

"Is it a secret?"

"Maybe."

"Maybe you will feel better if you let it out?"

"I made a promise," he said faintly. But I could see that he was wavering, reconsidering.

"Please, Daniel. Just say it."

"This afternoon after you left with your parents and sister . . . I went to his room to wish him goodnight. He wrote a note on a piece of paper. Begged me not to say a word. He knew you'd be back."

"But why beg?"

"Evelina, I don't want to cause your family any more pain, can't you see?"

"What are you talking about, Daniel? Aren't you the one in pain? And how could you have possibly hurt us?"

"Promise me you won't tell anyone."

"I promise."

"Years ago—"

"What happened years ago, Daniel?"

"Years ago…He and his daughter, your mom, she—"

"Yes? Daniel, please, don't stop now, keep going," I said, tugging on his hand that I noticed was starting to get warmer.

"When I went to the orphanage to look for my roots, the nurse gave me a picture. That picture is what brought me here."

"You are here because of a picture?" I asked. He nodded. "Whose picture?"

Daniel struggled to speak. "Of my pregnant mother, and her father."

"Can I see it?"

Daniel shook his head. "He has it now. I thought he would be happy to see me. Instead he was so shaken, like he was afraid of me. I think he wants to protect her. His daughter. Like you said, he always worries about her."

Blood drained from my face. Father's accusations of Mom's infidelity... her guilt, her pain... her perpetual, unexplained pain. Could it all have been related to Daniel's story? The answer became clear. Daniel was at the center of my family drama, and it took me embarking on this trip to discover it. This is why Punk said to me that if I went, I would find the thread that would lead me toward the truth, which had eluded me for my entire fifteen years of my existence.

"I am so sorry," Daniel said. "I only wanted to meet you. Not cause any problems."

My body constricted before two tears trickled down my cheeks. They were like the water of a spring welling up in a mountain, a spring that had finally found a way out. The truth was not painful to me. It was a release. Painful was Daniel's suffering.

"All this time," I whispered, "I sensed that something was missing. I just had no idea that he was my brother."

XII.

The room was quiet and the air still. Outside, the rain had stopped pounding the glass, the wind had subsided to a low hum, and in its stead snow began to fall. The candle had burned more than halfway down and the moon was already descending somewhere on the other side of the ecliptic. My fascination with Daniel and the shock of his revelation overrode my weariness. The only thing that bothered me, if Daniel's suspicions of his looming death were indeed accurate, was how much time we had lost and how little time we had left. Rena's wristwatch indicated half past one in the morning. I wanted time to freeze, wishing for the watch's hair-thin arm counting the seconds to stop ticking.

Daniel lay curled up on his side like a small child, his fists clenched, face expressing relief and regret. I sat cross-legged atop his tiny bed, where his feet would've normally been, my elbows digging into my knees, interlaced fists under my chin. We were both staring at the elongated flame reaching toward the ceiling like an inverted fountain pen. I was trying to make sense of things, but my ability to think was failing me. It was only the here and now. Only Daniel and Evelina. A brother and a sister. Reunited in secret under most trying circumstances. The past was a gaping hole wanting to be filled, sucking the fleeting moment into its hungry cavity.

"It's all very paradoxical, isn't it?" Daniel said shifting his gaze from the candle to me.

"Like having so much to say and yet not knowing where to begin?"

"I can only imagine the chaos this has caused you. I'm really sorry."

"Just the opposite," I said. "Finally things are starting to make sense. But I'm curious. How did you find him? How did you get a trace of Grandpa?"

Daniel's gaze returned to the flame. "When I went to the orphanage to find my roots, the nun who had given me the picture of Jan and his daughter had also told me of a trace she had found of the man in the picture. She knew his doctor and

92

gave me the doctor's name and the address of this clinic.

"When I arrived here and met the doctor in person I didn't want to just inquire about his patient. It would've been too intrusive. Plus, I wanted to have a chance to observe him, get to know him from a distance. So I told the doctor about having dizzy spells, which I'd get on occasion, and he agreed to admit me to run tests. In the days that followed, I looked everywhere for his patient but I had no luck. I was starting to develop severe migraines then. The blood tests confirmed I was fine, but I didn't want to be released just yet, so I asked for a brain scan. I wanted to find Jan, if he indeed was there, so I dramatized everything and he agreed to give me a brain scan. That's when he discovered something in my brain and suspected a tumor and asked to retain me longer if I wanted to be treated."

"I can't imagine how it must have felt getting such news."

"Sure, but it gave a change to stay and look for my family."

"I am still getting used to your way of thinking. You get diagnosed with terminal illness and feel glad."

"Eve, you muse understand. I didn't have much to live for."

"Did the doctor help you? Did he try at least?"

"Our relationship became an exchange of sorts once he realized I had the ability to see more than the average person. I would sometimes use my foresight to help him. But he would ask so many questions it soon became exhausting. And the more he got, the more he wanted. First it was about his career, then about his family, even about his wife. I couldn't help him sometimes. I didn't want to at others. He would get angry in those moments and threaten me to stop the treatment. The doctor was a very ambitious man," Daniel said. "He wanted to be become famous one day for his discoveries in neuroscience. But one day all this strive paid off because Jan returned and I finally got to see him."

"That must have been April."

Daniel smiled. "Indeed. I saw him while I was sitting on a bench in the garden. He was taking a walk with a nurse.

I was certain right away that I had found the man from the photograph. I could also tell that we were related. There was this strange aura around him, something mystical trailing him. I became very curious. But before I even had a chance to talk to him, he was released to go home and I lost track again. I could've checked the records and found his address, but at that point, I had no energy to even walk across the hall. I became bound to my bed. The doctor said that the cancer was progressing rapidly and he needed to operate quickly if I wanted to live." Daniel turned his head to show me the long scar on the back of his cranium.

"But he didn't get it all out?"

"No. He said it had metastasized. We were too late."

"So you stayed here waiting for death?"

Daniel nodded. "But the doctor didn't give up right away. He thought that maybe if I went deeper into the part of my mind that produced the visions, it could help him find a cure. So I did that. For days I floated in darkness inside of a saltwater tank that was meant to put me in a meditative state and help me access deeper parts of my mind. I wasn't even sure what I was looking for. I just floated, scanning pictures my brain produced like movies. At first it was a jumble of memories, then hours of silence. Then one day, my mind started to produce an entirely new set of images that seemed to be pointing toward the future. But even then I didn't know how many of the visions were actual foresights, and how many were just wishful thinking. In one of them I saw Jan return."

"Which he did. I remember. That's when things got very serious."

"Yes, and ironically with him came back my curiosity and zest for life. For awhile I thought I was actually getting better."

"But the mind therapy didn't work the way the doctor had hoped?"

"It didn't and it did. The doctor said that he couldn't cure me. But I did gain something through his therapy. Because of it I realized I had a real gift and I wanted to explore it further. Because of it, I saw you in my dream. I knew you were Jan's granddaughter and I knew that you were searching for something but didn't know what it was. Your soul ached for answers and you wanted adventure. I felt your sensitivity and knew you were able to see beyond the veils. You also had that mystical aura about you, which your grandfather possessed."

"What do you think that is?"

Daniel shook his head. "Don't really know. Still a mystery."

A seed of terrible guilt spilled inside my soul. So much time we had wasted. . . . Some things just didn't take sense. Why would Mom agree to leave a helpless baby? What if she hadn't listened to Grandpa? Would Daniel still have gotten sick? Would the disease have spared Grandpa, too? Daniel saw my struggle and asked what was on my mind so I told him.

"There are still so many questions left unanswered. I hope Grandpa will be able to speak soon."

"No." Daniel said. "You promised you wouldn't tell anyone."

He was right. I did promise. How could I break that trust? Yet it wasn't easy to live without being able to tell. My sense of alienation were already starting to sprout.

"How about your father? Did you find any traces of him?"

"Nothing." Daniel said that despite his vexing efforts, he was unable to find even the smallest clue to the most elusive part of his origin. He tried hinting at the question in a most delicate way after showing the picture to Grandpa. Grandpa held it in his shaking hands and stared at it with a contrived face, but offered nothing but a shrug and headshake, accompanied by a terse *I don't know.*

I shared with Daniel what I knew were facts. Mom had met Dad when she was seventeen and married him two years later, after getting pregnant with Rena. Their relationship was turbulent from the start. Grandma insisted it was the best she could do considering the paltry pool of local candidates. She must have had Daniel at eighteen. So something happened before she met Dad and had Rena. His date of birth confirmed it.

"Maybe giving me up was simply an act of parental protection?" Daniel said.

"Maybe. I know from Mom that it was Grandma who pushed for them to get married," I said. "She thought that with his name and wealth, my father would provide security for their only daughter."

Daniel looked at his open palm as if examining its value. "She was so young. What do you do when you have no one to turn to, and those who you go to offer no support?" he asked, throwing my head into a tailspin. I couldn't even imagine. But this complicated situation surely made me see my parents, and grandparents, in a new light.

Daniel wanted to know everything about Mom, from how she dressed to what she liked to eat. As I spoke, I felt the stories and vignettes, current and old, gain new dimension, with my father's suspicions gaining weight. True, Dad could be tyrannical sometimes, but his reasons now had more credence. Still, Mom's affair with a mysterious stranger had occurred before they were married. Further still, she kept denying the truth, never mentioning Daniel. Why? Was her desire to adopt that boy years ago a way to satisfy her sense of loss?

"It really doesn't matter who my father is at this point. I'm out of time to look for him."

"How are you so sure that you're out of time, Daniel?"

"Look at me, Eve. I'm a wreck, a hollow doll."

"But now . . . now things could finally get better. I mean—"

"There is nothing we can do. In fact, we'd better not. Your mother has suffered enough."

"I'm sure she'd love to see you. Even if for a moment."

"You don't know that. Sometimes it's better to leave things as they are. I've already made peace with it," he said firmly. "Having you here is the ultimate gift."

And so death was an uninvited guest that refused to go away. No matter how hard I tried to ignore its presence, it would continue to poke us with its scythe.

"Up until I had met the doctor, I thought I was going to live forever. Such a childish fantasy. . . . And then, one night in a vision, and maybe as a reward for my acceptance of it, I was shown that death was not even real," he lifted his head, and looked at me with a tired smile.

"How?"

"I saw an arching doorway between worlds through which a soul passes from one life to another. I stood right in front of it. Suddenly, a beautiful woman appeared, wearing a cloak. I knew she was the soul essence of my mother. She pointed at an inscription carved into the doorway and the symbols lit up. And at once I knew their meaning. Not only mentally, but viscerally. I felt it, Eve, with every cell of my being."

I was imagining it as Daniel spoke.

"What did it say?" I asked, leaning in closer.

"It said that nothing ever dies. Only the worlds change, forms change. We're like rain drops, falling into a vast ocean, before we rise again as clouds. The cycle goes on and on like that forever. There is no end, Eve. And death is only a long sleep."

I felt a strong urge to hug him, but each time my body readied itself to make a move, I'd withdraw. Caught in my own web of indecision, I told Daniel about the poem I had written in class, welcoming a reason to get off the bed and stretch my limbs. I unrolled the crumpled paper after recovering it from my coat's pocket and brought it to the flame. I read it to him, reliving the events of that day and seeing that the poem contained clues to my understanding. The moon, the feathers, the mirror… it was all there, as if a deeper part of me already knew what was going to happen.

"I used to write, too. My poems were sometimes prescient," Daniel said.

"Why did you stop?"

"Stanislaw, my adoptive father used to think that my words were blasphemous. He equated that to the worst evil. He'd say that only God could know the future. He'd call me the devil's child and burn my notebooks whenever I left them out to punish me."

"Punish you for what?"

"Sometimes reading his mind. I think I scared him.

The day he died, we had a bad argument. He got drunk and went through my room destroying everything that had value to me. When I saw what he had done, I looked him in the eyes and told him I wished I hadn't known him. He kept screaming at me but I shut the door and left the apartment. That day I met the person I told you about who had become my only friend. I came back later that night and found Stanislaw dead on the kitchen floor with a note in his hand. He was starting to write a letter to me but never finished it. The alcohol from the spilled bottle smudged the ink leaving only my name intact."

"What did you do?"

"A day after his funeral, Stan's sister came to claim the apartment. Things got ugly between us and I didn't want to be there anymore. So I packed my things and left. But I resumed my writing after that summer. In addition to the picture, the nun at the orphanage had given me another thing that belonged to Jan—his notebook. The picture was inside of it. She said that my mother left both behind in secret from her father."

"She probably hoped you'd find them one day. Do you still have it?"

Daniel shook his head. "I must have lost it. I've looked everywhere."

"That's too bad. I'd love to hear one of your poems."

"I do remember some parts quite well." Daniel sat up across from me and with a smile on his face began reciting: "*I open the gates, gazing inside the lion's den, unsure whether this fear is my foe or my friend. He speaks: the answer, my dear, is within your heart; so don't let illusions tear you apart. And as you gaze up into the light and look for traces of familiar faces, before you turn away, remember that most profound truths—*"

"*Hide in the darkest places.*" I finished the last words with him. My face was burning.

"How did you know?" Daniel asked in astonishment.

"Yesterday, after school, I went to my town library. I thought I would never find anything good there, but I went anyway, like I was drawn there. Guess what I found hiding between two books?"

Daniel shook his head.

"A notebook. It had the same exact poem in it."

"Maybe it was just similar?"

"The book had a black cover with an embossed circle on it. I remembered it had a drawing of soldiers on its first page. Now it made sense. It looked like on of Grandpa's drawings! And it was filled to the brim with poetry."

"Where is it? Do you have it with you?"

"Across the street. At the motel," I pointed out the window. "I wanted to bring it here with me but I dropped it behind a bed. But… I don't understand. How is it possible that we're talking about the same thing? What are the chances of that?"

"You were meant to have it. Please keep it," he said with certainty. "Write in it, please. It should still have few blank pages."

Daniel's facial expression oscillated between serenity and disturbance. Was he relieved the notebook was this close, or did its proximity bring him distress? Did it deliver more burden or respite? I didn't get the chance to ask. We heard a thud and turned our heads toward the noise. A thick white blotch of snow was melting on the windowpane.

"What was that?" Daniel asked.

I got up to investigate who could have thrown a snowball at our window during the darkest hour of the night. The streetlights shone down onto the asphalt, framing the hospital's territory within their beaded halos. Snowflakes followed spirals as they fell, and a thin layer of snow covered the ground. But I could see no one outside. Not even a trace of a footstep marked in the virgin blanket of snow.

XIII.

The hours before dawn are the quietest. Streetlamps outside flashed on and off like giant strobe lights before giving out and revealing sights above previously unseen. Looking toward the dark expanse of the winter sky, patched with yellowish snow clouds, I watched banks of clouds glisten with silver and beyond them, faint stars like pinholes float across the void. I listened to the whisperings of the air, my breath appearing and disappearing over the pane. With my fingertip, I wrote Daniel's name on the glass and then watched it fade into transparent nothing.

"There's no one there, only the night," I said, looking up again.

"Strange things are in the air, I can feel it. My whole body is on alert."

"Do you think it's because of the angel?"

"Yes."

"Do you think he will return?" I turned to Daniel and began walking toward his bed.

"That will depend on you."

"Ever since the dreams started, I feel more alive; life has more depth, more meaning. I don't know if I want it to go back to what it used to be, I—"

"Remember that he's a fallen angel, Eve. *Fallen.* Not a guardian."

"Fallen doesn't have to mean evil or dangerous."

"They lusted after human women and revealed their secrets to them," he said. "The comingling was forbidden. This is why they'd been cast into the pit of Tartarus."

"Maybe they were called fallen, because they fell in love?"

"No one can stop you from doing what you want, Eve. But it is obvious that the one you call Sariel wants something from you. And he has great forces behind him. All I can do is warn you," he said, and lowered his body onto the pillow. His skin looked almost see-through.

"I'm probably getting you more exhausted with my

questions," I asked, sitting next to him. "I'm like that doctor."

Daniel smiled. His lips were chapped and his lids as heavy as his breath. I brought the glass of water to his lips and he drank until it was half empty. I only managed to take one tiny sip, still not used to its repulsive taste. The candle had almost burned down to its base, its quivering flame feeding off the molten pool of wax. I set the glass down and laid my head by Daniel's side, listening to his breath, my ears soon picking up the distant cries of a child. I thought I was imagining it until I heard a fist pounding on a wall, followed by rushed footsteps on the floor, probably belonging to a nurse.

"She cries every night calling for her mother. She's been left here to die."

"Makes me think of a boy I met in the hospital years ago. He ate too many green apples and got sick so his parents took him there. But they never came back for him. The boy would come to my room and hold my hand when Mom used to read me stories," I said, and sank back into silence.

Daniel stirred and began speaking, his voice almost a whisper. "Before the nurse and her alcoholic husband adopted me, I met a little girl in a hospital. Her mother used to come to read to her. The boy held her little hand and imagined how it would feel to have a sister and a mother."

"She wanted to adopt him. But Dad wouldn't let her," I said, tears wetting my face and his pajamas.

"It's like she knew. . . . A mother can sense when her child is near."

"She still thinks of you, Daniel," I said through a curtain of tears. We were both shivering. "Why is it that the moment things come together, everything has to end?"

"I don't know," he whispered.

No longer indecisive, I leaned forward and enclosed his thin body in a cocoon of my embrace. Daniel's thin arms wrapped around me.

"It is time you let me go, Evelina. Let everything find its place. Return home, be with your family, and know I will be close when you think of me."

"How can you say such a thing?"

"I can feel the sleep approaching. I don't want to

fight anymore. You brought me so much happiness. You don't even know—"

"Please, stay, Daniel. Don't go yet," I was sobbing.

"I will never leave you. As long as you remember me, I will be close. I promise," he said, making me completely fall apart. "You are the best sister I could ever ask for."

"Daniel, are you really leaving me?"

"I can never leave. Remember? Nothing ever dies. It's just a long sleep," he said, and the light in the room dimmed until fizzing lightly in its final effervescent exhale, the candle gave up its flame. A moment later I smelled the acrid trail of drifting smoke.

I lifted my head and looked at his face, now illuminated by the faint light of the approaching dawn. A purple vein on his right temple pulsated softly under his translucent skin. I glanced toward the window and saw an inkling of blue in the sky—a placid lake with floating clouds of pink cotton.

"I love you, Daniel," I whispered.

It seemed that he was trying to say something but was struggling, his body quickly fading.

"Daniel?" I lifted my head to look at him once more, trying to read his lips.

He opened his eyes and looked at me one last time. "Nothing ever dies."

My head was pounding from crying so much; I felt exhausted and even speaking was a struggle now, like climbing a steep wall. So I curled into him, inhaling his faint scent, offering my warmth in return.

"Sariel," I whispered before sleep took me away. "Help Daniel. And I shall be yours forever."

Daylight stung my eyelids like the burn of a direct flashlight. I sensed a commotion in the air. I tried to move but couldn't, feeling pressed down as if by the weight of heavy sandbags. Resigned, I exhaled, sinking back into the veiny obscurity inside my lids. But not for long. I heard a loud noise, a door slamming, and my eyes blinked open. I saw a fogged window with milky stains on its surface. Low hanging clouds, dispersing bright autumn light. My skull hurt and my head was spinning. I inhaled and curled my fingers over the coarse texture of linen sheets, and pressed myself up. I was alone in a hospital room. Parts of the walls were scraped down to the cement and stained with rust. The room looked much worse in daylight. A crooked clothing hanger stood by the door, still holding my jacket.

"Daniel?" I called into the empty room, but of course got no reply. At least not the one I was hoping for. The doors opened and in stormed a plump middle-aged nurse wearing a white uniform and garish makeup.

"Finally, she wakes up. Grab your jacket and come this way," she motioned with her plump arm, "Time for you to go. Here," she reached out her hand. "Let's go. Now."

"Where is Daniel?"

"Are you coming or not? Your mother is in the hallway."

Slowly, I put on my jacket. "Where did you take him?" I asked, causing the nurse to lose her patience.

"As far as I can see, there is no one here," she turned with open palms, before pointing her finger at me. "So hurry out or I will report you to the head of security. And if you think I'm not nice, wait until you meet the man. Out you go!" she said, grabbing me by my shoulder.

I shrugged off her hand and slid off the gurney, nearly falling over as it slipped away on its rusty wheels. I opened the doors and left the room, the nurse following closely at my heels. Out in the hallway, I saw Mom pacing nervously.

"Eve! What happened? We've been looking all over for you!" Mom looked as if she was tallying whether it was more appropriate to be angry or concerned. She chose the latter. As usual.

Placing one of her chubby arms on her hips, the nurse pointed at me, as seemed to be her custom, and ordered my mother to take her unruly daughter before she caused any more trouble. In her eyes, I could have just as well been an arsonist or a murderer.

"Let's get out of here before things get worse," Mom said, eyeing the nurse and taking my hand.

"But I can't leave him here," I cried to Mom.

"Leave who?"

"Daniel!" I said, as if stating the obvious.

The nurse wrung her arms over her generous chest. "What did I say?" The nurse served me a deathly glare.

"What happened to him?" I challenged her again, feeling more confident with Mom around.

"Who's Daniel?" Mom asked.

"Listen, child," the nurse said, her finger approaching. "I have no idea what you're talking about. I do not know who you are or who Daniel is. Now out of my hospital."

Mom yanked my hand and began walking away, dragging me behind her, away from the nurse. "Eve, this behavior is unacceptable. What in the world possessed you?"

"I've been trying to explain, but you're not letting me!" I shouted. "Where are we going?"

"To the car. Your father and Rena are waiting."

"What about Grandpa? I need to see him!"

"You can't see him. He's in ER."

"Why?" I stopped abruptly, halting her momentum.

"He needs another surgery."

"What?"

"They said it's an infection," she replied, a dark cloud obliterating her strained forehead. "So you see why I am so stressed? And now this?" She let go of my hand and began walking without me.

"Mom, but this is . . . this will help you understand. Mom, just wait here, please? I'll be right back."

Mom called after me, but I was already halfway up the stairs that led to the second floor. Almost knocking over a nurse carrying a tray of food, I ran down the hallway and stormed into the room where I had spent most of last night.

The room was cold and bleak like a hollowed tree trunk in a winter forest. Daniel's bed was empty; there was nothing on the crooked hanger, the water pitcher was gone. I ran toward the object of my pursuit fixed atop the metallic surface. With my nail, I peeled off and placed in my pocket the thing that at least to me held the proof of Daniel's existence—the remains of the white candle. I placed the hardened wax inside my pocket, walked out of the room, descended the stairs, and entered the hospital lobby. The red haired nurse stood there scribbling something on a notepad. Upon seeing me she abandoned her task to personally walk me out before releasing me into the hands of my disheveled mother like a criminal.

Not saying another word, I hung my head and entered the car. Mom shut the door behind me and taking a seat in the front blew out a long sigh.

"Where is my watch?" Rena barked as I sat next to her. "You stole it!"

"The notebook!" I yelped in response, unfastening the watch to give back to my livid sister. "I left it in the motel room. Did anyone find it?"

"Eve, please," Mom said in a tired voice, her head sinking into her palm. "Your backpack is in the trunk. Enough already."

"But the book fell behind the bed! Did anyone find it? It had a black cover—"

"Didn't you hear what your mother said? Enough. You are grounded for a week," Dad said, and I knew it was the end of that discussion.

Rena grinned ear to ear. I didn't see it, but I could feel it in the way she moved her body, as if carelessly dancing on the seat next to me while I mourned the loss of a treasure. I pressed my lips together, feeling the urge to let it all out with a river of tears, but I wanted to be stronger than that. I wanted to be stronger for Daniel. I needed to think clearly and come up with a solid plan. Too many questions were left unanswered, and an innocent life had vanished without a trace—the life of my brother, the brother denied to me since before my birth.

I gazed at Mom's hand in front of me as she searched for a place to rest it in order to bolster her fatigued head, and noticed it was shivering. Dad, as usual, was grinding his teeth, and Rena acted as if she had won something of incredible value now that she had been proven right. Her younger sister, that little smartass, finally got the punishment she deserved. I exhaled and sank in the seat, casting one last glance at Rena who sat behind Dad, and preparing for the drive that I knew would take a torturous eternity.

The strike came out of nowhere. Rena screamed, Mom gasped, and Dad slammed the brakes, causing the car behind us to hit our back end. I watched it unfold in slow motion, feeling a surge of adrenaline shoot through my veins and sharpen my senses, but I remained calm and reactionless through it all. The glass next to me shattered into pieces, and the jagged rock catapulted in front of my face, landing on Rena's lap. Her hands were covering her ears. I felt drops of liquid stream down my cheek and when I reached out to touch my face and pulled my fingers back to look at them, they were crimson red.

Dad guided the car to the side of the road and stormed out of it, shutting the door behind him. Mom was soon unbuckling her seatbelt, leaping from the car, and opening my door to crouch beside me, gathering me into her arms. But I didn't feel anything. The accident had released a load of tension, and in a strange way I felt better, as if the impact had adjusted our flow after the muddled morning, setting my destiny on a new course.

I got out of the car, and taking advantage of a private moment with Mom, I addressed her while she held a kerchief to my bleeding temple. It was only a scratch.

"Please don't think I'm crazy. It is enough that Rena does."

"I don't think you're crazy, I just think you haven't been your usual self lately. First you want to go to a cathedral at night to pray, and then you break into a hospital. Churches and hospitals are the two places that repel you most, Eve. You shouldn't be surprised that I'm concerned. I don't understand what's gotten into you."

"I would tell you if you let me explain."

"Then tell me. For goodness sake, tell me." Here I was, exactly where Daniel stood last night, on the juncture of revealing the truth and breaking a promise. It was not an easy decision. My stomach churned, my heart fluttering against my ribs. "Eve?"

"Remember the boy we met at a hospital by the sea when I was little? The one who held my hand, the one you wanted to adopt?" Mom arched her brows and nodded her head. "Do you remember his name?"

"His name was Peter," she said, "Why?"

"Are you sure?" I asked, feeling her words seep out my hope like a pierced balloon quickly losing air.

"Yes. Why?" She looked at me, puzzled. Dad called to Mom, motioning for her to join him. "You'll tell me later." She excused herself and walked away, leaving me standing on the side of the road.

Rena bent over in her seat, looking out the open car door, and staring at me spoke one devastating word "Lunatic."

But her word didn't hurt as much as did Mom's response. The boy's name was Peter. How could I have forgotten it? And what did that make Daniel? A product of my imagination?

I brought my hands to my head to steady the flurry of thoughts. With my throbbing temple, it was a dizzying combination. What if Rena was right when she called me a lunatic? Wasn't a lunatic someone who goes insane around the time of the full moon? I bent over to try to meet my sister's gaze. I had the sudden urge to appeal to her, to have a conversation, not an argument. I wanted to ask her at which point last night she had noticed that I was gone, but she had her headphones on and was looking the other way. I reached in and picked up the rock she had placed on the seat next to her. Rubbing my fingers over it, I looked at its brown surface. There were a few red dots smudged on one side—my blood.

I paced around the car, hyperventilating, teetering on the edge of insanity. What was real? I tried to concentrate on what I was seeing so as not to let my thoughts take over. I glanced toward my parents. Dad was writing something on a piece of paper, the woman from the other car was talking to Mom and pointing at something in the distance. Then I looked at our car. The window on my side was missing.

I studied the rock again, and then the street and the intersection, watching the light go from green to yellow to red. I tried to determine where the rock could've come from. Spinning around on my heel I looked at the trees lining the sidewalk until I caught a glimpse of a black coat. He was hiding behind a tree.

A bare, gnarled hand was holding onto a tree trunk, a man's cold eyes fixed upon me as an impish leer spread across his face. There was no doubt in my mind as to who had cast the stone and caused the accident.

The old man tipped his hat at me.

Time stopped once more.

I read his lips.

I will find you.

PART III
SARIEL

XIV.

My eyes skipped across colorful lights of our freshly decorated tree. Amidst lingering smells of an earlier Christmas Eve feast that consisted of fried fish and mushroom dumplings with beet soup, I sat wrapped in a blanket on the sofa, sipping clove tea, while outside thick snowflakes covered the frozen ground. It was two in the morning and everyone but me was asleep.

With all the frantic preparations, the dinner served as a great distraction that held my thoughts and emotions safely tucked behind a wall of denial. Over the past month, I had managed to push my thoughts of Sariel and Daniel to the farthest recesses of my brain, keeping the memories in a firm lock down. It was easier to live this way, believing that they were a mirage, personified figments of my overactive imagination, too intense to ponder, too pointless to follow. It smoothed out my relations at home, eliminated tensions. I didn't want to wrangle with guilt and regret anymore, or trade my delicate sense of newfound order for another pandemonium.

But as I stared at the entrancing lights on the tree Rena and I had adorned with shining trinkets just this morning, I felt restlessness rise inside my heart. Maybe the exhaustion that ensued after a whole day of chores unraveled my focus? Maybe it was because of the tension I felt looking at Grandpa who sat across the table from me, avoiding my gaze? Besides a greeting and goodbye, we hardly exchanged another word. Whatever had caused it, all the thoughts I'd tried to hold back were now bubbling up to the surface at once. Too tired to resist, in a few short moments, my body relived what had taken me weeks of great effort and self-control to keep under wraps.

For several days after returning home from the hospital, I dreamt of my brother, each morning wondering if this would be the day I'd approach my mother with the question that might lead us deeper into the territories of the past. But by the time I'd have my breakfast and my opportunity, my tea and audacity would turn cold, and I'd postpone the task to the following day, until eventually forgoing the task all together. What would I tell her? After all, besides me, no one had seen the book of poems, the only proof I'd had to substantiate my theory. But even if I did tell her, and she didn't deny it, what would be the point of probing her, a line of questioning that may take on the tone of accusation or attack, adding to the living hell she already had to endure?

Since returning home, the tensions between Mom and Dad had taken a turn for the worse. The onslaught of arguments—some whispered, most shouted—were testing her ability to keep a semblance of unity over a shaky foundation, which held us together by the means of tearing threads. It reached a point where my father was rationing food money to us, the way the communist government used to with food stamps, making her rely more on aid from her parents. Grandma was angry with Mom for not knowing how to please her husband, which in her opinion was the true reason behind his prolonged absences.

Grandpa returned home ten days after we did, which was now well over a month ago. He was still too weak to get involved in the family squabbles. Not to mention, it would've been rather awkward since it was Dad who was commissioned with the task of driving out to the hospital to fetch him. I cursed myself later for letting Dad go there without me, missing a chance of going to the clinic to look for traces of Daniel.

After returning home, Grandpa convalesced under a protective dome of Grandma's care that consisted of pureed chicken soup, supplemented by a string of detective movies Grandma rented by the dozen from the town's only video shop. Grandma was adamant that we should not bother Grandpa with anything even remotely distressing for at least a couple of weeks, as the smallest upset—down to stray down feathers floating dangerously too close to his breathing passages— could cause a bout of coughs that would take a great toll on his recovering body. Grandpa's condition and delicate handling resembled that of a newborn child's. He slept a lot, ate pulp, and was discouraged from speaking and emotional engagement that could throw his healing off course.

But I couldn't restrain myself for that long before

talking with him, which proved disastrous for both him and me. The evening he came home I was already by his side and holding his hand, waiting for Grandma, Mom, and Rena to leave the room. When they left to prepare supper in the kitchen, I got my chance to ask him, gently of course, for the reason why he cried that afternoon at the hospital, breaking Grandma's cardinal rule of no disturbance. I thought I saw his pupils dilate with remembrance. With a scratchy voice that had lost its tone, he responded by uttering one word, *children*, before his chest exploded in a storm of coughs.

Grandma rushed in, and holding a kerchief to his mouth, patted his back. With each pat, my hope dwindled, cooler air entered the room, shapes lost their definition, and shadows elongated. I had to let it go.

Later that night, I concluded that Grandpa was crying for all the children that had to suffer the pain of premature mortality, not one specific individual, and put an end to it. Maybe there was never a Daniel, as the nurse had insisted. Maybe I had seen a movie about an orphan boy years ago and my subconscious mind made it into my story. Maybe I got high on drug fumes wafting through the hospital ventilation system and experienced a grand hallucination. With a tight fist pressing down my will, I forced my thoughts to leave my mind even though the effort resembled laying a basket of grenades under a bed covered with a dozen mattresses to muffle their successive explosions.

In any case, it was not my time or place to get my answers. I knew I should just forget it and let normal existence replace the shaky turf of navigating my way to the core of my family mystery, which could've been not much more than a manifestation of a teenager's wish for an extraordinary experience in what was nothing more than an ordinary town. After all, even Ben had we make real where we choose to put our faith.

Soon, my initial resignation became an obsessive need to make anything that even hinted at the mystical leave my life. Especially since I grew a suspicion that something in the vein of impish forces had invaded my room shortly after our return. Coming home from school, I'd notice that objects had shifted on my desk; books on ancient history or the occult that no member of my family would ever consider reading would be left open; different cassettes would be left in my tape player from the one I had left in the night before. The pages of my diary bore the marks of liquid smudging the ink.

One Thursday, I detected the scent of smoke from an extinguished candle. The wax around the wick was still warm and easily gave in under pressure. Rena was at school, and Mom at Grandma's apartment. The following day I found the shape of the waning moon painted with red lipstick on my windowpane. As I tried wiping it off with a sleeve cloaking my trembling wrist, the thought of Sariel kept crossing my mind. Was he back? Or was this a warning, much like the red wax effigy that Paula and Marta insisted represented the devil?

What if they had been right?

That Sunday I attended the eleven o'clock mass before joining my family for lunch at grandparents' place. I attended another mass two days later, and then again on Friday, feeling noticeably better with each day. No more surprises waited for me after that. A new space was opening up inside of me, making it easier to concentrate on more earthly matters. The more I filled up my life with concrete spiritual practice rooted in tradition, the less I thought of the events from November. Consequently, my fantasies about Sariel and memories of Daniel receded, giving way to more peaceful nights and focused, practical days. Mom seemed relieved to have her old daughter back and Rena finally stopped teasing me. And when the next full moon came along, I slept through the night without a single dream disturbing my tranquility.

At school, gossip about Ben and me went from shimmering intrigue to shameful dismissal, inspiring a self-imposed exile. I felt too raw and sensitive to partake in any act of self-defense. Fragments of stories soon reached my ears. People spoke in hushed voices in the hallways about how Ben had left me because I was playing with demonic forces. The stigma of witchcraft was effective enough to keep most people at bay. I knew that once Marta caught hold of any buzz, she would spin and embellish it until it caught the wind and spread like coal fumes across our town.

From disjointed strings of chitchat I quickly discerned that Ben got a new girlfriend—much prettier than me, and a talented musician to boot. I didn't see him behind the theater, but that was mainly my choice because I didn't have the nerve to go there.

Day after day I'd leave school and trudge through the alley lined with naked oaks, loaded with the weight of my existential concerns crushing my budding sense of elusive identity. Occasionally, a thought would cross my mind of encountering the familiar stranger who, with a single glance, would notice the seeds that lay dormant within my soul. Punk's knowing gaze would chase away my doubts, catalyze recognition, and make the whirling chaos raging under my skull settle into a kaleidoscopic pattern ripe for exploration. I would imagine us looking deeply into each other's souls until our separateness melted into a puddle of common understanding. Words would be superfluous and serenity would replace confusion, anticipation edging out boredom. I desperately craved closeness with someone who would dare to understand what I was going through.

But Punk had left my sleepy town, quite possibly with no plans to return. Instead, one murky afternoon I encountered someone else, a meeting that filled me with terror and motivated an even more pronounced act of renunciation. The man in the black coat followed me home.

I hadn't seen the man in the coat since he promised to find me, after hauling a rock at our car on our way back from the hospital. As I quickened my pace, so did he. His footsteps were soon on my heels, hands eagerly reaching. I could feel the chill of winter emanate from his body.

He would have had me in his grasp if a neighbor had not happened to drive by. I waved her down and she stopped, chuckling at me and asking why I was so distraught. As we drove away, I turned around to look through the back window of her car. The man was standing empty-handed in the middle of the road looking straight at me. I turned back around and sank into the back seat of her car, shivering.

"Pretty cold out today, eh?" she asked and

laughed again.

"Did you see that man running after me?" I asked, once my breathing calmed down. But she only looked at me strangely and said that there was no one else on the road besides me. The incident made me think of Mom who also didn't see the man at the candle altar in the cathedral.

Despite plunging myself into hot water and drinking a whole pitcher of hot lemon tea at home, I couldn't free myself from the frozen grip of the man's presence. Not until I aimed my trembling arms at my collection of my music cassettes, which people like Marta no doubt deemed came from hell, and cast them into a plastic garbage bag. My collection of hard to find esoteric books followed. I put them in a box, with the intention to donate them to the library. The activity warmed me up and I slept better that night. Maybe it was because of the music?

As much as I relished peaceful moments in the dark, I resented them in daylight. I used to love being alone. But having nothing left to explore, no mystery to untangle, and no music to listen to, silence became more of an aching burden than a welcome respite. Besides school, homework, and church mass, I had nothing left to do. Too much television left me feeling lobotomized, and too much sleep exhausted me more than its lack. My world became flat and predictable and I indifferent and numb.

As I sat reminiscing and watching the tree lights twinkle, the growing shield of oncoming tears distorted their radiance. But my crying only opened the gates to a much deeper release. I felt the saltiness burn my cheeks, and I opened my mouth to take in a shaky gulp of air, my first real breath in hours, if not days or weeks. I was reawakening, reuniting with all that I'd been trying to reject as mere fantasy. It was time to surrender and free myself from the chains of my own self-righteousness.

Much like a child learning to walk, I let myself stumble across the minefields of my mind, perceiving the past events as real instead of imagined, and watching my body's reactions. To my surprise, there were no big earthquakes or tsunamis. In fact, my body seemed to open and root, stirring back to life. Tiny waves of resurrected emotions pulled me in their tides. Exhaling over a month's worth of stagnant air, I was beginning to feel again. What if what I had discovered was true rather than imagined? What if I was sane and everyone else lived in some sort of a lie?

Casting the blanket to the side, I unraveled my joints that creaked from my sudden movement. I walked into my room and put a second pair of socks on my feet and a wool jacket over my shirt. I opened my desk drawer and took out a small object wrapped in aluminum foil and put it inside my pocket. I walked into the small foyer that smelled of shoe polish, laced up my boots, quietly turned the doorknob and slipped outside.

Dry snow cracked under my feet. I drank the frozen air in large gulps, the pain of cold serrating my lungs, waking up every cell. Inside my pocket, my fingers kept rubbing over the smooth surface of the one thing I had refused to forego— Daniel's last relic—the hardened puddle of white wax.

Approaching the same stack of pipes I had used to check the shape of the red wax that revealed the profile of Sariel, I suddenly felt as if I had just stepped into a pool of hot water, a vortex that never closed. The heat shot up my legs, rising through my belly and back, exploding in my head. Before I knew what was happening, I was on my knees, sobbing like a child. My bare fingers gripped the snow. I realized that over the past weeks I had let others dictate my destiny, letting them take away my fledging sense of self, direction, and purpose.

The cold of the snow was sobering and I rubbed it into my face and hands until they stopped trembling. Taking out the piece of wax from my packet, I peeled the foil and placed it atop my open palm, snowflakes melting around it. Fearing what the contours would reveal, but even more fearing my own doubt, I brought the object toward the curved wall of a pipe to catch its shadow.

I had to turn it around and try multiple angles before my mind finally caught up. At first, I thought it was a jagged heart, then a leaf, but none of the images fully matched the concepts they invoked. The shadow's transmission was a subtle inkling, a distant afterglow.

"Open your mind, Eve," I said to myself. "See it."

And then I did. The wax was an effigy of a wing—an angel's wing. The physical and the mystical snapped into one giving rise to new questions.

Was there more of a connection between Daniel and the angel than I had allowed myself to consider? Was Sariel present with us in the room that night? The thoughts stirred more heat in my body. Familiar desire began to simmer my blood, engorging my veins. I held the wax as if it were my key to salvation, paving a way toward a deeper understanding.

But the subtle illumination also contained a shadow, a threat of danger. I didn't want to burn myself on this fire, and again be cast into the pit of isolation and confusion, the pit of enigma. The pit out of which, like steam, raised a love—nascent and ancient, innocent and sinful—love that tasted like the mixture of sweet honey and bitter wine. But it alone was a taste worth living for, a feeling worth losing days of sleep for—a joyous celebration, and a mournful elegy.

Why did life need to be this complicated?

Once more I was caught in a war with myself. I could take being the outcast in school, but could I withstand that feeling at home? Clearly these were nothing but delusions. Or were they? Here I was, alone, but surrounded by a supernatural presence, while at home I would be surrounded with faces of people who I was discovering lived in denial. I was starting to fully comprehend what Daniel meant when he said that the truth would make me the loneliest person in the world.

But also in that moment I realized that my desire to know was stronger than my need to belong. That unless I took a leap of faith to find out what really happened before my sister and I were born, I would always live with an unanswered question frozen on my lips.

I gripped the wax too strongly, denting its shape. What if exactly the opposite was real? What if perception was a mirror reflecting an opposite image, as my vision at the castle showed me? Like the moon, always half-shrouded in darkness. I watched my nails pierce through the wax, my fingers curling into a fist, bending the effigy into pieces.

Which was true? My burning emotions or the cold hand of reason? Was there room for both?

White bits of wax fell off my open palm and vanished in snowy whiteness. There was nothing left to do here, so I turned back home.

Tearing off my coat and unlacing my boots in haste, I walked into the living room and reached inside a credenza, filled with a jumble of books on one side and videotapes on another. There I found it—the Bible. It had a polished blue leather cover and gold embossing on the front and spine. It was a present from Grandma for my first communion.

I peeled open the cracking pages, its glued bonds stretching. Lying down on the sofa under the blanket, I leafed through its pages until I found the passage in Genesis:

Now it came about, when men began to multiply on the face of the land, and daughters were born to them, that the sons of God saw that the daughters of men were beautiful; and they took wives for themselves, whomever they chose. The Nephilim were on the Earth in those days, and also afterward, when the sons of God came in to the daughters of men, and they bore children to them. Those were the mighty men who were of old, men of renown.

It was true then. They existed.

I read the passage over and over until the words burned in my memory. Soon the weight of my lids obscured the text, sealing in the content and carrying the silent outcry of my soul into the darkest depths of my being, where only He could hear me.

XV.

I'm bound. There is nothing but darkness here. I call out, but the hollow silence deafens my voice. No sight, no sound, no reference point in this place—it's an imageless sleep, like being dead while awake, with no place to turn.

I hold still and watch, I wait and listen, until my breath becomes a wave upon which I drift.

From afar, I catch a whisper of a sound, like a breeze carrying words, an invocation. Rise up and fall in love. . . . Rise up and fall in love. . . . The speaking grows louder and I recognize my own voice.

"Eve, wake up!" Mom's hand gently shook my shoulder.

I opened my eyes and stretched out my arm. I was on the living room sofa. Everyone was already up having breakfast. The smell of coffee and poppy seed cake drifted in the air. Dad was preparing his pitcher of tea—I could tell by the banging of his spoon on the glass. Upon seeing me awake, relieved Rena turned for the remote control and plopped on an armchair.

"What time is it, Mom?"

"It's past noon. Phone call for you."

"Who is it?" I asked with a yawn.

"Not sure. Should I ask him to call back later?"

"No, I'll take it," I said, rolling off the couch and walking toward a small bureau in the hallway.

Who could it be? Was Ben coming back around? I would never tell him to his face, but I was beginning to miss him. A lot. I missed the conversations we had, the music we shared, and the questions that took us beyond the mundane. I missed all that and more, down to my daily anticipation of him knocking on my door around suppertime, and the knowing that the best part of my day was just about to begin. The lack of Ben in my life, the lack of simply knowing that he was there and thinking of me, was becoming more devastating than I could ever admit. I used to take all that for granted.

"Hello?" I said into the phone.

"Hey." It wasn't Ben, but the voice gave me a taste of familiarity.

"Hey Rock."

"I was wondering if you're free later today."

"I am. What's happening?"

"Nothing really," Rock said. "I was just hoping for a guitar lesson or a jam session. Or whatever. But it's okay if you are busy, I mean—"

"Works for me. Wanna come by in an hour?"

"That would be perfect," he said, and we hung up.

It had been weeks since I touched my instrument, and while I was hardly in the mood to play music, I did crave company. The prospect of another day in front of the television eating holiday leftovers was unbearable. I showered and changed, and by the time Rock arrived, my hair was almost dry and my amp buzzing.

"What's new?" he asked, untying his polished boots in the foyer.

"Nothing exciting," I said and Rock followed me to my room.

"What happened to all your tapes?" he asked, taking notice of my empty shelves.

"Gave them away," I said to avoid unnecessary explanations, before plopping down on the revolving desk chair. Still, part of me wished I could just tell him they were in the garbage and how I wished I hadn't thrown them away.

"All of them?" His eyes were wide with disbelief, as if asking why I didn't think of him first. I really had amassed an impressive collection.

I plugged the amp jack into my guitar, which made the sound of crumbled plastic, ending with a fiery pop. Rock sat on my bed and unzipped the black bag that held his wooden, tan-colored acoustic guitar with red trimmings. "What would you like to work on?" I asked.

"I thought that I could practice the pentatonic scale while you hold the chords," he shrugged, and I swapped my electric guitar for his instrument. It was easier to solo on an electric.

"Sure thing."

"And then I got this new song and was hoping you could help me rip off a riff or two."

"What is it?" I asked, taking the tape he pulled out of the inside pocket of his leather jacket.

"It's a demo by this new band, Daimonion. Out of this world."

"I could try."

"Ben got it from Fly. Apparently Fly met these guys at some festival and now can't stop talking about them."

Fly was the nickname of the rhythm guitarist, vocalist, and songwriter of Sirrah, a local doom metal band that was experiencing quite the measure of success.

"So, what's Ben up to these days?" I asked, trying to hide the eagerness in my voice.

"He's been up in the city a lot, sitting in on rehearsals with Sirrah. They will be playing in our little village at the beginning of February. You should come."

"Is Ben part of the band now?"

"He wishes. But sometimes he jams with them," Rock said, getting up. We needed to swap places, as the cord that connected my guitar to the amp was too short to reach my bed. Rock sat on the chair and scooted it toward the amp while I settled on the edge of my mattress. He cranked up the volume but immediately turned it back down after the deafening squeal of feedback ripped through the air.

"Oops, sorry."

"And Art?" I asked while strumming his six-string acoustic. It was in need of a tuning. "What is he up to these days?"

"Art moved up north to live with his father. But he said he would be coming back to town for the New Year."

"I see."

I asked Rock to strike each of my freshly tuned strings, bottom to top, while I twisted the pegs of his instrument in search of matching notes. Once both of our guitars sounded the same, we began our lesson. I picked four chords to play in sequence as a background for Rock's solo improvisation. But it was hard for me to keep the chords clean. My head was too preoccupied throwing off my rhythm, and we had to start multiple times. Finally, we decided to take a break.

Rock plunged the Daimonion tape into my player, pressed play, and turned up the volume.

"The track's called 'Night,'" he said, before the sounds reverberated with full force, rattling the glass in my windows and door.

It had been weeks since I started my music cleanse and even longer since I had heard anything new. The combination of melodies and lyrics spilling in lilts and thuds into my room gave rise to astounding visions and sensations. The bass, strings and drums tore up the air, and the vocalist's gloomy vocals grabbed a hold of my soul. As much as part of me wanted to resist it, hearing this track was like medicine, unlocking a deep longing, reconnecting me with my essence.

Night, night, her sister took away your waking days, the vocalist sang. *And the moon, it lights up my path, while you sleep,* went the chorus, freeing me from last vestiges of my self-imposed renunciation.

Take me, deliver my life into your heaven. Night, night, her sister took away your waking days . . .

The song ended and I looked at Rock, who was grinning ear to ear.

"Pretty dope, huh?"

I nodded. "I will rip the whole thing for you, but you will need to leave the tape with me."

"This is your copy," he said, pointing at the player.

After another shot at a solo jam, way more fruitful this time, Rock left, and I spent the rest of the afternoon locked up in my room, wearing out the six song demo tape with successive replays.

Belly on the floor, feet wiggling in the air, I immersed myself in biblical study, highlighting passages with references to fallen angels. By the time the night reached its darkest hour, I had listened to the tape more than a dozen times and had more than half of the holy text marked and annotated.

Two lines I found in Isaiah inspired an idea. I paused my research and stared at the words I had circled with a pencil:

How you are fallen from heaven,
O Day Star, son of Dawn!
How you are cut down to the ground,
You who laid the nations low!

The passage pointed toward a link between the morning star and Lucifer. I pulled out a clean sheet of paper. Near the top, I drew a star to represent Venus, and angel wings below, connecting the two images with a weaving image of a serpent. *Lust. Astrology. Myths. Rites of Passage,* I jotted down beside it.

My body responded and for a split second my vision cleared.

There was no evil in nature. There was only massive human misunderstanding. There were those people who used stories long ago in an effort to convey to others the steps of human evolution. This was the true purpose of mythology and religion—to unite people in common understanding on our individual quests for truth, to point a way toward a path, not easily found in a world that muddled our senses with incessant distractions. And then there were those who used those same stories to scare those who might be seeking answers. People like me—those who swam against the current.

I was standing on a precipice of change. I felt it with every fiber of my being. This moment called for drawing from the well of my own strength and not relying on anyone when making decisions. This quest required faith and strong will. My old views would need to be deconstructed—hence the association with destructive forces. But the only thing that would be destroyed was the old self hypnotized by status quo, no longer relevant, no longer useful, and preparing me to question even more.

I looked at my sketch of the wings ascending up the serpentine spiral toward Venus. In it I recognized a map guiding me toward my personal rite of passage. The angel was my catalyst, the agent of change. I knew there would be people and signs guiding me onward, but ultimately it would be a lone journey.

On the last day of 1995, I paced around my phone for hours before mustering the courage to dial Rock's number. I wasn't used to being the one to initiate a connection. Ben usually took care of that part. It was already twilight when I finally called. Rock's mother picked up and told me that he had gone out with Artur. Of course, it was New Year's Eve. Art was back in town. Fighting initial reticence, I donned my coat and went outside. For all I knew they could be anywhere, but there was one place more likely than others. For the first time since the unfortunate kiss between Ben and me, I ventured to the theater.

The town was desolate, frozen in time, save an occasional vehicle rushing to a party at someone's house. A light drizzle of snow and rain was falling. I walked wondering whether I would be riding into the New Year with my old pack of friends or hunched over the scripture, collecting new insights, my investigation interrupted by drunken neighbors shouting their felicitations toward the heavens. There could even be a firework or two.

As indicated by a poster with a two fizzing champagne glasses hanging on the front door, tonight the theater would house a private party upstairs, where I knew Rena would be boogieing. Rounding the corner, I entered the plaza, just as a group of four guys were splitting a pack of beer. Two punk rockers I knew vaguely, Sasha and Kal, sat on the concrete stairs while Art and Rock remained standing, likely to not dirty their coats. Feeling a bit as if encroaching upon a closed circle, I approached with a weary gait until Rock noticed me and waved.

"How's our secret project?" he called.

"What secret project?" Art perked up and turned in my direction. "Long time no see."

"Eve is helping me rip the chords off the song Ben wants to cover with Fly. I want to beat him to it."

"I smell rivalry," I cast toward Rock. "You didn't tell me that part."

"You could've said no," Rock said.

"Anyone got a smoke? It's been ages," I said to fill

the silence. Kal extended his pack and Rock offered his light. I leaned into the flame, feeling Art's piercing glare.

"Surprised you're not with Ben tonight," he murmured. "I heard there is going to be a mad party in the city."

I shrugged with overstated indifference, sensing that all four of them knew more about what happened between Ben and me than they were willing to admit.

"Where are you guys going from here?"

"My garage," Kal said. "Wanna come? It will be mostly guys though."

"She shouldn't have a problem with that," Rock said, the guys laughed, and Sasha handed me a bottle of beer he had just opened for me.

I felt much better.

About a dozen of us lingered inside the makeshift space Kal referred to as his *living room*. Band posters covered the garage's metal walls floor to ceiling. The music was blaring from a guitar amp connected to a tape player; there were blankets and pillows in each corner and wood stubs for tables atop which rested bowls with potato chips and pretzels. While the food offering was paltry, cases of booze made up for any lack. We must have had enough alcohol to inebriate half of the neighborhood.

As the current music track was coming to a close, we heard a loud slam. The doors parted with a bang and in rushed Crass with his entourage.

"What up, motherfuckers?" he shouted from the open doorway. I stepped behind Rock to get out of his view.

"What is he on today, you think?" Rock elbowed Art.

"Probably everything he could get his hands on," Art said and called toward the disheveled youth. "Hey, Crass, come over here and join us for a shot!" It didn't take much for the youth to saunter over and wedge himself between Rock and Art, and plant a loud kiss on Art's cheek, which Art ostentatiously wiped with the back of his hand. "Easy, man. Easy."

The difference between them was staggering. Art, polished and tidy in his gray coat, green scarf, and shiny boots, and Crass, unkempt and wild—frayed hair, flannel shirt poking out of his bomber jacket, mangled black skinny jeans. Crass greeted Rock with a high-five and turned to look at me. "Good evening, Madame," he said, tipping an invisible hat and extending his hand. Warmed by his gesture, though not without reluctance, I gave him my hand, which he slowly raised to his mouth. Looking me in the eyes, he turned it palm up, and traced its length with his wet tongue.

"Eww, man! Gross!" Art laughed.

I withdrew my hand quickly and wiped it on my pants, chagrined by the sudden arousal that shot through my body.

"Felt good, right?" Crass whispered, making sure no one besides me heard him. "It could be even better."

I walked away but before Crass had a chance to call me out on my sheepishness, I returned with a full bottle, jamming a shot glass into his hand. I wouldn't let Crass intimidate me.

"Here, drink with me," I said, pouring us shots.

"You really are something," he squinted his eyes and raised his glass. "The joke's on me."

Rock and Art joined us in a round and the four of us went outside to smoke. As the guys talked about some new band they had just discovered, I drifted off thinking about Sariel and what I could possibly do to prepare myself before the next full moon. It was time to initiate a meeting. My eyes landed on Art. I knew he was well read and had dabbled in philosophy.

"Eve is good at ripping music," Rock said, breaking my daze. "You should ask her."

I looked up. "What are you guys talking about?"

"Crass wants to know how to play the guitar. He needs to learn a chord or two that he can repeat over and over until it sinks in. That should last a few months, right buddy?" Rock slapped Crass' shoulder.

"Hey, stay back," Crass reacted, pointing his finger at Rock. "Hands to yourself!"

"Calm down, I was just trying to help," Rock blushed,

raising his hands in surrender. I sensed we were all thinking the same thing. One wrong move could send Crass reeling, throwing fragile objects at walls and killing innocent animals. "Somebody give me a fucking drink!" Crass growled, his eyes burrowing through Rock with that hollow gaze that frightened me so much.

Rock glanced at Art, and then back at Crass. "If you want a drink, let's go in," he said, and Crass followed him inside the garage. I breathed a sigh of relief.

I asked Art for another cigarette. "Sorry, I came completely unprepared."

"At this rate, let's just say you owe me a pack," he said and we lit up.

The alcohol was surging through my veins and the smoke was making me lightheaded. I swayed to the side, shamelessly ogling Art's face.

"What?" he finally asked.

"What do you know about fallen angels?"

"You mean the myths?"

"Not myths. The real stuff. Did it really happen, you think? Did the angels have, you know—?"

"Intimate relations with women?"

"Right," I said. With Rock gone, it was my turn to blush.

"Well . . . first off, if something is a myth, it doesn't mean it doesn't represent something true. The original function of myth was to explain the complexity of life, the underpinnings of existence. It used to serve as a road map to help navigate reality, to give people an idea how to live, how to move through cycles."

I stared at Art, who had just reiterated what I had recently discovered through my drawing. If only I had had the courage to talk to him earlier. . . . Clearly, alcohol helped break the ice.

"With time, and as science took over, the whole thing reversed," Art continued. "So now when we say that something is a myth we often mean that it is false and superficial, completely the opposite of what myths used to stand for."

"So do you think that the story of the fallen angels is true?"

"I don't know that. But it could also be a metaphor that describes something transcendent, like a change of state."

"A rite of passage, maybe?" I asked.

"Exactly. Why do you ask?"

"I feel like they've infiltrated my reality." Art raised his brows so I continued. "I agree with you that they might point toward something deeper. . . . But I also think that they could actually exist," I said, feeling an onset of nausea. It was not the best idea to drink and smoke on an empty stomach.

"You know they exist or you want them to exist?"

"Is there a difference?" I asked.

"When you want something bad enough, I guess it can seem like you're making it real. Is that what you mean?"

"Right. And the more you know you are not supposed to have something, the more you want it," I noticed that I was beginning to slur my words. "The angels are cursed because they evoke the forbidden aspects of the feminine. They are all male, you see, and they carry with them this raw feeling of lust and desire and we are supposed to stay innocent, you know, we are supposed to be pure," I said, fighting a wave of queasiness and hoping I was making sense. "We are not supposed to go there, you see, into that place of temptation and pleasure and—" I was so caught up in my rhetoric that I didn't notice when Crass joined us, dropping my cigarette onto the snow.

"Keep talking. I'm captivated," he said, handing me a shot glass.

"I don't think she should have any more," Art said.

"She should and she will. Cheers!" Crass bumped his glass with mine. "Just returning the generosity," he winked.

I knew that Art was probably right but I didn't want to appear weak so I tipped the glass and felt more of the warm liquid spread through my chest.

"So you were saying? Temptation and pleasure?" Crass prompted.

I blushed. "Art and I were just discussing the story of the fallen angels."

"My favorite topic," he burped and smiled.

I was pleasantly surprised by how much my peers knew about the subject. Art said that he was cold so he excused himself and went inside, leaving Crass and me alone.

"So what do you know about the fallen?" Crass asked, handing me a new cigarette.

"Very little. But you sound like you do," I inhaled the smoke. For a moment, Crass went out of focus.

He nodded. "I do. And I know how to experience them directly. Would you like to know what it's like?"

I couldn't believe my ears. Crass knew how to contact a fallen angel?

"Why read a book if you can take a field trip, eh?" Crass smiled and I shivered. "Don't look away. Don't move. Just watch me. Right in between my eyes." With his middle finger, he tapped the space where his nose began to jut out from his forehead.

I squinted, trying to focus with all my will, but my vision was blurring while Crass' face kept growing larger, his brows furrowing, mouth parting. The next moment one of his hands was gripping my jacket, the other reaching between my legs, his wet mouth surrounding my lips.

"Stop!" I screamed, pushing him away as I stumbled backward.

"You wanted me to show you," he laughed. "So I did!"

You know nothing, I thought, falling to the ground.

XVI.

"Happy New Year!" Dad entered my room with a half-filled champagne glass in his hand, finding me sitting on my amp in pajamas, lifelessly plucking the strings of my guitar. He held out the glass toward me. I looked at the sparkling liquid and gagged.

"Thanks, Dad, but I think I'll pass."

"Really? You don't want champagne?" he asked, withdrawing his hand in disbelief.

I shook my head again. "Positive."

"I see you are more exemplary than I thought," he said, and guzzled the drink in one gulp. "You should get dressed. I think we're leaving soon to have lunch at your grandparents' place," he added and left my room.

I was still shuddering at the thought of alcohol. Exemplary? If Dad only knew. . . .

Last night after Crass made his move, I awoke lying under a blanket and over a stack of pillows and in a corner of the garage with a throbbing headache, trying to remember what had happened. The party was in full swing with more people still arriving. Sasha noticed me and sauntered over.

"Want some pretzels?" he held out a bowl.

I shook my head.

"Better eat to sober up," he said, popping one into his mouth and biting down.

"Okay." I sat up, reaching my hand into the bowl, the world spinning. Rock came over and handed me a can of Coke. I drank and ate, swaying side-to-side, feeling cold and then hot. But when the memory of Crass' cigarette-stained lips closing over mine returned, I couldn't hold back anymore. I tried to get up and go outside but I only managed to stumble over a few steps before throwing up all over Kal's pillows.

The meal Grandma prepared for us was truly festive, though it was more suppertime by the time we got there. Mom cast glances at me from across the table. It seemed she suspected what had happened to me last night, but said nothing. Grandpa was slowly regaining his voice and color had returned to his face.

After we finished eating and everyone retreated to the living room, Grandpa felt enlivened enough to make a sketch for me on a piece of wrapping paper. I sat on the floor by his feet and watched him draw. The television was on, replaying last night's celebrations.

"Your Mom told me of how supportive you've been to her. She really needs you now," he said, sketching a human figure. "I always thought you were the most mature of the whole bunch," he added in a hoarse whisper.

Lifting my head, I smiled at his appeasing comment before lightly rubbing his wrinkled hand, lined with bulging blue veins. "Thank you, Grandpa. I try."

"And you've been attending church, I hear. That's really something."

I smiled in response. Last time I was there was for the Christmas Eve service, well over a week ago, but after my recent realizations and growing desire to continue with my quest, I had no intention of entering the holy ground for some time. I kept that detail to myself. My playing the role of an obedient Catholic girl must have provided a relief to him. I was one less to manage as the conflict between my parents raged on. I also stopped questioning his behavior at the hospital. But he knew so little of what I'd been through and I knew almost nothing of whatever knew he was hiding. Since he was feeling better, I decided to take a risk and test the waters.

"Grandpa, I want to tell you something," I spoke in a quiet, confessional tone. "Weeks ago, I had a peculiar dream. It put strange thoughts in my mind."

Grandpa peeled his eyes from the paper, his eyes alert, eyelids quivering. "What kind of a dream?"

"I dreamt of a fallen angel." Grandpa's hand jerked as if electricity had shot through it, making an intentional line across the body of a soldier.

He took a deep breath and straightened his back, his stern eyes glued to my face. The tension between us grew, like clouds gathering before a storm.

"The dream haunted me and made it hard for me to concentrate on anything. It made me exhausted. That's when I started to pray. I wanted the thoughts to go away. And they did," I said in an effort to stir the conversation back to safe waters.

Grandpa kept looking at me with squinted eyes, nodding his head.

"I'm no longer haunted," I smiled.

"That is very good," he said and patted my hand, but his austere eyes remained fixed to the space between my brows. I became viscerally aware that Grandpa was looking at something no one else could see.

Slowly, his gaze returned to the paper. He folded it and handed it to me before turning towards the television. I followed suit, but was not in the least interested in the singing and dancing taking place on the screen. I retreated to the cave of my thoughts, digesting the exchange that had just taken place between us. He knew about the angel. His body betrayed him.

After returning home, from my desk drawer I took out my notes, sketches and the Bible, and put on the only music tape I had in my possession. Nodding to the track I'd gotten to know so well, from the back pocket of my jeans I took out the sketch Grandpa had made for me this evening and placed it open on my desk under a small lamp. His unique drawing style of curved streaks and pronounced shadows, reminded me of the drawing in Daniel's notebook. I wished I hadn't lost it. It could be so useful now.

The newest piece was of a soldier looking at smoldering embers of a dying fire in front of him, a common scene during the war, Grandpa had once told me.

"We'd roast potatoes found in frozen fields under the fire," he said, referring to the fire's dual function of providing warmth and serving as an oven.

But there was another person in the drawing—a man consumed by ecstasy, dancing around the fire holding a drum and a stick. The man evoked a certain atmosphere, the presence of a spirit, something I couldn't quite put my finger on. Was Grandpa familiar with magic rituals? A close examination of the drawing seemed to confirm so.

The Sirrah concert Ben helped organize in our town's theater fell on the night preceding the full moon. Letting the store clerk believe it was a gift for my mother, I bought myself a new red lipstick for the occasion. After pleading with her all day, Mom agreed to lend me her red leather gloves and her beautiful belted, ivory knee-length spring coat, as long as I wore a thick sweater underneath to protect me from the biting cold. As I was tying my boots in the foyer, Rena came walking in from the garage.

"Going out?" she asked, and I nodded. "You look nice," she said, and left, leaving me stunned by her generous comment.

I walked trembling from excitement. The live music reached my ears before the building came into view, banging drums and distorted guitars jabbing air molecules. The opening band was already on stage. I reapplied the lipstick, checking for smudges in a random car's side view mirror.

A crowd of people in black clothing encircled the theater's walls. I had Rock meet me on its steps, and teased him for being a slacker. While I had the entire Daimonion album memorized to the tiniest lyric and note, Rock never came back to learn the chords. And this is how Rock was, excited in the beginning, his eagerness declining before he even got a chance to get a basic grip on the very thing he was trying to master.

"You look ten years older with that stuff on," he said, pointing to my lips.

"Exactly the image I was going for," I said to him, and handed my ticket to the doorman.

Inside, humid scent of agitation, sweat, and cigarette smoke saturated the air. The place was so crowded it seemed that people from all the surrounding towns and villages were here, packing the theater to the brim. It would be hard to run into Ben in these frenzied circumstances, I thought, feeling both relieved and disappointed. Part of me wanted to see Ben and tie up some loose ends, but another part preferred to avoid him.

Halfway down the hallway between the entrance and stage, I had already lost Rock in the thick mass of enraptured strangers, but I caught a glimpse of Mila, edging in the same direction, though few meters ahead. I called to her, standing on my tiptoes, and waved my hand. She turned to look at me, but then quickly turned away aiming for a tall figure that had just appeared in the doorway. Ben reached out his arm and helping her bypass the line, pulled Mila inside the stage hall. I felt a pang of jealousy and anger. I remembered when it was me who skipped lines and got to see great shows, often without a ticket.

"There you are," Rock's voice blasted my eardrum. To avoid getting lost again I grabbed his hand, something I wished that Ben could see. "I brought you something," Rock said, his check turning crimson, and handed me a tape.

"Who is it?" I asked, flipping it in my free hand.

"Hildegard something-something. Some nun chanting Robin Hood tunes. Ben left it at my house a couple of months ago. And since you don't have much to listen to, I thought I'd give it to you. It's not my cup of tea, but I think you'll like it."

I let go of Rock's hand the moment we entered the room with the stage. It felt too awkward and I didn't want to risk more gossip. We found a spot in a corner where Kal and a few more guys from his New Year's party had gathered. The music was loud.

Sasha was presently on stage with our town's band, slapping and plucking the living daylights out of his bass. I watched him but couldn't get the image of Ben and Mila out of my head. I kept imagining what they could be doing backstage at that very moment.

Mila's brother's band took the stage next. They played only three songs, each very long and technically impeccable. While they lacked a vocalist, my music teacher's guitar made up for the deficiency. His Satriani-esque solos, one seamlessly bleeding into the next, left many standing with their mouths agape. I moved toward the stage until I reached the front row, showering my teacher with awestruck gazes. I even went as far as to imagine him and me in a romantic scenario, and the shock painted on the faces of his sister and her new beau, my lost friend who used to be exclusively mine.

Once the band was through, Ben approached the microphone and announced a brief intermission to give the guys from Sirrah time to set up. I wanted to get away from his sight but Ben already noticed me. Instead of walking backstage, he descended the side stairs while I stood in place waiting, bumping one boot into the other.

"I didn't think I would see you," he said, now standing across from me, the tips of his fingers stuck in the pockets of his jeans. "I'm glad you made it."

He looked different than when I saw him last, more normal and lacking the blue aura, and yet I couldn't take my eyes off of him, our good memories trailing him like a shadow.

"It is good to see you too."

"You've been hiding out."

"Not really. Just reading."

Ben paused and looked at me. "I'm sorry, I've had my hands full with this thing," he motioned backstage, "but I'd really like to talk to you, or visit you, if that's okay."

"You can walk me home."

Ben smiled and said he'd meet me by the stairs after the show. We said our goodbyes and I rejoined the circle of my friends in the corner. Rock handed me a glass of cold beer, which I hoped would help me relax before the walk.

By the time I finished the glass, the first notes from Sirrah's tear-inducing repertoire sounded across the room, evoking ecstatic screams from their fans. Masses of people rushed to the front. I stayed back, swaying to the rhythm of the melancholic tunes enriched with live violin.

As the evening came to a close, Ben joined the band for their encore, guitar strap over his shoulder, and showed off his skills covering Daimonion's "Night." I stood in the crowd singing along with Sirrah's second vocalist, whose velvety voice glided over the notes.

After the concert was over, I waited by the stairs for Ben to arrive and walk me home, declining an invitation to hang behind the theater. Only when most people had already departed and the cleaning crew arrived did he come out.

"Sorry it took this long," he said, putting on his coat.

"I could've just walked alone, but I didn't want you to look for me," I said, rubbing my gloves. But in reality, I wanted him to accompany me. The silence between us had grown too stale.

"I keep disappointing you," he said, idly pacing next to me.

"No, you just have your hands full. Like you said."

"I know," he scratched the back of his neck. "But I miss seeing you."

"Then why didn't you come over? You know where I live."

"I thought you didn't want to see me after what had happened."

"Only for few days," I whispered, unsure whether he heard me.

We walked absorbed in our own thoughts until we reached the bridge. Cars were passing us by, mud and water splashing from under their tires. I worried about Mom's jacket getting dirty while trying to come up with something to say. Ben switched places with me so that I was further away from the traffic, strangely busy at this late hour. I was trying to increase our pace, but Ben kept slowing us down.

"Why are you walking so fast?" he asked.

"Trying to get away from the cars."

"No, you're running away from me. Admit it."

I stopped and turned toward him. "If you want to know the truth, I think you have it all backwards," I said. "I think that it's you who's been running away and not just from me. Clearly, you've found yourself a whole new crowd."

"Oh, Eve, please. Not you. Don't say that. It's enough that Rock keeps bugging me about this. I mean… I'm sorry I didn't come to see you, but I really got the sense that you just wanted to be left alone."

"And what made you think that?" I asked and began walking again. We were approaching my neighborhood.

"You said that to me that night in the car."

"That was months ago."

"Eve, why are you acting so cold? I told you I was sorry!"

"I know. Like a million times already. But those are just words."

"What else do you want me to say?" Ben asked, scuttling closer to me. We had entered the quiet neighborhood street among houses.

"If you're this good with words, could you please explain to me why Mila hates my guts?" I turned to him, wringing my arms and walking backward.

"What are you talking about?"

"I saw the two of you tonight. And in case you haven't noticed, gossip in this town travels faster than the speed of light. Congrats. You've found yourself a beautiful girlfriend."

He looked at the ground, hesitating. "I don't know what to say."

"You don't have to say anything, Ben. Just admit it."

"It really doesn't change how I feel about you," he said, dragging his feet.

I felt a pang of sorrow. "Forget about it. Anyway, thanks for walking me home," I said, and turned to walk faster. "Goodnight."

"I promised I'd walk you home so I'll take you all the way."

We traversed the last few blocks without uttering a word. I felt bad for saying all those things to Ben, but also relieved for not having to carry it inside me anymore. Part of me was feeling victorious that tonight Ben chose to be with me instead of Mila. But the idea of holding hands with him still felt odd, even though, deep down, I wanted him to wrap his arms around me and beg me to forgive him. Maybe even try to kiss me. I was as confused as Ben.

"Hey, Eve?" he asked, as my body turned toward the stairs of my house, "I hope you are not mad. But if you are, I completely understand."

"Why should I be mad?"

"Because obviously I failed you. I hope you can forgive me one day."

I shrugged, pausing with one foot on the first stair. "It's okay," I said. "You are not the only one to blame." This was his last chance for him to do something, make a move. I waited counting to ten.

"Thank you for saying that," he said, when I was half way through my count. "I should let you go. Goodnight." "Night."

I sped up the stairway, opened the front door to my house, and went inside without looking back at Ben. After shutting the door behind me loud enough for him to register my emotion, I leaned into it and tightly closed my eyes. I felt like crying. I could picture Ben still standing there at the bottom of the stairs where I saw him last, looking up after me. What was wrong with me? Why didn't I stay to talk with him more? How could I be jealous of Ben and Mila while resenting the very thought of becoming Ben's girlfriend? How could I blame him for choosing to be with her if I was incapable of reciprocating his feelings? Why the hell did it hurt so much? *What was wrong with me?*

I took off my boots and making sure it was pitch dark all around me I looked out the small foyer window through the lace curtains. Just as I suspected, Ben was still there standing in the street. His hands were in his pockets, legs slightly apart, head facing the door behind which I had just vanished. I didn't have the nerve to go outside and invite him in, even though part of me wanted to do it.

After turning away to catch a few solid breaths, my racing heart calmed. Seeing Ben stand there was a confirmation that he really must have felt something for me, must have cared. All those thoughts made me feel better. But as much as I missed Ben, I knew the old days were gone, and that precious thing we had before—whether born of innocence or ignorance—had died. Let him mourn now, I thought. I had already done my grieving. I needed to move on and get a fresh start. There was no point in trying to mend something this damaged. One more time I turned to look through the window. But Ben was no longer there. I felt a jolt of guilt and disappointment.

In the living room, Dad was sleeping on the couch

with the television still on. I turned down the volume and walked into the kitchen to make myself a cup of tea. As my water was heating up, I climbed onto the counter and with trembling hands reached toward the highest cupboard to take out a partially drunk bottle of port wine and a crystal chalice, parents' wedding gift. Back in my room, I placed both items and my steaming tea on my desk and tiptoed into to the basement to retrieve a tall votive candle with a blackened wick, not used since my first communion seven years ago. I was going to improvise. But first I needed to calm my nerves. After taking a relaxing bath, I rubbed fragrant oil into my warm skin, while directing my thoughts toward Sariel, the one whose presence I intended to invoke this very night. Unlike Ben, Sariel not only didn't have a body, he also wasn't at the mercy of moody ebbs and flows that come with having one. He was also exclusively mine.

I put on Mom's old nightgown, which I had found in a basement closet, and looked at myself in the mirror. It was white, trimmed with lace, and made me look like a young woman. I brushed my hair, reapplied the lipstick, and left the bathroom. In my room, I queued the tape Rock gave me. The music was perfect: soothing, saintly, and uplifting. Adjusting the volume so I wouldn't wake anyone up, I lit the candle, opened the window, and gazed at the moon.

"Sariel," I whispered, raising the wine glass toward the moon. "If you are real, and if you still want me, come to me. I am ready." I drank the wine and set aside the empty glass. Reclining on my mattress bed and listening to the chants, I spread my arms open and repeated the words from my dream.

Rise up and fall in love. . . . Rise up and fall in love. . .

For the longest time, nothing happened. I only felt the gentle caresses of the night air swirling over my skin. But before sleep took me away, I knew he had arrived. He was here, in my room, though I didn't dare open my eyes. Suspended in the hazy state between dream and reality, I floated, offering my body to his feathery caresses. And when I awoke the next morning and stretched my arms wide, my hand came across something soft and light.

On the pillow next to me rested a long, snow-white feather.

XVII

The next day turned out to be a beautiful, sunny Sunday. It was still winter, but as I walked on an unannounced visit to Grandpa, sunrays warmed my face. On my way there, I passed by Ben's apartment and glanced at it, wondering if he was home, last night's conversation fluttering through my mind. Rounding the corner, I saw Marta and Mila walking her dog. They ambled toward me. I crossed the street in hopes of evading them, but my preventative measure didn't work. Known for her loud mouth, Marta couldn't restrain herself.

"You're too late! He isn't home," she called out through cupped hands.

"I wasn't looking for anyone, Marta."

"Strange, I could've sworn you've been stalking Ben for awhile," Mila added. The girls were much closer to me now. We were almost passing, the street spreading between us.

"If you are talking about last night, I'm afraid it was the other way around," I turned toward her.

"He was with you last night?" Mila's voice raised an octave. In her conquest of Ben, she must have lived with the hard reality that he and I shared a deep bond that would not be easy to dissolve. After all, Ben and I had been inseparable for over a year. Not to mention that not too long ago, he wanted to make me his girlfriend.

"We had a really good time."

"My brother says he doesn't want to give you any more lessons. He says you lack talent and are a drag to teach," Mila called after me.

The comment about her brother stung, even though I suspected she had made it up to hurt me.

When Grandma answered the door, I saw a look of concern flash across her face. She let me in and sat me down, asking what had happened. In neutral terms I relayed to her a summary of what had occurred between the girls and me. She waved her hand. Unless I was physically injured, there was nothing to worry about, she said. Theirs were just meaningless words.

"Where is Grandpa?"

"Went out on a walk with the neighbor from upstairs," Grandma declared, placing a steaming bowl of soup on the table. "Eat, child, eat. It will warm you up and make you feel better."

I dug in my spoon and stirred the colorful medley of cooked vegetables.

"How come Grandpa speaks fluent Russian?" I asked. "Did he learn it during the war?"

"Oh, no." Grandma danced around the kitchen. "He's spoken it since he was a child. Do you want a slice of bread with your soup?"

I shook my head. "I thought he was born in Poland."

"He was. But his father was Russian. He was an old medic from Siberia."

"A medic?" I asked, realizing how little I knew about my own origins.

"Oh, yes. He was a strange man. A good man, but very strange. Burly and robust. But he had a gentle soul, a good heart. Jan called his father a magician."

I sensed I had just stumbled onto something very important. "What happened to him? How come I never met him?"

"He died before you were born. Jan was but a child. He, his brothers and his mother arrived here alone."

"That's terrible. To lose a parent so soon, I mean."

Grandma shrugged. "Times were hard. People died like flies. But I don't know. He never talked about how he felt. Not like people do nowadays. People these days are much more concerned about feelings. I like this, I don't like that, she hurt me with this, he made me sad, on and on like that. Back when we were young, different things were a priority. Like survival. Do you want more soup?" Grandma stood next to the pot, holding a dripping ladle.

"No, thank you. I'm getting full," I rubbed my belly, clearly disappointing her.

"You are too thin. You should eat more," she plunged the ladle back into the pot.

"Tell Grandpa I'll be back tomorrow," I said, putting

on my jacket.

"You're leaving already?"

"I have some research to do," I said to avoid making up a lie. If I was on a quest for truth, I needed to practice telling it. It was too easy to make things up for the sake of convenience; something I saw was running rampant among my family members and my peers, each day adding to the Gordian knots of falsehood tightening all around me. I kissed Grandma goodbye, and flew down the stairs.

He was a strange man. . . . Jan called his father a magician. . . . I kept thinking on my way home.

Once I was in my room, I took out the drawing Grandpa had made for me with the man dancing around the fire. Could this be how he remembered his father? Magic. That was it—old pagan magic. That was the atmosphere, the underlying current running through Grandpa's sketches.

I was so absorbed in my world that I didn't notice my parents arguing in the kitchen, until Dad slammed the door to the basement so loud I was sure it would come off its hinges.

"Why don't you just leave for good?" I heard Mom's angry yell. "Go back to your mistress and never come back!"

My nerve endings coiled up like fire-singed hair. After a month of relative peace, they were at it again. I heard Dad running back up the basement steps before stopping right outside my door.

"Oh, yeah?" he screamed. "And what are you going to eat? Dirt?"

"I can manage fine without you!" she cried. "I'd rather live on air than have you infest this house with your poison."

"I don't think so," he laughed. "And frankly I think your parents are sick of having three more mouths to feed!"

"Get out!" Mom screamed. "Get the hell out!"

I heard them grappling and I stormed out of my room before anyone got hurt.

"Stop it!" I screamed. "Stop hurting each other, please! I can't take it anymore!"

"Go back to your room!" Dad ordered, looking at me over his shoulder. He was holding Mom by her wrist but she managed to wrestle herself out of his grasp.

"I won't go anywhere until you stop," I said, and wedged myself between them, to shield Mom with my body. I had no idea where all this courage was coming from.

"Of course!" Dad burst out, throwing up his hands.

"They are always on your side. My own children," he said, and turned away. Mom and I stood there together, trembling, until the sound of the car engine was beyond the range of our hearing.

"Are you okay? Did he hurt you?" I asked Mom.

"I'm fine. I'll be fine," she nodded, wiping her tears.

"Let's just run away."

Mom laughed. "To where?"

"Anywhere. Just away from here."

"He is right. How will I feed you?"

"You'll find a job."

We entered the kitchen and Mom sat down at the dining table. It hurt to see her looking so battered and helpless.

"I've been trying for years. It's harder than you think for someone as old as me."

I spent the afternoon with Mom in the kitchen. While she drank the tea I made for her, I plotted our escape routes all the way to the Baltic Sea. When a television anchor announced a travel documentary, Mom went to the living room, her attention quickly absorbed in a narrative about a mountain trekker. Painted on her face I saw a desire to be free.

My parents' fight, and my earlier squabble with Mila, affected my mood but not enough to pull me away from my goal. With the night of the full moon approaching, I was hoping for an opportunity to make contact with Sariel, but I had no idea where to begin. Up to this point, he was the one who came to me. Still if the investigation into my ancestry was on the right track, I may have had the blood of a magician running through my veins. I looked at Grandpa's drawing hoping it would open the door to his mind. I wanted to go deeper, but I was getting a strong sense that Grandpa would be highly against me using my ancestral power, if I had any, to invoke a fallen angel.

I reached for the feather I had hidden under my

pillow. It was as real as my own hand, and as soft as his touch, a gentleness that stood in stark contrast to the volatility I had just witnessed play out at home. How could Sariel ever be thought of as dangerous, when my own parents were capable of hurting each other so much? All that the angel wanted was to be free. Was this desire really that dangerous? One would think that in a world marred by possessiveness, control, and violence, the desire to be free would be revered.

Later that night Mom made supper for the two of us, and afterward sat down on the couch to escape into the fictional world of a novel. Conducting a small reconnaissance, I asked her about Rena's whereabouts and she said that my sister was spending the night at our cousin's house. I knew that meant that both girls, who were roughly the same age, were going to sneak to a discotheque, taking advantage of carnival before Ash Wednesday, which marked the beginning of Lent. Without the need to say it, we both didn't expect to see Dad home tonight. She said that she suspected Dad wouldn't be coming home tonight.

The phone rang, startling us both. Since I was standing next to it, I picked it up.

"Eve, hi, it's me."

"Hi, Ben."

"Will you be home tonight?"

"Yes. No. I don't know. Maybe. Why?"

"I need to see you. Can I come over?"

I had no intention of spending my entire evening with Ben. I had preparations to make. After being left a feather, I had high hopes for the night. Sariel was listening. His presence was near; I could feel it. Still, hearing the near-desperate need to see me in Ben's voice made me feel like I had won something.

"What time?"

"Not sure. Ten maybe?"

"Eight," I said. He agreed and we hung up.

"Are you and Ben friends again?" Mom asked without lifting her eyes off her book.

"Sort of."

"I'm glad. He's a nice guy."

Ben knocked on the front door a half hour before eight. He looked distressed when I opened the door. Mom made us lemon tea, and on a platter arranged whatever she could find—stiff raisins, cracked marquise cookies, leftover pieces of hardened marzipan. We didn't even touch the plate.

Sitting in my room in silence, me on the revolving stool, he on the carpet, our eyes meandered without aim. It was like the old days and yet very different. Occasionally, our gazes would brush against each other, he would smile and I would catch a glimmer in his eyes, which made the eight-hundred-year-old Hildegard von Bingen composition playing softy in the background sound more like a requiem than a celebratory hymn.

Ben extended his lean arm to set his empty cup to the side. "I need your help," he said.

"With what?"

"Help me break up with Mila."

I raised my eyebrows. "You've got to be kidding me."

"I'm totally serious. It is not right for her or for me."

"What isn't right?"

"Me staying with her, keeping her around, while she thinks this can actually go somewhere."

"Please, Ben, be specific."

"She's just . . . so different from you," he began, and soon the dam cracked and he went on and on about how she is becoming jealous and obsessed, constantly checking his whereabouts, how he feels trapped and even bored, all the things I knew that would happen.

I didn't hide the hint of a smile dawning on my lips. Though, on the other hand, I feared that he was here not only to figure out how to end it with Mila but also how to rekindle things with me.

"She doesn't understand the things that come so naturally to us. It's like I have to explain everything to her a million times before she gets what I'm trying to say."

"How am I supposed to help you? Isn't this something that's entirely up to you? If you don't want to be with her, why don't you just tell her?"

"I wish it were that simple."

"It is, Ben!"

"No, it's not. She is too sensitive. Too delicate. It will break her."

"Then I think you only know half of her."

"No, you don't understand," I saw desperation in his eyes. "She threatened she'd hurt herself if I broke up with her."

"And how am I supposed to help you prevent that? You can pick pretty words, but the meaning will remain the same."

"I don't know," he said, looking lost. "Maybe I just needed to talk to you again, to feel you still cared about me. You do, don't you?"

"Is this why you really came, Ben?"

"I wanted to see you again. Last night I felt like we ended on a bad note."

"You asked me for forgiveness."

"I did."

"I forgive you, Ben. But past is past. We can't go back," I said, simultaneously feeling the urge to hug him.

"I wish we still could."

"Unfortunately time moves only in one direction."

"Evelina?" He reached out his hand and touched mine. "Yes?"

He held it, rubbing my skin with his thumb.

"I'm sorry."

"Why do you keep apologizing?"

"I don't know," he said, slumping briefly before he withdrew his hand and stood up. "I guess it's because I have nothing else to say to you."

The sadness in his words made everything around us go cold and still. Part of me wanted to believe that we could recover the connection we once shared, to mend things, before we lost it all. But another part of me already gave up. I was caught between wanting him to stay and go away.

"I'd better go," he finally said. "Thanks for the tea."

Alone, standing in the middle of my room, I listened to Ben put on his shoes in the foyer before exiting my house. I squeezed my fists and took a deep breath holding back my tears. I missed him already. And yet, it was so hard to be with him these days. When he wasn't around, I wanted Ben near me, but when he got too close, I'd push him away. It used to be so easy between us. So much had changed. I knew the direction in which he wanted to lead us. He wanted the language of the body to play a part in our communication. But I only wanted that with Sariel, the one I couldn't have, or even touch.

I checked on Mom, who was in the living room watching a movie, and quietly went to the bathroom to wash the crystal wine glass in the sink. Tidying up my room,

I waited for the moon to rise above the neighbor's roof and for Mom to go to bed. Once the house was quiet and still, I began lying on the bed with the feather resting on my heart.

From the moment I shut my eyes, things were not going the way I had hoped they would. Halfway down my descent into a dream state, I was losing control. My visions of flying, and my chant, *Rise up, fall in love,* became *Descend, fall into the pit.* I searched for Sariel, stumbling through the endless expanse of gray rocks, ground splitting underneath my feet, the hollow abyss trying to swallow me whole. Until, it happened. I fell in.

My body hit the bottom of a pit. Bruised and aching all over, I shivered as pairs of shining eyes blinked around. Creeping out from the darkness, demonic bodies crawled toward me. Claws, fangs, distorted faces, torn, decaying bat-like wings growing out of their backs.

There was no place for me to run. The demons surrounded me from every side. The ground beneath me was translucent. Below it, in the subterranean pit, blazed an inferno. The surface separating me from the fire was thin, and soon the flames broke through and my body began to burn. I felt the scorching heat sear my skin and smelled the stench of burning flesh. The creatures howled at the inevitable loss of their prey, their shrieks threatening to explode my brain.

Sariel! I called, but no reply came. I kept calling his name until I lost my voice and my call became a distant echo.

The loss of my body was painful but also liberating.

The fire vanished, the burning sensation receded, and I found myself drifting through an empty void, free and no longer in pain. Would I find him here? I looked up and down and all round me, but I saw nothing but blackness. That's until my sight caught a white speck floating in the distance. It became larger as it drew closer. I instantly recognized the moon that was hurling at me with unbelievable speed. I shuddered and opened my eyes.

I was still on my back and in the same position as before the dream. Besides my aggravated breathing, I could hear another sound, like a muffled commotion. My father had returned and he was hitting my mother, trying to do so quietly. I heard her stifling cries and my heart sank, giving rise to a wave of deep-seated anger.

Tearing off the sheets, I ran out of my room and into the kitchen. Dad had his back turned toward me. Mom was seated on a chair, covering her head with her hands. His arm was raised, ready to strike.

"Stop now, or I'll kill you," I said with a tone that was as foreign to me as it must have been to them. Dad froze and turned around slowly. My eyes must have been shooting daggers because even though his mouth opened, he couldn't say anything. He simply walked away, slamming the doors to the garage behind him, as he usually did when he had nothing left to say or do. Mom removed her arms and I saw that her face was red, bearing marks of Dad's fist.

"He hit you?" I asked, although I already knew the answer. The rage boiling in my veins compelled me to run downstairs after him and hit him with my own small fists. But Mom stopped me.

"He is drunk and could be dangerous. We have to get away. Go to your room and change. Hurry."

Mom and I jumped out of the back balcony onto a blanket of fresh snow. Crouching, we ran along fences until we reached the street. We had to be wary, as Dad could've been lurking inside any of the passing cars. Chased by fear, adrenaline pumping through our veins, we made it to Grandma's apartment an hour later. Their lights were already on.

"Oh, thank goodness you're finally here," Grandma lamented, opening the doors for us. "I tried calling you. The ambulance is on its way." Her face showed great distress. "My God! What happened to you?" she added, seeing Mom in bright kitchen light. Mom's hand ventured to her temple.

"Dad did this," I said, hoping this would convince her of his true character, which she kept defending. "How did you know we needed help?"

Grandma looked confused. "I didn't. I called because Jan has another attack. He couldn't breathe."

Mom rushed to his room and we followed. Grandpa was still coughing violently. Upon seeing his daughter's battered face, his coughing increased. I could see anger in his eyes and a terrible sense of hopelessness.

"Don't worry. I will not let him touch her ever again," I said, taking his hand into mine. He looked at me and for the first time in my life, I saw fear in his eyes. Mom sprang to action, piling pillows behind his back to prop him up while Grandma gently patted his back.

The ambulance came and took Grandpa, his wife and daughter away. I stayed behind in my grandparents' apartment and bolted the door. Crouching beside it, hands on my forehead, body slumping in shock and exhaustion, I let out a loud cry and a long stream of tears flowed from my eyes. When the emotional storm passed, I got up and went to the living room where I curled up on the sofa and shut my eyes.

When I awakened, it was already late afternoon. Grandma was home and busy in the kitchen. A mouthwatering smell was seeping into the room. Through the glass doors that separated the kitchen from the living room, she saw that I was up and came in to tell me that she had made pancakes. Sitting at the table, I asked about Grandpa, and she said his condition had stabilized. The doctor said that he had contracted pneumonia and needed to stay under medical supervision for a few days. I asked her about Mom, whom she said had gone to her brother's house to ask him to get Rena.

I picked at the food on my plate while a movie was playing on the television, but once the sun had set and darkness of the night began creeping into our town and Mom was still not back, I told Grandma I, too, wanted to go home to fetch clean clothes and get my textbooks, since we would likely be spending another night here. I was not afraid of Dad. I knew he wouldn't hurt me and that the most vulnerable person before him was Mom, never me or Rena. If anything, he sought to make amends with us, hoping that we'd side with him.

Reluctantly, Grandma conceded under the condition that I wear warm clothes and come back right away. I did not plan to hover at home for long. My plan was to get my things and turn right back. But most of all, I felt a pull to go outside and clear my head. Putting Grandpa's ushanka hat over my head and surrounding my neck with an extra layer of wool, Grandma sent me off with a wave and a request to hurry.

Traversing the desolate streets, I crossed the market center, catching shadows of people on foot scurrying to get somewhere. I passed by the town's castle and a small lake with plastic bottles and empty wrappers lining its shore. After that, there were no more people or cars in sight. I quickened my step, passing by an entrance to our town park, shielded from the sidewalk by thick shrubbery. It was a rather low-spirited place with old chestnut trees, rusty swings that hung from their frames like discarded pieces of scrap metal, and a broken fountain that for as long as I could remember had not spurted a single drop of water.

Brushing against the bushes that fenced the park from the street, I felt a sudden pull toward the yawning entrance to the park. I lost balance and almost fell sideways. I panicked, but before I had a chance to utter a sound, an icy hand covered my mouth and stifled my cry. The attacker dragged me into the lightless belly of the park. Struggling to free myself, I waved my hands until they also became immobilized.

"Calm down. I won't hurt you," his voice broke through my muffled calls. "I only have a message to relay." His clothing smelled of mildew, and metabolized alcohol.

The fact that his voice lacked malice calmed me slightly, but it took a few long breaths to steady my breathing. He turned me to face him and placed both of his hands on my shoulders. I looked at him and noticed that his face was serious but not threatening. He was the coated man from the cathedral, who not too long ago had followed me home. I shivered again. It was always so cold around him.

"What do you want from me?" I asked, my fear returning. "Why have you been following me?"

"I have something to tell you," he said in a low whisper. His voice was coarse and dry. "But you keep running away." The man reached inside the flap of his coat and produced a flat object, which he handed to me. A book. I ran my hand over its rough surface, detecting an embossed circle.

"You thought you lost it, but it found you again, see? Every object will eventually find its rightful owner."

"But how? How did you come upon it?" I pressed the book to my chest.

"I promise to leave you in peace and never return if you promise me one thing," he said, evading my question.

My mind raced. I had so many burning questions. Who was this man? How did he know so much about me? "What do you want me to promise?" I asked, hoping that his reply would reveal more than one answer.

"That you will find Daniel and help him."

I felt my eyes widen. "Daniel is alive?"

"Daniel is in terrible danger. He needs help or he will die."

"But where is he? How can I find him?"

"The answers are in this book. You should read it carefully."

"Daniel need help," I repeated. "He's alive."

"But you mustn't tell anyone about this. People will only slow you down. And don't be afraid. It will slow you down, too."

"I am not afraid. Not anymore."

"Good. Now go home, and start getting ready. There isn't much time."

"I will do that."

"And when you finally find him, please tell him I am very sorry," the man said and took a step backward. "That's the favor I ask."

"But wait! Who are you? Can you at least give me your name?"

"Stanislaw," a whisper echoed through the park after his silhouette blended with the shadows of trees.

Where had I heard that name? And why was he sorry? What had he done to Daniel? Holding the book close to my chest, I stood shrouded by the steam of my breath.

And then I remembered. Stanislaw was the name of Daniel's adoptive father. The truth reached me slowly like the hum of the engine in the approaching car outside the park. No wonder Mom hadn't seen this man in the cathedral. No wonder the night Stanislaw followed me on the bridge, my neighbor thought I was running from cold when I asked her to drive me home. The neighbor couldn't see my perpetrator. This would explain why he left no footprints in the snow outside Daniel's hospital window.

Stan was long dead, a ghost haunted by guilt, seeking redemption through Daniel's forgiveness.

<h1 style="text-align:center">XVIII.</h1>

I returned home with my mind in deep thought. This quest I was on was not a matter of dreams any longer, of choosing whether to attend a church mass, or whether to plunge headfirst into the abyss. In such a place where ghosts walked the streets like living men, fallen angels sought to be free, and objects were lost and found in mysterious circumstances, nothing was trivial, no detail insignificant. While I had received clues, what I needed was information to help me chart my course. I hoped that Stan was right and that the notebook I held in my hands could help me find my way through the maze that my life had become.

The house was dark. Dad was not home and I didn't have a key. I walked around the back of my house in search of a window that might have been left open. Mom always slept with her window cracked regardless of the season, so I dragged a ladder from behind a neighbor's house and climbed inside. Turning on lights in the kitchen and hallway, I walked into my room and flicked on my desk light, re-lit the votive, and without even taking off my jacket, immersed myself in reading.

I opened the book on its first page, written upon which, with grandfather's hand, was the poem Daniel had recited to me that night at the hospital. Below the poem, I recognized Grandpa's style in a sketch of a fire pit, and if that wasn't convincing enough, the J.G. initials beneath it fit Grandpa's name. But looking at the drawing even more carefully under the bright stream of light, I noticed something else far in the background. Just beyond the figure of a soldier, with a long rifle pressed to his chest, was a silhouette that at a quick glance could've been mistaken for a raven, had it not had human-like torso and extremities. It was not human, nor was it a bird. It was an angel.

The floor shook a little, announcing Dad's arrival, his car pulling into the garage. I closed the book and hid it under my pillow. He climbed the stairs and soon I heard his footfalls outside my bedroom. He paused in the open doorway, looking surprised to find me on my bed with a textbook in my hands.

"Oh, you're home?" he asked, though the way he said it sounded more like a statement. I nodded, considering that his earlier anger had left him.

My father had a penchant for quickly switching his mood once he blew his fuse. He could scream and shout at Mom, only to cast smiles at Rena and me standing nearby. It infuriated Mom. Looking straight at him, I noticed I was not afraid of my father. His appearance felt more like a nuisance interrupting my reading, rather than a threat.

"Are you hungry?" he asked, lifting a paper bag he held in his hand. I nodded again, as the smell of roasted chicken reached my nostrils. "Come to the kitchen. Let's eat."

A moment later, Dad and I sat at the table, bones piling on our plates. Not a single word was spoken. When we finished he made a pitcher of hot tea and went to the living room to watch the news. I called Grandma, who was mad that I still wasn't back, and I asked to speak to Mom.

"Yes. He's here and all is fine," I told Mom, my voice low, hand shielding the phone's receiver. "I'd rather just stay here for the night than walk back to Grandma's at this hour."

"Okay sweetheart," she said after a brief hesitation. "But if at any point you feel uncomfortable, call me and I will have your uncle come and get you."

"Deal, Mom. I love you," I said.

"I love you, too."

"And, Mom? Can I stay home tomorrow? I'm not ready to go to school."

"Don't you have your winter break next week?"

"No, that's the following week," I said, relieved at the recollection. It was better than finding cash in my pocket.

"Yes, of course. Stay home. I am sorry you had to witness all this," she said, and we hung up.

Back in my room, the book in my hands, I turned over the first page and entered Daniel's territory. His earlier poems reiterated what he had told me at the hospital. Those writings had the character of descriptive storytelling—vivid words bringing to life the search for his roots. The pieces gained a contemplative dimension as they progressed, his attention shifting from trying to find his way in the outside world to focusing toward the within, giving his passages an almost metaphysical quality. I came across philosophical passages like, *Nothing is absolute, especially belief.* There were also those disturbing passages through which I could feel what Daniel was going through: *I discover my humanity through you, Spirit of Pain.*

It was easy to lose myself in his words: *And fear shall cast no more veils over the eyes of The Seeker. Death's elusive faces, their essence untrue...* Many passages pointed to Daniel overcoming hardships. Over time, he seemed to have found the ability to let go and make peace with what life kept dishing out. He seemed to believe that he needed to suffer so that he could better understand himself, integrate the parts he might have lost or forgotten.

As Daniel's own search for clarity and understanding began to bear fruit, so did his verses: *Life has no meaning unless one can face the lies and look without blinking.* He believed he had to dissolve the walls that sheltered his innermost being to gain insight into the workings of his soul.

Daniel was coming back to life on the pages before me. What's more, in his words, I was recognizing my own struggles. It was getting harder to keep my eyes open but I wanted to keep reading, aware of the fact that his beating heart was close to fading. That thought gave the burst of adrenaline I needed. I read every page that night, following Daniel's alchemy of words that kept conjuring a spirit of a quest.

I blinked my heavy eyelids, exhausted, and fanned the pages once more. Unless I had missed something or his location was written in code, I saw nothing concrete in the text beyond the evolution of Daniel's soul. But maybe my oversight wasn't as much due to my inability to penetrate the verses, but rather boiled down to the simple fact that Daniel had lost his book weeks, if not months, before he had met me. He had had no opportunity to add anything to the text that would indicate his current location.

I stood up and approached my window, hoping to see Stan waiting outside, so that I could ask him again. But there, I only met the wind rustling branches of trees. Holding the book in my hands, I reclined on my mattress. The dawn was already breaking, faint light of a new day seeping into my room.

As I lay drifting, fragments of Daniel's last poem floated through my mind. It was a short and peculiar piece, its meaning elusive, harder to grasp. Holding the text above my face, I examined each word once more. The way they were strung together, the way they teemed with contrast, seemed to give rise to an equation. Like a plus and minus, one verse cancelled another. All of the rest of Daniel's poems led somewhere, except for this one, and yet it alone contained an indication of a possible location:

> *Weeping in the darkest hour, not knowing,*
> *I teeter over the precipice of all knowing.*
> *Fear is nothing but a shadow of the sun,*
> *Darkened light of twilight, such is early dawn.*
> *Find me where light reaches not.*
> *Find me where light fills the void.*

Reading the last two lines over and over, my head spun in circles like a cat chasing its tail. I was going nowhere. It led nowhere, yet Daniel's request to be found could not be more obvious. What place was light and dark at the same time? Had Stan—the person who was already dead—not told me that Daniel was alive, I would've thought that Daniel was describing the place where people went after death. But of course Daniel could not have written about that when he was still alive. Numbness spread through my body, inciting doubt. I was back to questioning my sanity.

Under closed eyelids, my tangled, emotionally charged thoughts turned into a vision of snow-capped mountains. I was flying over a chain of ragged peaks. Descending lower, I spotted a lone figure sitting still on a plateau, high in the land of endless winter. His eyes were closed. So immersed was he in concentration that his body generated enough heat to melt the snow around him. Daniel's features were as serene as they had been the last time I saw him. Falling flakes evaporated before touching his skin. I noticed that his lips were moving, soundlessly reciting the lines of his poem: *Find me where light reaches not. Find me where light fills the void.* I wanted to ask him where that was, so I descended lower. My feet touched the ground and I approached until I stood facing him.

The air grew dense. Electric sparks stung my skin. I heard the sound of approaching thunder and saw the shadow of a bird circling above me. Its wingspan was enormous. And then a roaring came, like that of a plunging waterfall or an avalanche. The mountain shook beneath my feet and a blizzard obliterated my view of Daniel before I had a chance to ask him anything. The bird descended to where I stood and enveloped me in its wings to take me away.

The dream dissolved into nothingness until I awakened to my room bathed in the gray light of a winter day. I couldn't tell what time it was, only that the clouds had returned. The grainy ceiling appeared to be slowly shifting, like veins of quicksilver. *Find me where light reaches not. Find me where light fills the void.* I recalled the vision of the meditating Daniel, and an idea popped into my head.

I need to see Paula.

"You want to learn to meditate?" Paula looked at me with her big brown eyes. She was standing in the doorway of her apartment, the door-chain stretching at the level of her throat. "Like, now?"

"The sooner, the better. Could you just give me a few pointers? Please?"

Paula looked at her watch. "I have loads of homework, but I suppose I can spare fifteen minutes before supper. Come in." She undid the chain and held the door open for me before shutting it with a long creak. She led me to her bedroom. Two twin beds lined the two opposing walls, and wedged beneath the parapet of a solitary mirror was one desk Paula shared with her sister, my classmate. The room was half the size of mine, but it was very cozy with blue patterned wallpaper covering the walls.

"The first thing you'll need to do is empty your mind of thoughts," Paula said as we each sat down on the edge of the beds, facing each other, her hands on her lap. "Which alone can take years."

"Bummer," I said. "I don't have that much time."

"What are you doing this for?"

Daniel had inspired me, sitting in deep focus on the mountain plateau in my dream. I hoped to learn how to meditate to forge a mental connection with my brother, which could lead me to him. But I didn't want to share my reason with her, or anyone for that matter.

"I want to learn to concentrate better. And it takes however long it takes. Sorry. Please proceed."

She drew in a deep breath. "The best way to begin is to focus on one thing. Like repeating a phrase or listening to your breath."

"Okay, focus on one thing. Got it. And once I get this part down, then what?"

"Then you wait," she instructed.

"Wait for what?"

"The visions," she said, spreading open her hands like it was the most obvious thing. I really felt like I was entering a foreign territory. We barely started and I was already falling behind.

"Visions? You mean like having dreams while awake?" I asked.

"Not at all. Dreams are the product of the unconscious. A jumble of all sorts of things." I didn't agree with that part, but kept mum about it. "Visions come after you clear the slate. You don't make them, they come to you."

"What do you see in a vision?"

"Depends. Often it is light. But you have to be able to stay in the no-thought zone for a long period of time to achieve that."

"Have you seen it? The light, I mean."

"Only little flickers," Paula said. "Like mini fireworks."

If it took so long for Paula, who sounded like she was quite the expert already, it would probably be awhile before I'd see anything. Too much time. The time I didn't have. But maybe it's because she didn't have the urgency I did?

"By the way, what happens to me will be different

from what happens to you, but there is a place where we all link up," Paula added, confirming to me that I had done the right thing coming to ask her for guidance. I was after that link.

"Can you please elaborate?"

"For example, once both of our minds are empty, we should be able to connect to the same thing no matter who we are. I like to call the ocean of consciousness."

"That would make telepathy possible," I said, wanting to go home and try it as soon as possible.

Paula smiled. "Exactly."

I stood up. "Thanks so much. I really appreciate you taking the time to explain."

"Remember to sit still. Think of one thought or feel your breath and try not to flinch. And most importantly, be patient. Things of value take time to achieve."

I nodded. "Can I ask you a favor?"

"Sure."

"Will you please not tell anyone about our meeting?"

"I never talk about such things to anyone. Most people don't understand. Especially Marta," she said, and walked me out of her room into a likewise tiny foyer.

The smell of supper coming from her kitchen wafted through the air, making me hungry. Her sister, my classmate, walked out of the kitchen and gave me a puzzled look.

"How come you missed school today?" she asked.

"Not feeling too well," I replied, thinking I should've asked her about today's homework, but school was the last thing on my mind.

"I see you're better already. Coming tomorrow?"

"Yeah. Probably," I waved at the girls and turned toward the stairs.

Walking home, I tried to get a head start by concentrating on my breathing, but aside from creating steam clouds, I hadn't succeeded in gauging how empty my mind had become as a result of my efforts. But one thing—the beauty of our world—did strike me just before I entered the street to my neighborhood. I stopped to breathe in the wondrous view spreading before me. The snow-covered fields to my right seemed to go on forever as the line between earth and sky blurred into obscurity.

Darkness was quickly approaching so I rushed home. Dad wasn't there and as tempted as I was to ask Mom for another day away from school and spend the night practicing meditation until dawn, I knew that the more time off I took, the more catching up I would have to do later. With reluctance, I brought a textbook with me to the kitchen to get an idea of what I had missed today, and made myself toast and hot cocoa.

It was close to midnight when I shut the book and went to the bathroom to brush my teeth. I only managed to get through a page and a half of the dense read. I was lagging and unprepared for tomorrow. Lying in bed, I tried to breathe, but a flurry of thoughts kept getting in my way. I wanted to make that leap to the visions already, but to my chagrin, I realized that Paula had been right. It would take time and practice. I grunted and rolled over to my side. I needed help from someone who understood this better than me. Ben was out and so was Art. I sank into my mattress and called for Punk.

Forgetting to set my alarm, I woke at eleven in the morning. Taking it as a sign, I stayed home rereading Daniel's poems. Spending all day in a quiet, empty house made me feel disconnected from the rest of the world. I could stare at a wall for hours on end and not come up with a single thought worth pursuing. This was very different than focusing on one thought with the aim of eventually letting it go to dissolve in nothingness, per Paula's instructions. This was my version of a languid avoidance of responsibility. This was my mind turning into a mush of confusion, teetering on the verge of despair. My dreams that night were also devoid of concepts or foresights, and I had no energy to change that. All that was bad news in light of Daniel dying in some mysterious place I had no ability to pinpoint.

On Thursday, I mustered enough discipline to get up on time and go to school, but even there, I felt like a shadow of myself, and people were hardly noticing me. On Friday afternoon, Mom and Rena returned home. That evening, my immune system collapsed with my body temperature climbing to dangerous levels. Mom called in a doctor, the same one who would usually come to Grandpa's house when he had an attack. The doctor examined me and prescribed six days' worth of antibiotic shots.

The medication made me groggy so I spent most days sleeping. As much as I disliked being sick, resting did have its advantages. My mind quieted down and soon I was making progress in keeping my mind solely focused on my breath for longer stretches of time. But I still had no visions, no new ideas of where else Daniel could be. The only thing that kept coming to my mind was returning to the very place I saw him last—the hospital—and pestering the nurse to force her to admit the truth about my brother.

Grandpa was released from the hospital the day I received my last shot. Mom left with Rena to visit him at home, leaving me on the sofa in my pajamas, with a remote in my hand. Shortly after they left, I heard a knock on the door.

"Who is it?" I asked through closed doors.

"It's a surprise." I heard a male voice, muffled as if he was speaking through a piece of fabric.

"Who is it?" I repeated and sneezed.

"Bless you," the voice was clearer this time. I thought I heard a chuckle.

"Thanks, but I'm still not opening the door until I know who's on the other side."

"I told you it's a surprise," the voice said. "So I can't say. That would ruin it, wouldn't it? Not to mention I don't really have a name."

I turned the handle and pushed open the door. "Punk!" I exclaimed.

He stood smiling with his hands in his pockets. This time his jeans were not torn up, his black jacket not made of leather nor stained with paint, and his hair not modeled into a blue spike. He looked tidy and clean, his black hair loose and falling in long streaks to the side of his face. If he had passed me on the street, I couldn't have guessed it was the same person as the raggedy youth I had met in November, though in no way would I fail to notice him.

"I heard you needed help," he said.

XIX.

"This is such perfect yet imperfect timing," I said.

"You're sick. I know. And yes, you should definitely apologize!"

My teeth were starting to jitter. Hoping that I would be left home alone for some time, I invited Punk inside.

"You can tell, huh? I must look terrible," I said standing back. "I don't want you to get what I have."

"Don't worry, I don't get sick."

"How did you know where to find me?"

"I have my ways," he replied.

"Always elusive. Can I make you some tea?"

"Would love some."

I invited Punk into the kitchen. It was hard to call him by that name, as he didn't look like a punk anymore. He wore a black turtleneck underneath his jacket and a pair of purple cords. I, on the other hand, was a complete mess in dire need of a shower.

"When did you arrive?" I asked, filling the kettle with water.

"Just now," he said as he leaned against the counter. "Literally just got off the train."

"How did you know I needed help?"

"Picked up your message floating through the ether." He made a gesture as if catching a speck flying through the air and I almost dropped the kettle into the sink. Punk was not an ordinary person and it didn't take long for me to feel the space around and inside me fill with his ardor. I had so many questions to ask him. But I also felt that since we last met, I'd made progress on my own, which allowed me to understand him better even without words.

"You can communicate using telepathy?" I asked, placing the heavy kettle on the stove. The air was growing thicker between us, the air charging with electricity.

"You can call it that, but rather than complete sentences, the message is more of a feeling right here," he said, tapping the middle of his chest, "and a vision right here," he pointed to his head. "Plus, I was planning to pay a visit anyway. I made friends in this town back when we met," he said, his words sounding almost too earthbound. "So, what's new with you?"

"Where to start?"

"Anywhere. You choose."

I began by telling him about how right he was by advising me to go with my parents to the hospital where I met Daniel, who turned out to be my half-brother. I told him about the secret that weighed down my family like a storm cloud and often made me question my own sanity. I told him about Stan, and after our tea was made I had him follow me to my room and showed him the book Stan's ghost had given me. Running his fingertips across the black leather cover, Punk absorbed my words without a hint of surprise. It was a relief to be heard and not be thought of as a lunatic, although I was also hoping for a degree of astonishment in response to my discoveries. "I think my grandfather has supernatural abilities. I can't know for sure, but when I put the pieces together, he seems to be an intricate part of everything," I said.

"Sounds like you are on the right track. And the angel? Any more visits? Or clues?" he asked, looking up at me.

"Yes. In fact, I got another gift," I said, and opened Daniel's notebook to the middle of the tome where I had stored the feather.

He took both into each hand. "Interesting."

"I need you to help me find Daniel. This book belongs to him."

"This is why I'm here."

"You already know that, too?"

He nodded. "Told you. Your message stabbed me in my chest," Punk used the tip of the feather to show me just how it had done it.

Based on what he had told me about picking up messages from thin air, Punk seemed already well versed in the practice I was trying to master. I relaxed knowing I no longer needed to strive to perfect it, compressing years of effort into days or perhaps even hours of concentration pasted with intent.

"And do you happen to also know where he is?"

"I'm afraid that part remains obscured."

"Can you find out? Somehow?" I asked with pleading eyes.

"I need something that belonged to him. It would help with the visions—cut the time, shorten the distance."

"You are holding it in your hands," I said, pointing at the book.

But Punk shook his head. "Too long in the hands of a ghost."

"I don't have anything else," I said, dismayed. Just when I thought all hope was lost, I remembered an object. "It's a slight chance, but maybe I could find the picture that helped Daniel find my grandfather? Daniel told me he gave it to Grandpa at the hospital. If luck is on our side, the picture should be somewhere at my grandparents' apartment."

Punk inclined his head. "That would help."

"I'll go there as soon as I'm well enough to leave the house," I said. "Grandpa's just gotten out of the hospital. It would be a disaster if he got whatever I had."

Punk nodded once.

"How is Daniel? Are you able to tell?"

"Not good." Punk's expression became strained. "When I first heard your call and connected the dots, my body went numb. I think he might be in some induced sleep. Or a coma."

"I wish we could get on our way immediately. Darn! Why did I have to get sick?"

Punk set the book down on my desk. "Give me your hand," he said and reached for my cold palm to take it into his warm hands.

"What are you doing?"

"Giving you my energy. So you get better faster."

I could feel his heat transfer into my body. The feeling was much like that of placing cold hands under the stream of hot water. My skin covered with pleasant shivers.

"By the way, you are no longer contagious."

"You have many talents," I said.

"They are useless unless I can share them."

"Who are you, really?"

Punk sighed. "I mistrust labels and adjectives. I'd prefer you get to know me and draw your own conclusions. It's better to read a whole book rather than its summary, don't you think?"

As usual, what he said made sense.

"I sometimes wish to hear what you really think of me. And yet, part of me is afraid of what you'd say."

Punk smiled and looked at my hand. "True power comes from self-discovery and not being afraid to be you. How could I ever rob you of that with a paltry comment or a meaningless personal opinion?"

I looked at his hands cradling mine. The heat was now radiating to the rest of my body. His words inspired me to wonder about how this would could be if more people thought like him. But Punk wasn't the only person encouraging self-exploration. Back at the hospital, Daniel told me about a friend he once had who encouraged him to search for his roots. Daniel said that they were of the same kind. The same kind... This was a long shot, but I felt the significance of this memory magnify the reason behind Punk's coming to help me find Daniel.

Could it be that he knew my brother before he even met me?

"Your family is back," Punk said, letting go of my hand. Soon I heard the percolating engine of my uncle's truck outside the house. "I'd better go now."

"Will you come back again tomorrow?" I asked.

"I may. In the meantime, try to find the picture."

I walked Punk down to our basement and let him out through the garage door just as Mom and Rena were entering the house through the main entrance upstairs.

"Daniel was right. You are an extraordinary friend," I said, taking a chance.

Punk stopped and turned around to look at me with surprise. "Can't hide much from you for too long," he said with smiling eyes.

The next morning, I awakened feeling rejuvenated, not even

a lingering trace of my illness left. Without wasting any more time, I got dressed and went to see Grandpa. The day was wet, gloomy, and cold, but a sense of purpose added a spring to my step. I felt proud of myself for figuring out the link between Daniel's only friend and the familiar stranger who came to my hometown, looking for a girl that showed up in his dream. I made another leap. But what filled me with the most joy was the fact that I had managed to surprise Punk. All this time, I felt like I was at the mercy of his insight.

Grandma told me that Grandpa was asleep and took the opportunity to feed me more chicken soup. I ate, albeit slowly, still not having worked up much of an appetite. A half hour later, while Grandma left to the adjacent "cold room" that served as a provisional refrigerator during winter to finish making her batch of homemade pasta, I went to their bedroom to check on him. Sitting by his side, I took Grandpa's veiny hand into mine and closed my eyes to administer my version of Punk's therapy. As heat collected in my palm, Grandpa stirred and opened his eyes.

"Oh, look who's here," he smiled.

"How are you?"

He groaned. "Much better now that you're here."

"Can you feel the energy I'm sending you?"

He nodded. "Feels good."

"Grandma told me your father could heal people. I thought I'd try it too, since I'm his great granddaughter."

Grandpa winced. "Heal. That he could do. And more."

"Was he a doctor?" I asked.

Grandpa shook his head. "He was a shaman."

I straightened my back, wondering whether my blood lineage was at least in part responsible for my ability to see ghosts and attract fallen angels.

"Is that who you drew, that figure dancing around the fire?"

"No. That was me," he squinted his eyes. "He trained me in early years. But we never finished our lessons."

"Are you also a shaman?"

Grandpa smiled. "Let me show you something."

He asked me to help him sit up and then go retrieve

a small wooden box from a top shelf of the adjacent closet. I did so and handed him the box, flicking on the bedside lamp.

"I am not nearly as skilled as my father was, but there are a few things I still remember. These are his tools," he said, opening the box with a dignified gesture. I wished for Punk to be here and see this. Carefully weighing each object with swollen-from-age-and-labor hands, he took out each treasure. "A veil for protection," he spread a square of black sheer fabric over the comforter before him. "A wand to summon the spirits," he placed a gnarly stick on top of the cloth, "and a stone for listening."

"A stone for listening?" I said, peering at the black, glass-like piece he held in his hands reflecting light like a polished piece of coal.

Grandpa looked at me. "People lie. But an obsidian will always tell the truth." I was trying to imagine how it was possible when Grandpa added, "My father knew how to hear the whisperings of stones. He'd say that they are the oldest living organisms on Earth. If you seek truth, which is every Shaman's aim, you should learn to listen to stones. They are the chroniclers of history."

"Where does this one come from?"

"Anatolia. Land far away, in the east, the place of my origin. And yours on this side of the family. All three artifacts have been passed over for generations."

"A wand for summoning spirits?" I asked, nearing my fingertip toward the next artifact. But I didn't dare to touch it. "How do you do that?"

"First things first," he said, folding the veil over the wand. "This is not to be taken lightly. In the wrong hands, magic can do more harm than good, mostly to the uninitiated practitioner. This is why preparation is critical."

I nodded fervently. I was willing to do anything to gain access to his knowledge. "Why are you sharing this knowledge with me?"

Grandpa sighed. "I know you've been dabbling in esoteric books—and I don't mean the scripture. I also know that once someone like you takes a step in this direction, she is not likely to stop."

"Is this why you decided to share this knowledge with me? Because you know I won't stop?"

Grandpa smiled. "You naturally sense the presence of spirits around you. And you are not afraid to go to dark places as some people are. Every shaman must make peace with his darkness before he can command the light. It's not an easy process."

It seemed that I was more transparent to him than I had thought. A massive weight lifted off my shoulders. Until now, two parallel versions of my life—the mundane and the magical—had to remain separate, at times even antagonistic. But this sharing brought down a wall, allowing me to dwell in the world of spirits and images, without feeling like I was losing my mind or alienating my family.

"Thank you. Your words mean that I don't have to hide anymore."

He smiled. "I don't know how much longer I will be around. So I'd like to teach you what I know so that my knowledge, as scant as it is, doesn't die with me."

"How do we begin?"

"First, you need to know how to protect yourself. The world is permeated with invisible forces. If misused or treated with disregard, these forces can bring chaos and destruction. Still, it happens all the time. Some people get careless. The shaman's task is to help restore harmony," Grandfather said, his countenance austere. "That is what we do. This is now also your legacy."

"How do you do that?" I asked. "How do you restore harmony?"

"It depends. Most often with a prayer or a blessing. But sometimes more drastic measures are necessary," he said, putting the tools back into the box.

"Like what?"

"A sacrifice."

"You mean death?"

But Grandpa didn't answer.

"What about the protection? Will you teach me now?"

"We will have to leave that for another day," he said, and handed me the closed box. "Your grandmother is coming."

I put the box back where I found it. "Could we ever restore harmony between Mom and Dad?" I whispered, closing the closet door.

Grandpa's expression shifted. He suddenly looked a hundred years old. Worry distorted his face, shadows moving across it, lips quivering.

Grandma entered the room.

"Look at my Jan! He is all up and talking," she chirped. In her hands, she carried a metal cup and a kitchen towel. "I brought soup," she said to him. "And you," she spoke to me. "You should go to the kitchen and pour yourself some. You must eat more. One gust of wind and you'll be swept away."

I stayed over until Mom and Rena came for dinner. While they ate, I began my search for the photograph. I checked drawers, shelves and even under the sofa. Lacking success, I was tempted to just ask, but Grandpa was in a precarious state and Stan was very clear in his instruction. I was not to talk to my family, as that would only slow me down. I took Grandpa's recent benevolence in letting me in on our shamanic lineage as an added bonus, not the foundation upon which to build my case. At the moment, finding Daniel took precedence over all else, including my growing desire to contact the angel and help my parents find harmony with each other.

Part of me still felt like I was operating blindly, though it was a great relief to now have a partner in Punk regardless of how little he was willing to share. Punk was a tough nut to crack. Not in the least concerned about the perceptions of others, he had no trouble blending in to remain hidden. I could only imagine the two of them—Daniel and Punk—one lost and the other nudging his friend to keep on searching. I got up and discreetly checked inside a credenza filled with papers and documents. I shuffled around the piles but found nothing. Quietly, I snuck into the cold room and looked inside every drawer. But I didn't find any photographs there either. Only stacks of napkins, plates and extra sets of boxed utensils.

Not wanting to go home empty-handed, I asked Grandma if I could stay the night. Mom was concerned that my recent illness might still be lingering, but I told them I felt great and there was no need to worry. I slept on the sofa and felt well that night, my body warm and my stomach filled with soup.

In the middle of the night, I awakened to a ring of light piercing through the ceiling. The light pulled me upwards and out of my body. As I ascended, I looked down and saw myself sleeping on the sofa, the angel stroking my hair that fanned over my pillow. I wanted to reciprocate his touch, but I couldn't move. All I could do was look at him, and myself, from above, his sad smile accentuating the deep shadows on his face, dim yellow eyes tracing my resting features.

Sariel, how am I supposed to help you if I can't even touch you? I thought in my dream. The futility of my contact with the angel suddenly hit me. He was an immaterial being that visited me in my dreams. And I was starting to have real feelings for him.

The angel kept stroking my hair until I heard his whisper: *Ninsal, come back to me. Come back, Ninsal. . . .*

The following morning, when Grandma was giving Grandpa a bath, I set off to rummage through his closet and dressers. I even checked under pillows and in his pajama pockets. Everywhere I looked I found no trace of the photograph. Just before my grandparents staggered back into the bedroom, I reached into the drawer of his end table and retrieved a copy of the Bible, planning to read a little to reset my brain before trying again. I took it with me to the living room to get out of their way.

Sitting down, I closed my eyes and asked for more clues. Maybe my eyes would land on a passage that could illuminate things? Flipping all the pages to one side, I fanned them until my eyes stumbled on something odd. Grandpa had used the picture as a bookmark, marking a page in Ezekiel. I spotted a faint dot marked in pencil next to a passage:

The soul that sinneth, it shall die. The son shall not bear the iniquity of the father, neither shall the father bear the iniquity of the son: the righteousness of the

*righteous shall be upon him, and the wickedness of
the wicked shall be upon him.*

I heard Grandpa's muted voice calling me into his
room. Leaving the photograph inside, I closed the holy text,
tucking it between the cushions, and went into his room. He
reached out his arm for mine and told me how much he liked
my being here, keeping him company.

"Evelina, I'm feeling better today and wanted to
continue our teaching," he said. Looking into Grandpa's
almost translucent blue eyes, I felt a pang of guilt for wanting
to go home now that I had located the object of my search. He
wanted to pass his knowledge on to me, but all I could think of
was Punk coming over to see me, and the two of us devising
a plan to find Daniel.

"Thank you, Grandpa," I said with downcast eyes.
"I'd like that very much."

"The first law of magic is self-knowledge," he said,
"Most young practitioners are very sensitive, too sensitive.
Self-knowledge allows you to feel another's feelings without
mistaking them as your own. It also helps to discern when to
trust, when to confront and when to turn away. So before you
even get to conjure anything, you need to know where you
end and others begin. It will help you protect yourself better."
"Is it the same with spirits?" I asked, thinking of Sariel and the
dream I had this morning.

"Yes, but it is best to not engage with spirits unless it
is absolutely necessary. Spirits never offer anything for free.
They always want something in return; there is a price to
pay. If you used them for some purpose, it is very difficult to
reinstate the order of things that existed before."

"Why is that?"

"Once they depart, the spirits leave behind a void that
needs to be filled, often at the expense of the living."

"The sacrifice," I muttered.

"Please do not speak of this to anyone."

Grandpa's sharing put many things in perspective. He
expressed his desire to protect me, and our family, from harm.
But the spirits were already among us. As he looked at me

with his tired eyes, the image of the angel flashed before my eyes. Was it too late? Neither of us said anything.

Even if I still could, I knew that if I turned away now, abandoning my search would only lead to more questions later.

I needed to know not only why Sariel came into my life but also what was it that he was making me remember. I also needed to know why Grandpa never brought up Daniel's existence, and what was an angel doing in his drawing, not to mention the words *forgive me* underneath his cryptic poem. So much still didn't make sense.

"Have you ever practiced any spirit magic?" I asked.

"Once, when I was younger," Grandpa said, his eyes fixed on mine. "But I made a mistake. I spent the rest of my life paying for it. This is why I'm cautioning you."

I was tempted to ask about Daniel but then I remembered Stan's words.

"What did you do?"

"I summoned a spirit in a moment of fear and the effects are plaguing me to this day. I just hope that it all goes with me," he said.

"But there must be another way! If you feel you did something that bad, there must be something equally good you can do to balance it, right? Restore harmony?"

"Dear Evelina, you are a smart girl. But I have reasons to believe that I alone must pay the price for my deed and no one else must be involved. There, I said it. If I were to share more, the curse would spill and infect the very ones I want to protect. Please don't ever bring this up again or mention it to anyone."

The pain on Grandpa's face said it all. But what he didn't realize was that whatever he had done already affected us all, and I was getting close to peeling the scab that grew over his secret. It even made me wonder whether perhaps this long unexpressed anguish was what had solidified into the cancerous cells that ravaged his body.

Grandma came into the bedroom to help Grandpa walk into the kitchen where she had prepared their midday meal. I returned to the sofa, took out the Bible and reread the marked quote. *The soul that sinneth, it shall die.* Ezekiel's words were starting to gain more meaning. Did they point to Grandpa's guilt?

I wished I could make him realize the absurdity of keeping things secret from us. Maybe what he needed was Daniel's forgiveness but felt he didn't deserve it after what he had done? After all, it is what he wrote in the journal. That must be it! Besides the picture in my hand, I felt that I held a key to Grandpa's healing.

I put the Bible back in the drawer, said goodbye to my grandparents, and stuffing the photograph deep inside my pocket, flew down the stairs, anxious to share my discoveries with Punk.

XX.

Coming on the heels of a quaint and snowy January, February resembled the exhale of an angry beast. Storm clouds simmered above our town, winds wailed and thick raindrops pounded roofs and heads at regular intervals. I was almost halfway home when the clouds emptied their contents, drenching me to the last thread. I ran as fast as I could, gasping for air and holding the photograph under my shirt where I moved it so as to not let a single drop reach its surface. Upon seeing me climbing the stairs to our house, Mom scolded me saying that I should've called her and she would've had her brother come get me. Her impatient hands were soon all over me, helping me out of the wet clothes clinging to my skin.

"Mom, please, I can do it myself," I pleaded, unwilling to move my hand that was pressing the picture.

"Fine. Hurry, though. I don't want you getting sick again. I'll get a hot bath ready."

I removed my hand with care. The photograph's edges were already curling from moisture. Slipping the picture between the pages of my own Bible, I left my room, got the rest of my clothes off, and eased myself into the tub, my body thawing with delight. A feeling of liberation came over me, a sense of achievement for directing my own destiny, though my enthusiasm was tinged with angst.

I knew I was walking on thin ice when summoning Sariel, but what I felt when I thought of him had already gone beyond mere thrill of novelty. Sariel had inspired me to be brave and bold, which I knew could help me find Daniel.

"Call for you." Mom knocked on my door. "Should I ask him to call later?"

"No, I'll get it! Just have him wait a moment," I said, already suspecting who it was. With a towel wrapped around me, ends of my hair dripping water, I walked to the phone.

"Hi. It's me." I heard Punk's voice. "Did you—?"

"I found it. Now what?" I said in a hushed voice.

"Given the weather, we need to either get creative or wait it out."

"Let's get creative. I feel like we've already waited too long," I said. "Any other ideas?"

Punk was silent for a moment. "How about we meet in your garage and talk it over?"

"My garage?" I whispered, stepping further away from the kitchen where Mom was busy preparing something. "Are you out of your mind?"

"Why not? All we need is some place dry."

"Sure if you want to risk a month-long holdup when my Mom sees you. It would only delay things."

"Who's at your home now?"

"She and me."

"We will be quiet. Don't worry. She won't know."

"My sister's room is in the basement and she's with her cousin. It's Saturday so they'll probably go out to a disco."

"Perfect. Her room then?"

"You better activate your sixth sense. If anyone finds us, I'll never hear the end of it."

"I'm on my way. Be by the garage door in ten minutes. I will knock three times."

I peeked into the kitchen where Mom was now peeling onions. She was sitting with her legs apart, a tall bucket on the floor by her skirts, thick tears dripping to the floor, the radio droning a sad song she seemed to know well—her lips were mouthing the words. Seeing her like that made me want to cry, too, but for a different reason. I loved Mom so much and desperately wanted to help free her from the chains of sadness that seemed to hold her captive. In fact, everyone around me seemed to be haunted or imprisoned by something.

I went to my room, finished drying myself off, put on sweat pants and a T-shirt, and retrieved the photograph from between the pages of the holy text. The picture was yellowed and aged. It showed my mother as a young girl, not much older than I was now, standing next to Grandpa who was in his glory years, tall and with a thicket of dark hair crowning his head, his hand on Mom's shoulder. Her beauty was striking, and innocence predominant, but her eyes and mouth betrayed her. I saw lines of worry and distant longing. One of her arms was hanging loose by her side, the other slightly bent at the elbow, fingertips brushing her growing belly. I turned the photograph and read the date written on the back: *August 1976*. Daniel was born in January of 1977. In this photograph, Mom must have been four months pregnant.

I jerked, remembering the impending visit. On my toes, I descended the stairs and put my ear to the garage door. Just as I did I heard three knocks, and twisted the knob to let Punk in, careful not to let the door creak. We glided across the short corridor on our tiptoes like a pair of professionals.

Rena's room was in complete disarray. I rarely came down here, and when I did it was usually to carry a message from upstairs, such as to inform her that dinner was ready. Clearly I wasn't the only one who bypassed this place. For all their faults, my parents left us alone, affording us much personal space, each for a different reason. Mom was respectful, father not present. But what I saw that gloomy afternoon made me wonder if it might be a good idea to bring Mom down here to see things for herself. We all knew Rena liked to have a good time, but the evidence on full display relayed a deeper story. Empty liquor bottles crowded the floor next to her open closet, which was almost entirely devoid of contents, her wardrobe mixed in with her bed sheets in a colorful cocktail of mess. The room reeked of alcohol fumes and putrid cigarette ashes.

"And I thought I was the one who misbehaved." I looked at Punk, who picked up one of the bottles and smelled it. His eyes were penciled with black liner, making them look twice as large.

"Whiskey," he muttered, and set it down. "Your sister has a sophisticated taste."

I moved several layers of clothes off her desk chair, bras and shirts falling to the floor, and made room for Punk to sit down, while I plopped on her desk.

"I don't know when Mom might start looking for me so we'd better hurry," I said, and handed him the picture.

"Nice work," he said and closed his eyes.

I saw his countenance shift, all expression wiped from his face. All that remained was the sound of raindrops tapping against the windowpane. He remained motionless for about two minutes, at which point he brought the picture to his forehead and remained still for another minute. He took a deep breath and opened his eyes.

"What did you see?" I asked.

"I know him."

I smiled. "Yes, you were once friends. He told me about you the night at the hospital. By urging him to search for his parents, you helped him find us. And then you encouraged me to go the hospital so that I, too, may find him. So in a way, you helped unite our family."

Punk leaned back into the chair. "There is still more to do."

"It is thanks to you that I met Daniel."

"When I met him, his name was not Daniel," Punk said, shaking his head.

"No? What was it?"

"His name was Peter."

Peter. . . . Peter! The name of the boy I met in the hospital as a child. The name of the boy Mom had wanted to adopt. Mom had said that Peter was his name. And I thought I had gone crazy. Punk's revelation would imply that Peter and Daniel were the same person. If so, it would explain a lot, making yet another puzzle piece fall into place. I shared my thoughts with Punk.

"Maybe he needed a change. Maybe it was his way of marking a new beginning?" Punk said. "Maybe it better matches his identity? Daniel interprets dreams, after all."

Again, Punks ideas made sense.

"Where is he? Did you get a location?"

"I saw a dark place, like a dungeon. I heard beeps in the background."

"Is he conscious?"

"No. He's sleeping."

"What do we do?"

"We board a train," he said.

"When?"

"Tomorrow morning. You can come, right?"

"Of course. You can count on me," I said, and looked out the window. It had stopped raining, the clouds parted, and a beam of sunlight bounced off Punk's blue iris. "Do we know where we're going?"

"Not completely. But that will unfold once we get on the road," he said, and stood up, looking around. He smelled the air. "I'd better get going now."

I followed him to the door. He hesitated before turning the knob, but when he finally opened the door, Punk's chest almost knocked the wind out of Rena's lungs.

XXI.

Upon seeing Punk, Rena froze in place with her mouth agape. She seemed oblivious to the fact that we had just walked out of her private sanctuary, desecrated or otherwise. She stood watching us disappear in the garage, where Punk bit his lip and said goodbye. "Good luck," he muttered.

"Who was that?" Rena asked, as I walked past her on my way upstairs.

"A friend."

"Does Mom know you are having boys visit?"

"It's none of your business, Rena."

"Who let you into my room?"

"I did. It's a total mess. You should clean it up before she sees it."

Rena squinted her eyes at me.

"Why don't you at least take out the empty bottles?" I asked. "I could help you, if you want."

"Because when I have a bad day, it reminds me of all the fun I've had." Her comment made me wonder whether my sister, as tough as she was acting on the outside, was struggling inside. The thought awakened in me certain tenderness toward my sister, a rather rare occurrence.

"How come you're home? I thought you were going to spend the night out?" I asked, following her into her room. I could smell alcohol on her.

"Yeah, we were going to. Then Mom called and asked me to come home. Apparently she's been all flustered that I haven't been home enough. But what sort of home is this?" she asked, lifting a bottle and taking a swig of the remains. I stared at Rena in disbelief. "It's a broken home! An empty shell," she dropped the bottle with a bang to the floor and watched it break, pieces scattering in all directions. The action dislodged tension from her face. "Look at us," Rena said. "We are like two orphans. Haven't you noticed? No one cares!"

"That's not fair," I said. "Mom has been trying very hard to keep us all together."

181

"Oh? Then why is Dad never here?"

"It's more complicated than you think," I said, looking down at the pile of broken glass. "Here, I'll help you clean up. You can't be living in filth like this."

"Whatever you say," she said, falling backward onto her mattress bed and covering her face with her hands.

"You've been drinking, haven't you?"

"That is what you do when you plan to go out," she said, confirming my suspicions. "What? You never drink, Miss Perfect?"

"That's beside the point. Get up, Rena! I'm not doing this without you. You're going to help me. And then you will follow me upstairs and the three of us will have a nice dinner together, the one Mom's been slaving all day to prepare," I said.

"What's his name?" she muttered.

"Huh?"

"What's the name of your new boyfriend? Don't worry, I won't tell Mom."

"He's not my boyfriend."

"Thank you, holy mother of God!" she cried out, raising her hands toward the ceiling. "He's quite cute," she said, turning to me and propping herself on her elbow. "When is he coming over again?"

"I'll tell you if you help me clean up this mess."

Rena rolled off her bed with a grunt and setting the radio tuner to the Top 40 hits, began picking her clothes off the floor. Hoisting a bag of laundry out of her room and leaving me to collect empty bottles, I thought to myself how ironic the situation was. After all this time trying to disentangle my family dynamics and melt the ball of wax that occluded our past, it had escaped me that Mom and I were not the only ones struggling. So was Rena. And apparently Dad.

"Do you drink often?" I asked Rena when she returned.

"Of course not. Only on the weekends."

"It looked like more than that to me."

"That's not even mine," she said, pointing at the empty whiskey bottle. "It was Arek's."

"Are you still seeing that jerk?" I asked. The boy she was referring to had a rather tainted reputation in our town.

"I used to be in love with the jerk."

"Used to?"

"That's until I was illuminated by true handsomeness earlier today. That cured me. Arek lost his crown. What's the name of this rare human phenomenon?" Rena asked.

"Umm . . ." I tried to think quickly. If I told Rena that he didn't really have a name, it would probably start an avalanche of questions I'd rather avoid. So I decided right then and there to give Punk a new name, one not too common, but not too eccentric either. In the period of time it took me to draw in a single breath, I ran across the names of the four archangels: Michael, Gabriel, Rafael, and Uriel. The last one was by far the most mysterious of the bunch. "The phenomenon's name is Uriel," I said to Rena.

"What? Uri? Is he Russian or something?"

"No. I don't know," I shrugged. "Maybe."

"How come I've never seen this Uri before?"

"Because he's not from here," I said, and before she had a chance to ask another question or insist that he must be Russian, I added, "I didn't know you liked those types of guys."

"Are you blind? He's really good looking!" she said, and I chuckled inside, thinking of Punk's look the day I met him, wearing his painted mohawk and torn-up clothes. Rena would collapse in shock if she ever saw him dressed like that. "This guy is not at all like what's his name—"

"Ben?"

"Yeah, Ben. All philosophical and brown. Ben is *waaay* too brown—brown hair, brown eyes, brown cords. Though I like the guy who comes to play his guitar here sometimes. The one with the black ponytail? He's cute, too." Rena's assessment of my friends was quite comical, but as far as I could tell she was dead serious. I handed her a towel to dust off her desk.

"But I thought you were more into, you know, the techno, preppy kind with flashy shirts and fitted jeans."

"Those guys are assholes."

"Really? I could never tell," I said, throwing the last bottle into the garbage can.

"Check this out. Just last week when we went dancing, this group of guys pulls up in a brand new Mercedes and one of them calls me over. So I'm like, cool, and I go to talk to him and he gives me every indication that he is interested in taking me for a ride. We talk and then his other friend starts to make fun of me for some unintelligible reason, but because I like the guy I'm talking with, I get kind of nervous and don't know what to say to the second guy. Like I got tongue-tied, you know? I hate that feeling. I wanted to just leave at that point, but then this other guy comes over and slaps my butt in front of the guy I am talking to and—"

"No!"

"I know, right? I hated it! Oh, how I wished I had an older brother to come over and kick his ass!"

It was not easy to imagine gentle Daniel kicking anyone's ass, but I tried anyway. My dear brother… in a coma, somewhere in a dungeon. The thought stirred concern, and remembrance of the call I was supposed to get any moment from Punk, now also known as Uri, to add Rena's spontaneous twist on the archangel's name. The more I thought of him as Uri, the less the name Punk fit him, the new moniker becoming a much better match. I wondered what he would say when I told him I had decided to rename him.

With the music spewing out of the radio, we missed Mom's multiple calls for dinner, prompting her to come downstairs to catch an uncommon sight: Rena and I hard at work. While I was dusting her shelves, she was fighting the vacuum cable that was too short and kept coming unplugged. The work was a panacea for Rena, who sobered up rather quickly. Not only was the fact that we were cleaning highly unusual, but also seeing Rena and me doing anything together was, in her own words, best grade medicine for her ulcers.

"Nothing makes me happier than seeing the two of you love each other," Mom said, placing a sizzling pan over a cutting board in the middle of our dining table. It was sautéed onions with bread on the menu this evening, poor man's food—simple but delicious.

"Don't get too used to it. It won't last through the night," Rena said, making us laugh. Having humor replace animosity was refreshing.

Just as I was about to put away my dish, the phone rang and I rushed to get it.

"Hello?" I said, walking as far away from the kitchen as the cord permitted.

"I found the right train."

"When?" I asked in a whisper.

"Be ready at five in the morning. I will meet you right in front of your house and we'll go from there. Try to make sure no one sees you."

"Anything I should bring?"

"Food would be nice. You make good sandwiches."

"Hey, Punk?"

"Yes?"

"I decided to give you a name. Do you mind?" I asked, a bundle of nerves tying my gut into a knot.

"Depends on what it is."

What if he didn't like it? What if he thought it was ridiculous, or worse that I was ridiculous for coming up with it? This was a big deal. Names carried energy with them, a power that could influence an identity, he told me that night by the castle.

"Hello? Are you still there?" he asked.

"Yes, sorry," I cleared my throat. "The name I came up with for you is Uri." I held my breath. "Short for Uriel. One of the four archangels."

There was nothing but a quiet crackling on the line. Seconds ticked and I was growing more anxious.

"The angel of repentance," his voice finally reached my ears and I breathed out.

"What do you think?" I asked. "Please be honest."

"I like it," he said. "Thank you. But do you realize what you've done?" he asked.

There it was. He was going to say it now. I made him become someone he was not, forced an identity on someone who wanted to remain free of labels.

"I'm sorry, I—"

"You've turned me into the one who holds the key to the Tartarus," he said. "And Tartarus, as you know, is the place where your angel has been imprisoned."

Later that night, with Mom watching some show and Rena back in her basement room, I was in the kitchen preparing provisions for our trip, trying not to make too much noise. Uri's words were slowly settling in and growing roots around my heart. If Uriel was the angel who held the key to the underground where Sariel was imprisoned, maybe, just maybe, by giving Punk his name I had evoked the archangel's spirit, and that could help me free him.

I wrapped four butter and cheese sandwiches in parchment, and hid them out of sight inside one of the refrigerator drawers. Just then, I heard the garage doors creak open and a car pull inside. I walked into the living room. Mom muted the television and we looked at each other, exchanging trepidation. After a long absence, his longest yet, Dad had returned.

I sat down next to Mom, who turned the sound back on, and we waited. Soon Dad entered the kitchen, and with two loud slams set heavy items on the table. I got up to go there to see what he was doing.

"Good evening," he said, smiling at me. "I went shopping," he added, pointing at the bounty. "Lots of chocolate and bananas. Just for you." My eyes widened. I only got to taste bananas on very rare occasions, as the fruit was hard to come by in my hometown. Dad patted my shoulder and walked past me and into the living room.

Curious, I peeked into the bags, amazed at the cornucopia of color. I'd never seen so many items swathed in shiny wraps at once, unless they were stacked on the shelf of a western store in a city that sold imported goods from the west.

Rena burst in, her eyes bulging at the sight. "Should we unpack it?" she asked.

"I'd wait," I said. "Want some tea?"

We sat at the kitchen table, staring at the bags in front of us, sipping the hot drinks and eavesdropping on our parents' conversation. While we couldn't hear the exact words, their tones were calm. But I could only imagine Mom's internal conflict simmering beneath the surface. She'd been betrayed so many times, yet she kept welcoming him back for the sake of our security.

I looked at my sister playing with the string of her teabag when Mom entered the kitchen.

"Girls, I need your help with the groceries," she said, motioning at the bags. I looked at her and she gave me a sad smile that seemed to say *I know, but what else can I do?*

I let Rena lead the pantry project while I followed Mom into the bathroom.

"Why do you think he came back?" I said, leaning into the door.

"He said he wants to make things right. Being away from us made him realize what he had been taking for granted."

"But isn't that what he always says?" I asked.

Mom sighed. "I want peace for you and your sister, and I want us to have a *whole* family again. You shouldn't bear the burden of our problems."

"I just think you deserve better, Mom," I said looking down. "And if he ever lays his hands on you again—"

"Thank you," she said and hugged me.

Thinking of the impending journey made it hard to drift off that night. Just as I fell asleep, my alarm rang. I got, dressed, and put the sandwiches I had made the night before, along with three apples, a carton of juice, and a handful of sugary treats into my backpack. In my room, I decided to also pack Daniel's notebook, Sariel's feather, and a roll of cash I had saved through my ear piercing operation.

At one minute to five, I was locking up the garage door when a pair of headlights swept across my house. I recognized the black Audi.

"Ready?" Uri asked, stepping out to greet me. I nodded and smiled and he held the passenger door open for me, but I told him I preferred to sit in the back. Rock was behind the wheel, fulfilling the role of our driver this morning. "How do you know Rock?" I gave Uri a quizzical look.

"I told you I made friends when I came here last

time," he smiled. "He's one of them."

"Does he know about where we are going?"
Uri shook his head. "Even we don't know that yet."

I thanked Rock for his help and he offered to come get us when we returned.

Rock dropped us off at the train station and a few minutes later we boarded a southbound train. It was a cold, crisp morning with a cloudless sky.

We found an empty car and took our seats, setting our backpack on the floor by our feet. Uri handed me a ticket. "Thanks. How much do I owe you?"

"A sandwich."

I opened my backpack and reached inside for his breakfast, wrapped in white paper, just as I had done that morning we met back in November.

"Déjà vu," he smiled. "We've come a long way since that morning. Who would've thought?"

I smiled and looked at the ticket he handed me. "Katowice? This is the same city where Daniel and I last saw each other."

"Is it?" He lifted his brows, chewing. "It was the first train out we could get on."

"Are you serious? You bought us tickets on the first random ride out?"

"It felt right," he said. "And if you say that this was where you last saw him, it must mean that my hunches should be right on target."

At this point, I wasn't even that surprised. This is how he operated and the best thing I could do was to accept it and come along. While Uri ate, I leaned into my seat and watched the landscape before me change from rusty rails to open fields in their last hour of sleep before spring tilling.

The journey to the center of town was going to take no more than three hours. Half an hour into the ride, my exhaustion set in, making my eyelids sink. Before I knew it, the outside faded into obscurity, the light shaking of the train lulled me, and I drifted off with my head resting on Uri's shoulder.

My mind lifted above the train and flew southward to the place where I last saw Daniel. The sun had set and night befell the world in my vision. I was with my brother again, my head resting on his chest. I saw my face drenched in a rain of tears as my fist clenched the fabric of Daniel's shirt, and I whispered, *Sariel, please help Daniel. And I shall be yours forever.*

But in that moment of remembrance, I knew that it was not the first time that I had given myself to the angel.

My mind ascended through the roof of the hospital and I soared toward the clouds. Breaking through the milky barrier of condensation, I flew higher until the sky grew dark and I could see the Earth's curvature, the moon shining above, its position in perfect zenith pointing toward a location I kept returning to, a place I felt I knew so well: the frozen lake in the mountains. I aimed for a precise location and slowly descended, gliding through the air. I was beginning to remember.

Ninsal. . . . I heard his voice echo in a breezy whisper. *Ninsal, remember your promise.*

I wanted to surrender to his will and relax in his embrace. I wanted my body to touch his body, for all the space and time barriers between us to disappear. Imagining how that touching would feel sent electric ripples through my core and awakened more memories.

It happened during another lifetime, millennia ago. And it was here by this lakeshore where Sariel and I saw each other for the last time before the Earth was consumed by a war between kingdoms that brought utter destruction to all.

He was waiting for me on the banks of the frozen lake, his wings folded behind his back, dark cape and long black hair protruding from beneath his hood, billowing in the cold wind. I caught the elusive glory of his face, the light of my attention skimming across the polished surface of his pale cheeks, the amber shine of his flaming eyes drawing me into his world. Falling into an embrace, I wanted to forget about the foreboding conditions shaping our destiny. The opium smell of his skin opened a new dimension, a gateway in time. The journey of my soul came into focus through an array of feelings that kept surfacing in an orchestrated succession.

But our love was doomed. Close relations between angels and humans were forbidden, and so it carried through to my present lifetime. Their kind and ours could not coexist, and no matter how much I wished for it to be so, my dreams of flying with him remained just that, dreams.

Sariel and I met for the first time when I lived as a young priestess at a valley temple in a faraway land. My name was Ninsal, and just like my temple sisters, I was a scholar consumed by an unquenchable desire to glean the mysteries of creation. My closest friend, Saneel, was also a priestess, few years my senior, and responsible for guiding me in my studies. She was like a mother to me in many respects, and my closest confidant.

Using the sacred rituals of our forefathers, our secluded community began a series of ceremonies that lured the celestial entities to our temple. First they came to us in our visions, until finally we met in flesh. The angels were very tall and their skin glistened in light, shining bodies towering beneath the domed roof of our temple. At first it was enough for us to just look at each other and revel in how different we were. This was how our first teachings were transmitted. But soon we were busy sharing with each other what we knew, using signs and symbols.

The Watchers told us they came from the stars. Later we learned that while their chieftains supported their learning about us, any physical comingling was strictly forbidden. But this group wasn't interested in studying us. They wanted to possess us.

As one of the youngest initiates at the temple, I found the presence of the angels somewhat intimidating. But there was one in whose presence I felt serene. His name was Sariel and he taught us the mysteries of the moon. Saneel also found a teacher. Her angel shared with us the secrets of universal forces and the power that ignites roaring thunders.

Due to the nature of our teaching, Sariel and I met

after dark, outside on the land surrounding the temple. While he taught me how to read the sky, I showed him what it was like to feel with my body. Sariel was most gentle when he first laid his hands upon me. It was at my own asking, as I was running out of words trying to describe the feelings his presence evoked in me. I wanted him to experience it too.

Once my body tasted the radiance of his touch, I wanted more. Each month I waited for the moon's entire face to illuminate, preparing for his arrival. We would sit on the grass in the garden's orchards and sometimes venture farther out to the meadows. There, bathed in moonlight and alone at last, we'd trace our hands over each other's faces, the secrets of creation coming alive beneath our fingertips.

Years had passed and our feelings deepened. Our temple thrived under the angelic influence, but one day everything changed. The king of the angels and the king of men entered into a deadly conflict, cursing our relations and turning our allies into deadly enemies. Accused of clandestine desire to control us, the angels were banished from our lands. But for many, it was too late. A new breed of beings was on its way and I was one of the human women carrying the fruit of his seed.

On the eve of the battle of kingdoms, I set out to see Sariel one last time. I walked to a lake high in the mountains, half way between our land and the place where the shining ones once dwelled. Standing on its bank and cross from him, I felt his fingertips touch my face. I closed my eyes and leaned my head into his shoulder, and he embraced me before his hands travelled to my round belly and an excruciating pain pierced my body.

My body jolted and eyes blinked open. The train was starting to move, leaving behind one of many stations at which it had stopped to let off and pick up travelers. The car Uri and I were in was filling up. I looked at my companion, his large blue eyes glaring at me.

"Are you sad to see him go again?" Uri asked, and I frowned. But before I had a chance to ask him how in the world he knew what I had just experienced, he added, "You were talking in your sleep."

XXII.

Grandpa's warning words ran through my head.

Once they depart, the spirits leave behind a void that needs to be filled, often at the expense of the living.

This is exactly how I felt now. Empty and missing Sariel more than ever. The more I remembered, the more I wanted him near. But what if there was danger in giving myself to the angel? There was fear, each time I did so, most recently when I was faced with the fear of losing Daniel, something that Grandpa had warned me about. A feeling of dread spread through my body, like the frost lacing the windows of the train. What would happen now? I wanted to ask my companion, but it was turn for Uri's eyes to fall shut. I was tasked with keeping watch of our whereabouts and was supposed to wake him when we reached our destination.

I was so wrapped up in my thoughts that had it not been for the fact that the majority of the passengers were disembarking at our own journey's end, creating an impossible-to-ignore commotion, I would've made us miss our stop. I shook Uri awake and helped him sling his backpack over his shoulder. I then took his hand in mine and pulled him out before the train started to move again. We got out in the nick of time. He shuffled behind me, still half asleep.

Outside, merchants selling gadgets and trinkets lined the sidewalks, while others walked in haste, shoving past them in a trance as if the former never existed. I coveted them having an agenda, a clear path to follow. As far as I could tell, we still lacked a plan. The turmoil abated as we entered the city streets. By then Uri was fully awake and walked fast and with unsurpassed confidence, dodging the onslaught of rushing amblers and leaving me behind.

"Where are we going?" I called out, once the distance between us grew too wide.

"To the park," he said, and paused to wait for me to catch up. He reached for my hand and pulled me forward. "I'm gonna need your help because I've got no clue what to do next."

"Still no plan? Seriously?"

"My portion of the plan was to get us here," he said. "It's your turn to get involved because frankly, I'm drawing a blank."

I was out of breath by the time we found a suitable bench in the heart of the park. The surrounding trees reached their crooked arms in all directions, poking through thick morning fog and forming a porous fence between the urban jungle and us, two lone souls dwelling in the Elysian Fields encircled by layers of concrete walls.

"We need to find where Daniel is. I need you to try to make contact with him since you are the one who saw him last. I can't seem to be able to get through," Uri explained. "My brain is all fogged up," he said, looking around. "Just like this park."

"What do I do?"

"It is simple. Just think of him and wait for visions," Uri said, squatting next to me, his gaze scattering in all directions. "You have to really focus to go deep. I'm here to keep watch so you don't have to worry about being interrupted."

"But how do I know the difference between my imagination and an actual vision?" I asked, thinking of Paula, the most disciplined teenager I knew, trying to rummage though her instructions, but my memory vault remained shut.

"It's no different than when you connect with the angel," Uri said, and cleared his throat. I kept staring at him.

"What? I'm just assuming."

"I know you are more skilled than most of us mortals, but please promise me you are not able to read my mind!"

"I promise, cross my heart. I only see what you want me to see and even that takes effort. Besides, what I do isn't all that prodigious. Most people could learn to do what I do if they wanted to. It's actually not that hard, only takes practice,"

Uri squinted his eyes at a passerby that entered our field, crossing the park. My eyes trailed his silhouette, while my fingers tapped a wooden plank of the bench as if that alone would make him move faster.

"Here we have a perfect opportunity to practice discerning fact from fiction," Uri said.

"How so?"

"You know how we tend to put labels on things all the time? Try to just look at the guy without throwing any of your own preconceptions over him. What does it look like he's doing?"

"Walking."

"Walking where?"

"Home?" I guessed with a shrug.

"You don't know that."

"This is pointless. Of course I don't know where he's going. Do I look like a prophet?"

"It's simpler than that. He's walking to the other side of the park. Period. End of story."

I snorted. "Duh. That's obvious."

"That is all truth is. Obvious simplicity. People make things complex and then get lost in the chaos they themselves created," he mused, and then continued, "Okay, let's dig a level deeper. What might he be thinking about?"

"How in the world am I supposed to know that?"

"Take a guess! Be bold."

"No clue. Why don't you enlighten me?"

Uri looked at me with his crystal blue eyes and then stood up to look at the man. He contorted his body to match the man's posture and took a few steps to imitate his walking rhythm. "Mind and body are one," he said over his shoulder. "The man has a guilty conscience. He's fighting with himself, can't find peace."

"Reminds me of Stan."

"Reminds me of most people. He's specifically thinking about something bad he has done. It preoccupies his mind. He's trying to escape. See the wobble in his step? See the hunch? This is a hunch of remorse."

"And you can see all that just from the way he walks?"

"You start with the closest thing to a fact you can find—thoughts that feel right, pieces that belong with the story you're building—and then the rest falls into place."

"And you get it right each time?"

"Let's just say it's a bull's-eye at best, educated guess at worst," Uri clapped his hands once. "Ready to contact Daniel?"

I nodded. Resting my palms on my lap, I closed my eyes and tried to conjure the vision of my brother's face. For weeks, after last seeing Daniel, I did my best to train my mind to forget him. The tall wall of resistance I'd erected between us made it difficult to bring him back at first. But when his big green eyes began to come through the haze, they seemed as real as if he were standing right in front of me.

Keeping my eyes closed, I nodded to Uri. "I've got him."

"What do you see?"

"Just his face, mostly eyes."

"Anything around him?"

"No, nothing. Only darkness." Just then it occurred to me that I could expand my scope of vision. I panned around but seeing nothing tangible, I returned to Daniel's face. "Wait! Now his eyes are closed."

"Good. You're on the right track. He's sleeping."

I opened my eyes, "This is pointless. I don't know how to do this."

"But you were doing fine! C'mon, Eve, don't give up now. Please try again."

I closed my eyes again, but my self-doubt made it harder to focus this time. I kept seeing the hospital and nothing new would come to my mind. "I'm afraid I'm confusing memory with vision, Uri. I see nothing other than that dreary clinic."

"Well, I guess that's where we need to go."

"But he was gone when I woke up the next morning."

"It's a big building," Uri said.

"You have that much faith in me?"

"You see the hospital. I see nothing. Only darkness, cables, and a blurred body. If we put two and two together, it makes sense that he's somewhere in there," Uri said, joining me on the bench. He was scanning the space with acute concentration. "Cold?" he asked, looking into the distance.

"Freezing," I said, turning toward him. "And hungry. Could we please find some warm place to eat? I have money."

"Not yet," he replied, still looking ahead. "The air

feels frozen. We should wait until it thaws," he said, squeezing my arm in comfort.

Of course it feels frozen. Because it is winter and we need to eat something warm, I thought but kept it to myself. Uri was by far the most eccentric person I'd ever met. Besides Daniel. No wonder they once were friends. The thought that there was someone other than me, with an even more peculiar way of looking at the world, was comforting. Especially now that I had lost Ben.

"Okay. Let's go now," Uri said, signaling me to follow him.

We traversed a few city blocks at Uri's rapid pace until I stopped in my tracks, pulling Uri by his hood. He turned to me with a puzzled look and I pointed toward a plump red-haired woman standing on the edge of a street in front of us, waiting for the light to turn. I recognized the nurse who had kept denying Daniel's existence.

"Bingo!" Uri asked me to wait by the nearest building while he snuck up behind the unsuspecting woman, briefly matching her stomp, and pulled a large envelope sticking out of her brown tote bag. He was by my side before the nurse reached the other side of the busy street. Grabbing my hand, he led us in the opposite direction. Once we were a safe distance away, he said, "This is what I mean about good timing. And this," he shook the rolled-up envelope in front of our faces, "this was just begging to be taken."

We settled in a milk bar, a diner that served a limited menu, usually a soup and a main meal that rotated each day of the week. Despite the paltry offerings, the food in such places was always made from scratch and very tasty. I ordered tomato soup while Uri requested the goulash.

The pale sun streaming through the windows had just about reached its highest point in the winter sky, which at this time of the year was not very high. I thought of my parents sitting down to lunch at my grandparents' house. I had left them a short note, attributing my absence to joining a student-organized tutoring circle in preparation for school tomorrow. As much as I disliked making up stories, I didn't want Mom to worry in vain, and in my heart I promised myself that if

I succeeded at bringing Daniel home, this would be the last time I fictionalized anything. I asked Uri if he thought we would be heading back before the end of the day, but he said he didn't know. He and I sat side by side, the smell of food making our stomachs growl, and opened the envelope.

Inside we found a small pile of papers, a brief letter and three pages of handwritten notes related to an experiment performed by a doctor whose name looked familiar, despite the difficult handwriting. The envelope was addressed to him, bearing a stamp, CONFIDENTIAL, in bold red lettering. Based on the letter, Uri and I surmised that the nurse was delivering a report to her superior who was attending a medical symposium in the city when we intercepted her. The letter referred to a series of unusual events outlined in the report that had commenced yesterday in the early evening hours in reference to a particular patient. The thus far predictable and controllable state of the patient had been disrupted, with the subject's vitals and mental responses reaching an alarming state. The nurse requested the doctor's prompt return to the testing chamber where the subject was being held.

"Testing chamber," I said, looking at Uri. "Sounds dark and secretive."

Lines of medical jargon filled the accompanying report, and while it was difficult to penetrate through the details, it pointed toward a project at the hospital supervised by the doctor that had tested the responses of a patient endowed with some form of Extra Sensory Perception.

The nurse emphasized that the subject, whose name was never mentioned, had been on a series of drugs, as ordered, with the aim of upholding the subject's stable and docile condition until the doctor's return. Then, at about 16:22, the subject began to display symptoms of violent agitation in the form of seizures, significantly disrupting the stability of his vitals. Heightened brain activity was recorded, despite heavy administration of tranquilizers minutes prior to the event. The second wave of seizures commenced at around five o'clock in the morning, when the subject's eyes opened wide, and he tried to rip the monitoring cables from his body. A double dose of sedatives had been administered, but before the subject receded back into the docile state, several times he repeated a word that sounded like the female name "Evelina." Uri and I looked at each other with dread. Our eyes returned to the page.

Ever since this morning, the subject's brain wave activity had been closer to that of a waking state rather than sleeping, though no bodily movement or changes in heart rate had been noted. Here again, the nurse requested the doctor's prompt return and advice, as the subject's responses made no sense to her, and she did not want to damage his internal organs by administering stronger doses of drugs or upping the intensity of the electric currents that kept his heartbeat from fading. The report ended with an appendix listing drugs and their dosages, a timed log of administration, and an alarming statement that raised the hair on my arms. If all else failed, the nurse suggested a procedure that would sever certain nerves in the subject's brain and prevent future seizures. But of course, that remained to be discussed, and the final decision would be at the doctor's discretion.

"What are they planning to do to him?" I asked, my face as pale as the whitewashed wall behind me.

"I don't know. But this is highly disturbing," Uri said, shoving the papers back into the envelope with a bitter expression on his face. "This is why we waited in the park. We needed to get these in our hands. And I wouldn't be surprised if he wasn't even sick. These monsters are only interested in what he can do."

"Part of me wishes I didn't know this much. He's been drugged, poked, and prodded. An electric current? Reading this has made me lose my appetite."

"You need to eat. We have a long night ahead," he said, picking up a knife and checking its sharpness with his thumb.

"He knows we're coming," I said, stirring my soup that was no longer steamy. "That's hopeful."

"You know how to get there?"

"I know the name of the place. We can look it up on a city map. I also know how to enter in through the basement in the back."

"Perfect," he said, stabbing a piece of meat with his fork.

Two hours later we stood in front of the hospital, hands in our pockets, clouds of steam vaporizing in front of our faces. There was much commotion in the front, people in white uniforms rushing about, patients walking in and out, and visitors standing outside smoking cigarettes. A couple of cargo trucks rounded the corner to get behind the building.

"We need to wait until it gets darker. Otherwise it is too risky. Everyone will see us," Uri said.

"Can we pretend we are just visitors and take a look around?"

"No need. I think I know where Daniel is."

"Where is he?"

"In the basement. When you mentioned the back entrance, it finally clicked."

"What if the doctor gets there before us?"

"He could."

"Maybe you could, you know, use your special talents and see?" I said, and then suggested we get some hot tea in the motel cafeteria across the street. Despite the sunny skies, the temperature outside was subzero.

We entered the cafeteria. The smell of lunch still lingered in the air, but besides us there was only one person behind the counter. Looking across that empty room brought back memories. I would never have guessed that I would return here in three months' time, once more planning to break into the clinic.

We ordered our tea, a plate of sliced bread and cold cuts, and Uri closed his eyes, one hand on the envelope, and focused until droplets of sweat began forming on his temples.

"The nurse is confused by the disappearance of her damn report. And she hasn't found the doc yet. He's not at the conference anymore," he said and opened his eyes.

"Any of them across the street?"

"Don't think so."

"How much time do you think we have?"

"We have enough," he stated with conviction. I believed him.

I pulled out Daniel's notebook and showed Grandpa's drawings to Uri, twirling the feather between my fingers. Uri leaned forward and tucked loose strands of his hair behind one ear.

"He is a true artist."

"Do you think he knows about the angel? He seemed to react strongly one time when I barely mentioned I dreamt of one," I asked, pointing the sharp end of the plume at the hovering figure behind the soldier with a rifle pressed to his chest.

Uri's eyes widened. "He probably knows more than he admits," he said, closing the notebook and sliding it toward me.

"And this? Do you think it belongs to Sariel? Do you think he left it for me?"

"If I was an angel on a mission to seduce a girl, that's what I would've done. Unless, of course, a swan flew into your room at night."

I smiled. "I often wonder what it would be like to be him, to have wings and fly."

"Well, this one can't fly. I can tell you that much."

"Why are you so against him? And please save your protection speech. This is my life and I will do with it as I please."

"Just trying to save you from an epic disappointment."

"I didn't know you were such a pessimist."

"I'm not a pessimist. More of a realist."

I laughed. "One thing is for sure, and that's that none of us—not you, not me—are realists. If anything, we are idealists."

Uri shrugged. "Fine by me. Just remember that he is dark and fallen before you commit yourself," he said, picking on a slice of bread.

"But has it ever crossed your mind that the punishment was too severe and that the whole darkness thing in general is overblown? The angels were sharing sacred knowledge with human women. What's wrong with that?"

"It was dangerous and you are indeed an idealist."

"Why was it dangerous?"

"They interfered in human affairs and promised something they couldn't deliver. Angels and humans don't mix, just like oil and water don't mix. You can't cross there and he can't cross here. It will be futile if you try. It will only lead to suffering. Why not just be content with what you have here closer to the ground? Is that not enough?"

"You are right. It is not. This world is boring and flat. And I happen to believe in love, as a force that makes everything possible. Even for oil and water to mix."

"Have you ever considered that your version of love might be different from his?" Uri asked.

I squinted my eyes at him. "Why do you have to be so cynical? Do you even know what love is?"

"That has nothing to do with what I know or don't know."

"Well I think it may. Is lack of love the reason why you ran away from your life and your name?" I asked, and immediately regretted saying it. "I'm sorry. I shouldn't have—"

"Maybe that's the crux of my problem. I was never loved. Mommy and daddy were never there to give me that. You're right. What do I know?"

"I'm sorry."

"No need," he said, and began impaling pieces of ham on his fork.

"You remind me of Daniel," I said quietly. "He told me you and him were of the same kind. I often wonder what he meant," I said, with more tenderness this time.

The earlier aggravation was melting off Uri's face, but his voice still carried an edge. "Knowing how driven you are, I bet you'll figure it out."

"Why are you being so secretive? You warn me of danger in one breath and then when I ask for clarity, you clam up."

"Listen, Eve," Uri put away his fork, leaned closer and lowered his voice. "There are things that when explained will do absolutely nothing because you don't have the whole picture yet, only certain parts. Your mind will misinterpret what I tell you, your imagination filling in the gaps. And we already know the disastrous consequences of that. When people take action based on fear or assumptions they only create more chaos. Because they still feel wounded and victimized by their stories, be it abandonment or harassment or feeling unloved or whatever, their emotions are not healed so they go on hurting others and spreading the harm. This only perpetuates the cycle of misery for themselves and others."

"Then could you please tell me more about my whole picture? Maybe that could help me make better decisions. I take it you know more than I do?" I asked.

"Eve, can't you see the beautiful paradox of it? I can walk next to you but it would be no good for me to tell you what to do or how to do it. No one can walk this path but you. This is why Daniel went on his quest. It was through the journey and facing the darkest parts of himself that he found his self."

"Yes but Daniel almost died!"

"True. But if you live according to what others tell you, you are dead inside. Also his sister had come searching for him, in the meantime perhaps salvaging a lost part of her own soul."

"But we don't know how the story will end,"
I scowled.

"Why should we? Life would be boring that way, don't you think? There would be no real stakes."

I thought for a moment about what Uri had said. "So it's true what Grandpa said. It all begins with knowing ourselves."

Uri nodded. "That's the true awakening. It's not about finding what makes us the same but rather what makes us different—finding that essence that is distinctive from everyone else. If you don't have that, you become a copy of someone else."

"Funny. And we concern ourselves with how to fit in."

"Exactly."

"You sound like you know who you are," I whispered.

"I do," he said. "And you are very close yourself."

XXIII.

At the motel phone booth, I hesitated before calling home. Lying to my parents was something I was not accustomed to, as I never before needed to do that. Mom let me be out as long as I was with people she knew and as long as my grades at school didn't suffer. In this particular case, I failed on all counts. I was prodding the depths of my family's secrets with someone she didn't know even existed, far away from home, and after having already fallen behind in my studies. But since I knew that there was no chance that I would make it home before bed, I had no choice but to call. I had to at least let them know I was safe.

I put a coin in the slot, and dialed the number. Dad picked up. Crossing my fingers I told him that we were extending our study session since there was a lot for me to catch up on. He said it would be better for me to come home sooner than later. Grandfather had another attack. The doctor was on his way to determine whether he needed to be taken back to the hospital. Dad relayed to me how Mom was concerned because she had no way of contacting me all day. I told him I'd do my best to get there soon and hung up before another untruth escaped my lips.

"I hate lying to them," I said to Uri.

"You could have told them—"

"Grandpa had another attack," I said quickly. "It seems to be happening a lot lately."

Uri and I went outside and paced in front of the hospital, monitoring for activity. People and cars were still abounding, though less so as the light outside grew dimmer. Once the sun's disk was almost skimming the Earth's skyline, its orange glow making the piles of snow on the side of the streets glisten like gold, we entered the premises and rounded the building.

Scattered coal, broken glass, and scraps of paper littered the blackened cement floor of the back plaza, where three piles of the black rock stood still and silent like small pyramids. Without Stan to aid our journey, but sensing no

204

lurking danger, I walked toward the back entrance, opened the door, and went inside. Uri followed me in, shutting the door behind us. Inside, the scent of burned coal and sulfur brought back memories. In darkness, I turned my head toward Uri, my face almost slamming into his chest. I told him that if we went in the direction away from the heating room, we would eventually reach a set of stairs leading to the main floor of the hospital.

"In that case we should go the opposite direction." He found my hand and pulled me toward the blazing furnaces.

The temperature inside was climbing until we passed the roaring flames, rounded the corner, and entered a narrower arm of the hallway. Uri stopped us the moment we heard the squeak of doors opening, followed by rushed footsteps that sounded like woman's heels stomping over polished stone floor. Uri and I looked at each other and let out our long breaths once the footsteps retreated.

"Now. Quick," Uri pulled me forward. We took another turn and ran until we reached a set of doors with an eerie dim light blinking and buzzing above its frame. Uri caught the doors just before they shut in front of us.

"Lucky," I whispered, once we were both inside. He placed his finger on my mouth, signaling me to keep quiet.

Pacing forward on our tiptoes, we looked around. Dim lighting illuminated the corridor, lined on both sides with small windowless rooms. One looked like an office with piles of papers stacked on a desk. Another was empty, save the floor-to-ceiling metal filing cabinets. The lights in the corridor grew darker toward its end where we noticed a set of closed doors with a small, round window like a porthole on a ship.

"Is he here?" I asked Uri.

He nodded.

We approached quietly, wary of our surroundings. Before we reached the end of the corridor, we passes another room that looked like a cross between a morgue and a classroom, with square metal drawers on one wall, and a blackboard on another. In the center stood an empty hospital bed, surrounded by all sorts of machinery and monitoring devices and a large model of a human brain. Uri and I exchanged glances.

"This is it," I said, placing my hand over the knob of the last door.

"Are you sure you want to do this?" Uri asked.

"More than anything in my life," I said and pressed down the lever.

We entered a dry, sterile room that smelled of chemicals and a moment later, the lights flickered on automatically. It was a small foyer, an interim space. Heavy steel door with a square glass window separated us from one more room. Uri pressed a button on the wall and the lights went off, allowing us to see a dim red glow coming through the small glass opening.

"It looks like a darkroom for developing photographs," I said.

"Or an aquarium," Uri said, and opened the doors.

He was right. The air inside the room was warm, moist, and thick. At first, my eyes travelled to the source of light—a red bulb in a far right corner of the room—and then to the large object dominating its center: a rectangular glass container filled with liquid, just like an oversized aquarium. Walking toward it, I reached for Uri's warm hand and he responded with a light squeeze. I was beginning to tremble. Inside the water floated a body.

"We found him," I said, released my hand, and reached for the glass enclosure.

"Daniel," Uri said, leaning over the tank. "It's been so long, my friend," he said.

Daniel looked frozen in time. His eyes were shut, features expressionless, skin whitewashed, and aside from a pair of underwear he was naked. All but his face and toes were submerged. A ganglion of cables like dendrites extended from his temples and chest, linking patches of electrodes to a beeping monitor, the active brain of this chamber.

I bent over the glass wall, just as a tear descended down my cheek and fell into the water, causing concentric ripples that nudged Daniel's hand. I reached my hand and touched Daniel's cheek. His skin was warm, the same temperature as the liquid. I touched my wet finger to my lips and tasted salt.

"How are we going to take Daniel out of here?" I

asked Uri. "It's freezing out."

"I brought an extra set of clothes," he smiled at me. "We travelers always come prepared. But he's very weak. We will have to carry him."

Uri picked up a clipboard with a sheet attached to it, lying on an adjacent table. It was a log of medication administered to Daniel.

"Looks like he was just given some sort of a sedative."

I looked at the sheet. "I know what this is," I said, pointing at one recent entry. "My grandpa used to take it. It's a muscle relaxant." Flashing back to the day I last saw my brother, I realized that the reason the water in his room tasted so bitter was perhaps because it was tainted with medicine.

That's why I was so sleepy. "We can't count on him walking or responding much after what he was given. What do we do?" I asked, panic seeping through my words.

"Keep calm and improvise. Fast."

The idea of losing fragile Daniel during our mission cast a dark cloud over my already taxed mind, a cloud that became even darker with Uri's somber reminder that we better act quick if we don't want to risk getting caught.

I looked at Uri, and then at Daniel, before reaching into the tank and ripping the patches off Daniel's skin. I was angry at the people who brought him here, angry at the whole world for allowing such injustice to take place. Because he didn't have a family to protect him and because he possessed a brilliant mind, he became a target. I blamed myself for not acting sooner and giving into my doubts.

Uri was gently tearing the bandages off Daniel's arm before withdrawing the IV needle from the inside of his elbow. The thought that we had no clue what we were doing crossed my mind and stalled my movement. What if we were endangering his life rather than saving it? I looked at Uri with teary eyes.

"Let's take my brother home."

"This is why we're here."

Floating unattached, Daniel was ready to be lifted out of the water. We did so together, Uri holding Daniel under his arms and I by his feet, and we placed Daniel on a table covered with white linen. Daniel weighed as much as a feather.

"Quick, we need to dress him," Uri said, asking me to dry Daniel's body with the sheet while he took out the bundle of clothes from his backpack. "We used to be the same size. Now he's merely half of me."

Uri and I worked in haste, bumping into each other, dressing Daniel. His body was limp. While I held him in my arms, Uri put his thin legs through the opening in his trousers, wrapped a scarf around his neck, put a wool hat on his head, and slipped a pair of ski gloves over his thin hands. I wanted to have a moment with my brother, hold him tight, cradle him, whisper to him how happy I was to see him in hopes of him hearing me, the way an unborn baby hears its mother's words in the womb. But the pressure to leave the hospital without getting caught was mounting. At any moment, someone could return and find two intruders stealing their research subject, and with it a load of secrets. With Daniel dressed, Uri and I agreed that I would carry our backpacks while he carried Daniel in his arms.

"Almost out of here," I said, hearing the third set of doors slam shut behind us as we shuffled our way across the dim hallway. Both of us were breathing heavily.

We didn't stop moving, not even to look over our shoulders, until we exited the building the same way we came in and reached the fence surrounding the hospital. All I could do was hope that no one saw us. We waited in the dark before crossing the street, away from the lamplight, until the front of the building was clear of people, taking a moment to think and catch our breath.

Daniel's eyes were still closed and his body lifeless. The only indication that he was alive was a faint cloud of steam coming out of his mouth and nostrils. I adjusted the hat on his head to make sure it covered his ears and added my own scarf around his neck.

"Daniel," I said to him. "If you can hear me…This is not a dream. You are coming home now. Your mother waited nineteen years to see you again."

Daniel's head steadied a bit and his eyelids quivered.

"Let's go before he gets too cold," Uri said and

lifted Daniel.

Noticing that Uri was following my lead, I aimed for the closest bus stop. "I hope we luck out with the return train," I said. Laying Daniel on a bench, we checked the map and schedule displayed inside the small waiting area. The bus arrived in less than five minutes and while it meandered a bit, skirting the edge of the city, the train station was its final stop. Taking up the entire back row of seats in an empty bus, I kept looking at Uri and Daniel, two friends connected by a mysterious cord. Both had their eyes closed, but sensing my gawking, Uri spoke.

"We are a good team."

"Thank you for everything."

"Things might get a little heavy now, more complex at home. Don't expect a rosy welcome. Be prepared."

"Thanks for being an optimist," I said.

"Just practicing being a realist."

With a seven-hour wait at the train station (the next train was scheduled to depart at four in the morning), we located an empty bench and positioned Daniel so that his head was resting on my lap. I stayed with my brother while Uri bought our tickets and called Rock to update him on our estimated time of arrival. I held one palm over Daniel's chest and the other just under his head, hoping to pass my warmth to him. When Uri came back, we switched places. Uri covered Daniel with his jacket and I offered mine to place under Daniel's head to serve as a pillow. It was warm inside the station but Daniel's skin was as cold as ice. He was sleeping, his breathing faint but rhythmic and steady. Leaving Uri with my brother, I left in search of something hot to drink.

When I returned holding the biggest cup of hot tea I could buy, and three pastry buns, Uri was bending over Daniel, whispering something to him. I set the food down.

"Is he awake?" I asked.

"He seemed like he was trying to wake up. I told him we were with him and then he turned limp and fell asleep again. I'm growing concerned."

"You think he's gonna be okay? What if his body needs the medication?"

"It might. Let's hope he heard me and is just resting."

"I brought us some food," I said, suddenly realizing the absurdity of trying to feed Daniel anything solid. I ate half of my bun and Uri devoured the rest. When the tea had cooled off, we sat Daniel up and I tried to give him the liquid with a plastic spoon. He was swallowing, so I continued until his cheeks became a little warmer to the touch.

"I have no clue what we're doing. The rescue mission was almost too easy. Will things get a turn for the worse now?" I asked Uri.

"Better not tempt fate."

At two in the morning, Daniel's body began to fidget, waking both of us up. He was lying across our laps, his head on thighs and his legs on Uri's. I tried to give Daniel more tea, which had gone cold, but he barely drank any. Soon his whole body was trembling.

"He must be going through a drug withdrawal," Uri said. "He was pumped full of stuff, his body is probably dependent on it."

Not knowing what else to do, I kept stroking Daniel's head and asking him to hang on a little longer. Soon both Daniel and Uri were sleeping again. I kept checking Daniel's pulse and breathing. Both were feeble, but present. I saw an inkling of a smile on my brother's face and the sight warmed my heart. I did not fall asleep until the train arrived. We had half an hour to board. Carrying Daniel's body, Uri's step was wobbly.

We grabbed the first empty car. Each side was lined with three joined seats. We set Daniel down and stretched him across all three, lifting the arm rests, once more using our wardrobe to make him comfortable. For a brief moment, he opened his eyes and looked at our faces in astonishment, and then his head rolled back and he lost consciousness.

When three hours later the train pulled into the final station and we saw Rock waiting outside his car through the window, I wanted to cry with joy for being so close to home at last. I did not want to even think of the upheaval that Daniel's arrival could cause. The train stopped with a loud screech. I gathered our things. Uri picked up Daniel and we were off.

"You can't take someone off medication and expect that they'll just wake up and go back to normal," Rock said, navigating us home as I continued stroking Daniel's head. In the morning light, his skin was the color of snow.

"This is why we have doctors," I said. "The good doctors."

It was almost eight in the morning when Rock pulled up to my house. I opened the garage door, which squeaked louder than ever, as if broadcasting my arrival to the whole neighborhood. Dad's car was not in the garage. Rock wanted to help, but we thanked him and sent him home with a promise to call later with an update. The less people, the easier it would be for Mom to cope.

We climbed the stairs from the basement to the main floor, which took us a long minute of hard effort. We were both exhausted. Daniel kept waking up and we kept pausing. He looked disoriented, but seeing our faces seemed to put him at ease. When we finally entered the main floor, the house was quiet and cold. There was no sign of anyone inside. We laid Daniel on my bed and I went downstairs to turn up the central heating.

"Maybe we should give Daniel a bath?" I asked, walking into my room.

"Excellent idea," Uri said. "It will warm him faster."

"You think I should try calling them?"

"It is your decision, Eve."

I took a deep breath and nodded. "It is time."

I started the bath for Daniel and put a pot of milk on the stove. I then walked to the phone and dialed Grandma's number.

Mom's sleepy voice answered.

"Mom, it's me. I'm at home. I'm so sorry I didn't come to be with you last night," I said, my voice breaking.

"It's okay, sweetie. I knew you were studying. Grandpa is home with us. He's sleeping. He's going to be okay."

"I called and Dad said you wanted me home—"

"I was just worried but I was also glad you were preoccupied. I didn't want you to witness any more of this.

You can come see him after school. Is your father home?"

"No. His car is gone." I heard Mom take a deep breath. "What happened. Mom?"

I detected a brief hesitation. "He left. I think this time for good."

Pressing the phone to my ear, waiting for her to fill the silence, I leaned on the wall behind me. Dad left us. This is why the house felt so empty and cold when we arrived. It was more than physical vacancy and the heating not being on.

"I'm sorry, Mom. Are you holding up okay?"

"Yes, fine. We actually had a good talk last night. He tried but he's just happier elsewhere. And it's wrong to force him to stay."

We both fell silent. To me, the news was relieving in light of whom I'd just brought home. It was better for Dad to be away. "I'm sorry for robbing you and Rena of your father."

"Please Mom, never think that."

"Still, I feel guilty."

"Mom, could you come home?"

"Aren't you going to school, honey?" she asked.

"No. And I wasn't studying last night. I lied. I'm so sorry. I just need you at home. And Rena. Please come quick," I said, trying to control my emotions.

"Did anything bad happen? Are you all right?"

"Yes, I am fine. But you have to be here to understand. It's too hard to explain. Please hurry." I hung up the phone and ran to the kitchen, barely catching the boiling milk from spilling all over the stove.

Holding the cup, I knocked on the bathroom door. "I brought some milk."

"Come in," Uri said, and opened the door for me. Daniel was floating in a bath full of foam. "We could've done without so many bubbles, you know."

I smiled and entered. Daniel was awake, looking at me with his large green eyes, which seemed even bigger on his emaciated face. I set the cup on the tub's rim and squatted next to my brother.

"Daniel." His name was all I could say before my voice broke.

"Thank you," Daniel said faintly, and closed his eyes. He seemed weak but no longer in danger of losing his life.

I gazed at Uri. "He looks like he's not even sick. Just starved."

Uri nodded. "We are stronger than most people. He is going to be fine."

"We?" I asked standing up. "Please, Uri, I can't take anymore withholding."

"I won't withhold. You are ready to know." Uri walked closer to me. The pupils of his eyes were almost as large as his irises, which were now but tiny blue outlines. "We are not exactly human. And you remembered right—Daniel and I are of the same kind," he added, looking at Daniel. "That's how I know that your brother will be fine."

"Not exactly human? What are you?" I looked at Daniel, whose eyes were closed, and then back at Uri. "Please, tell me," I asked, the current emanating from Uri's eyes making me dizzy.

"We are the Nephilim. Sons of fallen angels."

PART IV
NINSAL

XXIV.

Beneath the visible surface of forms pulsed a seraphic vein of shadows, an underground haven for bodiless souls eager to enter our world, a thrilling force, for which I had become a vessel. Grandpa was right. Obscure forces permeated our world, and those who didn't believe it, simply weren't ready to face this truth. What even I had once suspected as the product of my overactive imagination, turned out to be more real than the common perceived reality that could be nothing more than a sliver of a fleeting dream.

Uri explained that by understanding where we came from, we gained access to reservoirs of our inner potential. But before this power could be fully absorbed and expressed, dramatic shifts would have to take place, a challenging process, akin to walking through personal inferno. For me, Uri's revelation was like taking a plunge into icy water—momentarily unsettling but ultimately empowering. It also put Daniel at peace, confirming what he already knew.

Daniel had found the missing key to his origin in the hospital basement of all places, at the moment when his mind had almost left his body. The fact that his father was one of the fallen angels confirmed why Daniel couldn't find any traces in the outside world and reacted so strongly when I told him about Sariel. All Nephilim would likely react this way. Unbeknownst to them, they held the memory of the angels within their cells.

"What do I do now?" I asked Uri.

"I know you've been tapping into an archive of memories. I don't know their contents, but I can feel that you and the angel share more than a dream. I have a feeling you will follow that thread."

I looked at Daniel, who seemed like his mind was floating in another world.

"Once, in another life, I carried his child. But I think I lost it. That story is still incomplete. And then there is Mom and Grandpa ad their secret. I just don't understand how they had managed to keep so much hidden for so long."

Uri nodded. "You have a big story to disentangle. But you have an real ally now," he said, looking at Daniel who appeared to be sleeping again.

Uri helped me walk Daniel into my bedroom where we sat him on my bed with his back against the wall, and covered in blankets, cup of warm milk in his hands. Despite being nineteen years old, Daniel looked like a child. As he drank, color was returning to his face.

Uri reached for his jacket. He looked like he was anxious to leave before Mom and Rena arrived. I gave him a sad smile but I understood, thinking of what Mom just said to me about not forcing someone to stay. He and Daniel said their goodbyes but neither of them seemed shaken by the parting. It was probably because they would always remain connected with each other, regardless of their physical proximity.

I walked Uri to the entry door and before I had a chance to say anything, he swept me into his arms and held me in a tight embrace until all the tension left my body.

"You're strong," he whispered into my ear, and without turning once, walked down the stairs. I watched him until he went out of my view.

In my room, Daniel's eyes were scanning every detail in sight.

"Is this your home?" he asked.

"Yes. And it is not also your home. I promised I would bring you here."

"Thank you," he whispered, bringing the cup to his lips. He took a tiny sip and smiled. "You were right at the hospital about the meaning of the prophecy. I did come home."

"I always knew it," I said, also realizing the fragility of that statement. Had Uri and I been any slower, we could have never made it this far. "Why did you change your name to Daniel?"

"It's my real name. The name my mother gave me."

"How do you know this?" I asked.

"It was written in Jan's notebook. Not knowing I already had a name, the nuns at the orphanage named me Peter, after the one who never loses faith. But once I knew my real name was Daniel, I let Peter go. But they were right. I never lost faith that I would find her."

While Daniel spoke, I reached for my backpack to retrieve the black book and handed it to Daniel, taking the cup from his hands.

"You found it," he smiled, caressing the front cover with his fingertips.

"Stan gave it to me. He asked me to help you. He was a soul tormented by guilt, just like you told me. He asked for your forgiveness."

"I'm here because of Stan?" Daniel asked, incredulous.

I nodded. "In a way, he saved your life."

Daniel closed his eyes and mouthed a few words I couldn't hear. I could see new radiance emanate from his skin.

"Now he is free," Daniel said, and opened the black book to its first page. "Right here," he pointed at the inner flap.

Tucked inside and seeming to be glued to the cover was one additional page, easy to miss. Daniel slipped his fingernail underneath the sheet, pulled it out, and turned the book upside down so I could see what was written there.

To Daniel—the beat of my heart, the light of my soul.

"I believe that my mother wrote these words and left the book and the picture in secret from her father so that one day I could find her," Daniel said.

"I believe you are right. It does look like Mom's handwriting," I said, and paused to listen.

Just then I heard a double car door slam, followed by footsteps galloping up the front stairs. The two of us listened to the key turning in the front door and two people entered the house.

Daniel sat still, his eyes watchful.

"Mom, I'm in my room," I called into the foyer, my voice shaky, eyes fixed on Daniel.

After so many years, this was it. Would she even recognize him?

Mom and Rena appeared in the doorframe. Rena's

gaze kept shifting from the frail figure of Daniel to me and then back to Daniel. She looked confused, with a hundred questions on her lips.

Mom's face revealed a mosaic of shifting emotions. I saw an avalanche of thoughts running through her mind and animating her features. It was as if some force was peeling off layers of masks that held my mother's outer disposition together, the persona she strove to present to the world. I watched the shocking realization finally settle in and transform her face. After guises of convention and customary facades melted away, her face revealed a wounded woman with a broken heart. I'd never seen her look this vulnerable. Her features trembled like a meadow flower in the wind.

"Mom," I said. "It is all right to cry."

Keeping her eyes on Daniel, who was weeping now and reaching his thin hand toward her, she approached the mattress and dropped to her knees, a sob folding her body at the waist. It was a moment of release and reckoning, an instant where much fell apart but perhaps even more was mended. She placed her hands where Daniel's feet rested underneath the covers, her head bowed in anguish, and his hands traveled to her head.

"Mother," Daniel said to Rena's utter shock. Her hands were covering her open mouth.

"I am sorry," Mom sobbed, her back shuddering. "I am so sorry," she kept repeating.

Daniel leaned his fragile body forward, his tears falling over Mom's hair.

"Could someone please explain to me what's going on?" Rena finally said.

I looked at her through a screen of my own tears and said, "This is Daniel, our brother. Someone to, perhaps, one day stand up for you. But until then, we must stand up for him."

Seven textbooks and five notebooks towered high on the kitchen table. Some were closed, others open, with pencils and markers scattered about. It was a quiet, sunny Monday morning and everyone but me was asleep. But in truth, none of us had slept much that night. We stayed up talking, mostly me describing the rescue story to Mom and Rena, in whose eyes I had grown to the stature of a heroine.

After we broke up to let Daniel rest in my bed, I curled up on the living room sofa, but regardless of how tired I was my restless mind would not let me sleep. So instead of trying to force myself, I abandoned my blanket cocoon and settled in the kitchen to at least try to catch up on my studies. My progress was scant.

Unable to bear rereading the same paragraph for the umpteenth time, I closed the textbook and tiptoed toward my room. Standing in the hallway, I peeked though the crack in the door and smiled. Daniel was sleeping on my bed, the pale rays of the sun skimming over his face.

I heard a commotion behind me and turned around. Mom appeared in the doorway tying the belt of her rope around her waist. Her face was raw from her earlier outpouring of emotions, and eyes tired, but her countenance had visibly shifted and she appeared less burdened though somewhat disoriented.

"Coffee?" I asked, and she nodded.

Mom sat down at the table and rubbed her face with her hands, as if to clean away something obstructing her view.

"How did you sleep?" I asked, scooping coffee into a filter. "Did you sleep at all?"

"Hardly. You?"

I pointed toward the pile of textbooks, "I've been trying to catch up. Not easy, given the circumstance."

"This must be very disturbing to you. I'm sorry."

"Must be much harder for you," I said.

Mom sighed. "So much is coming out at once. So much has been repressed," she rubbed her forehead.

"I'm amazed you managed to hold it inside for this long."

"You know, when something terrible happens to you, you try to forget. It may sound selfish to everyone outside, but that was the only way I could cope."

"Terrible? What happened, Mom?"

Just then Mom wrapped her arms around her waist and began to bawl.

"Oh, Mom! I'm sorry, Mom."

She sniffed and sobbed, "I just feel like I'm coming completely undone. My world is shattered. I feel like I'm drowning in this welter of joy and sorrow. It's like I don't know who I am anymore. I don't know how to handle so much at once. So much guilt and grief. It is all coming out. And I can't stop it. And yet, I am so grateful, so profoundly grateful for what you have done. I've carried this deep loss for so long, it had become a part me, coloring everything."

"It's okay, Mom. It is good to feel all those things, to let them out."

"But how can those things be good? I feel like hell is consuming me, like some terrible form of punishment is imminent."

"What are you talking about, Mom? You've been punished long enough. This is the release; this is the beginning of truth and the end of a nightmare. Can't you see?"

Mom wiped her swollen eyes with the sleeve of her robe. "I just had a dream. I was burning alive and falling into a dark pit. It must be hell, I'm sure of it. Like I'm being punished for abandoning my child. I've wasted so much time . . . so much time."

"You dreamt of falling into a pit?" I asked, tightening my grip around the thread that I all too well recognized. I was eager to find out more about her own relationship with the angelic force. Mom, after all, was a direct recipient of something I myself was hurtling toward, bearing a tangible fruit of the forbidden union in this very lifetime. Did Mom remember what had happened to her the night she conceived her son? Based on what she just said, she'd rather not remember.

Mom blew her nose into a kitchen towel I handed her and looked at me with a crooked smile. She seemed a little calmer.

"Good thing it was only a dream," she forced a smile.

But after a moment of silence and me staring at her,

a new wave of sobs shook her shoulders. "There was some presence there, something I cannot define. It existed beyond a wall I couldn't penetrate. And there was all this pain and something else, something forbidden waiting for me there. Something that promised to take away all this pain. I want to touch it and know it, but part of me believes that if I do so," she looked up at me, "I will die."

"Mom, is this the first time you've had this dream?"

"No, I think I've had it at least once before. But I can't remember when. It might be one of those recurring nightmares."

I got up to pour us coffee and handed her a cup. I was convinced that in her dreams Mom was skimming the surface of her repressed memories of the angel.

"Mom," I began, sitting across from her and taking her hand in mine. Since Daniel and Rena were still sleeping, I used the opportunity of being alone with her to ask the ultimate question. There was no time to waste. I needed to quickly decide if it was safe for me to let Sariel come inside my world. "Ever since meeting Daniel and learning that he's my brother, I've been wondering about his father. I assume it wasn't Dad."

"I don't remember who it was," she said, her facial expression blank, eyes distant. "And I am glad, because I'd rather not know. It was a terrible accident and you shouldn't concern yourself with that. It is enough you found Daniel. We need to focus on him now and forget everything else."

"Were you forced to forget? Did Grandpa help you?"

"Evelina, stop, please!"

"I just don't understand how you can't remember!" I raised my voice. "Or why you don't want to tell me. Haven't I proven to you that I can handle a lot?"

"I don't want to talk about it."

"Why not?"

"Because I was raped!" Mom shouted and we both went quiet, the echo of her statement dispersing in space. The angel was sounding more sinister by the second. Rape was not something that was ever even implied in my interactions with Sariel. That's unless my angel had deceived me or Mom's memory was skewed.

"Raped?" I whispered.

"I can't believe I'm telling you this," she said and looked at me. "But maybe it is best you find out sooner rather than later."

"What happened, Mom?" I asked, fear creeping into my mind. Could the angel be that cruel? Why would he inflict so much pain on an innocent girl? It made me see Sariel in a different light, and I didn't like it.

"It was like being under a spell. I was lured. It is all that I can recall."

"And what happened after?"

"He found me in a meadow that night. I was asleep on the grass under the stars, my father said. He tried to wake me up, but I had fallen unconscious and remained asleep for many days. And then one day I found out I was pregnant. Father tried to purge the baby with herbs, but it was too strong. "

"And all this was happening while Dad was courting you?"

Mom nodded. So I got that part right. "My parents were adamant that I give up the baby or otherwise I would lose your father and likely never have a husband or a normal life."

"And you agreed?"

"Not initially. I wanted to keep the baby. Every mother does. And then my father took me away. A vacation, he said, to help me rest. But when we got to the mountain cabin, I was slowly becoming convinced that he was right and I needed to let this baby go. I was too young to care for him. The pregnancy was very difficult and nearly cost me my life. Father had to cut up my belly before he was due. He said I would've died from too much bleeding had I waited for the labor. The baby would've been to big."

"Soon after Daniel was born, he drove us to a local orphanage. My heart broke that day." I could tell that it was getting harder for Mom to speak. "That's the whole story. Now you know."

"But do you recall what it was that led to the meadow?"

Mom shook her head. "No but my father later told

me that the encounter was so traumatic, it deeply affected my psyche and distorted my memories."

I nodded, absorbing her words, but I was getting a strong impression that there was much more to the story. I could sense it. I wanted to show her Daniel's journal and Grandpa's drawing to help evoke earlier memories, but having already brought her to the edge of a nervous breakdown with my inquiring, I decided against it. Instead, I leaned in closer and hugged her.

That afternoon, Mom had our family doctor come to the house to check on Daniel. The doctor recommended running tests, which in conjunction with shopping for new wardrobe and rearranging furniture to welcome Daniel into our home, preoccupied Mom to the point where she didn't even notice that Rena stopped coming home. When one afternoon, freshly from school, I entered our empty house, I decided to go downstairs to check if she was there. This time her room was much tidier than mine and for a good reason. Most of Rena's things were gone, her desk empty save a handwritten note simply stating that she had moved in with Dad.

The news devastated Mom. She couldn't reach Rena as she lacked Dad's new phone number, so she wanted to try to find her at school. But I advised her against it. "Let her be," I said to Mom. "This is her way of coping. She will come around when she's ready." Mom eventually conceded and started to seek my guidance in other matters as well, like asking me how she should break the news about Daniel to her own parents. I could see she was frightened of them. But I could only tell her what Uri and Daniel had taught me—that she'd need to go within herself to find what felt right.

During his first days with us, Daniel remained introverted and soft-spoken. He often sought solitude. This was a different side of Daniel than the one I saw the day I had met him. Back then there was urgency in his communication with me; a burning desire to share that must arise in those who are facing their imminent mortality, perhaps similar to the impulse that had prompted Grandpa to share with me his shamanic past.

The Daniel who had come home was obscure and mysterious. Maybe his withdrawal was Daniel's attempt to find himself again? Despite the still cold temperatures, each morning and evening he'd go outside to be in nature, politely declining Mom's proposals to join him. But the more I watched him, the more I had the growing sense that rather than abate, something within him was mounting, some invisible force gaining momentum, and he was protecting it from the outside world.

Much like Daniel did at home, I became more introverted at school. Alienated from most people, my social world had become a desert. Ben seemed to have vanished from the face of the Earth, Art had moved away north again, and Rock was, well, I didn't know where Rock was. After everything I had gone through with Uri and Daniel, casual conversations didn't excite me. Still, part of me craved company and variety. So when one day a classmate invited me to Kal's party, I made sure to get all the details.

XXV.

Standing in the foyer outside my grandparents' front door on a Friday afternoon, Mom was visibly shaken. She had dreaded this day but delaying the inevitable was like trying to keep a lid over a boiling pot. Mom lifted her hand and knocked on the door. Daniel stood next to her, his head bowed, hands in his pockets. He looked very handsome sporting a new pair of jeans, a clean shirt, and a secondhand jacket. As usual I dressed in black feet to neck, I stood in between them and slightly behind, eager to witness the coming reactions that would reveal information about my family's past.

Grandma opened the door and upon seeing Daniel, her carefree smile quickly contorted into a look of surprise. Before a single word was spoken, Mom's demeanor was seething with defensiveness. She became a she-bear, ready to annihilate anyone who would dare to hurt her young.

"Come in," Grandma beckoned, strange ambivalence in her voice. The kitchen was all steamed up with the food percolating on the stove. Grandpa sat in a chair at the table and looked directly at us. But, contrary to his spouse, his face did not betray even a hint of stupefaction. It seemed as if he was expecting Daniel's arrival. He stood up and to my surprise, approached Daniel and embraced him with open arms. In that very moment, Mom broke down and Grandma turned to her daughter to serve as a shoulder for her to cry on. "It's okay now, it's okay," she kept patting Mom's shoulder.

Despite the outpouring of affection, the atmosphere in the kitchen seemed charged. Everything within me protested as I watched Daniel sway in Grandpa's arms and Mom receive her consolation. I felt angry, unable to accept the fact that years of unfathomable anguish could be pacified so easily with a hug and a few pats on the back.

"Why did you deny meeting Daniel in the hospital?" I asked Grandpa. Grandma looked at me, as if I had just accused her husband of killing someone, but I only called Grandpa out on one of his untruths.

He released Daniel and looked at me, his eyebrows

drawn. "I didn't deny anything," he said coolly. "You asked me why I cried and I answered, 'children.' Remember?"

In that moment, I knew I would not be staying for dinner. "You keep covering up the truth! You wept because you felt guilty. You knew he had found you."

"Evelina!" Grandma shouted, but I ignored her.

"Even after you came home you didn't tell us about Daniel. You kept it a secret from us, silently denying his existence."

"What? Is that true?" Mom asked.

"Mom! Can't you see this family has been brewing in a cauldron of lies? No wonder it has fallen apart."

"This is not as simple as you think," Grandpa said in a waspish tone.

I looked at Mom. "This is the true reason Dad left. He couldn't take *this* anymore, or your constant self-loathing."

"Evelina, stop!" Grandpa roared, his post-surgical voice shaking the windowpanes. The kitchen fell silent before he spoke again. "You wanted the truth, you got it," he said, a long wheeze following. "Give it a rest now. Everyone has suffered enough."

Daniel looked like he could faint at any moment, the storm raging in the kitchen too volatile for his battered soul.

But inside me a volcano was about to burst. Weeks of stifled questions and pent up frustration had reached a saturation point. I forced myself to speak calmly.

"I will give it a rest once I understand why you left Daniel." I looked at all the faces around me. Daniel was shaking his head, as if asking me to stop before things went too far. But I couldn't stop now. I needed to drive it to the end. "And why all these years you have hidden from your own daughter his father's true identity."

"Evelina, compose yourself right now!" Grandma intervened, but I continued.

"All I want—all I've ever wanted—was for you to tell me the truth," I said through tears. "But I keep feeling like you are constantly hiding something and I can't understand why. Is it so bad to want to know?"

At that point, I didn't even care about what he would say. Seeing Daniel's pleading eyes not to say anymore, I felt alone and inept. I wanted to get out of that place and run away as far as I could, and straight into Sariel's arms.

"Sit down, Evelina," Grandpa ordered with thunder, and I did as he said. His stature seemed to double in size and he exuded a power I rarely witnessed. "I wanted to teach you, tell you everything I could, in time. But you've been moving at your own speed. While I do believe that there is a time and place for a man to interfere with the order of nature, more often things are better left to the command of higher powers much more intelligent than we can ever be."

"It sounds like you'd prefer we lived in perpetual ignorance," I said quietly.

"You know you've crossed a line, young lady, and I don't only mean the demeanor in which you speak."

To everyone's surprise, I stood up and faced my grandfather, pointing my finger straight at his chest. "You are right. I have crossed the line. And I am glad I did. Because he is the only one left who cares about how I feel. He had found me and I will not turn away from his call."

"They are not what you think," I saw lightning in Grandpa's wary eyes. "And you don't realize what you have done. This will trail you for the rest of your life."

"Why?"

"Because they are hunters. Destroyers of youth and innocence."

"Jesus! God! Help us," Grandpa called toward the ceiling. Daniel was pacing nervously until he stopped by the window and stood there looking out and balling his fists. Mom was standing with her arms folded over her chest, a horrified look on her face. Every few words, her hand would travel to her forehead, as if experiencing flashes of remembrance.

"How do you know that?" I asked.

"I know, and that fact should suffice. I don't want to hear another word."

"That is not enough of an answer," I said, moving closer to the door. Grandma was moaning.

"Don't do this," Grandpa said. Lightning was

crackling inside of his irises. I could see a powerful energy well up within him and did not want to be a recipient of the coming thunder. I placed my hand on the doorknob. "He's a wolf in sheep's clothing. Not what you think," Grandpa added.

"I don't believe you," I said, and stepped into the foyer. "I know there is more you are not telling me. And since you deny me the truth, I'll just have to ask him directly," I shut the doors, and fled down the stairs and onto the streets, Sariel's name on my lips.

XXVI.

It was drizzling when I entered the cold winter night. I ran splashing through puddles, battling air currents that pushed against me. By the time I got home, I was faint from exhaustion and the effort it took to keep my thoughts at bay. I was growing a suspicion that the angel in Grandpa's drawing was a representation of Daniel's father, and that he feared that through my interaction with Sariel I would end up replicating Mom's fate.

I entered my house, kicked off my boots, and wobbling on my achy feet fell onto my mattress, my head spinning. The walls echoed back my thoughts. Why was everything such a struggle? Didn't he see that I all I wanted was to help restore the equilibrium? Or was I going mad again? The succession of thoughts gave rise to a deluge of emotions. I turned over and screamed into my pillow, letting my tears soak the sheets and cleanse my body like a torrent of rain. If I wanted to see Sariel again, I needed to do something now before my grandfather had a chance to stop me.

I wiped my face, sat up on my bed and took a deep breath, trying to think. I was home alone, but I could pick up a certain residue of something or someone's fleeting presence. That's when I noticed a huge plastic bag on my desk. How could I have missed it?

Crawling off the mattress on my hands and knees, I reached out my hand for the sack, pulling it down the way a child yanks down a toy from a shelf. I didn't expect it to be so heavy. It rattled and fell onto the floor with a crash. I jolted, aware that I may have broken or at least damaged what was inside. My impatient hands ran across the plastic surface searching for the opening. Finally, I tore the bag open, and peeked inside. All the tapes I had thrown away and thought I'd never see again, all my music that I thought I'd lost was there. My mood experienced an instant uplift. I searched around my desk until I found a note that read: *Miss you, R.* My sister never ceased to amaze me.

Outside, it stopped raining but dark clouds continued

to obstruct the setting sun. I turned on the lights and got startled by the mess in my room. Rolling up my sleeves, I brought in the vacuum and began going through everything, bookshelves to windowsills. My shelves went from disheveled to spotless, all items rearranged into aesthetic tidiness, tapes put back in their rightful place. Clothes were refolded and rehung according to varying shades of blackness.

Wiping my brow, I let the eye-pleasing symmetry penetrate my mind. And by the time I stood under a warm shower, thinking of which tape I wanted to listen to first, my mind was ready to receive new visions. The next full moon was only two days away. I didn't want to miss a chance. I wanted to draw him in, push against any opposing forces grandfather could have unleashed.

Cleansed and dressed in a dry pair of black leggings and a T-shirt, I lit a candle and placed it on top of my wardrobe for its light to fill distant corners. My space sparkled from all the care I'd given it. I dropped a cassette into my boombox, pressed play and before the first notes sounded out of the speaker, I was supine on my bed, curling my toes, ready for the melancholy melodies to set off my imagination.

I landed inside of an old gothic cathedral alight with the radiance of a hundred burning candelabras. The flames bounced off the gold-accented rims of paintings and altarpieces, puffs of myrrh smoke wafted through air, the echo of my footsteps traveling to the main altar where he stood waiting for me. Dressed in a red satin dress, I glided down the long walkway of the nave, from the narthex to the altar, carrying a bouquet of white lilies. As I approached, the closer I came to the angel's tall figure, the air between us grew denser and warmer, pressing on me from all directions. But I kept on, the thick air not affecting my resolve.

"Is it true this love will only bring me pain?" I asked and reached out my hand, but my fingertips encountered an obstacle; the barrier of air solidified into a pane of glass. "Sariel!" I cried. "Why can't I get through?"

"They won't allow it," he said, the sound of his voice

vibrating the pane.

"Who won't allow it?"

"Your ancestors. They believe I want to hurt you."

"Do you? This is what I need to know."

Sariel approached the glass from the other side and placed his palm, nearly twice the size of mine, on the pane. I looked into his glowing eyes that looked at me from beneath black, arched brows, like wings of a bird in flight. His hair was loose, falling over his shoulders and sparked like coal. His skin was pale, exposing multiple scars. My eyes skimmed his nose and stopped on the lips that looked dry and cracked and in need of a kiss.

He opened his mouth to speak. "All I want is to feel your love. I can't get enough of it. It is the only thing that keeps my spirit alive this long."

I dropped my bouquet to the ground and pounded my fists on the glass, igniting sparks over its surface. "Why can't they just leave us alone?" A rumbling thunder roared inside the cathedral shaking its foundations.

"It's against the law. But you can break it."

"How?"

"By surrendering yourself to me," he said.

"Will that make you cross into my world?" I asked, my heart filling with hope.

Sariel shook his head. "The only way is for you to cross into mine."

"But how?"

Sariel remained silent until I comprehended what he meant. Death. The only way I could cross into his realm was by leaving mine. All the warnings I had received along the way were screaming inside my head at once.

"I am scared, Sariel," I whispered. "I want you more than anything and yet I'm now terrified of your words and their meaning." My legs grew weak and my hands were starting to slide down the glass. I collapsed to the ground, the white lilies already decaying at my feet. "I thought you wanted me to free you."

"You did. You transformed me from a cold image—a thought buried within the collective memory, into a living being. Though I shall remain cursed in my loneliness."

"I'm so sorry, Sariel, I don't know what else to do. What can I do?" I asked. Part of me regretted this sobering encounter and wished I had remained in blissful ignorance, daydreaming about my angel, feeding my old desire to escape the mundane.

"Shatter this pane and stay with me." A wind blew across the nave, tousling the feathers behind his shoulders. I felt an instant implosion within my belly that yearned for surrender. "I met you in your temple. Do you remember that day?" he asked.

"The memories are returning," I said and stood up, placing my hands back on the glass. Next to his towering stature, I felt so small and fragile. Sariel reached his hands toward my face. His eyes ignited with light. I was no longer merely besotted with him. I was in love.

"I had never felt more pleasure sharing myself with anyone," Sariel said, "the way I did with you."

"And I had never felt more pleasure than when I shared my warmth with you."

"Ninsal . . . you were always so hungry to know all the secrets of the universe. For so long your desires have been denied."

"What happened to us? Why were you taken away from me?"

"Close your eyes," he whispered, "and you will see." A cool breeze skimmed my forehead. I blinked and looked around.

Sariel and I stood on the banks of the frozen lake high up in the mountains, no more barriers between us. He reached his arms to greet me and I leaned into him, his wings forming a protective shield around me. I was no longer Evelina. I was Ninsal, the earthly priestess in love with an angel.

"This will be the last time we meet," Sariel said to me. "I received my sentence for transgressing the immutable law," he said. "I must leave and will not be coming back."

I moved away and looked into Sariel's eyes. "Where must you go?"

"Away from the Earth," he said, and I could sense

a hint of fear in his countenance. I'd never seen him afraid before.

I looked down and rubbed my round belly. "I won't go back to the temple," I cried. "It is no longer my home. The priestesses have been taken to the king's castle as prisoners."

Sariel took my face in his hands. "Take me with you," I said to him.

"Where I must go, dear Ninsal, you could not survive."

"I'd rather die than go on without you."

Sariel found a place for us away from the lake under a solitary tree. There he took off his long cape and set it down on the ground. We knew we were only delaying the inevitable but every moment was precious. We settled beneath the tree, embracing until night befell the cold mountain valley.

"Look up," Sariel gestured at the full moon.

I opened my eyes to see the moon's face crowned by a pale arc of stars. Just then an intense stab pierced my body. I folded in half and moaned. "Sariel, I think it is time. . . . The child."

He tried everything to save me. He offered his heat and whispered magical words of love. But the baby could not be delivered without me passing away. I bled and bled until the snow around me was tinted with crimson and my vision faded away.

"Last time you died in my arms. I don't want the same fate to befall you twice," Sariel's voice brought me back to the cathedral.

"What happened to the child?"

"He became a warrior who united with others of his kind. Together they formed the first nation of the Nephilim."

"And what happened to you? Where did you go?"

He smiled at me with tenderness. "Look up."

The cathedral did not have a roof. Past the rugged edges of the building that had collapsed under the weight of time, was the black expanse of the night sky. Directly above our heads I saw the glowing face of the moon.

"I've been watching you for a long time Ninsal."

"My faithful companion," I whispered.

"Tartarus," Sariel said. As he spoke, a rock fell from

the edge of a roof and shattered by the altar.

"What's happening, Sariel?"

"They are coming to shut the door between us. You need to make a choice."

The cathedral was crumbling before my eyes. "Sariel, I can't," I said, watching all the gold in the altar turn to lackluster stone. The more it came undone, the more it resembled the ruined castle I once visited with my friends. Another stone fell to the ground, rattling its foundations.

"Come with me, Ninsal," Sariel said, and opened his wings and arms. A gust of wind swept the space.

"But what if I cannot become her?" I said. "I am Evelina now, not Ninsal. She is dead." I noticed that his body was starting to dissolve.

"Her memory lives within you," he said. "You can bring her back. Or forget I had ever existed."

"Sariel, please don't go yet. I am not ready to let you go! And I am not ready to die. Please, let me see you again."

"The shaman will not allow it," Sariel said through the rumble of a wall that collapsed behind him. He was becoming a shadow.

"Doesn't he owe you his life?" I asked. "Didn't you save him from death?"

His image was but a faint afterglow when he answered. "It was Ramiel, the angel of truth and thunder."

My hands traveled to my face. It, as well as my hair and the pillow, were drenched in tears. I felt dizzy and emotionally spent. I lifted myself on my elbows. The tape had long stopped playing, and the candle flame was jumping, pulling the halo with it. "I will not let you go just yet," I whispered, but to my great distress I noticed I was quickly forgetting what Sariel looked like. All I could recall was his immense stature and burning eyes.

The outside was pitch dark and I felt cold and lonely, suddenly missing Mom, Rena, Daniel, and even Dad. I went into the living room to look for my brother but he was still not home, so I poked my head into Mom's bedroom. She was in her bed sound asleep. I approached her bed.

"Ramiel," I spoke the name of the angel into her ear. Was he the one who conceived Daniel? I wondered, closing the door to her bedroom.

I stumbled back into my room, grief stymieing my motion, seeping the life force from my cells. The void Sariel's departure left radiated cold emptiness. Lying down on my mattress, I curled up on my side and closed my eyes, wishing for sleep to come quick so that I didn't drown myself in loss. After months of Sariel's presence filling my life with mystery and magic, it was hard to imagine that it would all end this way and I would never see him again. I contorted into a tiny ball, trying to shut off the pain.

"Uriel, please come back. I need your key."

XXVII

Having barely slept that night, I glided into the kitchen like a zombie, finding Mom bent over the kitchen sink washing dishes, soap foam up to her elbows. Upon seeing her face, it became evident that I wasn't the only one suffering from a lack of rest.

"Good morning," I said, plopping onto a chair and rubbed my face. "Is there any coffee?" She nodded and pointed with her head toward the drip. "Where is Daniel?"

"Stayed at Grandpa's last night."

"Did you have a nice dinner?"

Mom looked at me, shaking the water off her hands. "What do you think?"

"Sorry, Mom."

"No need," she said, but her voice betrayed her.

"I just don't understand all this secrecy."

"There is no secrecy," she said. "I already told you everything I know. It is us who don't understand your motives. What you are trying to get at?"

"Same thing as always, Mom." I looked pointedly at her. "Plain truth."

"You want the truth? Then let me ask you to share some with me," she said, wiping her hands with a towel. "Have you been practicing black magic?"

"Oh Mom, what in the world did Grandpa tell you?"

"He said you've been experimenting with dangerous things."

"Like what?"

"Like some form of sorcery."

"Mom, listen. I got a book of spells from Ben once, but I gave it back. I swear, I never conducted a single ritual in it."

"He said he's been trying to teach you how to protect yourself. But apparently you've been conjuring spirits on your own. Do you realize the danger of that? Do you realize what you may have exposed yourself to?"

"No, Mom, you got it all backwards. I didn't conjure

anything. I had only answered a call," I said in my defense. I didn't understand why Grandpa would say such things to Mom. And if me practicing black magic was the conclusion of the discussion they had after I had left, then the hurt was double because obviously Daniel did not volunteer to straighten the facts. It made me feel very alone again.

"Who are you talking about? Who called to you?" Mom asked.

I swallowed. My noble quest was turning my life into a living pandemonium. Here I was again, tethering on the edge of revelation and insanity. Could the pursuit of truth make one crazy? Mom's brain was probably wrapped in layers of stories Grandpa had told her. He had the advantage of really knowing what had happened; I was still lost in the maze.

"An angel, Mom." A deep crease in Mom's forehead relaxed. It seemed as if a flash of recollection ignited in her mind, so I quickly added, "And I have my reasons to believe that the same thing happened to you before you had Daniel."

Mom's eyes skimmed across the floor.

"Does the name Ramiel sound familiar?" I asked. But the wrinkle between her brows was back and she looked at me.

"What are you insinuating? That my pregnancy was the result of some angelic intervention?"

"I don't know for sure. You see, this is what I've been trying to figure out and why I need you to try to remember what happened. And once the truth is out, Grandpa won't be able to hide it from us anymore. Then all of us, including Daniel, can give it a rest, because then we will know, and Daniel will reclaim the second half of his origin—"

"Eve," Mom said, approaching me. She squatted next to me and put her hand on my lap. "Baby, it's not what you think. You are mistaking fact for fantasy. I appreciate you trying to romanticize the past but the past is painful and you need to let it go before you involve yourself too deep in my story."

I tried to say something but my words failed me. I was back to pushing rocks up a hill. I looked away, feeling the urge to leave the house. The walls were pressing down on me from each direction.

"Eve, look at me," Mom said. I did so, but my eyes were blurry with rage and disappointment. "What happened twenty years ago is not something I want to analyze. I was raped. Believe me, if something like this happens to a person, they want to forget and move on." Mom squeezed my hand. "Please, Eve. Help me do that. Help me forget."

I stood under the shower, the rush of hot water muffling my groans, my insides contorting in protest. Either Mom was brainwashed or I was operating under a spell. Which was true? Should I swallow my pride, go back to Grandpa and beg him to talk to me? I intuited that no matter how mature I would make myself sound, he would stick to his story. Grandpa would not open up to me. I grunted and left the shower. In my my room, put on the heaviest piece of music I could find, cranked up the volume and got dressed for Kal's party. I had to get out of the house. It was making me claustrophobic.

Kal's garage was empty. Probably because I was too early. Inside, crackling sound seeped out of an amp in the corner of the room, and a small heater exhaled its orange heat, breathing scant warmth into the chilly space. I walked outside through the back door, and into Kal's orchard bathed in twilight. Above my head a vortex of a sinister mass was brewing in the partly overcast sky. The air was moist and unusually warm, the evening light taking on sepia tones. I longed to see the stars.

"Look who's here," I saw Crass emerge from behind a tree, exhaling a plume of smoke. "Want one?" he offered me a spare cigarette he pulled from behind his ear.

"Sure. Thanks," I said, and he lit it off his own. The filter was wet where his mouth had touched it. "Are you the only one here?"

"They left to get the booze. I'm holding down the fort," he coughed and spat. "So what's new, temptress?"

"Temptress?"

"You don't get it do you?" he said, spraying more saliva from between his teeth.

"I guess I don't," I said, and took a drag. The cigarette tasted nasty, but I didn't want to offend Crass by throwing it out, so I kept holding it between my fingers. At least it gave me something to do with my hands.

"It's like a veil of smoke around you, all sweet and musty," he said, tracing an outline around my body with his hands. "Smells fucking delicious," he said, making me look away.

I heard a peal of raucous voices coming from the street and glanced behind me with relief. "They're back," I said in an effort to diffuse some of the tension, dropped the cigarette, and went inside the garage.

Grabbing a spot in the corner with a bottle of beer in my hand, I reclined my back against the wall, watching as people trickled in. Soon I was catching up on town gossip and learning about new bands that had recently popped onto the metal scene. But Sariel kept coming into my mind, making me miss a lot of what was said. Finally, it dawned at me. What if the whole struggle between what I heard from Grandpa and what I felt for Sariel was a test of my will? There could be no test without opposites! The tenderness with which he spoke to me, the way he held me, were in such stark contrast to what Grandpa would have me believe. It had to be a test.

I needed to see Sariel again to tell him he had my allegiance. We belonged together and nothing could change that. And if what he said to me was true, we would find a way to be together somewhere, somehow.

I dumped my empty bottle into a makeshift trashcan, spotted Crass taking shots across the space, and pulled him outside to come smoke with me.

"What do you know about magic?" I asked, after he offered his light. It was completely dark outside.

"Depends what kind."

"Don't know. Any kind. How many are there?"

"Many. But for me, the darker, the better," he grinned.

"Black magic then," I said. "Do you practice it?"

"You bet. C'mon, you saw. Don't play dumb."

A vision of the hung cat flashed across my mind. "You're not afraid of something bad happening to you after?"

I asked, taking a drag. Another nasty smoke. Or maybe I was losing my taste for it.

"Like what?" he seemed confused.

"Like a swarm of demons descending upon your bed at night?"

Crass laughed. "That would be a dream. Why? What's your deal with black magic?"

"I'm trying to contact a spirit."

"A ghost?" he asked, but I shook my head. "A demon?" Crass arched his brows and smiled.

"A fallen angel," I said, shaking off the ash. "Could you help me do that?"

Crass squinted his eyes at me. A chill ran down my spine but I didn't give in to fear. He brought his face closer to mine, but I didn't withdraw.

"Maybe I could," his smoky breath pushed the hair off my face. "In fact, invocation is my specialty," he neared his mouth to the crease of my neck, making all the little hairs stand upright. "The sacrifice you saw was for them."

"Is this why you killed that animal?"

"Believe me, it made them very happy." Crass slid his hands into his pockets and with a head gesture pushed the bangs off his eyes. "When?"

"Soon," I said, too overwhelmed by what I had just heard.

"You know where I live," Crass said, spat, and vanished inside Kal's garage.

I didn't follow him in. Instead, I decided to go straight home, thinking of how strange it was that creepy characters like Crass were more eager to help me than the good people I loved and wanted to trust. Crass was a gamble. I didn't so much doubt his abilities but the intent behind them. But I had to see Sariel again at least to discern once and for all what was truth and what manipulation. And with is young warlock power, Crass could help me break through the barrier.

To get back home, I took the shortcut that led through unlit back roads and farm fields. I was alone in the desolate night, so I quickened my step. My eyes travelled up toward the sky. In front of me drifted the nearly full moon, most of which was obscured by clouds.

"I can barely remember your face. Have I lost you already?" I whipped.

I stopped in the middle of the road, closed my eyes and stretched out my arms. The birch trees that grew alongside the road rustled in the night breeze. The air smelled of moisture and earth. Keeping my eyes closed, I imagined the energy of the moon enter through the crown of my head. At once I felt clearer and empowered. I opened my eyes just as the clouds parted.

"Thank you," I whispered. "Tomorrow I shall open the gates."

XXVIII.

I awakened with a growling stomach but no appetite. All night I kept going back and forth trying to decide between two options: surrender to Grandpa's safe guidance or follow my own precarious path.

I walked into the kitchen. The house was quiet and a note was waiting for me on the dining table. It was from Mom. She went to my grandparents' apartment to fetch Daniel. Under an inverted bowl, Mom had left me a plate of scrambled eggs, but they didn't look very appealing. Instead, I made myself tea, feeling a particular desire for lemon. I ended up squeezing three whole ones into a pitcher. Sitting down on the table and sipping the tart drink, I put together a rough plan of my day. I knew that engaging Crass in my ritual carried a risk, but thanks to the moon's energy I had received last night, I felt a certain power. I took it at Sariel's way of calling me home. All I needed Crass for was the invocation.

I looked at the clock. It was almost noon. I tidied up my room, got dressed, and went outside to think some more and avoid bumping into Mom and Daniel, possibly even carrying grandfather's reprimands.

The neighborhood was quiet, most people attending the Sunday mass. Two ravens circled the network of streets. The trees were naked, with nascent spring blooms poking out of their branches. Passing through my backyard, I aimed for the river. Halfway there I needed to take off my jacket. The sun was bright and the temperatures quite warm for March. The air smelled of fecund earth. In eight days, I would be turning sixteen. It would be the first time that I had no plans for my birthday. By the time I paused at the riverbank, I was down to my black short-sleeved top. The day was serene and nature was beginning to awaken after months of slumber. Making a pillow out of my jacket, I laid down on a patch of moss, letting the sun caress my face in splashes of light that streamed between braches. I felt profoundly alone in my quest.

Perhaps this was, after all, the way things were. Paths

244

to truth had room for only one traveler.

I must have fallen asleep for some time. When I finally awakened, the sun was much lower. I was hungry, but I did not want to go home to eat, as surely Mom and Daniel were already back. Instead, I followed the banks of the river southward, the direction of a neighboring house development where Crass' family lived.

Crass' house stood at the very end of a narrow street and faced the river. His parents had taken over the uninhabited plot of land on its banks and had made it into a vegetable garden. Years ago, I'd see their hunched bodies working the land on the days when I'd venture too far in that direction, picking flowers for Mom. They struck me as hardworking, quiet people who mostly kept to themselves.

When I approached, Crass was in the garden, freshly plowed for sowing, smoking a cigarette, his head toward the rushing body of water. He was wearing a black long sleeve shirt with a white pentagram on the front with a skull in the middle. His hair was tied at the nape of his neck. He looked like he was expecting someone. The thought was both exciting and scary. I wavered. This was my last chance to turn around. But the only other option was to relent and submit to the will of others. I took a step forward and cleared my throat. Crass looked in my direction and dropped the butt to the ground. He waited for me to walk up to him.

"Follow me," he said and turned toward his house.

We passed the open gate in the fence and I caught a glare of television screen through one window. We skirted the decaying rose garden and walked upon a smaller unit behind the main house. The door to his room was left partly open. Entering after Crass, I was taken aback by the intense smell inside. It was a mixture of stale tobacco, incense, and something else, I couldn't tell. The walls in his room were painted black and covered with posters of metal bands, monsters, and creatures that looked like the living dead, with rotting flesh peeling off their glistening skulls.

"Your own private lair I see," I said, looking around.

"I call it my Hades," he murmured, rearranging a few objects on a low glass table that stood in the middle of the room. It was cluttered and covered in grime, which looked like dust and cigarette ash. On the edge, tied with a red ribbon, lay a bundle of dry chrysanthemums.

"Nice bouquet," I said.

"Fresh from the cemetery," he smiled at me. "Ready to take a walk on the wild side?"

I gulped the air. "I think so." Crass was starting to make me nervous.

"I need a definite answer," he added. "Maybe a little more enthusiasm, too?"

"Yes. I mean yes," I said, wary of Crass' persuasive powers.

"Good. Make yourself at home. I'll be right back," he said, and left the room.

After wrestling with it for a while, I managed to crack open the room's only window, which was in dire need of washing. Crass' interest in the occult was clear. I counted more candles in his room than we had ever had in my house. Most were half-molten, made of yellow or red wax, and scattered around the room, over shelves and stools, one of which stood next to Crass' unmade bed. His desk was encrusted in splashes of wax with symbols carved with a sharp object. On the floor, leaning against a wall, I counted a row of thirteen more candles. I looked up and saw the hand drawn image of a downcast pentagram on a fragment of a wall.

"My altar," Crass said, carrying two steaming cups in his hands. "Have a seat." He motioned to his bed, and set the cups on the table before locking the doors behind him, which must have led to the rest of his family's domicile.

"What's in them?" I pointed at the cups.

"A tea we will be having after I find the fucking lighter."

"Your pocket maybe?"

He reached into his pocket, pulling out the lighter. "Ha! Clever or clairvoyant?"

"Pure logic," I replied, watching him light every single candle in his room.
"Are you warm?" he asked, and I nodded. "Then take off your jacket."

I obeyed again, not wanting to offend, or worse anger, Crass. "How long is this . . . ceremony going to last?" I asked, setting my wool jacket next to me.

"You'll be playing hooky tomorrow," he said, kneeling next to the table and picking up the final unlit votive. "And likely will miss your Sunday supper with mommy and daddy." I told him that "daddy" was no more. "Whatever," he shrugged, and dug his fingers into the candle to retrieve its sunken wick.

"What are we going to do?"

"Curious, are we?" he said, pulling out the wick and lighting it up. "One thing I can guarantee," he held the flame to his face, deep creases lining his forehead, "is that you'll be on fire." Crass threw the lighter onto the bed and walked to his stereo to put on a heavy metallic tune.

In an effort to appear comfortable, I leaned back on my elbows over Crass' bed, and looked around for the tenth time, thinking. What would happen tonight? Would I manage to reach Sariel? In order to find him, I was willing to work with a young warlock. This was true devotion, I thought to myself.

Crass touched one of the teacups. "Okay, it should be cool enough now. Let's drink," he said, handing me one of them. "Bottoms up."

"This is not the first time you're doing this, I take it?" I asked, staring into the cup.

Crass glanced at me through a veil of steam and began to laugh. "Do I look like a novice to you?" he said and blinked. "Don't be afraid, have a sip."

The fact that he saw my fear was not a good sign.

"What's in it?" I asked.

"Magic."

I smelled the rising steam that hinted of sweet earth and fungus before dipping my tongue in it.

"This tea of yours tastes nasty," I said, experiencing an acidic aftertaste.

"You have to finish the cup if you want to see your fallen angel tonight. Drink up!" He came toward me and held the cup to my lips. "All the way. That's right," he said. I kept swallowing while making a sour face. For Sariel, I thought and that got me through. I blinked and a tear fell down my cheek.

"That bad, huh?" Crass laughed again. Once my cup was empty, Crass drank his in three loud gulps, wiped his mouth with a sleeve, and went outside to smoke. I sat on his bed twirling my fingers, feeling increasingly more out of place. But it was too late. The substance that would catalyze the visions was already inside me. Not wanting to face the rising guilt for having submitted to Crass' influence, I decided to join him outside.

He stood silently, looking toward the backyard of a neighboring house, its gray wall covered with climbing vines. Feeling slightly nauseous, I passed on a smoke and started to dig a hole in the ground with my boot.

"So what's next?" I asked to fill the void. "What do I do?"

"Nothing. It will happen by itself."

"What will happen?"

"The going deeper part," he said, shaking the ashes off his cigarette. "Until you find what you are after. Don't worry. I'll help you light the fuse."

I looked up at the twilight sky and got dizzy. I noticed that my hands were tingling and my stomach churning. The panorama in front of me jolted and began to shift. The trees, the stacked boxes by the fence, the wall with the vines—for a moment I couldn't tell which layer was closer and which was farther away from me. Lines began to vibrate and circular patterns spun around their center. I looked at Crass and noticed he had four eyes. I blinked and saw them overlap and become two again.

"You feelin' it?" Crass asked, the end of his cigarette sparkling like the end of a magic wand.

"I think I'm starting to see things." I said, clutching my stomach.

"You sick?"

"Yeah."

"That's normal. Soon you'll be flying."

"What exactly was in that drink?" I asked, watching a

cluster of transparent bubbles float through the air.

"Let's go inside." Crass extinguished his cigarette and led me back into his dark temple shutting the door behind him.

My legs bucked under me and I fell straight onto his bed. I closed my eyes and everything spun.

"I already told you, it's magic. The tea is full of magic," Crass said, positioning himself behind me, his hands clutching my waist. I could feel both of us shiver. Not knowing what to do or how to navigate my changing mind, I kept my attention on the music, which seemed to be coming from some place far away. Or straight from within me. I heard a whole new spectrum of tones outside the normal range. There were high treble sounds like chimes that invoked the image of stars, and bass melodies so low and deep they seemed to emanate from the earth's subterranean chambers. One song ended and another began. And then another. It felt as if it had been hours since I first laid down.

"When will I see him?" I muttered.

Crass stirred behind me. "After the blood is set free," he said out of nowhere. "Then he will come."

"What?" I opened my eyes, the blood in my veins curdling.

"Can't access the forbidden without a proper sacrifice," he said, lifting himself up and pressing my shoulder down to turn me onto my back. His ponytail had come undone, the loose tendrils of his hair falling toward me.

"Are you planning to kill another cat?" I squirmed. I wanted to get away from him, but Crass had me trapped underneath him. I felt like I was losing my grasp on reality. Trying to think, my thoughts were slipping like bare feet over ice.

"No, there is no need for that," he said. "It's a different kind of blood he wants," he intoned with a raspy voice. "Once it's set free, the gates will open," Crass said, slipping his hand underneath my shirt and bringing his face closer to mine.

"Stop!" I turned my face and tried to push away his hand. But he was too strong.

"C'mon. He's waiting. The fallen wants to

come through."

"No," I cried out, and shut my eyes.

But then something strange happened. Crass' body froze above me, becoming completely still. Slowly, I turned my head to look at him. His eyes were partly closed, exposing only the whites, a dim smile dawning on his face. I got a strange feeling that he wasn't here anymore. The more I looked at Crass' face, the more it seemed to be losing its substance until nothing but a milky haze remained. Out of that haze emerged two small flames.

"Ninsal," I heard him hiss.

"Sariel," I gasped, watching more of the angel's features come through. My lips parted and I opened inside, a surge of energy rushing from my belly down, like a river of nectar. I lifted my head and our mouths connected. My back arched and I felt myself falling through the sheets like clouds. Soon I was soaring like a bird; at last I knew what it felt like to fly. Sariel kissed me deeply. He tasted bitter, but it didn't matter. I finally had him in my arms. His lips traveled to my neck.

"Blood," he whispered into my ear. "I need your blood."

"Go ahead, take it," I said, and tilted my head back even farther.

Sariel's hands moved down to unbutton my pants. Just then something shot through me like a lightning bolt. *Evelina, no!* I heard Daniel's voice and opened my eyes. Instead of Sariel, I saw Crass hard at work to get me undressed.

"What are you doing?" I groaned, trying to push Crass away.

"Taking your offering," he said, and looked at me with bloodshot eyes. I shivered. "You're a virgin, right?"

"Get off of me!"

Crass' hair was covering my face and his hands moved swiftly like snakes, wrestling with my clothes in an effort to tear them off. I squeezed his wrist that was reaching in between my legs and redirected it to the side.

"Please stop," I called, but it was getting harder to resist him. Sariel had awakened a fever in my body and part of me wanted to surrender.

"This is going to be glorious," Crass sighed.

"Help me, Daniel," I said to myself, and kept fighting to regain control over my senses. What I used to think of as solid reality has completely liquefied, disintegrated and turned inside out. Images were fluctuating, juxtaposing, melting and congealing into new shapes, all in the blink of an eye.

But Crass was entranced as much as I was, if not more. So I tried another tactic—to move with him, instead of against him, all in an effort to find a way to slip out of his grasp. With my languid maneuvers, I managed to switch places with Crass and turn him on his back. Draping my body over his, I looked to the side. On his walls, the faces on the posters were coming out before retreating back, dissolving before reappearing again. They were demonic and grotesque, tongues lashing out, and vines growing between them, weaving everything into one seamless web. The doors seemed exceedingly far away. Crass' hands reached for my hips. I slowly peeled them off, rolled off him, and ambled toward the door.

"Come back," he called after me. "Come back to me."

"I need air," I said, opened the door and stepped outside taking in a lungful of cold air. I had left my jacket on his bed but I had no intent of turning around to get it. It was a small loss compared to what Crass was after.

I was in his garden now, not completely out of his reach but far away enough to free myself from his spell. The fresh air sobered me up, but not for long. There, too, a procession of visions crawled between foliage, with elves flying across the darkened sky, gnomes staring at me from beneath berry bushes, and snakes wriggling on the ground. The earth's veils had lifted, revealing another face full of eerie guises, a surreal spectacle.

"Come back," I heard Crass call through the open door of his room. I turned around and saw him crawling toward me.

XXIX.

It was completely dark now, and I was struggling to find my way. *Evelina, you must get away from there,* Daniel shouted inside my head. A tide of desire was still coursing through my veins, raising the temperature of my blood. A sweet, musky smell lingered about me—Crass' kiss. He could be right behind me but I didn't dare to turn. I walked fast, aiming toward the river. Soon I heard the rush of water and searched for the path that would take me home. When I found it, I broke into a run. But soon I was lost again. I stopped to listen, but instead of the trickling of water I heard voices and whispers. I looked around and saw lights popping around me, like glowing eyes or night creatures. Hallucinations, I thought. Which way? Daniel, help! I spun my body around, on the verge of panic. *This way,* I heard him and headed toward the lights, which turned out to be the glowing window lights of my neighbors' homes.

Stumbling, I ascended a small hill and entered the paved road of the cul-de-sac with the five houses, one of which belonged to my family. The lights in our kitchen were on. I looked up toward the blinking streetlamp, which had been on the verge of dying since November. The bulb flickered violently until it cracked and went out in smoke. Darkness descended over the street. I kept on until my eyes could discern a tall figure standing by the side of my house. I stopped, wary of being seen. But soon, my step quickened and before I knew it, I was running toward him.

"Daniel!" I called, falling into his arms. Upon contact, our bodies wrapped themselves into a tight knot and I knew that from this point on, I would never doubt him again.

"I've been looking everywhere for you," he said.

"I'm sorry."

"No, I am the one who is sorry. I should have stood up for you," he said and withdrew a little to look at me. "What happened to you?"

"It's been such a bizarre night," I said, reaching my hands toward my temples. "I feel like everything is out of control." The images around me were still shifting and I could see circles of light surrounding Daniel's head. "I tried to contact Sariel."

"You never give up, do you?"

"He did come through. But then the whole thing turned into a disaster."

"I'm sorry I abandoned you."

"No, it's not your fault. If Grandpa would only open up to me and hear me out, maybe I would listen to him more."

"He did."

"What?"

"Are you ready to hear his story?"

"He told you what happened?"

Daniel nodded and, catching a glimpse of a moving curtain, suggested we go inside and away from the eyes of peering neighbors.

"Is Mom home?" I asked, climbing the stairs.

"No, she's with her father. It's her turn to hear it."

I couldn't believe my ears. Grandpa was speaking to Mom!

"Tea?" Daniel asked as I sat down at the table.

"No, I'd rather not. I think I need a break from tea," I said, wincing at the memory of the pungent taste of the drink Crass had given me. I told Daniel about it, sparing the ghastly details.

"I'm sorry. I left you vulnerable to the predators."

"It was my choice. I take full responsibility."

Assuring me I would be fine, Daniel filled a small pot with water and put it on the stove.

"So tell me, what happened?"

"After you left, Jan was very disturbed. He wouldn't even eat anything. I knew he was on the verge of breaking down so I decided to stay there. But he waited until after Mom went home before he finally started speaking," Daniel said, sitting down across from me. "Had you not said what you did, we would probably wait who knows how long to hear anything, if at all. So thank you for being stubborn."

"Oh, Daniel, all this time I felt so guilty for bringing anything up."

"But you were right about him. He knew more than he was willing to share. You were also right that he did it to protect us. But you made him realize that withholding the truth was creating more damage than good."

"But what was it that finally made him open up."

"There was only one thing he needed to let go. Forgiveness."

I thought of the passage in Ezekiel and smiled to myself.

"How is he now?"

"He's tired. Very tired. The weight he's been carrying had almost crushed him."

Daniel's words filled me with hope that grandfather's condition would begin to improve now that he purged his system from secrets. That's if it wasn't too late. My brother leaned his elbows over his knees, and reached for my hands. Light emanated through his skin and I could feel the tingly warmth of their golden corpuscles. Daniel's heat traveled up my arms.

"So tell me," I squeezed his hands. "What did he say?"

"What he had been telling us was true, but only half of the story," Daniel said. "Mom was indeed violated the night she conceived me. The part he didn't tell was that the soul of the man who had done it was possessed by the spirit of a fallen angel. Since they don't have bodies, they take over others. It's like a feast for their spirit," Daniel's face expressed deep sorrow. "This is probably not what you wanted to hear."

I shook my head but the revelation shattered the last bit of faith I had in the virtuousness of the angel. "No, but the truth's purpose is not to make one feel better," I said and closed my eyes. It was my turn to feel tired.

"I'm sorry, sister."

"I thought he really loved me. But because of my gullibility, almost the same thing happened to me tonight," I said, thinking of Crass' advances to take my virginity.

"So you see how devious the fallen can be?"

"I still don't see how someone devious could create people like you and Uri."

"That's because you don't know what it means to live in our skin. It's been a struggle since we were born. Each time something good happened to us, the rug was pulled out from underneath our feet. It was only thanks to our inner faith in some greater purpose and the generosity of people that allowed us to get this far."

"But why?"

"The fallen want the souls of their children to return to them. This is how their spirit survives. They take back what they beget. But as Uri had told you, we are strong. Stronger than we may seem. Still, both of us came close to losing our lives. Numerous times." Daniel narrowed his eyes. "The world is filled with demons seeking to possess people. The doctor who held me in the hospital, the parents who never came to pick me up when I was little, Stan, all of them were suffering from some degree of possession."

"How about Grandpa?"

"Jan is a shaman, a spiritual warrior. But unlike his predecessors, he's resisted his fate."

The water began to boil and Daniel got up to turn off the flame and set the pot aside. He reached for a small pouch that rested on the counter and withdrew a handful of dry herbs, which he threw into the water. A pleasant aroma filled the air.

Just then all the lights in the house went out. The darkness made the glow around his body shine even brighter. I went to my room and retrieved the candle that was still resting up on top of my wardrobe where I had left it two days ago.

When I returned to the kitchen, Daniel was waiting with a box of matches in his hands.

"Rena came by the apartment yesterday," he said, lighting a match. "She thinks we're all nuts." His comment made me smile.

Daniel and I returned to the table, our faces inside the flame's circular glow. Metal objects sparkled, and Daniel's face once more looked otherworldly.

"Sometimes I feel like I'm losing my mind," I said, reaching my hand toward my forehead.

"I've been there many times myself."

"I bet Rena never feels that way." It was my turn to

make Daniel smile.

Grandpa's box and notebook were on the table. Daniel reached for the notebook and opened it on the first page. "Our mother's story begins on this drawing," he said, and turned the book around presenting it to me. It was the drawing of the two soldiers. One was pressing a gun to the other's chest. A faint figure of what looked like an angel hovered in the background. Right above Grandpa's initials was his request for forgiveness.

"It was a cold winter night. Jan was in a war, fighting against the Soviets. The man with the gun is a Soviet soldier," Daniel pointed. "The other person is Jan. He said he came close to dying that night. The moment he captured in this drawing marked a turning point in his life. He summoned a spirit in fear, and everything changed from that point on."

I thought of Grandpa trying to pass his knowledge onto me, warning me about asking spirits to do anything for us, emphasizing the debt that such action always caused.

"What made him so afraid?"

"To fully understand it, we need to go back a little further."

As Daniel spoke, a rich story unfolded.

Our grandfather was born the middle child of three sons in a small village in the north of Russia. His mother, Julia, was of Polish descent. Jan's father, Mir, our great-grandfather, was born in the Far East in a region known as Anatolia, into a small community of shamans. When Mir was sixteen years old, the local government began its campaign against the community, forbidding their shamanic practices and thus forcing many families to abandon the village. They claimed it was a campaign against charlatanism, though Mir was of the opinion that their plan was to use the shamanic knowledge for their own political purposes.

In order to increase the likelihood of preserving their spiritual heritage, the elders of the tribe decided it would be best for them to scatter. Mir's family was to travel west. Caught under fire, Mir's parents and younger sister did not survive the escape. Alone and frightened, young Mir fled in mourning, eventually reaching the Siberian taiga. He endured a harsh winter by hunting animals for their skins and food. After months of wandering, Mir stumbled upon a Siberian village and spent most of the summer watching its inhabitants from a distance. He soon realized that most were war deserters and labor camp fugitives from the First World War. By that fall, Mir was fully assimilated into the life of the small community. There, he met Julia, a recently orphaned daughter of Polish labor camp escapees, and they were married by the next summer.

Unable to deny his heritage that had led to his family's demise, Mir began to heal residents of the village using his shamanic knowledge. Aware of her husband's escape story, Julia tried to remind Mir about what could happen once his practices began to extend beyond their small circle. As his healing powers and popularity grew over the next two decades, Julia gave birth to three healthy sons. But few years later, his wife's warning came to pass and history repeated itself when a government official from a nearby town heard about Mir's abilities and sent his spies to gather information.

In an effort to protect his family and avoid working for the enemy, he and Julia plotted an escape. She had distant relatives who lived in western Poland, assuming they survived the war. Before their departure, Mir and Julia spent the night apart, Julia and the children staying with a neighbor, while Mir was busy making last preparations at their cottage. As it had been in the past, Mir's intuition was sharp, although not sharp enough to spare his life. Their home was invaded that night and Mir was captured. With the help of the neighbor, Julia and the children escaped. They hid in the woods, awaiting the arrival of the neighbor and Mir. When one day the neighbor indeed came, he delivered sad news: Mir had been shot while attempting to flee.

After a long and grief-filled journey west, Julia and her sons returned to Poland where she found the village of her birth. While no family members awaited their arrival, there was an old house, almost in ruins, with an attached plot of land, waiting to be claimed. There, Julia and her three sons began their life anew, away from war and magic. But unbeknownst to her, her middle son, Jan, who was only fourteen at the time when he lost his father, had been already indoctrinated into the shamanic ways. According to what his father had told him, Jan had an inborn ability to invoke spirits. And soon those seeds started to sprout.

As the boys grew, Jan's older brother moved north to a city by the sea and the youngest of the three brothers married the daughter of the local farmer and settled happily in an adjacent village. But Jan was unsettled. He wanted to go back to Anatolia, the homeland of his father, to better understand his strange heritage. When the Soviets invaded Poland a few years later, overtaken by inner rage and a desire to avenge his father's death, Jan joined the Polish army. Thus, our grandfather journeyed east.

It wasn't long before Jan realized not only the perils of war but also the true cost of his desire for revenge. Captured by the enemy, the members of his platoon became prisoners of war and faced imminent death. The night of his planned execution, using his still nascent abilities as the last resort, Jan invoked a spirit, calling upon his ancestors from Anatolia. To his great surprise, the spirit he invoked was that of an angel. Consumed by the terror of dying with a soldier pressing his rifle to Jan's chest, Jan begged the spirit to spare his life. The angel agreed, asking for an offering of his firstborn daughter in return. Jan conceded to the angel's request, not fully understanding just what kind of an angel came to him in his vision or what exactly his request meant. The angel directed his hands at the soldier holding the rifle, and a line of lightning shot toward the soldier, causing him to misfire and Jan to lose consciousness.

The following day, Jan awakened in the forest. Unsure of how he had gotten there, and scarcely remembering what had transpired the night before, Jan started to run towards the setting sun. He never found out what happened to the rest of his platoon, but he suspected the worst.

"So the angel saved his life," I said.

Daniel nodded. "But there was a price to pay."

"That's why he wrote 'forgive me' beneath the drawing, " I said, finally grasping the true weight of those words. "He sacrificed Mom that night."

Daniel nodded again before continuing the story.

Famished and in shock, Jan roamed the foreign woods looking for a way out of Russia. But the farther west he got, the more the mystery of his lineage and the angel's appearance haunted him. Thus, after crossing the Polish border, he chose to stay in the woods longer in hopes of finding peace within.

There, he built for himself a modest dwelling. Spending his days collecting herbs, one day he stumbled upon a young woman foraging in the wild. Reserved at first, over time each made a step closer to their ultimate acquaintance. She lived nearby with her father. She was beautiful and kind and soon Jan was enamored.

After months of courting young Maria, Jan learned that her father was very much against the budding romance. He viewed Jan as an alien and a mad man, too dangerous to be around, too damaging of an influence. In an effort to dissuade her from visiting with the interloper, Maria's father told her he often saw strange lights hover outside of Jan's dwelling, and heard appalling noises, like murmurs and incantations of ghosts and animals scowling in entrapment. But Maria wanted to hear no such nonsense, and continued seeing Jan in the groves and meadows that lined the forest's edge. But in her mind, Maria had finally come upon a kindred spirit.

As autumn encroached upon their little world— dimming colors, deepening echoes, and dampening scents— so grew the young lovers' longing to embrace by the hearth in the open. Jan was well aware that Maria was her father's treasure, one that he refused to relinquish. He was an ailing old man, a widowed man who had lost his wife prematurely, and was deathly afraid of loneliness and Maria's curiosity of what lay beyond the forestland they inhabited. With Maria as his only family, Jan posed a threat to the old man's stability. Taking things into his own hands, Jan hunted down a boar and prepared a feast for Maria and her father. As the scent of dinner steaming on a platter filled their home, Maria's father's nostrils flared and his heart opened. With many such feasts in line, Jan ingratiated himself enough to have the old man bless their union.

The following summer Maria's belly was big enough

to suggest a newcomer into their world. While the change delighted the young mother-to-be, it terrified Jan, the angel's request resurfacing from the ashes of memories. He tried everything to disrupt the pregnancy by sneaking herbs into her teas and stews, all to no avail. In the end, she gave birth to a healthy boy and Jan breathed a sigh of relief. Two years later, their second son was born, though not without another wave of terror. Maria's father passed shortly after the second son's birth, and Jan looking at his blooming brood, adopted a belief that if the angel's request was true, maybe he had changed his mind and had taken the old man's soul instead.

With Maria's daughterly duties unchained, Jan decided it was time for his wife to meet his mother, Julia. The journey was uneventful and the reunion joyful. Julia was relieved to see her son alive, let alone married and with children. For almost a decade, the expanded family lived happily in old Julia's house and flourished. More animals were acquired and a new cottage was built. That was until Maria's belly swelled once more. Plumped from age and prosperity, she hid her state from her husband, aware of his strange fears, until she delivered their last offspring while Jan was away visiting his older brother, Viktor, by the sea.

The child was a girl, feeble and small. Receiving the news via a telegram, Jan was beside himself with concern and returned home promptly. The scab that occluded his meeting with the angel broke open, recharging his anguish.

From the moment Jan met his daughter, his heart belonged to her. He vowed to guard her with his life, both against worldly ills and otherworldly afflictions.

As the girl whom they christened Krystyna grew, and their two sons married and moved out of their parents' home, Maria would catch her husband looking at his daughter with increased sadness. In the attempt to hide his anxiety, he slowly lost his abilities to cope with ordinary affairs and withdrew within himself. Confused, she approached Jan to inquire about his strange moods. Bit by bit, and pushed to the brink of despair, he revealed to her the shamanic origins of his lineage, told her what had happened to him during the war, and described the angel's apparition. He even shared with his wife his guilt over not complying with Mir's warning never to summon spirits while in fear, and especially the agreement he had struck with the angel.

Jan considered talking to young Krystyna about his encounter with the angel but Maria strongly objected. She thought it was unnecessary to disrupt their daughter's youth with disturbing stories that may not even be true. She was not convinced of the story's full validity, suspecting that Jan's fear of being shot by the soldier may have incited a hallucination, or that he had embellished what had happened, his growing fear distorting the memory.

When Krystyna reached her teenage years and began spending more time with her school friends, which to Maria's relief spared her daughter the constant vigil her father kept over her, Jan's gloominess seemed to lessen a bit. That's until Jan's older brother Viktor came for a visit, and the two of them began reminiscing about their forlorn childhood in the east. That night, Jan learned that his kin had a dark side.

According to Viktor, in an attempt to preserve Jan's innocence and untainted talent for healing, Mir purposely omitted to tell his young son apprentice about a certain branch of the tribe that practiced sorcery. Viktor first found out about the dark sect by accidentally stumbling upon a ritual deep in the woods that was so chilling, it scared the boy and he waited a few years before asking his father about it. Mir kept away from the sect, directing his gifts toward the betterment of humanity. He called himself a true shaman and wanted nothing to do with the dark priesthood.

The ritual Viktor had witnessed was meant to invoke the spirits of the tribal ancestors, and included animal sacrifices and the usage of ancient symbols and chants, in order to keep their magical powers strong. Many birds were slaughtered that night to make cloaks that looked like wings. Viktor later gathered from several sources linked to the tribe's high priest that their Anatolian tribe's legacy reached back to the times of the Nephilim, its elders believing to be direct bloodline descendants of the fallen.

"That would mean that Grandpa himself could be a descendant of the Nephilim," I said, startled by the discovery.

"It's very possible and would explain a lot," Daniel said.

"And if it is so," I whispered, my eyes burning, "it would imply that so am I."

Daniel and I looked at each other, currents of energy moving through the air. I felt like we were getting very close to disentangling my family saga, so I asked my brother to please continue.

Having realized that he was dealing with powers that were beyond his control, Jan's inner state oscillated between despair, denial, and acceptance. He began having dreams of rumbling storms and consuming fires, out of which arose the angel's apparition, coming to claim young Krystyna. When Jan tried to chase away the angel, it would turn into Mir, as if reminding him that he was chasing away his own. Coming to terms with his own impotence in the face of a great power, Jan shifted his focus from prevention, which would've been futile unless he chained his daughter to the bedpost, to planning post hoc, in the event the worst came to pass.

When, much to Maria's delight, a young man had been spotted two evenings in a row walking Krystyna home, she shared the news with Jan. The young cavalier was from a good family, known around town by their high status and prosperity. Jan responded to the news with nothing more than a shrug and continued his ghostly existence. On the evening of the autumnal equinox he couldn't take his eyes off his daughter, sensing a strange presence around her that trailed her like smoke, a clandestine air that made him suspect the worst. She ambled around the kitchen, preparing a supper, humming a strange tune.

No amount of delicate questioning made Krystyna open up to her father, as the girl and her parents consumed their evening meal. Grandma scolded her husband, insisting that their daughter was embarrassed, as she had obviously fallen in love. But Grandpa knew his quiet truth. Fallen, yes, but neither in love, nor with the one Grandma had believed. Their daughter had fallen into the trap of lust and enchantment.

Her blank stare and dreamy smiles confirmed it.

That night Jan refused to drop his guard. So when

still dressed in her sleeping gown, Krystyna left the house just before midnight, he followed her. She passed the neighboring blocks and garden patches and entered the surrounding woods. The night was unusually warm, the sky cloudless and the moon full. Jan followed her until she settled in a corner of a glade.

From behind a hedge, Jan watched his daughter murmur something toward the sky, lie down on the ground, and caress the skin of her face with a feather. He decided to step out of his hiding and interrupt the process sooner. But to his anguish, he encountered an invisible wall of resistance he was unable to cross. Pounding on the barrier with his fists, he called her name, as storm clouds began to gather over his head. There was no rain, only thunder and lightning bolts, one of which must have struck Jan and he lost consciousness, just as he saw a silhouette of a man approaching his daughter's body. He awakened at dawn, to find his daughter on the grass with bloodstains on her legs. He carried her home, silently weeping. It was done. He had failed.

Through the coming months, until the birth of Krystyna's child, Jan worked tirelessly to help his daughter come to terms with what had happened. With Maria as his accomplice, Jan took his daughter away and lived with her in a remote mountain village until she delivered a son, whom she named Daniel. After giving the child up for adoption, he tried to help restore a semblance of normalcy in her life. Hoping the worst was over, some of Jan's earlier vigor returned.

Delivering his daughter to the longing hands of her suitor, he stepped back, wishing for the couple to find happiness. But things did not go as smoothly, as he had hoped. From the start, Mom's fiancée felt that her heart belonged to another. And he was right. Beneath the layers of repression, she longed for her angel, the "shining one" who would come back one day and take her to the stars.

Daniel reached into the box and took out a white feather and handed it to me. "Jan was the one who took away the feather Sariel left you in the meadow when you were little. Now you know why."

"He was afraid that the same thing that happened to

her, would happen to me."

Daniel nodded again.

"Grandpa wanted Mom to forget him so that she could have a normal life with my father."

"Makes sense right?" Daniel asked. "According to him, the angel had shattered her young soul. She couldn't find herself after that."

"But I don't understand one thing. I've been remembering so much lately . . . my meeting Sariel epochs ago as a priestess. Was this all false? Is this memory just a figment of my imagination?"

Daniel took a deep breath. "I don't know. All I know is that the spirits of the fallen still hover in the space between heaven and earth, reminding us of their presence. But we must never forget that they are the perpetrators and human women are the victims."

"So in your view they are just monsters that take possession of naïve women only to ruin their lives?" I asked.

"Not to mention that they leave their children fatherless and in the throes of constant danger," Daniel said. Hearing all that from Daniel, did not convince me that Sariel was evil. To me, the angel was as lost as the rest of us.

I shared my thoughts with Daniel. "I feel like there is more to this story that still doesn't make sense. I need to see him. At least one last time, or I will always be haunted by it."

"You must do it then."

"But that leaves only one option," I said.

"I know," Daniel said looking at the box resting on the table. "I'm prepared to take you to the gate."

XXX.

The concoction brewing in the pot was meant to catalyze my shamanic vision quest. According to Daniel, it was very much unlike the potion Crass had given me. This mixture came from our great-grandfather, Mir, and contained herbs that only grew in Anatolia. The shamans used them in their sacred ceremonies. The herbs would cleanse the body and mind of false perceptions, offering a peek into the timeless world of spirit.

I hoped for a deeper insight that would tie up loose ends and fill the yawning gaps in my understanding. I sensed that vital memories were still missing, significant pieces of the story locked in my unconscious. This was my opportunity to reclaim those obscure parts, unearth old links to a broken chain. Under Grandpa's tutelage and with his blessing at last, my brother was prepared to guide me.

"Maybe it will help me find that harmony the shamans seek to restore," I said, taking the cup from Daniel's hands.

He smiled.

I took a sip and then another. The drink tasted pleasant and lightly sweet, the after flavor hinting of mint and cinnamon. Daniel said that this mixture would relax me while delivering a light rush of energy. I finished the drink and feeling sticky and stained, I excused myself to the shower. Daniel said when I was ready he would take me outside.

Standing under the stream, I closed my eyes, steadying myself with my hands on tiles, and watched my mind get swept by a vision. It came in a flash. . . .

The inside of the temple was buzzing. Females of all ages were preparing for a visitation. I was among them, arranging flower bouquets. I heard footsteps, turned and saw her—my dearest friend, my mentor and guide—Saneel. She was walking towards me. In her hands, she held a black veil. I stood up and faced her and she put it over my eyes. *Their radiance can be blinding to unaccustomed eyes,* she had said to me. I hadn't realized what she had meant until much later.

I turned off the water and exited the shower.

After drying myself off, I darted out of the bathroom and into my room to look for something to wear. I opened my closet and easily spotted it between rows of black—Mom's lace trimmed white nightgown. In my mind's eye, I saw her wearing it the night she was with the angel. I didn't know whether that was indeed the case, but the thought made me hesitate. Finding nothing else festive enough to wear, I slipped it on and covered my shoulders with a woolen scarf. I then tore a sheet off my bed and folded it under my arm, looked at my desk, and slowly opened the drawer. I picked up the red lipstick and curled my fingers around its shiny enclosure.

"Ready to peel back the veils?" Daniel asked when I entered the kitchen. He was ready to go, the box in his hands. *Peeling back the veils. . . .*was that what this quest was about? I nodded and followed him down the hallway of our unlit house toward the front door, spying eyes trailing us from dark corners.

Daniel paused in the foyer to put on his tennis shoes. I glanced at my boots but they looked weighed with too much mud. I chose to leave my feet bare. We exited through the front door and walked down the stairway. The bottom arc of the full moon was brushing against the oaks' crowns. I trailed my brother's footsteps in the warm night, temperatures resembling those of May rather than March. Or maybe it was just I who felt warm? But even Daniel was dressed lightly, wearing a white T-shirt, which tonight glowed with opal luminescence. We skirted the house, walked through our garden, across a small empty field, and down lower toward the creek.

The meadows . . . I thought. Back to where it all started.

We entered the short wooden bridge. On the other side, young grasses sparkled with moisture. I walked hugging the folded bed sheet and squeezing the lipstick, careful not to let the gown catch any splinters. The night was serene and even though it was dark, nature seemed aroused and awake. A delicate breeze played with tree branches, the rustle adding to the ambient sounds of the flowing water. I thought I could hear the song of sirens downriver.

Stepping off the bridge, Daniel reached his hand toward me and upon our contact the singing vanished, the song once more becoming a subtle trickling of the stream. My feet touched the solid ground and Daniel pointed ahead.

Uri stood in the middle of an open field, outlined by a circle of light, hands in this pockets, head towards the moon.

"You came!" I called to him.

Handing the sheet to Daniel, I lifted the gown to my knees and ran across the grasses, to greet him. Uri turned toward me and I fell into his embrace.

"I heard your call," he said squeezing me tight.

"I feel so much better that you are here."

Daniel joined us, and the two Nephilim brothers embraced without a word. I suspected they were in a constant thought exchange so speaking was superfluous.

"I guess there is no question as to where we should settle," Daniel pointed toward the spot illuminated by a ring of moonlight. He unrolled the sheet, opened the box, and with Uri's help arranged upon it the three shamanic artifacts: the veil, the wand and the stone. While they did so, I discretely applied a layer of crimson to my lips.

When everything was set, Daniel and Uri kicked off their shoes, and all three of us stepped onto the sheet. Together, we formed a triangle. Daniel bent forward and picked up the black veil of protection and carefully placed it on my head. We stood quiet for moment, their faces solemn and eyes on me, before we linked our hands and my lids fell shut like two heavy curtains.

Interlaced with mine, their fingers seemed to elongate, plowing beneath my skin, threading through gaps between veins, reaching for lungs, before gaining a stronghold on the heart. I took a deep breath. They were with me.

Daniel spoke. "Tonight you will walk the shamanic path. We are here to help dispel the obstructions so that you may find the gateway of your soul."

Uri took over. "The journey will unravel memories encoded within your cells, the serpentine wisdom leading you back to the time before your birth."

"I, Daniel, will take you to the threshold."

"And I, Uriel, will provide the key."

Beneath my closed eyes, I saw two distinct auras forming in the place where Uri and Daniel stood. Daniel's was golden like the sun and Uri's silver like the moon. I felt their light rush into my body. Daniel's flowed downward, anchoring me to the earth, while Uri's spiraled upward towards the sky.

"Dear sister, descendant of El," Daniel spoke. "May the ancestors of the renown guard you on your journey into the finer dimensions."

"And as the gates open before you, may your truth be your guide," Uri said, and our hands reached toward the sky. At once, the wind picked up force and the river surged onward. The rushing sounds merged with an oscillating vibration moving through me, becoming the ambient current of my spirit flight. The earth trembled beneath me. My soul and nature were merging.

Just then, I heard a voice. It belonged to a man.

"A true shaman owns her darkness," he said. I recognized grandfather. The shaman came to offer his guidance. I sent my silent thanks. "To summon an angel, you must give up your stance. Your path will split, it will diverge. The elements will rage, as they must rearrange. Nothing will be the same. Are you sure you want to take this flight?"

"Yes," I cried into the vortex spinning around me.

"Then ascend!" the voice ordered.

I felt a cord extend through my feet and burrow down into the very core of the Earth. At the same time, my mind expanded with such velocity that in no time it reached all the corners of the universe, where it witnessed a glowing theatre of instantaneous creation.

Soon the elements settled, movement slowed and a tapestry of floating galaxies unfolded before me.

Focus now. See the gate, Daniel's voice echoed through space.

Concentrating on his words, my mind contracted into a point-like singularity. It separated from the cosmic matrix, and I became an entity again.

I spun around on my axis to scan the cosmic panorama.

In one area, where the vacuum folded on itself, I saw an outline of a round gateway with a cavernous wormhole at its core. I noticed I was orbiting around it, feeling myself drawn to it like a speck of iron toward a magnet. The closer I got, the faster I approached until my ethereal body passed through the funnel-like boundary.

Physical sensation returned to me when my bare feet touched the cold stone ground. A shiver rippled up my spine, snapping my mind into my new body. I was standing inside a dark chamber in front of an arched portal made of stone with two pillars on each side. I looked at my pale, glowing hands.

"True knowledge withstands the test of time—no part can ever be lost. True knowledge is unborn—what has been, always will be," a female voice echoed. "True knowledge can be known only if it rests outside the confines of time."

I could not see her but I did recognize that voice. And even though she spoke in a different language, I understood every word.

"Goddess of night, Lord of light—open the gates to your eternal knowledge so that our minds may dwell in pools of undisturbed clarity."

I knew that prayer. This is how the temple priestesses began each ceremony.

From a distance, I saw a glimmer of light approaching, like a bright star that kept getting bigger. Once it was close enough for me to discern its shape, I noticed it was a torch flame carried by a woman dressed in a silver robe. Her hair was fair and flowing past her waist. Her eyes were blue and bright.

"I was summoned to serve as your guide on this journey," she said settling on the stone floor, next to where I stood.

I bowed my head and looked at her radiant face.

"I know you," I said, in the same language.

She smiled. "Of course you do."

XXXI.

The robed lady inclined her head. "Even though you meet me outside the confines of time, we had once met on Earth and in the flesh. Dear Ninsal, you recognize me because I was your guide at the temple."

"Saneel," I said. "How wonderful it is to see you."

Seeing my friend compressed all the years between this meeting and our last into a distinct sense of knowing. I was her again, a young neophyte preparing for an initiation into the mysteries of the cosmos.

"You found the gate," Saneel said, and raised the torch to the arch that towered above the gate. The stone crescent was inscribed with symbols.

I looked up. "What do they say?" I asked.

"It is your task to decipher them so that you may cross to the other side."

"But how?"

"It's simple," Saneel said with a glimmer in her eyes. "You must use your imagination,"

A row of characters made of crisscrossing lines glowed with an iridescence. Looking at them stirred within me a faint awareness of their meaning. Just as I knew her, I knew this writing. These were runes. Our forefathers brought the language with them when they ventured into the Far East to settle new lands. I glimpsed their long pilgrimage in my mind. The symbols, along with the rites and mysteries, were passed onto the priests and priestesses for safekeeping, and every neophyte studied them to use in rites and divination.

The more I looked at the symbols, the more intensely they glowed, their shapes burning into my psyche, rushing in like an avalanche of spells, opening internal channels. The veils lifted and the meaning came alive.

"Nothing ever dies," I whispered and looked at Saneel.

"Only forms change," she added.

"It is the same thing that Daniel told me at the hospital."

270

"Yes, I know that. He came here."

"You met Daniel?"

She nodded. "The doorway to truth is always open to those who seek it. And knowing that shall set you free," she said, and then pointed beneath the arch. "Look, Ninsal!"

The gaping void that spread beneath the gate had become a mirror. I approached it and saw my reflection. I was wearing a black robe. The veil Daniel had put on my head covered my face.

"You can take it off now. You will not need it anymore," Saneel said.

I looked at my pale hands and lifted them slowly to touch the veil with my fingertips. The fabric turned to ash revealing my face. In the mirror, I saw Ninsal. Her hair was light, long just like Saneel's, and features soft.

"Go ahead, take a step," Saneel encouraged. "You are ready now."

I reached my hand into the mirror and it vanished from my sight. I withdrew it back and quickly and looked at my hand, which was intact, and then at my companion.

"Do not be afraid," she said, her eyes gentle.

"Will I see you again?"

She smiled. "I am always with you. In a place where time is not, you shall always find me," Saneel said and her body slowly dissolved.

Looking into the mirror, I lifted my foot and carefully stepped through. My body swayed lightly and I passed to the other side.

I landed on a gray rock, my bare feet kicking up a small cloud of silver dust. The landscape around me was grim and gray. Up above, a myriad of stars danced across the sky's inky blackness.

"Just the way I remember seeing you in my dream— walking across the surface of the moon. Remember when I told you about it?"

Quickly, I turned to my side. "And you," I said to him, "are always materializing out of thin air."

"There is certainly not much of it around here," Uri grinned. He too looked different. Older perhaps, or timeless rather. Surely more regal. His black hair flowed down past his shoulders and his blue eyes shone with celestial brightness. He wore a long blue cape cinched by a belt from which hung a silver key. He had become Uriel, the keeper of Tartarus.

"I do remember when you told me that you dreamt of me," I said. "We were behind the old, gray theater. Next to my school."

"It was a gray cold morning. And now we are on a gray cold moon," Uriel said.

How distant that November morning seemed now. It was only four months ago, but it felt like so much more time had elapsed.

"Where is he?" I asked, and I knew he understood whom I meant. Will you show me the way?

"We must get to the dark side," Uriel said, and reached for my hand. Our fingers interlaced. I looked over my shoulder to catch the last glimmer of sunlight.

Entering into the area of permanent shadow, the black cloak I was wearing turned into a long white dress. Both of our bodies glowed in the dark. While I didn't feel cold despite only wearing a thin dress, I also didn't need oxygen to breathe. A frightening thought came to me.

"Uriel, am I dead?"

He looked at me and smiled. "Far from it. It is just that your mind is no longer bound to it."

"Is it like dreaming, then?"

"Not quite. You are fully conscious. In fact even more so than when you are awake."

I let go of his hand and paused our walk to stretch my arms towards the sky. I wanted to use my whole body to feel the essence of his words.

"'You yourself are even another little world and have within you the sun and the moon and also the stars,' once said a mystic," Uriel said and pointed upward.

The heavens above were riddled with thousands of stars, more than I had ever seen, spilling like shimmering diamonds over black velvet. All the knowledge of the universe was on display in front of me, its intelligence contained in the smallest speck of moon dust. And I knew at once what it was like to be free of trying to grasp, and one with it all.

"As above, so below," I whispered.

"If the whole universe can be reflected in a single drop of water, why can't it be the same with us?"

"I feel like it is exactly the same with us, " I said, looking at Uriel. His eyes were looking at something far in the distance. I followed his gaze. There, I saw a column of smoke rising from a pit.

"This is the farthest I can take you," he said. "You must proceed from here on your own." He reached toward his belt to untie the silver key and handed it to me. The key looked as if it was made of quicksilver. Opalescent veins shifted across its surface. "It will help you get through the barrier."

"How will I know how to use it?"

"The key will show you," Uriel said. "Now go. It is time."

I smiled, though my eyes remained solemn. I didn't want to go alone, and yet I knew that I had to. Uri placed his arm over his heart and closed his eyes, and I watched my companion disintegrate right before me, just as Saneel did by the gate. Holding the feather light object in my hand, I aimed for the gorge.

Not too far from where Uriel and I had parted, I encountered the invisible barrier, much like the one I had come across inside the cathedral. I leaned my body into it, sensing its composition. Its surface was neither smooth nor hard; I could press in deeper, to try to force myself through, but the deeper I got, the more resistance I encountered. I looked at the key in my hand. It was glowing blue.

Nearing the key towards the barrier, I felt it shift in my hand like a small snake becoming grandfather's wand. I curled my fingers around it and plunged my hand deeper. The wand ignited in a blue flame, which quickly spread, revealing the blockade's dome shape. I opened my palm and the wand melted like a snowflake. The moon's ground rumbled and shook, lightning crawled across the curved surface that was now rippling like water. I took a step back. When the shaking abated and the flames died out, the watery shell of the enclosure began to boil. It hissed, bubbles spreading across the entire enclosure, turning the liquid into vapor. At last, I watched the steam lift like a cloudy veil toward the heavens.

The passage was opened.

And then I heard them, the howling incantations from my dream.

The wails grew louder the closer I got to the gorge, the singing more feverish, carrying with it the restless thumping of my invisible heart. Besides the column of rising smoke before me, there was nothing else in sight but endless planes of gray rock swathed in silver dust. My glance traveled down to my bare feet stomping across the moon's surface, toward the ruptured ground. When I reached its edge, my toes curled over the precipice. Next to my feet, I saw a peculiar object. I recognized it and bent down to pick it up. It was the obsidian from Grandpa's box, the stone of truth.

The voices stopped wailing. I looked at the rock reflecting in its smooth, polished exterior the orange flames raging below. Curling my fingers around it, I directed my gaze down towards the pit.

"Ninsal. . . . " his call arose from the abyss like a long exhale. I found him. I found the entrance to the Tartarus.

Fear made me waver but not for long. There was no point in delaying the moment. My flight could be over soon and I had a quest to complete. If I wanted to see him, I needed to enter his domain. I leaned towards the gorge and squeezing the rock in my fist, let the gravity of the moon pull me toward its center.

XXXII.

I awakened to birdsong, the sun's rays tugging at my eyelids. I sat up quickly and scanned my surroundings, then looked down at my body. I was back in the meadow wearing Mom's gown. I had no mirror nearby, but I checked the color of my hair. It was brown. I must be back in my earthly body.

But Daniel and Uri were not with me. I called their names, but got no reply.

Was this it? Had I failed? I came so close to Sariel, but something must have gone wrong.

Just as I was about to walk toward the creek to see if my companions were there, the sunlight dimmed and with it all sounds went mute. I squinted my eyes and glanced up.

The moon was obscuring more than half of the sun. I had no idea that we would be having an eclipse. Cupping my hands, I tried once more to call for Daniel and Uri, directing my shout in all four directions. *They should be here to see this.* Alas, my ears registered nothing but deaf silence.

As a cape of encroaching shadow cloaked the grass fields and neighboring forests, the meadow lit up with flickering blue flames. One by one they ignited and arose from the grasses. Up in the heavens, the moon and sun's orbs locked together, leaving visible only a corona of fire. The trickling sound of the river returned and a symphony of crickets and birds filled the night air. My journey was not over yet.

Behind me, something was looking at me, luring me there. I felt their eyes piercing my back . . . Slowly, I turned around and saw it: the shielded glade from my childhood.

Nearly ten years had passed since I had first discovered it, and with it the blooming seed of my femininity. It should by now be overgrown and impossible to enter, the trees growing too tall and too wide to preserve the dome shape inside. But today, the glade seemed to look the same as it did back then, its trees young and leaning toward one another.

The ground was moist and water welled up around my bare feet as I walked. Holding the gown high to my shins, I followed a path marked for me by the tiny blue flames that hovered above ground. *What kind of magic is this?*

The soft tree branches parted, as if pushed aside by invisible hands, and I entered the clearing. White flower petals carpeted the ground. I counted sixteen candles swinging from branches in jam jars.

"I know your birthday is seven days away, but I thought you might like an earlier celebration," I heard his voice behind me. I turned and gasped. Sariel reached his hand out to me and gently stroked my cheek.

"At last," I sighed. "There are no more barriers between us. Does that mean you can stay?"

"Dear Eve. This is your spirit flight; this is why I am here. Remember what I had told you before. I am forbidden from coming into your world."

With trembling lips, I decided to ask the difficult question.

"Is it true what my grandfather said about you?" I asked. "That you are destroyers of innocence?"

Sariel smiled, but his eyes remained somber. "It is the awareness of death that erodes human innocence," Sariel said, "It is easy to blame the fallen for the ills of your world."

"Why did you break into my dreams?"

His eyes ignited with a glimmer of fire. "So that our legend could continue to live on."

"Do you speak of the legend of Sariel and Ninsal?"

"You and Ninsal share the same soul," His eyes were now glowing like two suns. "Your remembrance freed me from my chains."

"But how is it possible? How could we be the same? She lived so long ago and in a world that was nothing like the one in which I live."

"If you allow me, I will show you." He opened his arms towards me, and two black wings unfurled behind his back. "In my embrace, you will find the answers you seek."

Reluctantly, I stepped forward. I could feel the heat emanating from his skin and a scent that knew so well. I was falling under his spell again, but there was no point resisting. He was offering to illuminate me. And this was my quest.

"Allow me," he repeated, his wings folding around

me. "Allow me to show you what it means to fly.

Standing over a blanket of rich green grass, I watched moisture-bearing mist float low beneath a milky sky. The air smelled of the sea. My body was clothed in a green, flowing robe, and a wreath of leaves crowned my long copper hair. As I did each day since the start of fall, I had something important to do. But on this early morning it was more difficult to concentrate on my task. Nature was so alive, and speaking directly to me. I pressed the dry bundle of twigs to my chest and turned to walk toward a circle of nine stones, in the midst of which nestled a stone bowl. A small fire kindled inside of it. I gazed into it and with my freckled hands added a few small twigs. The moisture on the wood hissed before the flames caught. I added a handful of leaves and the smoke engulfed me in a familiar smell. I watched the fire grow and recited my invocations, holding my hands over the amber flames.

Just then a feather descended from the sky, landing directly over my extended palms. "My angel," I whispered, and looked up, but the skies were blank.

The scenery changed and I found myself in a land of perpetual snow. It was night. A large tower of fire burned inside of a circle, warming the faces of a dozen, keeping away the encroaching shadows. Their faces were red from the elements, their hair wild. Hands they held out toward the roaring flames were scarred and smeared with blood's rust, bodies covered with animal skins, feet stomping a rhythm, throaty sounds intoning a primal song of the elders. The ritual was coming to a peak. The voices rose to a crescendo, and hands ventured toward the sky. I thrust the charred end of a torch into the fire and sparks scattered at our feet.

It was sunset. The air was warm and arid, suffused with a scent of oregano. I stood inside an open temple of twelve pillars of stone. Rolling hills of green fields and olive orchards surrounded the temple, peppered with human dwellings and rock outcrops. I kneeled down and aimed the torch I was holding toward the flame. A heavy necklace weighed down my breastbone, and a golden diadem ornamented my forehead just beneath the hairline. The end of the torch ignited and I rose up to turn toward a cloaked man who stood behind me. I bowed and handed him the torch. But when I looked up I encountered his flaming eyes.

The music carried me around the room. My body felt open and free, bangles on my wrists chiming to the rhythm of drums. In the center of the room burned a fire. Flickering oil lamps patterned the walls. I was dancing for the shadow-cloaked audience that surrounded me in a circle. As I twirled, droplets of sweat trickled down my back, the ends of my hair sticking to my neck. The air smelled of heavy incense, musk, and the sweat of bodies, their eyes upon me. But in my mind, I only danced for one being—the dark angel for whom I waited each night in the garden.

The women screamed as the scorching flames devoured their wounded flesh. Tied to a post mounted over a stake, agony replaced my earlier rapture. Once my ally, the fire now seared my skin, filling the air with an unbearable stench. I looked at the crowd with bloodshot eyes, hoping the end would come soon. I spotted him from afar, his face hiding behind a hood. He pointed his arrow at me and soon I felt it pierce through my heart. Free from pain at last, my soul soared toward the moon.

I couldn't move. My arms were bound, tightly wrapped around my chest. Everything was white and the same. Snow? Sky? No. These were the walls. The fear returned with a memory of a man and a woman in white suits. It was what they did that left me so confused. They numbed my pain and made me forget. They severed the cord turning memories into fragments of a broken mirror. I let out a scream that tore away from my chest like a discarded scab. *You took him away from me!* I cried.

The lights flickered on and a man entered the room. In his hands I recognized the agent of amnesia. I knew that no amount of protest would make him hear me, so tossing my head to the side, I looked to a scraped white wall as the needle punctured my flesh. Soon I was fading into oblivion until only an inkling of awareness remained. A tear moistened the skin of my cheek and the hot flame that burned at the base of my spine dimmed to a whisper.

"This is not the first time," I said to Sariel, looking up toward his face. My whole body was vibrating as if plugged into an electric current. "I've been obsessed with you for lifetimes."

"You remembered me."

"Sariel, I am scared," I said, nestling myself in his chest, feeling conflicted again. It was so hard to resist him. "I feel that if I let this go on, I will vanish from the earthly plane of existence."

"Don't be afraid. I will never leave you."

"But this is a dream. And it will fade the moment I wake up."

"Then don't wake up," he whispered in my ear. "Stay with me. Merge with me."

"But I must go back. There are people I love who are waiting for me."

The angel let go of me. I shivered again, but this time from the cold. Sariel took a step to the edge of the glade, his eyes directed toward the eclipse.

"Your mother was once the beloved of an angel," he said. "I believe you knew her when her saga began. You two were very close at the temple. But she now chooses not to remember. One day, it will be the same with you. You will no longer remember me."

"Mom and Saneel are the same person?" I asked.

Sariel turned towards me. "History moves in cycles, souls reunite in new times and places."

"My mother was taken by force, Sariel. It nearly destroyed her," I said.

"You are wrong. Saneel gave herself to Ramiel willingly," he said, stepping closer to me again. "Just as you once gave yourself to me." The moon was beginning to retreat, letting in the first rays of sunlight. One by one, the candle flames were beginning to fade, leaving behind snaking tendrils of smoke. "If you stay with me, I will make you immortal."

"Which means death to my world."

"But eternal life in another world," he said. Sariel's body was becoming transparent, but his eyes were burning bright. "You now have the power to command the elements. Stay with me, Ninsal. Close the gate and remain."

"But I'm no longer Ninsal," I said and dropped to my knees. "She is dead."

"She is within you."

"No Sariel. I am Evelina, a girl who belongs to a world, in which you cannot live, a lost human who used to want to escape and go somewhere else. But she is beginning to see that all this time she thought of her world as mundane, it's been teeming with beauty, love and magic."

Sariel's body was almost completely faded now. More sunlight entered the meadow. It was so bright, the rays were blinding.

Sariel came closer and placed his palms over my face. My eyes fell shut and the darkening felt soothing. There, beneath my closed lids, I saw the truth and shared it with the angel.

"The awareness of death, the acceptance of our mortality is not the end of innocence," I said. "It is the end of ignorance."

When I opened my eyes, Sariel was no longer there.

In his place stood my grandfather.

"My dear granddaughter," he spoke. "As you approach the end of your quest, you can now see that the journey was not only about finding the angel. It was not even about finding the truth about Daniel. It was about so much more than that. And now that you have found it, no one can take that away from you."

"It was a journey back," I said to him. "To find myself again."

He smiled. "Herein lies your initiation."

XXXIII.

"Evelina? Eve, open your eyes," I heard Uri's voice. I blinked once and then again, his large blue irises slowly coming into focus. "Glad to have you back," he smiled.

I was in my room. The sun was still out, but its light was pale. "How long have I been out?" I asked, my hands reaching for my head. My body felt heavy and sore.

"You slept for a week. Everyone's been worried. Well, everyone but me."

"That long? Then it must have been the longest dream I've ever had. And the most amazing one yet."

"I can only imagine."

"Uri, it was most incredible. It felt so real. I saw so much," I said, propping myself on my elbows. I felt dizzy and collapsed down again. I wanted to share with him what I had seen. But the memories were fading so fast it was hard to hold on to them."

"I know what happened," he said. "You talk when you sleep, remember?" He smiled at me and pointed at a sheet in Daniel's notebook. It was covered in his scribbles. "I tried to write it all down. Sorry about my handwriting. I know it's terrible."

"You are a gem."

"That's a first," he said and winked at me.

"Where is Mom?" I asked, wrinkling my forehead. My head was pounding like an old bell.

"I believe in the kitchen with Rena, Daniel, and Adam."

"Who's Adam?"

"The doctor who treated Daniel. He is practically living here now."

"Adam, huh?"

"If it wasn't for him being here, your mother would probably have gone crazy with concern. He's a doctor after all. But even he was worried and wanted to take you to some clinic. But I wouldn't let him."

Someone opened the door. Upon seeing me awake, Mom was overjoyed. She kept hugging me and apologizing.

"I'm sorry I wouldn't hear you out," Mom said. "I kept pushing you away. But you knew. You knew all along."

"It's okay, Mom. Sometimes the most obvious things are the hardest to see."

"I got so afraid I would lose you."

"You can never lose me. We are bonded beyond this lifetime," I said and looked at Uri who seemed to understand.

Soon after, Adam walked into the room. He kept looking at me with keen eyes, but didn't interfere in our small reunion. I could tell he was relieved that I had finally awakened and quite puzzled by my mysterious affliction.

"We have news to share with you," Mom said casting her eyes at Adam. She settled on the edge of my mattress and gripped my hand. "All of Daniel's tests came back from the laboratory. They found no trace of disease."

From the day I met Daniel, I had no doubt in my mind that he had a long life ahead of him. But to have it confirmed by a doctor filled me with even more peace. I saw joy dance on Mom's face. I'd never seen her this happy before. My eyes filled with tears and one fell straight onto Mom's hand.

"Thank you for saving his life," she said.

"It was a team effort," I looked towards Uri who stood by the door. Daniel walked in next and held the door open for my sister.

"I heard today was someone's birthday," Rena walked in holding a cake with sixteen lit candles. "You'd better like it," she said, kneeling next to me. "It took me all day and two trials to make this crooked masterpiece. I almost burned down the kitchen."

She brought the cake closer to my face and I felt the warmth of the candles on my skin. My family and friends sang "Happy Birthday," though it seemed everyone knew a slightly different version. When the voices faded, Rena helped me blow out the candles.

"How did you know I'd wake up today?"

"He told me," Rena said, casting a sideways look at Uri.

I turned toward Adam. "How is Grandpa?" I asked, not without trepidation.

"Well on his way to recovery," he said. "He's been making steady progress since last week."

"He was here this morning," Mom said. "He sat by your bed for over an hour, holding your hand."

The cake Rena made was delicious, but it made me sleepy. Curled in my bed, I insisted on having Uri and Daniel stay with me for as long as I was awake. They were my closest friends, and we shared experiences no one else would believe.

"It is time for me to go," Uri finally spoke the words I didn't want to hear. Daniel and I exchanged glances.

"Why so soon?" I asked.

"Life beckons," he reached forward to hug me. "You are indeed a stubborn girl, Evelina. Thank you for bringing us together," Uri said.

"I will miss you," I said, digging my chin into his shoulder. "You will always have a home with us."

"Thank you. I will remember that," Uri said, loosening our embrace. "Before I go, I have something to give you."

He reached his hand into the pocket of his jacket. "This must be yours," he said, handing me a white feather. I looked at him and then at my brother in surprise.

"Everything else burned down," Daniel said. "One by one, all of the magic items turned to ash—first the veil, then the stone, and finally the wand. Even the box. This is the only thing that survived."

I was speechless. I inhaled the smoky air around the plume and ran its tip against the skin of my face.

"It will help you remember," Uri said. In a daze, I watched him get up and walk through the door.

"Bye, Punk," I called after him, hoping his old moniker would cheer me up, but my voice got stuck in my throat.

"Goodbye, Eve," he turned. "Until we meet again," and quietly closed the door.

I wiped away a tear and laughed. "I will never get used to saying goodbye to him," I said to Daniel. "Just in a short while I've felt so many opposing emotions. First I am happy and now I am sad again. It's endless."

"Life is like that," Daniel said, tucking me in. "And you've been through a lot. Now is a good time for you to let yourself rest and be taken care of."

"How are you planning to take care of me?" I asked.

"I heard that you liked stories."

"That I do. Do you have a good one?"

"That I do," Daniel smiled.

"What is it about?"

"A girl who wanted to fly."

ACKNOWLEDGEMENTS

Writing a book made me gain a deeper appreciation for the nature of this demanding craft and the work of other artists. In light of that humbling awareness, I'd like to begin by thanking Bri Bruce for her steadfast spirit and generosity in sharing her skill, knowledge, and publishing experience with me. Her editing helped make *Moonchild* much more cohesive, and her direction kept me from going off on too many tangents. My gratitude also goes to John Biscello for becoming the "Luna Baby's" self-proclaimed "crazy and proud godfather." His help with smoothing out the manuscript was key in transmuting my daily agitation into prolonged moments of tranquility and trust.

My heart goes out to those who cheered on my nascent literary efforts when I was taking my first steps: Jasmine Miller, Paula Cazares-Oberst, Joy Branford, Natalie Ullman, Toni Chartier, Prof. DeAnna DeRosa (when I was writing my first articles for the college newspaper), and my dear "other" sister, Hannah Allen. Thank you for your friendship, confidence, and encouragement.

Deep appreciation goes to my old pack of friends from Niemodlin, many of whom inspired the characters in *Moonchild*: Gregor, Slash, Zyla, my music teacher Tomek, Krzesa, Aga, Sasza, Saszka, the nameless punk with blue mohawk to stumbled upon our town one day, and the original Sirrah crew members. And thank you, little Peter, for holding my hand when I was small, ill and scared. I hope your parents did finally come to take you home.

I wouldn't have written the story without the inspiration that flows from music, the form of art that has always evoked the most potent visions. So thank you Jochan Edlund, Yorck Eysel, Peter Steele, and Carl McCoy for unknowingly contributing to this book.

And finally, I could have never gotten this far without the undying faith and love from my greatest fan, my mother. Thank you, Mom, for shining your light when I was overcome with doubt. Huge thanks go to my two awesome sisters, Ania and Aleksandra, who provided ample doses of humor when the going got tough, to my father whose support I've felt from across the ocean, and to my grandparents who always believed.

I dedicate this book to my parents and their parents, whose legacies I had endeavored to capture between the lines of the story. I hope I had given them the justice they deserve and in the process succeeded in entertaining the innocent bystanders.

ABOUT THE AUTHOR

EWA K. ZWONARZ was born and raised in a small rustic town in Poland as the middle of three daughters. As a child she was intrigued by the state of the world and inundated her parents and teachers with questions they were unable to answer. Thus, she set out on a journey to understand who we are, how we got here, and what had happened in our world to bring it to its current state of degeneration. In the process, a new passion was born: a desire to inspire others to question what is known and dig deeper. Ewa knew the only way to accomplish it would be through continual research and storytelling.

An avid investigator of myths, mysteries, and unified sciences, Ewa's passion is to hunt for ancient puzzle pieces left to us by our forefathers and seek out novel perspectives, often born beyond the perimeters of mainstream, with the aim to stumble upon patterns that would lead her to uncover the truth behind human origins. Through music, art, the study of physics and mysticism, as well as rummaging her way across town libraries and obscure bookstores, Ewa seeks to piece together Earth's story. Her quest continues and in a place where it merges with her imagination, stories are born.

Ewa is a recipient of several awards in journalism and film production, a published poet, and a blog author. She graduated valedictorian with a bachelor's degree in mass communications and works for a Silicon Valley start up. When she is not working, Ewa is traveling the world collecting morsels of inspiration for her future projects. *Moonchild* is her first novel.